Praise for Karen Kay's
The Eagle and the Flame

"I was so extremely touched by this story…there are parts of this story that…(will make) you cry so much your heart will hurt, and other parts that will fill you with joy.
Amazon Review by Cinderella 7

"…this is a superior story to most western stories or any stories for that matter."
Amazon Review by Janalyn

"No one writes Indian romance better than Karen Kay."
Amazon Review by Kathy

Look for these titles by Karen Kay

The Eagle and the Flame

By

Karen Kay

The Wild West Series

PK&J Publishing
1 Lakeview Trail
Danbury, CT 06811

The Eagle and the Flame
Copyright © February 2020 by Karen Kay
Print ISBN: **979-8-63686-333-5**

Cover by Angela Waters

Karen Kay

NOTES

THE SCOUT: Traditionally, North American Indian tribes called their scouts wolves. These scouts were the most trusted individuals within the tribe, belonging to a mysterious medicine society of their own. Upon their trusted word stood the well-being and safety of the tribe and every member in it. Even chiefs bowed to the wisdom of their scouts. These men were trackers, trailblazers and capable warriors if there were a need to fight, but most of all these were men of incredible skill and pride.

BUFFALO BILL'S WILD WEST SHOW, FROM WIKIPEDIA, the online encyclopedia: "**Wild West shows** were traveling vaudeville performances in the United States and Europe that existed around 1870–1920. The shows began as theatrical stage productions and evolved into open-air shows that depicted the cowboys, Native American Indians, army scouts, outlaws, and wild animals that existed in the American West....

"...In 1883, *Buffalo Bill's Wild West* was founded in North Platte, Nebraska when Buffalo Bill Cody turned his real-life adventure into the first outdoor western show... *Buffalo Bill's Wild West* toured Europe eight times, the first four tours between 1887 and 1892... In October 1887, after more than 300 performances, with more than 2.5 million tickets sold, (the tour) return(ed) to the United States in May 1888 for a short summer tour."

A Note on the Native American/American Indian Names as Used in Buffalo Bill's Wild West Show

Some of the Native American men in Buffalo Bill's Wild West Show had a European name, as well as an American Indian name. I don't know why this is, or how they got their names. But, what I can show you are many of the names of the real Native American men who worked and performed in Buffalo Bill's Wild West shows. Be sure to notice that the first name is European and the last name is American Indian.

Samuel American Horse; Joe Black Fox; Amos Little; Amos Two Bulls; Luke Big Turnips; Sammy Lone Bear; William Frog.

While the tale of *The Eagle and the Flame* is a story of imaginative fiction, I did try to mimic this tendency to add a European name in front of the American Indian name.

Author's Comment

At this time in history, the term "Native American" or "First Americans" did not exist. The Indians were called simply Indians, although within their own cultures, they were more usually known by their tribal name. Also, even in the present day, depending upon the tribe, Indians often call themselves Indians, and are proud of it and honored to be Indian: (The Blackfeet "Indian Days Pow-wow," etc.). This is true of the Blackfeet, the Lakota, the Assiniboine and several other of the Northern tribes. Indeed, I have first-hand knowledge of this. There are, however, several tribes that I know of in the southwest who prefer to be called, "Native American." But, this reference to "Native American" is a modern term, and simply did not exist at the time period of this novel.

SPECIAL ACKNOWLEDGEMENTS

I wish to thank Tom Brown, Jr. and his book, *The Way of the Scout*. It is through this book that I first learned of the phrase and its meaning, "The Spirit that moves through all things," as well as the mind-set and the skills of the ancient scouts.

As of this date, Mr. Brown still teaches a tracking class for anyone who is interested, and his school and its address can be found on the internet. In the book, *The Way of the Scout*, Mr. Brown calls his school:

Tracking, Nature, Wilderness Survival School.

Thank you Mr. Tom Brown, Jr.

And a Special Thank-you to my Warriorette Gals

Vickie Batton; Carolyn Benton; Christine Martin; Sharon Crumper; Janet Hughes; Starr Miller

You are the Best!

Karen Kay

Dedication

This book is dedicated to my husband, Paul, whom I love with all my heart.

Also, inspired by the music of The Beatles, this book is dedicated in part to James Paul McCartney.

The songs *Love in the Open Air* and *Here, There and Everywhere* just might be two of the most beautiful musical creations in the last century.

Also, I would like to thank the following recording artists for their inspiration:

Ed Sheeran, for the songs, *Perfect* and *Photograph*

Alyssa Baker, for her cover of Elvis's *Can't Help Falling in Love,*

and

Paul Bryant, excellent song writer and country artist. His songs, *I do, The Last First Kiss* and *Run to Me* are sheer beauty.

PROLOGUE

The Wild West Series

Book One

The Assiniboine Sioux Reservation

Northeastern Montana

May 1884

"*Run! Run to them! Help them!*"

Ptehé Wapáha, Horned Headdress, couldn't move. It was as though his feet were tied to the ground with an invisible rope. He attempted to lift his feet one at a time. He couldn't. Bending, he struggled to remove the shackles that held him prisoner. It was impossible.

Straightening up, he looked down into the Assiniboine camps from his lofty perch upon a hill, and he watched as a cloud of dust and dirt descended from the sky to fall upon the children of the Assiniboine. Helpless to act, he stared at the scene of destruction as each one of the children fell to the ground, their bodies withering to dust. Still, he stood helpless, unable to act in their defense. He heard their cries, their pleas for aid. He reached out to them, he, too, crying. But he couldn't move; he couldn't save them.

The cloud lifted. The children were no more; their bones had returned to the earth. Instead, in their place arose a people who appeared

13

to be Assiniboine outwardly, but within their eyes, there showed no spark of life. They appeared to be without spirit, without heart; they were broken—mere slaves.

From the cloud of dirt came the sound of a whip as the people cowered beneath its assault. Then arose the lightning strikes and the thunder. One by one even those soulless people fell to their knees—a conquered people, their heads bowed in fear.

And, then they were no more. All was lost; all was gone.

What force was this? Who or what was this faceless power that had killed the Assininboine people and their children? He knew it not.

He cried, his tears falling to the ground, but even the essence of this, his body's grief, was barren. His proud people were no more.

Jerking himself awake, Ptehé Wapáha, Horned Headdress, chief of the Rock Mountain People, sat up suddenly. His sleeping robes fell around him and sweat poured from his body. Tears fell from his eyes as he came fully into the present moment.

At once, he realized that what he had seen had been a mere dream, and, while this might have comforted a lesser being, Horned Headdress knew that there was more to the nightmare. It was a vision, a warning from the Creator: this was what would come to pass if he and his people didn't act. And now.

But, what was he to do? He didn't know who this enemy was.

It was then that, wide awake, he beheld a vision unfolding before him as the Creator spoke to him in the language of the sacred spider. And, as the spider weaved his web, pictures of a future time appeared upon that maze.

Astonishment and fear filled his soul. But, he soon came to realize that the Creator had not warned him in vain, for, upon that same web appeared visions of deeds that would thwart that future evil, if he could but do them.

He must act, and with speed. This he vowed he would do. But how? He was no longer a young man, conditioned to the rigors that would be required. He could not perform the skills necessary to accomplish what must be done.

But there are two youths among our people who can. The thought came to him as though it were his own, but he realized that the words were from the Creator. Moreover, he saw with his mind's eye, that there were, indeed, two young men who were strong enough and proficient enough to undertake this task.

With a calmness of purpose, Horned Headdress knew what he would do, what he must do....

CHAPTER ONE

"*Our* way of life is endangered, and our people might well be doomed, I fear — all our people — unless we act."

Twenty-year old Waŋblí Taté, Wind Eagle, of the Hebina, the Rock Mountain People of the Nakoda tribe, listened respectfully to his chief, Horned Headdress. The chief held an honorable war record, was honest beyond reproach and was known to be wise at the young age of fifty-two years. On this day, Wind Eagle and his *kóla*, Iron Wolf, were seated in council within the chief's spacious sixteen-hide tepee. There were only the three of them present: Horned Headdress; himself, Wind Eagle; and Macá Mázasapa, Iron Wolf, the chief's son.

"The White Man is here to stay," continued Horned Headdress. "Many of our chiefs speak of this. Already we have seen changes that are foreign and confusing to us, for their customs are not ours. I have asked you both to this council today because I have dreamed that our people will not long exist if we do not act as a united people. But allow me to explain.

"As you both are aware, the annuities, promised so easily in treaty by the White Father, did not arrive this past winter to replace the hundreds-of-years-old food source, the buffalo. Because of this, too many of the young and the old did not survive the harsh snows and winds that inflicted wrath upon this country; a worse winter cannot be remembered, not even by the very old. All our people are grieved, for every family amongst us lost loved ones, and, I fear that if we do not become like the beaver and act in a fast and well-organized manner, we, as a people, will perish from the face of this earth.

"The Indian agent is partly to blame for this; he put us at a terrible disadvantage, for our men of wisdom and experience, who have always ensured that our people remain alert to future dangers, were rounded up and placed in an iron cage that the agent calls 'jail.' He used Indian police to do this; they were young men from our tribe who listened to this agent's poisonous tongue, and, feeling they knew best for our people, acted for the agent and not us. They helped him to disarm us, not realizing that their people had need of their guns and their bows and arrows not only to defend their families, but to hunt for food. Later, these same young men lamented their actions, for they learned too late that the Indian agent is not our friend.

"Some of our young men, like yourselves, escaped by hiding until the danger passed. Then, stealing away into the night, these men left to find food and bring it back to supply us with needed rations. But in many cases, the food arrived too late, and the evil face of starvation caused the death of too many of our people.

"We have heard this agent laugh at our plight, but what are we to do, for we have no one else to speak for us to the White Father? We chiefs have spoken often of this matter and have pondered who among us might seek out the White Father and express our grievances.

"Recently I received a vision from the Creator. I have now seen that the danger is not in the past; I have learned that our children have a terrible fate and we might lose them all if we remain here and do nothing to change our future."

Wind Eagle nodded solemnly; no words were spoken, as befit the purpose of this council.

"I believe I know what must be done," continued Horned Headdress. "I have seen in vision that there is a white man whose name is Buffalo Bill Cody, who is now visiting our Lakota brothers to the southwest of us. I am told that this man, Buffalo Bill, is not a bad man, though he pursues fame and approval, as well as the white man's gold. Further, I am told that he searches for those among us who can perform feats of daring, because he would take the best that we have and parade those youths before the white man. It is said to me that this is the manner in which this man purchases the necessities of living.

17

"I have discovered that he offers a home for those whom he chooses, as well as the white man's gold and silver which can be traded for clothing, food and other comforts. He is soliciting youths who can perform trick riding, or who can run as fast as the wind or can shoot with precision. He also is asking for young men who are unparalleled in tests of strength and brawn. Wind Eagle, you have proven yourself to be unequalled in shooting the arrow straight, accurately and with a speed that no one in all the nations can match."

Wind Eagle nodded silently.

"And you, Macá Mázasapa, my son, are the best horseman in all the Nakoda Nation, performing tricks that even the finest riders of the Plains, the Blackfeet, admire."

Iron Wolf dipped his head in acknowledgement.

"I am now asking you to act for me on behalf of your people; humbly, I would implore you both to travel to the Lakota people on the Pine Ridge Reservation and enter into those contests sponsored by this man, Buffalo Bill." Horned Headdress paused significantly as though he were choosing his next words with care. "I have seen in vision," he continued, "that the White Father, or a man representing him, will attend one of Buffalo Bill's Wild West shows. If I could, I would go in your place, but there are reasons why I cannot. I am no longer a youth who might compete against other youths. Also, I am needed here to counsel our sick and our needy and to act against this Indian Agent on behalf of our people, for this man is still here, is still corrupt, and every day denies our people the food and supplies that have been promised to us by treaty."

As was tradition in Indian councils, neither young man spoke, both kept their eyes centered downward in respectful contemplation. Not only was it the utmost in bad manners to interrupt a speaker, but it was a particular taboo to volunteer one's opinions with an elder of the tribe unless asked to do so. At length, Horned Headdress continued, saying, "I have seen into the future, and I believe that both of you will be accepted by this showman.

I ask you this: when the White Father or his representative comes to this show, ask for a private audience with this man, who I believe will grant your request. But beware. I have also seen that all will not be easy for you, for there is a deceiver there. You may come to know this person by being part of Buffalo Bill's show. Have a care, and do your work well, for this deceiver might be the greatest threat to all the Indian Nations. This trickster, if not recognized and stopped, may bring about death and destruction to our children in ways that our minds do not comprehend. Look for this person, discover who it is, man or woman. Be alert that if we do not learn from what tribe he or she hails, this deceiver could bring disaster not only to us, but to all the Indian Nations, and we, as an Indian people, might die in spirit forever. Identify this person as quickly as you might and disarm him or her, for I do not speak lightly that the fate of our children rests with you."

He paused for a moment. "And now," he continued, "I would hear what you wish to say about this burden I ask you to shoulder, for I would know if each one of you stands ready to pit your skills against this ill wind of tragedy for our people."

Now came the chance for each young man to speak, and they both agreed that they would be honored to bear this responsibility. They would go at once to their Lakota brothers in the south, and yes, they would use all their cunning and strength to prevent any future harm from befalling their people.

Horned Headdress nodded approval. "It is good," he acknowledged, before adding, "Seek out another young man from your secret clan, the Wolf Clan, once you have been successful in joining Buffalo Bill's show. Take him into your confidence, for I have also seen that three is oftentimes better protection against evil than two."

Both young men nodded.

Wašté, good. Now, listen well, my young warriors, and I will tell you what I wish you to say to the white man's representative, and what I wish you to do...."

***

Wind Eagle looked out from his lofty perch upon a stony ridge, which sat high above the winding waters of the Big Muddy, or as the white man called it, the Missouri River. He faced the east, awaiting the sunrise, his face turned upward, his arms outstretched in prayer. Below him unfolded numerous pine-covered coulees and ravines, jagged and majestic as they cut through the mountains, a range which appeared to never end. The huge rock beneath his moccasined feet felt solid and firm, and, as he inhaled the moist air of the morning, he gazed outward, welcoming the beauty of the Creator's work.

He sought a vision to guide him on this vital quest for his people. Also, he hoped to ease his troubles, for as Horned Headdress had so elegantly said, the shared tragedy that had destroyed so many of their people had also struck Wind Eagle personally.

It was true that starvation had been the ultimate weapon employed by rogue forces within and without the tribe. Because both the Indian Agent and the Indian police had acted against the people, Wind Eagle's grandfather had died in those cages the white man called 'jails.' At the time, Wind Eagle and his father had been gone from the village, on the hunt for food. But game was scarce, causing his own, and his father's, absence to extend for too long a time. When they had returned to their village, they had found that many of their friends were now gone. Even his beloved grandmother—the woman who had raised him—had been weak when Wind Eagle and his father had returned. For a short while, it had appeared that she might recover, but it was not to be. Too soon, she had left this life to travel to the Sandhills, where she would join her husband. At least they would journey on that path together.

It was only a few days past that Ptehé Wapáha, Horned Headdress, had spoken to Iron Wolf and himself, setting the two of them into action. Quickly, they had made their plans and had talked of nothing else for the past two days, and, if they were both picked by the Showman to be a part of the show, each individually knew what his part would be in this vital task. Failure was no option; the life of their people must continue.

Because no delay could be spared, they were to leave this very night to set out upon the trail to the Pine Ridge reservation. They would travel by horseback, both of them taking two or more of his ponies with him.

But no such journey could commence without first seeking a vision, for only in this way could a man communicate with his Creator. And so Wind Eagle began with a prayer:

"*Wakaṅtanka*, hear my plea. I come before you humbly, having given away my best clothing to the needy. As is right for my appeal, I have bathed myself in the smoke of many herbs, and have spent many days in prayer. Show me, guide me, to see how I might best aid my chief and my people."

Then he sang:

"*Wakaṅtanka, wacéwicawecioiya,* (Creator, I pray for them)
Wakaṅtanka, wacéwicawecioiya,
Wakaṅtanka, ca jéciyata, (Creator, I call thee by name)
Wakaṅtanka, ca jéciyata,
Wakaṅtanka, unkákí japi. (Creator, we suffer)
Wakaṅtanka, oićiya. (Creator, help me)
Wakaṅtanka, oićiya."

He closed his eyes, inhaling deeply as the sun peeped up above the horizon. Already he could feel the sun's warming rays, and he sighed. It was good, and he became quiet, merging himself with the spirit of Mother Earth, hoping that he might be gifted a vision. Perhaps Wakáṇtaṇka was attuned to the cries of His people, for Wind Eagle was not left long to linger. As he opened his eyes, he beheld a pair of bald eagles—his namesake—dancing in the cool drafts of the air. Beautiful was their courtship ritual as they climbed ever higher and higher into the airy altitudes of the sky.

Then it happened, the dance of love: locking talons, they spun around and around, spiraling down toward the earth in what might seem to be a dive to their death. Still, neither let go of the other, embracing and holding onto each other in their twirling spectacle until the very last moment. From that courtship dance, the pair would mate and form a union that would last their lifetime, and out of that union would appear a new generation of bald eagles. So it had been for thousands of years past; so it was now.

Entranced by the exquisiteness of this show of nature, he didn't at first see what was before him, didn't realize the two eagles were now hovering in the air, within his reach. The sound of their flapping wings, however, was loud in the cooling mountain breeze, and, lifting his vision to encompass them both, they spoke to him:

"We, the eagle people, are sent here from the Creator to tell you that He has heard your plea. He has told us to say this to you.

"Learn from us, for we, the eagle people, marry but once and for all our life. Heed the advice of your heart, since it will lead you on a path that will ensure the well-being of your people. Beware the past mistakes of others. Beware also the one or the many who would hide within the cloak of deceit. Be strong, remain alert, for the way to help your people will be fraught with great danger.

"Opportunity will soon be yours, for your skill is the best in all the Nations. Use this to learn about your people's secret enemy, for it will be through this venture that the chance to free your people from a coming darkness will appear. If you are successful, your acts of valor will be spoken about throughout the Indian Nations.

"Trust your heart, for there is one there who might help you to find peace within your mind and spirit.

"We have spoken."

Wind Eagle outstretched his arms toward the eagles, and he might have sung his song back to them, but the two birds had already lifted away from him, soaring higher and higher into the sky. Once more, the eagles locked talons, repeating the ancient courtship ritual dance.

Breathing deeply, he watched their magnificent show with respect, until at last the eagles plummeted to the earth, breaking away from one another before striking the ground. Coming together again, they climbed high over the rocks, alighting at last upon their nest. Here, they would love, ensuring that their species survived well into the future.

What was the meaning of their verse? He would relay his vision to his chief, of course, for only in this way could he assure the success of his task. But, before he left, he sang out his thanks in prayer, saying:

"Wakaṅtanka, I thank you for the vision you have given me.

"Wakaṅtanka, I honor you. I honor your messengers.

"And now I would seek out my chief that I might ensure I understand fully your instruction to me."

So saying, Wind Eagle stepped back from the ridge and retraced his steps to his camp. The day was still young, and he felt renewed with purpose.

CHAPTER TWO

An infamous dueling field outside Bladensburg, Maryland
May 20th, 1888

 *T*he early morning's cool, gray mist hung low over the dueling field's short grass and the woods that surrounded it. The lawn and woods-scented air was heavy and moist here at the Bladensburg contesting grounds; and, because this notorious spot lay only a few blocks from Washington DC proper, the atmosphere was further flavored with the scent of smoke from the fires and the wood-burning stoves of the numerous houses in the city. The earth felt mushy and wet beneath her footfalls, and the grass both cushioned and moistened the leather of her boots, as well as the bottom edge of her outfit. There was a chill in the air, and Lucinda Glenforest wore a short jacket of crushed velvet gold over the flowery embroidered skirt of her cream-colored, silky dress. Her bonnet of gold and ivory velvet boasted a brim that was quilled, and the satin bow that was tied high on top fell into inch-wide strings that tied under her chin. The color scheme complemented her fiery, golden-red hair that had been braided and tied back in a chignon that fell low at the back of her neck. The entire ensemble had been strategically donned in the wee hours of the morning to allow for freedom of movement, which might be more than a little required for the sedate "battle" which was to take place.

Beside her reposed Lucinda's fifteen-year-old younger sister, Jane, whose condition being only a few months in the making, was, for the moment, hidden. But soon, in less time than Lucinda liked to consider, the consequence of Jane's ill-fated affair would become evident.

"Don't kill him, Luci."

The words served to irritate Luci — not because of Jane's concern for the swine who had done this to her, but because of Luci's involvement in a situation that should rightly involve male members of their family. But their father, General Robert Glenforest, had left for the Island of Hawaii on the urgent business of war, and this, because their family had no brother to uphold its honor, left only Luci to contend with the problem. The fact that she possessed the skills to tackle the dilemma was hardly the point.

Being the eldest child in a military family, Luci had been fated to mimic her father's profession, for General Glenforest had made it no secret that he hoped his firstborn would be a boy. To this end, he had carefully schooled Luci into the more male occupations of war, of shooting, of defense and of strategic planning. Luci's own inclinations — which had included dolls and pretend dress-up — were of no consequence to her father. With the feminist movement in full swing, General Glenforest had found favor in openly proclaiming that he hoped Luci would follow in his footsteps, or if this weren't quite possible, to marry a soldier as like-minded as he. He went further to state that he hoped his daughter would thereafter advise her husband wisely.

As Luci had grown older, she had protested, of course, but it hadn't done her any good, especially since she enjoyed and stood out in the sport of the shooting gallery. Her prowess in these matches had earned her many a trophy over her male counterparts, and, as time had worn on, she had gone on to win and win and win, even those matches where the man she was pitted against was years older than she.

Now, while it might be true that Luci enjoyed the thrill of shooting matches, it was not factual that she shared other traits of the male gender. After all, she was well aware that she was not a man, and outside of the marksmanship that she excelled in, she held few common threads with the male of the species. Indeed, she often found a boy's rather crude sense of humor extremely gross and very unfunny.

So it was that she had mastered a defense against her father, her resistance being to dress up and to act in as ladylike a manner as possible. Indeed, she flaunted her femininity, had done so even as a child, especially when her father was in residence. Her rebelliousness had earned her a treasure, though. She had come to love the manner in which she adorned herself. Even her day dresses protested the current trend of the dark colors of black, brown and gray—none of that for her. Her clothing consisted of vivid hues of blue, coral, pink, yellow, green and more. Indeed, she flaunted the style of the walking dress, cutting her version of that style low in the bodice. Tight waists, which hugged her curves, ended in a "V" shape over her abdomen in front and the beginning arc of her buttocks in back. These and other attributes of her clothing asserted her female gender quite vividly. Her bustles were soft and feminine and her dresses were generally trained in back, adding to the aesthetic allure of her costume, while the overall effect of her skirts, draped in gatherings of material, fell like a soft waterfall to the floor.

That this style was considered to be a woman's attire for only evening gatherings bothered her not in the least. Although she had often heard the whispered gossip doubting the truth of her maidenhood, no one dared to repeat such lies to her face.

Her father, when he was in residence, accused her of playing up her feminine assets too well. But when he had gone on to criticize her too greatly, Luci had merely smiled at him; revenge, it appeared, was sweet. Truth was, left to her own devices, Luci might have made much of her own inclinations anyway, for her heart was purely girlish. Indeed, secretly at home, she enjoyed the more womanly chores of baking, cooking and sewing.

It did bother her that her abilities with a gun appeared to frighten suitors, for at the age of nineteen, she had never known the amorous attentions of any young man—no boyfriends, no male interest in her as a young woman. She'd not even experienced a mild flirtation with a member of the opposite sex. Indeed, it might be said that she was nineteen and ne'er been kissed.

So it was with reluctance that Luci answered her sister's plea to "not kill him," saying, "I promised you that I wouldn't, Janie, and that's all I can assure you. You must admit that the brute deserves no consideration whatsoever. If Father were here, you know that he would demand a Military Tribunal for that man, since both Father and that viper are military. Even a firing squad would be too good, I'm sure. To think, that skunk told you he wasn't married —"

"He did propose to me."

"How could he? Janie, he was married when he proposed to you. He's nothing but a lying thief."

"He's not a thief!"

"He took your maidenhood, didn't he?" Lucinda whispered the words. "Once lost, it's gone forever. You must see that he deserves to be killed."

Jane blushed. Still, she persisted, entreating, "Please don't do it, Luci. Please. I love him so."

This last was said with such urgency and dramatics, that Luci's only response was a sigh. If it were up to her...

She still remembered back to a few weeks ago, and to Janie's confession.

Luci had found her blond and beautiful fifteen-year-old sister locked in her room, grieving. On inquiry, Jane had confessed her problem.

"I'm pregnant, Luci. We had planned a June wedding. But now?..."

"Pregnant? Had planned a June wedding?"

"He's married. I didn't know. I swear I didn't. He told me he loved me, and that we would be married in June. But when I came to him to tell him of the child, he laughed at me."

"He laughed? You're telling this to me truly? He honestly laughed?"

Jane cried and seemed unable to speak. She nodded instead.

"Who is this man?"

Jane hiccupped. "I...promise me that you won't kill him."

"How can I say that to you in view of what has happened? And with Father gone. Now, tell me, who is this man? You know I'll find out one way or the other."

"I suppose you will. But please, I can't reveal his name to you unless I have your word that you won't kill him."

Luci paused. She could force the issue, but she would rather not. Perhaps it was because Jane was more like a daughter to her than a sister, for Luci had taken on the role of "mother" at the age of four, when their own mother, shortly after giving birth to Jane, had passed on to the heavenly plane. Plus, their father had never remarried. Luci uttered, "I will do my best not to kill him, Janie. But that's all I can promise."

Sniffing, Jane blew her nose on the dainty handkerchief in her hand, then at length, she admitted, "I guess that's good enough. I think you might know him. It's Captain Timothy Hall. But please, don't be angry at him. I love him so."

Of course Luci knew the worthless snake. He had once courted Abagail Swanson, one of her best girlfriends, who also had been underage at the time. Luckily for her friend, she had discovered the truth of Hall's marital state before he'd been able to inflict permanent damage on her.

What was wrong with the man? Was his twenty-year-old wife already too old for him? Was he a pervert?

Oh, what she would like to do to him if the society around them would only allow it....

Well, that was all in the recent past; what was done was done. Today was the day he would pay. Today, that no-account slime would contend with her, and Luci pledged to herself that her sister's honor, as well as that of their family, would be avenged.

Once again, she thought back to the last few weeks. In less than twenty-four hours after her talk with Jane, Luci had challenged the bearded, black-haired degenerate, and had done so in as public a place as possible: a garden party. He had laughed at her, of course, when she had confronted him, and, using her gloves, she had slapped his face.

"You're a two-timing scoundrel, Captain Hall, and I challenge you to a duel. Make no mistake, I will protect and defend my family's honor."

"You? A woman? Dueling me?" He snickered. "I wouldn't stoop so low."

"Low? Are you a coward, then? Is your problem that your spine runs yellow? You know that no man has ever bested me in the skill of the shooting gallery."

His answer was nothing more than a loud hiss.

"My second will act at once, setting the time and place of the duel. And hear me out, if you don't show, I will ensure that all the country in and around Washington DC, as well as your wife, will know not only of your misdeeds, but also of your cowardice. And this, I promise."

Still, she thought, he might not come. For now, she awaited her second, as well as those in Hall's party. She picked up her pistol—a Colt .45—checking it over carefully, swearing to herself what she would do to him if the wicked man didn't show....

***

"The rules for this duel are as follows," declared Sergeant Anthony Smyth, a tall, dark-haired gentleman, who was Luci's second. Smyth was an excellent marksman in his own right, which was one reason why Luci had picked him to preside over the duel. That both he and his wife were close family friends had aided Luci in making the choice. But Smyth continued to speak, and said, "The match will go on until first blood is taken, and, regardless of how minor the injury, the match then ends. No further shots are legal, and will not be tolerated. The twenty paces, which were agreed upon in writing, have been marked out by a sword stuck in the ground at each side of the field. When I drop the handkerchief that I hold in my hand, you may each advance and fire. Lieutenant Michaels is on duty as the official surgeon." Sergeant Smyth glanced first at Luci, then at Captain Timothy Hall. "Are there any questions?"

When neither she nor Captain Hall spoke up, Sergeant Smyth continued, "Then it is begun."

Luci glanced down the field, estimating her distance, as well as determining where exactly she would place her shot. Having already decided that a shoulder injury would be the easiest to heal, she calculated the precise angle that would be required to obtain that "first blood," and end the match. Next to Captain Hall stood his older brother, James Hall, his second.

Behind Luci, well to her rear and out of shooting range, sat Jane, who had brought a blanket to cushion the soft ground upon which she sat.

Refreshments of cinnamon rolls and coffee, with plates and coffee cups, decorated a table next to Jane. As was expected by the rules of conduct for all matters concerning dueling, both Jane and Luci had brought the refreshments for the participants today, including that serpent, Captain Tim Hall.

Luci hadn't easily consented to the early morning snack, but her friend, Sergeant Smyth, had already determined that the duel would follow the rules of personal combat exactly, making her obligated to provide the food and drink.

She sighed as she awaited the signal to begin, but she never once glanced away from her target. To do so might be fatal.

Smyth dropped the handkerchief, and both duelists fired at will. Luci's shot hit Hall in the shoulder, as she had intended, while Hall's shot missed her entirely.

"First blood has been taken," called out Sergeant Smyth. "The match now ends as formerly agreed upon. All participants are to put down their weapons, and all are invited to coffee and rolls, which they will find at the far side of the field. A surgeon is on hand to deal with your wound, Captain Hall."

Luci turned away, setting her gun down on the table next to her.

Blast!

The explosion was unexpected. The match was finished, wasn't it? If so, why was Captain Hall still firing at her?

Boom!

Hall's next gun shot hit her in her left upper arm.

"Stop this at once!" shouted Smyth. "Halt! This is illegal!"

But Luci ignored her second-in-command; she was in a gun fight and under attack; his words didn't even register with her. With the quick reflexes of one who is in command of her weapon, she grabbed hold of her Colt, turned, and carefully aimed her shot to do the most damage to Captain Hall without killing him.

Blast!

She sent her answering bullet at Captain Timothy Hall, placing the slug high up on his thigh, intending the bullet to miss, yet graze his masculine parts. His loud cry indicated she had been successful. She turned her pistol on Hall's second — James Hall — who had picked up his own gun, as though he might consider using it against her, also, illegal though it was.

"Captain Hall, you and your brother must cease this at once. You will be reported. You and your second will likely be court marshalled if you continue firing," Sergeant Smyth yelled, as he hurried toward Luci, his own Colt drawn and aimed at the two culprits. But his threat fell on deaf ears. Hall had fallen to the ground, his shrieks indicating he was in too much pain to be of any more use in a gunfight. Hall's brother, James, however, looked ready to continue the match, except that when he espied Luci's Colt pointed directly at him, as well as Smyth's drawn weapon, James Hall instead dropped his gun and held his hands up in surrender.

Luci nodded. But that was all that she did. Without letting her guard down, she kept her weapon trained on both the Hall brothers as she paced to where Jane sat at the side of the field. Bending down, Luci grabbed hold of her sister by the arm and pulled her up. Then, without turning her back on Captain Hall and his brother, she made her retreat toward the street, where her coach awaited.

"Make a report of this at once," she instructed Smyth, as well as Lieutenant Michaels, the military surgeon. "Let all know what a cowardly slime Captain Hall truly is. My father must be informed, and he will thank you both for doing so."

Without cause to do more at the moment, Luci and Jane slowly withdrew, Jane leading the way to their coach, for Luci never once turned her back on her opponent. That the screams of Captain Timothy Hall wafted through the air was music to Luci's ears. By measured retreat, they gained the street and the carriage, and Jane practically flew into her seat within.

"Driver!" yelled Luci as she quickly followed her sister into the conveyance. "Take us to the army telegraph office as quickly as possible!" Seating herself with care, she continued, declaring to Jane, "We must send Father word of this at once."

"Why, you're hurt!"

It was true. The exact extent of the damage was yet to be determined, and it was only now, within the relative safety of their coach, that Luci realized her arm hurt unbearably.

Yet, to Jane, all she said was, "It is only a scratch, soon healed. But come, Jane, please tear off a part of my petticoat, and give it to me to tie, that I might stop this bleeding, for I fear it is staining my blouse."

"Leave it to you to consider only the damage to your clothing," scolded Jane as she did as instructed. It was also she who tied the tourniquet. "As soon as we arrive at our home, I will summon our surgeon to attend to you at once."

"After we send that telegraph to Father," amended Luci. "I fear we have not heard the last of Captain Hall and his brother. Though I feel assured that Mr. Smyth will also telegraph word to our father on any channel available to him, he may not be able to do this at a speed that would be required to ensure our good health."

"What do you mean?"

Luci sent her sister a cautious glance. With the duel having gone as badly as it had, it was not in Luci's nature to instill even more alarm in Jane, especially considering her delicate condition. Nevertheless, a word of attentiveness might be in order.

To this end, she patted Jane's hand, smiled at her and said, "When Captain Hall heals from the wound I inflicted upon him, he might feel compelled to seek us out for daring to expose his base nature to his fellow military officers. A man who would flaunt the rules of honor cannot be trusted. And I fear—"

"Luci, please," Jane cried, tears in her eyes. "What he has done is wrong, so very, very wrong, but please do not keep degrading his character to me. A scoundrel he is, I have no doubt, and I feel terrible that he has hurt you, but I am, after all, carrying his child. I wish I weren't, Luci, but it is done, and I must bear the consequences of my actions. However, I fear that, as he is the babe's father, he may have rights that even I don't understand. I should try to discover a good trait he might possess, for I fear that I may have to deal with him in the future." She pulled out a hanky from her purse and blew her nose. "Is it possible that he might have some logical reason as to why it was necessary to continue to fire at you when he should have stopped? Perhaps it was a reaction he could not control?"

"He fired two illegal shots at me, Janie, not one."

"Oh, how hard it is to love a man so much," Jane uttered with so much heartfelt passion that Luci was reminded of her sister's youth—and the hardship of being pregnant at so young an age. "I know it's true enough that he lied to me, but that doesn't make him all bad, does it? I once found good in him. It must still be there. Oh, Luci, it hurts to love him so. It hurts."

Momentarily, Luci felt at a loss for words. She made up for that lack by patting Jane's hand instead.

"It will get better," she assured Jane at last. "I know it might seem now as though the hurt will never heal. But it will." She sighed. "It will. And perhaps you are right. Maybe in the future we might be dealing with a good man. I guess one could say that only the future will declare the truth of his character. We can hope, Janie, we can hope."

Luci averted her gaze to stare at the closed, royal blue curtains that fell down over the windows of the carriage. Enough said. She would send this telegram to their father, then wait and see what might unfold. Reaching over to pull that blue, velvet curtain away from the window, she watched as the sun came up in the east.

CHAPTER THREE

Q Street, Georgetown, Washington DC

"*W*ake up, Luci!"

Luci returned to the land of the living with a start. Her left arm hurt like the dickens, and, for a moment, she couldn't remember why. Oh, yes. The memory came flooding back with the impact of a slap: the duel — the illegal shots. Doctor Keller, being a military man, had rushed to General Glenforest's red-bricked townhouse on the fashionable Q Street in Georgetown. Sergeant Smyth had summoned the man, and had brought the doctor to the townhouse in as quick a manner as possible.

Doctor Keller had accomplished the necessary operation without delay, having announced that the bullet had lodged itself only a fraction of an inch into Luci's arm. Her left arm still hurt like mad, however. Plus, the sedative the doctor had given her to ease the pain caused her to feel groggy.

"Yes, yes," she replied sluggishly. "I am awake now." Looking toward the lacy curtains that fronted the floor-to-ceiling windows of her bedroom, Luci calculated the time to be early evening, perhaps around eight o'clock, for it was dark outside.

"I fear we might be in danger," uttered Jane. "Sergeant Smyth has rushed to our home, and he brings news that James Hall and many of his friends and relatives are marching here."

"Here? Now?"

"Yes."

Luci swallowed hard and shook her head from side to side, trying without much success to clear her mind of the drug given her to dull the pain of the surgery. Luckily, her feeling of anxiety came to her rescue, and she sat up without her head feeling as though she had been spun in circles for hours.

"Is Anthony here now?"

"Yes, he is. He said he will help us defend our home against them."

"Does he know how many of them there are?"

"He said thirty, perhaps more."

Luci gulped. "Help me up, and please send Anthony to me at once."

"Yes," answered Jane, as she hopped to her feet and rushed to the door, opening it. Luci could hear her steps fleeing down the stairs.

Well, this is quite a turn of events. How many more deeds of evil was Timothy Hall to inflict upon them?

Anthony was not long in coming to her, for she had yet to stand to her feet when he quickly strode in through the door. Hurriedly he crossed the room and pulled up a chair next to her bed.

"It is because our father isn't here that Captain Hall feels emboldened enough to commit these wicked acts upon us. If my father were here…"

"Yes, it is true," confirmed Anthony. "But the Hall family has friends in high places; his father, as you know, is editor of the County Paper. That shot you fired as you were leaving the field barely missed Hall's masculinity, as I'm sure you intended, and he is in great pain."

"Good."

"Yes, I would agree it is good, but I believe there are already lies being spread about you, for the sheriff and his deputies are a part of those thirty or more men who are determined to take you and lock you up…or worse…."

"The sheriff? His deputies?"

He nodded. "I fear that until your father does arrive here—for both I and the surgeon have made full reports on the matter—you had best leave Washington DC with all possible haste. I already have a carriage arranged for you, and I will stay here to cover your departure."

Luci nodded. "So soon after my surgery?"

"It must be."

"But where will we go?"

"West," he advised. "Disappear into the west. There, you can lose yourself, but beware. Captain Hall's father is a powerful man, and he will have his bullies stationed at the carriage houses and the train stations. Perhaps you could disguise yourself and your sister."

"My sister? Do you think I need to take Jane, too?"

"Without doubt. I fear they may not hesitate to do away with her in whatever manner they feel necessary, for there will be blame and shame brought to them because of her condition. And he, the father of the babe."

"Surely they would not dare to — "

"As we sit here speaking, every minute they come closer. Remember, your father is not here to protect you. Please go. I will stay. I will do my best. Take your sister, for I believe that she, too, is in danger."

"Yes. Give me a moment to dress."

"There is no time. Go in only your nightclothes. You must."

What he suggested was akin to sacrilege to Luci, insisting that she go out not properly dressed. Yet, the urgency in his voice and in his gestures gave her to understand that in this, she must do as he asked.

"Very well," she agreed, coming up uneasily to place her bare feet upon the cool, hardwood floor of her bedroom. "Please lead me and Jane to your conveyance with all possible speed."

"Have you any money?"

"Yes, a moment please while I open the safe that Father keeps."

"There isn't time. I'm sorry. Here, Jane has already thought of the need for finance." Reaching into his pockets, he pulled out a purse and extended it toward her. "She opened the safe earlier and took out these few pieces of gold and silver. I added a little to it to ensure that you and Jane might obtain seating upon the fastest means of transportation out of Washington DC."

With a deep sigh, Luci accepted the purse, knowing that she and Jane could go nowhere without it. "I thank you, my friend, for your assistance and for your warning. Someday I hope to repay you and your wife."

"I am your second in this duel. It is my duty. Besides, being a sergeant with a wife to support, I have little enough silver to give you. What is here is mostly your own, my friend. Now go, and Godspeed."

***

"Why did you choose a general's daughter? It's not that these little affairs matter to me or to the family, but couldn't you have chosen a girl of no account?"

"She seemed of little account to me."

"You do realize, don't you, that a general's daughter could cause the army, even the government, to come sniffing around our family business. And what would they find?"

"What is this, a lecture? I know what would happen. I don't need your hints at it," snapped Captain Timothy Hall to his father, John Hall.

"You are in no position, young man, to back talk to me. Need I remind you that you have put our family at risk?"

Captain Timothy Hall set his lips together in a frown, and wisely said not a word. His father, head of the Hall family clan, ruled the family as though he were a god rather than what he was: a dictator engorged with his own self-importance. Worse, when it came to the family business—the financial side of it—John Hall wouldn't hesitate to pull strings, and send his son into the depths of hell, if need be. He'd done it once to his older brother, Seth, a man who was always referred to by other family members as "the black sheep."

"Why did you do it?" asked the elder Hall.

Tim Hall shrugged. "Her father was away," he explained. "Still is, and she has no brothers. How was I to know that her sister is a crack shot?"

"You should have found out. At least, when challenged to a duel, you should have come to me. Now we have trouble, and all because of a little, underage slut. When you found out that the girl was pregnant, why didn't you seek out my advice then?"

"I thought that I could easily triumph over her sister, and, when I'd done that, I could insist that the entire affair be swept under the rug."

"Well, it didn't happen that way, did it? You've left me with a fine mess, and now I have to do damage control. We'll run several stories in the paper about your honorable military record and your good public works, so that the general person in the street will question *her* virtue and not yours. That should help, but from this moment on, I must have your word that you will be on your best behavior. Need I remind you that you have been placed exactly where you are in order to control the army's response to our business, in the case it might ever be discovered? You must rise in rank in order to accomplish this. This you will do. But there must be no other hint, ever again, of stepping out of line. Do you understand?"

"Of course."

"I would have your word."

"You have it, all right?"

"Don't get snippy with me. Now, here is my advice when it comes to women: have as many affairs as you wish, but have them with women of no account. Do you hear?"

"Yes, sir, I do."

"Good. Now, we must find these two sisters. We must kidnap them, or at least the younger of the two, so that we might gain bargaining power over their father, General Glenforest. You understand that when he returns, he will learn the truth; he will try to convene a Military Tribunal, and, if he does this, not only your affairs, but mine and this family's business, could be made public knowledge. We would be ruined, and, since this is your inheritance, you would do well to mend your ways, just as you have promised to do. Do you understand?"

"Yes, sir."

"Good. Find those two sisters. Bring them to me…or at least, since the older one might be harder to subdue, if you can't take them both, bring me the younger one, the one who is carrying your child. It is my hope to buy her silence. Now, you must do this before their father, General Glenforest, returns to this country. Do you understand?"

"I do, sir," said Timothy Hall, with a mock salute. "I will see to it at once."

"See that you do, son. See that you do."

***

The young boy and his dark-haired "twin" sister stepped off the train at Grand Central Depot in New York City. Here, they hoped to rest until they could board another conveyance headed directly west. The only problem was that the next train going west wasn't scheduled to leave until a few days hence.

Luci was well aware that agents of the formidable Hall family were watching all possible means of exiting the East Coast, both by coach and by train. Also, because Luci was now officially charged with attempted homicide, she and Jane had no choice but to travel incognito.

It was startling how quickly posters had gone up for their capture—for both she and Jane—the price for their seizure being five thousand dollars cash. But it was not only the posters that had been set against them; every edition of the Hall's newspaper had carried pictures of herself and Jane.

It was this that had caused them to go to the extreme to hide their identities, and they had hatched a plan. Dressed as fraternal twins, they had escaped Washington DC without detection. That they were now in New York City, and were still being sought after by agents of the Hall family, gave them no option but to continue the charade. Jane, who was wearing a wig, had become a brunette, and Luci had caught up her hair in a bun and donned a hat, which hid her mane's length. Then, winding a tight, long piece of cloth over her breasts, she had attained the look of a "boy," especially after she had attained some secondhand boy's clothing, garnered from a Washington DC shop.

Hall's hirelings seemed to be everywhere, and the girls spotted them easily enough, for they usually hid behind an open newspaper. Almost every operative wore dark clothing and black frock coats. Their felt, bowler-style hats were almost always pulled down low over their foreheads, and the recognizable short, sideburn moustaches seemed to be a trademark between them, one and all.

As Luci glanced around the depot, she spotted one of Hall's agents to her right, about one hundred yards away. Another appeared to be positioned at the train station's exit.

What were she and Jane to do? They couldn't stay here in the underground terminal for two to three days. Not only would it be suspicious, but there would be little here to allow them to survive until the next train, for food and drink were only to be found upon the streets of New York City, not in the train's depot.

No, they would require a place to sleep and food to eat, as well as an apartment that would permit them to bathe. Yet, their meager finances wouldn't allow them to purchase a two-night stay in New York City, as well as two train tickets bound for Chicago.

As Luci glanced up at the one-hundred-foot iron and glass curved ceiling, she tried to envision a way out of this railway shed without alerting Hall's agents. But where to go?

They couldn't sleep on the streets; they couldn't afford housing. She bit her lip in concentration, bringing her gaze downward, and glancing off to the opposite side of the huge train depot. It was about two hundred feet across to the other wall, and she frowned.

Her scrutiny alighted upon a poster which was plastered on the other wall. What did it say? Buffalo Bill's Wild West Show? She turned around and gazed at the wall behind her. Sure enough, a few paces away, on their side of the tracks, hung another poster. Taking hold of Jane's elbow, Luci stepped as casually as possible toward the advertisement.

It gave her an idea — a long shot to be sure — but if Buffalo Bill's Wild West Show were here in New York, could she not approach Bill Cody and apply for a job?

After all, she was noted as being one of the best shots in all the DC area. Could she perhaps pass herself off as a "boy wonder"?

She was well aware that Annie Oakley toured with the show, which could make it difficult to hire another woman in the same profession. Besides, she needed to continue her and Jane's disguise, or risk capture, jail or worse. But if she applied as a young boy?...

Well, it was worth a try, and, at the moment, she didn't have any other ideas. Besides, even if Buffalo Bill didn't appreciate her marksmanship with a gun, couldn't she seek employment as a hired hand?

Did the poster include an address? Yes, it did: Mariner's Harbor in Staten Island.

"Jane, I have an idea," murmured Luci, pointing to the poster. "We could go to Mariner's Harbor, here in New York, seek out an interview with Buffalo Bill, and ask if he might hire us."

Jane glanced up at the poster. "I don't know, Luci."

"Please don't call me by that name in public, dear Sister. Remember that until this mess blows over, I am Louie, your twin brother."

"But the Wild West Show? They might hire you, Lu—ie, for you have a talent that might appeal to that show. But they would never be so silly as to take me on. I have no skill that would cause me to be hired, unless Buffalo Bill suddenly decides that displaying one's quilting proficiencies is part of the Wild West."

"You are my sister and as such, I believe that they might accept you as part of my family. We can tell them that we are traveling to join our parents in the West. It's not too farfetched, for I'm certain our father will find us and come there for us as soon as he is back in the country."

"I...I don't know." Jane frowned. "But I suppose it's worth a try, especially since we have no other options."

Luci grinned. "Yes, it might not be the haven we seek, but for now I can think of no other possibilities that might allow us to leave New York—at least not without incident. C'mon. Let's go there and see if we might talk to Colonel Bill Cody, himself."

Luci grabbed hold of her sister's elbow, and, leading the way, exited the New York train depot. Luckily, they passed by Hall's agents unnoticed.

CHAPTER FOUR

Mariner's Harbor, "Erastina"

Staten Island, NY

May 22nd, 1888

"Come in, come in, Charles."

Buffalo Bill Cody stood up from his seat within his office, a room which was as grand a tent as twenty-four-year-old Charles Wind Eagle had ever seen. Indeed, the showman's pavilion could have been a white man's paradise, for thick, woolen rugs covered the grassy earth, cushioning a man's steps, while furniture consisting of chairs, a couch and numerous tables decorated the "room." The tent was divided into quarters by canvas walls. This particular compartment, Cody's office, contained a large desk with numerous chairs stretched out in front of it.

Cody — known to the Indians as the Showman — gestured toward a seat on Wind Eagle's left. Two of the other chairs that had been set in front of Cody's desk were already occupied, and Wind Eagle gave those occupants a quick, although thorough, glance. What appeared to be two children in their teen years, one male, one female, were seated on his right.

As requested, Wind Eagle sat down and gave the Showman his attention briefly, although in his gaze, he took in Cody's pristine appearance, from his fringed buckskin shirt, to his shoulder-length, dark brown hair, mustache and short beard. Wind Eagle gazed downward, as was good, Nakoda manners. However, he hadn't missed the spark of excitement in Buffalo Bill's eyes.

"Wind Eagle," addressed Cody, "may I introduce you to a young gentleman who is as fine a sharpshooter as any I have ever seen."

Wind Eagle glanced to his right, his scan of these two adolescents quick. He looked away, bringing his attention downward once more, bestowing good etiquette upon the newcomers.

"Now, this young gentleman can shoot good—real good—so fine, in fact, that it has given me an idea," explained Cody. "But it would require your cooperation, thus my summons to you."

Wind Eagle nodded quietly.

"My idea is to stage a contest—a real one—between you and this lad. I have seen him in action, and I have realized that he's as accurate a shooter as—and maybe better than Johnny Baker, only this lad is a mere fourteen years of age. He's so good, that I got an idea while I was watching him perform."

Again, Wind Eagle nodded.

"Now, you're the only Indian that I have ever seen who can shoot an arrow as fast as a man can fire a gun. You're almost as quick with a gun, but not quite. I have a question for you: would you consider teaming up with this youngster? My idea is this: the lad here could help you to become a faster draw with a gun, and, under your direction, you could teach this young'un to discharge arrows as fast as you. It'll be a real shootin' match. With your skill and your popularity with the women"— here he winked at Wind Eagle—"it could be a show that could rival Annie Oakley!"

Wind Eagle nodded, yet he remained silent. He kept his gaze down and centered.

"What do you say? Will you do it?"

"*Hau, hau.*"

"Good, good. The boy here and his sister are going west in search of their father, a man who appears to be lost out there. Louis — that's his name — can become a performer with the show, travel with us back to Nebraska, and hopefully find his father all at the same time."

Wind Eagle didn't speak, his only communication being a slight nod.

"Good. Stand up now and shake hands with the lad. Louis, this is Charles Wind Eagle."

The boy stood to his feet.

"Now, I'm counting on you, Wind Eagle, to take him under your wing. Teach him well. What a show this will be! What money we'll make!"

As was proper manners, Wind Eagle acted as instructed, and came up onto his feet. Turning toward the lad, he held up his right hand, palm outward, which was his custom of acknowledgment, but when the boy reached out with his right arm, Wind Eagle met the gesture and took hold of the boy's hand.

At once, Wind Eagle felt the lure of deception jerk him to instant attention. What was this? A test from the Showman, Buffalo Bill? Or was this person before him trying to deceive them both?

This was no lad. Were Wind Eagle not trained as a member of the Clan of the Wolf, a scout; were he not proficient in detecting even the faintest of scents — those elusive pheromones that a man supposedly could not distinguish — he might have been deceived. But there was no mistaking the faint, almost indistinguishable fragrance of this person who stood before him. This was a woman, not a lad. Additionally, she was no youngster. This was a woman of child-bearing age. Her natural perfume proclaimed it, and this, alone, declared her true gender.

Gazing down quickly at her hand for another indication of her true gender, he beheld the obvious: her index finger was the same length as her ring finger. It was the mark of a woman's hand. While not always an accurate test, a man's index finger was generally shorter than his ring finger.

He frowned. What was this woman about, pretending to be a boy? Was she the trickster that Horned Headdress had warned him to beware of? The fraudster who would spell disaster to their nation?

He nodded an acknowledgement, dropped her hand, and turned back toward Buffalo Bill, pinning him with a sharp, quick glance. Did he know?

No. Wind Eagle could detect no duplicity about the Showman. The woman had tricked him, too.

What about the other woman, the young, dark-haired girl who was still seated? Was she, too, pretending to be someone she was not? No. He could detect no subterfuge in that one.

But this lad… This one meant to deceive.

Wašte'. It was good that the showman had asked him to keep this imposter close to him. He would teach her to shoot with a bow, yes, but that was not all he would do.

He would watch her, test her, and, if he were wise, he would determine as soon as possible what she was hiding, and why. He inhaled deeply at the same moment that he felt himself relax. Indeed, at last, he felt as though one of his major tasks in joining the show was to be revealed to him. He was ready.

***

It would have been an understatement to say that Luci was pleased. She was ecstatic. Not only had she been successful in her disguise, she had been accepted as part of the show. That her pay would include her own private tent for Jane and herself, complete with meals, as well as a good salary, seemed too good to be true. At least in this, their father had ensured their future, for without her skill, what would they do?

"Shall I accompany you tomorrow morning?" asked Jane, as soon as the two women had arrived "home" to their own tent.

"I don't think so," answered Luci, as she, in her role as brother, pulled back the canvas opening into their quarters, allowing Jane to precede her into their lodging.

"Are you certain? You know what Father says about Indians; they're all beggars, thieves and worse, they will kill you just to look at you. While the two of you must practice, it might not be safe to be alone with him. It could be true, Luci. He might try to kill you."

Luci grinned at her sister. "Yes, I am certain our father would say this were he here. But, I think not. Father also told us that the Indians have been recently tamed by the cavalry and the good agents on their reservations. And, although they put up a good fight several years ago, they have been conquered now. He said that without the white man's help, their race would be extinct."

"Maybe. But I will worry about you, knowing that you will be alone with him for many hours each day."

"Why? You know I can defend myself."

"Yes, yes, I know. But remember, our father also said that the Indians can be cunning and dangerous."

"Yes, he did. But he also fought against them before you and I were born, in a war he called Red Cloud's War. Perhaps his judgment is in error on their character. Besides, Buffalo Bill told me that Mr. Eagle has been with the show for a couple of years now, and that he toured with their entire troupe throughout England and many of our different states. Surely, if there had been any problem with the man, Mr. Cody would not suggest that Mr. Eagle and I work together."

"I don't know." Jane frowned.

Luci shrugged. "Come with me, then, if you wish, but I think it is unnecessary. Besides, perhaps you might remember that he and I have agreed that each day we will start our practice early in the morning, long before sunrise. If you think about it, you, in your condition, might wish to gain those hours to enhance your sleep. After all, the day will come when you will need your strength."

Jane continued to look doubtful.

"I understand your concern, dear sister," said Luci. "But why don't we continue our talk after supper? I, for one, am hungry, since we have not eaten yet today, and it is already early evening. Come, let us go find the mess hall, and see what kind of food we can expect to be served to us while we are with the show."

It was Jane's turn to shrug. "All right," she replied after a few moments. "So much has happened today that I had forgotten that I, too, am hungry. Truly, I must remember that I eat now for two."

"Yes, indeed," agreed Luci. Then she repeated, "Yes, indeed."

***

As Luci prepared for bed, slipping into her boy-like pajamas, she felt happy, lucky. Glancing around their new quarters, which was a tent furnished with nothing more than a couple of cots, two pillows and two woolen blankets, she saw that Jane, who lay on an opposite cot from her, was already asleep. Gazing about her, Luci decided that she and Jane might decorate their new home...at least a little.

She conjured up a mental picture of her new "partner," Charles Wind Eagle. Tall and handsome in an exotic sort of way, she wondered what her father would say if he knew that she had pledged herself to the company of this man. Would he understand that she'd had little choice?

She was reminded that Mr. Eagle's people, or people like his, had once fought a desperate war with soldiers whom her father had led into battle. Her father called these skirmishes the Indian wars, and he spoke derogatorily about the people whom he had been ordered to subjugate, and, if necessary, to kill.

If Mr. Eagle ever learned of this aspect of her family, would he seek to do her harm, as Jane feared? Perhaps, but somehow Luci doubted it.

Luci thought again of the handsome, young warrior she had so recently met. He had left Cody's tent-turned-office together with herself and Jane. Once outside, Mr. Eagle had turned to her, and said, "We meet tomorrow morning before the sun rises in the eastern sky. We will practice in a wooded area outside of these grounds, where any noise we make will not awaken or disturb others. It is at the southwestern side of the camp. You will know it when you see it."

Luci had responded with little more than a nod.

And, then he had smiled at her, and Luci had thought her heart might surely explode, for it had suddenly beat much too fiercely. Why? Did she fear him?

Of course she didn't. It was true that he came from a culture that seemed to thrive on murdering her own people, but—

She hadn't finished the thought at the time because suddenly he had winked at her. Winked? Somehow that simple action was horribly at variance with both her thoughts and her father's descriptions of these people. It was as though Mr. Eagle were…human, not some degraded degenerate.

And then, Mr. Eagle had said, "Don't be late. I will know if you are even if I am not there to greet you." And, with that said, he had turned and walked away from Luci and Jane without another word.

Luci had watched his slim figure trod swiftly away, acknowledging that his stride was oddly elegant. He was the first American Indian she had ever met, and she hoped that if he ever did discover that her father had led troops against Mr. Eagle's people, that the young American Indian might forgive her.

Sighing, she lay down on the cot and sought solace in sleep.

***

The three young scouts sat cross-legged around the small fire they had kindled within Wind Eagle's tepee. Present were Wind Eagle; Iron Wolf; and Wakiŋyaŋ Paza Tosaŋ, Blue Thunder Striking. Blue Thunder was also a member of the Clan of the Wolf, a scout, but he represented a different Nation, the *Húŋkpapȟa* Lakota. He could not be beaten in a foot race or a horse race within his own or any other tribe. Plus, he was a trick rider, his skills fitting closely with those of Iron Wolf and Wind Eagle.

As Horned Headdress had bid them to do, both Wind Eagle and Iron Wolf had taken Blue Thunder into their confidence, stating their purpose in being with the show, the risks they were to take, and what was at stake for their tribes. Blue Thunder had understood the special responsibility offered him, and he had agreed that he would accept and be a part of this deadly mission, even, if need be, to his own death.

As all three young men sat in council, they were clothed in their riding clothes, which consisted of little more than breechcloth and moccasins. It was a warm evening, and, with the fire heating the atmosphere within Wind Eagle's lodge, not one of them reposed with their buffalo robe thrown around their shoulders. Instead, each one sat on his robe, as though it were a hide.

As was the way of the Nakoda, both Wind Eagle and Iron Wolf wore their hair braided at each side of their face, leaving the rest of their hair loose in back, yet all was pulled together behind the head and clipped there with special fasteners of beads or feathers. As was their style, they each had cut a section of their hair's forelock, and wore it shorter and pulled down over the forehead and almost to the nose, creating a particular and unusual kind of "bangs." Such a style distinguished them from the more numerous Lakota Indians, who populated the show, and who generally wore their hair parted in the middle.

Because Blue Thunder was Lakota, he generally styled his hair in the tradition of the other Lakota men, parted in the middle, leaving the majority of his hair long. But, because he and the two Nakoda men were of the same secret clan, the Wolf Clan, and, because they were all three bound to do their duty to their tribes, they had become a threesome. To honor this, Blue Thunder now mimicked the Nakoda style of "bangs," cutting a forelock so that a section of it, too, fell down over his forehead.

At length, Wind Eagle took up the pipe of peace and lit it, since it was a necessity for any council, regardless of how informal that gathering might be. He took a short puff on the pipe, and then passed it to his friends to do the same. He then awaited the pipe's return to him before beginning the council.

When at last it was done and he held the pipe in his hand, he began, speaking in a hushed voice. "We have now blessed the four corners of the world, the four winds, the Above Ones and the Creator, and we three have inhaled the sacred smoke," he said. "We may now begin our council, but heed this, that all said here must be true."

Both Iron Wolf and Blue Thunder nodded.

"I believe," began Wind Eagle, "that I have possibly met the deceiver. Since we have been warned that this person will cause the downfall of our people, it is right that I inform you of this meeting. The possible trickster is a woman who is pretending to be a boy. She is a sharpshooter, and Buffalo Bill has asked that she and I compete in many different kinds of contests."

"*Hau, hau,*" murmured Iron Wolf.

"*Hau,*" repeated Wind Eagle. "It is good. Our practices will demand that she be with me each day, and thus, I will seek to learn more about her reasons for being here. I hope to discover soon what sort of danger she might cause our people, if she is, indeed, the deceiver whom we must beware."

"*Hau, hau,*" echoed Iron Wolf. "And while you uncover her true nature and expose her, I will discover, if I can, when we might expect the white man's President to attend one of our performances, so that we might practice our speeches and deliver our words to him without error."

"This is all very good," Blue Thunder stated. "But there is doubt in your voice, my brother, when you speak of this deceiver. Do you question that she is the one?"

"I do," replied Wind Eagle. "When we met, I became aware that she was not a boy, but I detected little, if any, evil in her manner. That is why I will keep her close to me, for she might be skillfully and carefully hiding her heart. I must determine it."

Blue Thunder nodded. "*Hau, hau.* And so you must, but consider our problem if she is not the one. Therefore, I will do all I can to observe others in the show, so that we might identify if there is another whose purpose is to deceive others, and, by this trickery, to gain access to our people to destroy them. If you do not object, I would attend one of your practices that I might see this deceiver for myself," declared Blue Thunder.

"*Hau, hau,*" answered Wind Eagle. "You are welcome to do this. In truth, I believe you speak wisely, for although this woman dresses herself in a manner to mislead myself and other members of this show, there is doubt in my mind that she is the one, for I am not well enough acquainted with her to know her heart. Still, I must follow this path to the end, for if she is the destroyer, and I do not discover it until too late, I will have failed our people."

"*Hau, hau.*" Both Blue Thunder and Iron Wolf spoke as one. But it was Iron Wolf who continued, and who declared, "It is good that we each have our paths to follow as we determine how to bring down this foe. Let us continue to speak to each other of these matters when we feel it is right to do so, and let us keep each other informed of the truth that we unearth."

So they agreed, and it became Wind Eagle's obligation to close the council in the good and sacred way. Announcing the end of their meeting, and scattering the ashes of their pipe upon the earth, their council came to an end.

***

As Lucinda gazed around the clearing where she was to meet up with Charles Wind Eagle, she continued to bask in her good luck. Despite Jane's fear of consequences, Luci felt certain that Charles Wind Eagle would do her no harm. If anything, her own emotions were more ecstatic, for she rejoiced in the prospect of working with a man who was known to be the best archer in this part of the world. But more so than that, was the knowledge that her disguise was good, and that Mr. Cody had not asked or had even seemed to suspect that she and Jane were on the run from the "law."

Or so she hoped.

Of course, she would be required to learn and to practice shooting an arrow as accurately and as fast as her instructor, Mr. Wind Eagle. And that would take some practice. But Luci felt certain that within a few weeks, she'd be firing off arrows as well as the best.

His would be a shorter learning experience, she assumed, for she was fairly certain that she would find that he could draw and pull the trigger of a gun almost as fast and as accurately as she. There was little she could do about their upcoming and uneven learning experiences. However, she made a promise to herself that she would practice hard in order to shoot an arrow as fast as he, even if it meant arising earlier in the morning than usual and working on the skill until late into the evening.

He had chosen well for their first practice. These wooded grounds were as far apart as possible from the living quarters of the rest of the troupe. As Mr. Eagle had said, it was here that the noise of their shooting would draw as little attention as possible.

To her chagrin, Charles Wind Eagle was already standing and at ease at their designated point when she stepped into the clearing. Drat, she had assumed that she would beat him to these grounds, but she had been wrong about that.

It was early morning, six o'clock to be exact, and the sun was only now starting to peep up in the eastern sky. Still, that light, dim though it might be, was enough to allow her to see the man clearly.

He turned when he detected her presence, and paced toward her casually. She frowned. Was that the hint of another smile upon his countenance?

Yes, it was. She wondered why. Wasn't it disconcerting enough to have to be taught a skill by a man who was uneducated, a possible heathen, and whose people had been at war with her own? That he should grin at her so easily didn't fit in with her father's learned lectures on the nature of these people. Indeed, if her father were here right now, he would remind her that there was nothing to recommend the American Indian—not socially, not mentally or scholastically, and certainly not morally.

Yet, as she looked outward, taking in Mr. Eagle's tall form as he slowly paced in her direction, she thought he might possibly be one of the handsomest men of her acquaintance. Odd, that. From her father's colorful description of the Indian, she had thought that this race of people was ugly beyond description.

But if this were so, her father had undoubtedly never met a man like Mr. Eagle. Despite herself, her eyes were drawn to his tall, dark looks. As she gazed at him now, she decided that he might be in his early twenties, and she calculated that he must stand at about six foot tall, maybe a fraction less. With black hair, dark brown eyes and a tanned complexion, his image was purely exotic. His eyebrows were sparse, though groomed perfectly, and his nose was not hawk-like as was commonly assumed where Indians were concerned. Rather, his nose was straight; it was not long and it was, in fact, good-looking; his lips were full with a well-defined cupid's bow. His shoulders were so broad that the "V" which so distinguished the masculine chest and waist seemed exaggerated. His leg muscles seemed thicker and more muscular than what she more commonly observed in the male of the species. But what she couldn't understand was how he seemed to move with a grace that defied logic for a man of such masculinity.

His choice of clothing deepened his good looks, also. He wore a light blue bandana tied around his neck, and a short string of blue, white and red–beaded earrings fell from his earlobes. The effect of those earrings, however, was not feminine; rather on him, it exuded manliness.

His figure was slim, with lean hips, but his long legs seemed to be unusually muscular, and he wore navy-blue trousers that looked to be made of cotton; they were beaded and fringed, and, at the bottom, disappeared into his moccasins. That this particular piece of clothing was tight-fitting drew too much attention to his legs, and she quickly decided not to look there. The American Indian breechcloth that he wore was made of deep blue and white cotton; it was fringed in light blue and fell to about mid-thigh. She had never before witnessed a man dressed in breechcloth and trousers, and she wondered why the style was not more well-known, for the striking look of it was quite masculine.

His feet were shod in blue, white and red beaded moccasins which were obviously made of leather. His hair was braided and pulled back from his face, where an attachment held his braided hair together, while feathers stood up at the back of his head. Long bangs fell down over his forehead; an odd style for a man.

His shirt was a deep red in color with a white, beaded vest pulled over it. That vest was tied in front with what appeared to be buckskin strings, and four squares of blue beads with a white, beaded cross in the middle of them decorated the vest, front and back. Arm guards, made from metal, were placed above the elbow and at the wrist. Luci, who had never seen an Indian up close and personal, was impressed not only with his good looks, but she thought that if she were a boy for real, she would not want to face this man on the battlefield.

"Mr. Lou-ie." He pronounced her name in his deep voice with a slight accent, although it was pleasant. As she gazed up at him, she caught a gleam of humor in his eye, as he continued, "Later, we will see to your accuracy with a gun. For now, we will begin your training with bow and arrows. You will need a bow to start your training, and we could borrow one of mine for today, but, I think not, for you are smaller than I."

She nodded, and pulled her hat down over her eyes. His voice was low, slightly hushed and baritone; there was also a quality to it that caught one's attention. What she really needed, she decided, was to stop gaping at him. He was, after all, beneath…

She didn't finish the thought, for this man certainly did not fit that lowly description she had often heard in her home. Even though she loved her father dearly, she realized that if Mr. Eagle were at all representative of the Indian people, then her father's accounting of them left too much unsaid.

But Mr. Eagle was continuing to speak, and he uttered, "We will look in the midst of these trees for a piece of wood," he gestured at the stand of trees behind her, "that will be of the kind we need to make your bow and arrows."

"But—" her voiced squeaked, and she lowered it as she continued, "I thought we were going to practice shooting."

"We are," he agreed. "We must, as soon as we make a proper bow and some arrows for you."

"But couldn't I borrow or pay for a bow and some arrows from you, or your own people? After all, it seems a terrible waste of time to go to the trouble of making my own, when I would gladly pay for a product already made."

"And have any of these people you mention ventured to suggest that you are free to borrow them or purchase them?"

"Well, no, but then I don't know them or — "

"Among my people, it is considered ill-mannered to ask for an object of some value that has not been offered. So we will not take that path. Instead, we will find the right wood, and I will instruct you in how to make the bow and the arrows you will need. Come," he clapped her on the shoulder, causing her to trip forward. He *tsk, tsked* at her. "If we are to compete in these contests, you will need to build some muscle there, my young fellow. I will teach you." His words were filled with so much humor that she thought he might be laughing at her. But when she gazed up at him and looked into his eyes, his countenance appeared to be somber…except for that slight gleam in his eye.

"But that will take a long time."

"Not too long," he replied, then he winked at her. "Come, let's see what kind of wood we can find for your new bow." With this simple utterance, he turned and stepped into the woods.

CHAPTER FIVE

The bow with which they are armed is small, and apparently an insignificant weapon, though one of great and almost incredible power in the hands of its owner, whose sinews have been from childhood habituated to its use and service. The length of these bows is generally about three feet, and sometimes not more than two and a half. They have, no doubt, studied to get the requisite power in the smallest compass possible, as it is more easily and handily used on horseback than one of greater length. The greater number of these bows are made of ash, or of "bois d'arc" (as the French call it), and lined on the back with layers of buffalo or deer's sinews, which are inseparably attached to them, and give them great elasticity.

— George Catlin, *My Life Among the Indians*

"*Do* you know your trees?"

She coughed, obviously lowering her voice. "Not as well as you, I think."

Wind Eagle chuckled. Humor, teasing, poking fun at her disguise might be his only means of declaring war against this deceiver, and he determined that he would enjoy this act of discovery and the unmasking of this woman's true intentions. For the moment, he ignored his past experiences and the memory of other women—two women who had been close to him—who had chosen a similar path as this one.

Oh, to be sure, if he found this girl to be the one who meant harm for his tribe, he would act. But meanwhile, he intended to tease her about her deception as cleverly as possible, and often.

Knowing well that the East harbored many ash and hickory trees, and that this was the wood in this area of the country that made the best bows and arrows, he deliberately led her astray, and suggested, "The willow tree might do well for your bow. What do you think?"

"If you suggest it, it must be so."

He grinned at her and was barely able to contain his laughter. "Well, come then, let us gather much of its wood and set you to work. Look for branches littering the ground, for these are already dead."

"Already dead? Is that important?"

He grinned at her. "You wouldn't wish to kill a tree, would you?"

He watched her as she frowned. At length, she said, "I...have never thought about it."

"Then you must consider it, for a tree holds the same sort of life that we all do, only in a different form."

"I'm not certain that's correct. Aren't trees and other life forms here for our ease as human beings?"

"Perhaps, but that doesn't mean that one should take a life without due regard."

"Why?" she continued to argue. "They are only plants, and you must admit that a man must kill a tree in order to build houses, and, since all people need shelter, there is no shame in that."

"Of course you are right, and there is no shame in that...but..." he trailed out the expression, "...it does not follow that one should take a life without need. Ask yourself: is the tree not alive? Does it not enjoy the thrill of life flowing through its many branches?"

"I...I don't know," she sighed. "Is it important? I mean, all of the homes that you see here in this town, all of the businesses, the structures on these streets—they are all made of wood. Without this, where would civilization be?"

"Much better, I think," he replied. "But we will not argue that. Consider, if you will, would you kill a tree or its limbs, only to make yourself a bow? Is your need greater than the life of this tree?" He gestured toward the weeping willow tree.

"I…but clipping the limb is like cutting hair, is it not?" Why she seemed compelled to continue their argument, he didn't know, and he could only speculate that the reason might be because his point of view was foreign to her. ut she was continuing to speak, and he gave her his attention as she muttered, "It doesn't hurt the tree, after all."

"And you know with certainty that this is so?"

"Of course I do."

"I might argue with you about that. But, at present, that is another point we should not debate. Instead, let us approach the tree, and ask it if it hurts to trim its limbs."

"What? Surely you jest."

He gave her a serious look. "Would I tease you?"

"I…I don't know you well enough to be able to give you an honest answer about that."

He smiled at her. "Perhaps I tease you. Maybe I don't." Grasping her gently by the shoulders, he prodded her toward one of the many weeping willow trees that grew in these woods. "Listen to the tree as we try to discover whether it has feelings or not. You must spread your arms around it, for a tree lives in a different time than we human beings."

When she held back, he urged, "Come, get closer to it; spread your arms around the tree, and listen."

He heard her sigh, yet she did as asked and stepped up to the tree, spreading her arms around it. However, like a woman's arm span, they reached only a little about the circumference of the willow. Then he asked, "Do you hear it breathe?"

"No."

"Do you feel its life?"

"No… Wait. I do feel something."

"*Hau, hau.*"

"What did you say? What does that mean?"

"Good, yes, fine; also a greeting. That is what *hau, hau* means."

"Oh." She repeated, "*Hau, hau.*"

"Ah, but that is how Nakoda men say those words. Women say, *'haŋ, haŋ.'* Can you repeat that?"

"Of course."

"And which of those expressions would you say, if you were to be honest?"

She gave him an odd, startled look, but she said, "That's a strange question for you to ask me. *Hau, hau,* of course."

He winked at her. "Of course."

***

"With any wood, you must look for as straight a piece of it as possible. Try to find one that is free of offshoots and knots. You will want as large a log as you can find and is easy to manage."

"But I thought that one had to fell a tree to get the wood needed for a bow."

"Sometimes, that is true," he replied. "But this wood that surrounds our camp is full of large branches that have only recently fallen, and these will do. Over there—" he pointed, "do you see that big one?"

She nodded and followed him toward it. He picked it up and presented it to her.

"Do you perceive that it is still wet? It would make bad firewood, but good material for bow. Do you have a large, firm piece of flint?"

"Ah...no."

"Here, use mine." He pushed a piece of flint into her hand, where she stared at it, dumbfounded.

"Ah...all right," she acknowledged. "But, couldn't I just go out and buy a bow and some arrows? If not from your people, there might be a store in this big city that would carry what I need."

"Not good. Do we compete Indian-style, fairly matched, or do you wish to cheat?"

"Ah..."

"Think well on what I ask, for your answer will determine your character, I think."

It was a serious question, yet within his gaze, his eyes twinkled as though he were sharing a good joke with her. Even one side of his lips slanted upward, in a half-hearted grin.

She sighed. It would appear that learning to shoot a bow and arrow as accurately as he did was going to be a little harder, and require more work than she had assumed. Yet, she would not be turned away, and she would not be bested by him on a personal basis. Angling him a sharp stare, she confessed, "I suppose I would rather buy a bow and some arrows, but, if that is cheating and if that gives me an unfair advantage over you, a man who has shot a bow and arrow for all his life," she continued sarcastically, "then I will do all I can to make a bow and some arrows as you instruct, but—be warned…." She turned the sarcasm in her voice into as low and as stern a manner as she could, and said, "I don't trust you. There is a light in your eyes that makes me doubt your sincerity. Although we have only just met, there are now many times when I have seen humor in your manner as you speak to me. Do you think that I am stupid?"

"*Hiyá,* I do not." He laughed, the action making light of his words. "But," he continued after a bit, "I believe that you might be hiding a truth that I have yet to discover."

"*Baaa…*" She made the sound as she blew out a disgusted breath. Nevertheless, she looked away from him.

"That is what I suspect, but come, we will let the future tell us the truth. For now, let us set to work and make that bow. Then I will instruct you on the best way to create arrows that shoot straight every time. Are you ready to begin?"

She glanced up at him suspiciously, if only because he had given in to her doubts much too quickly. All she said, however, was, "Yes, let's start."

For answer, he merely winked at her, and, clearing a spot on the ground on which they were to work, he showed her how to use the flint he had given her as a tool to separate the bark from the wood. And, as the sun arose in the eastern sky, showering her in its light, she threw herself into the chore, ignoring for the moment that the task was labor intensive and that the temperature was getting hotter, and hotter....

***

"The day is warm," he observed after they had been working over the making of the bow for several hours. It was true. Had he deliberately given her a seat in the sun, while he basked in the shade? Even now, she could feel the beads of sweat that were gathering over her brow, several making paths down her face, and dripping down the end of her nose.

"Why don't you do as I do," he suggested, "and take off your shirt?"

She glanced up at him to witness again that ever-present gleam of humor in his eye. As her gaze met his, he again winked at her. She looked away. Why did he seem to be so perpetually in a good mood? And why did he appear to be continuously laughing at her? Hadn't her father said that these people were glum and sullen? She didn't answer his question.

He continued. "Let us take our leave from this task and journey to the water that is hidden from the many eyes of the Showman's performers. There we could cool off from this heat by swimming as nature intended, as naked as the day we were born."

Momentarily, she paused, shocked. At last, however, she managed to mutter, "Ah...no thanks."

"No?" Again that note of humor entered into his expression. "Then perhaps we might journey to the arena, where we can both show each other the strength of our skills."

The idea of ceasing this project, if only for a moment, seemed to her to be a gift from the gods, and she at once agreed, saying, "Yes. That would be most welcome."

"Then come, follow me," he encouraged, rising to his feet. "I will show you the way to the arena that the Showman uses for his exhibition. That place is somewhat distant from here."

"Yes, good. How many weeks do we have for practice before the show begins?"

"Several, I believe. Do you worry about that?"

"Absolutely not. I am certain I can learn to shoot an arrow as well as you in only a week." She frowned at him as she sarcastically added, "Although you have had a lifetime to perfect your skill."

His only answer to her ill-humor was a round of what appeared to be good-hearted laughter, and, truth be known, it was given at her expense....

***

"You're good."

The praise from Wind Eagle was not easily won. She'd shot accurately, and from the many different positions he had indicated: from standing, lying down, squatting, upside down, even backward, using a mirror—all this she had done with precision, and had been done in the heat of the day. How long was it, now, that they had been standing here, with her having to shoot over and over, in order to prove to him that she was an excellent marksman? It seemed as though it were forever, standing as they were beneath the oppression of a noon-day sun.

If she had felt overly warm this morning, as both she and Wind Eagle had fashioned a bow for her, it was worse now. But she would expire from the heat before she'd ever let him know it.

She did, however, send a frustrated glance up at him where he stood next to her, on her left side. "And now," she uttered, her voice as low as she could muster, "it's your turn to show me what you can do."

He grinned at her, that delicious laughter ever present in his gaze. Worse, he winked at her, again. "All in good time." His tone and his manner mirrored what seemed to be his continual amusement at her expense. "Show me how fast you are on the draw."

"What?" She squinted up at him. "I don't understand. Annie Oakley doesn't have to perform a quick draw. And she's a main attraction here."

"But you and I will. Do you not recall what the Showman said? We will compete. That includes fastness of draw. So far, you've only shot at unmoving targets. In nature, your game does not await your pleasure."

"You doubt me?"

"Show me." He grinned at her.

She sent an impassioned glance up to the heavens, as though the sky itself were to blame for her ill mood. Nonetheless, she told him, "Set up the clay pigeons, and watch an expert at work."

He laughed, and she frowned.

She asked, "Well, are you going to do it?"

"Of course."

"And when will I have the delight of watching you at your work?"

"In good time." His words carried that ever-present smile. "Are you ready?"

"Are you?"

"*Hau, hau.* Gun in your holster now," he instructed as he moved in front of her and to her right, getting himself into position and out of the line of fire. He picked up a clay pigeon. "Ready? Draw!"

And so it went for what must have been a good half hour. On and on it continued, as though the concept of breaking for the noon-day dinner were a foreign idea to this man's mind. But she couldn't shoot over and over forever, and at last, he seemed satisfied. As he paced toward her, he said simply, again, "You're good."

She sighed. It was probably the best praise she would ever get from him. Incredibly, she smiled.

She glanced down the length of the grassy field of the arena. The place was huge. She guessed its size at about one-hundred and sixty feet to two hundred feet wide, and maybe six hundred feet long. A bleaching-board type of seating arrangement lined the field on both sides, and there were large, canvas tents placed above the seating, as well as at entrances. These "doorways" into the arena lined each end of the field. The grasses inside this space were matted from use and the ground was hard, probably from the constant hammering that took place here.

"And now," she began, "I think it's time for dinner, and once that is done, let's see how good you are. Hopefully, we'll be done before the supper hour."

"*Wašte'.* This is good. We will meet back here after the noon hour, and its dinner of good food."

She nodded and watched as he turned away, where he paced toward the side of the arena, where sat about ten, maybe more, white women. Women? It was the first time she had noticed them.

What were all those girls doing here watching their practice? Two other young Indian men sat among the giggling females, and, even from where she stood, she could hear the laughter and the welcoming words as Wind Eagle strode purposefully toward those ladies.

"Come sit with us, Charles," encouraged one girl. "I have brought some country-style fried chicken for you. My grandmother made it for you boys this morning."

"Well, my mother baked an apple pie for this occasion."

"And I have a blueberry pie, especially prepared for the three of you gentlemen."

Luci could barely believe what she heard. Why were these women here, doting on Wind Eagle and the other two men as though these Indian showmen were some sort of royalty?

Realizing her question would not be answered here, she turned her back on the scene and trod away in the opposite direction. Hopefully, the noon-day meal would still be warm.

CHAPTER SIX

*Many ladies were offering them their hands and trinkets – some were
kissing them, and every kiss called forth the war-whoop (as they called it a
"scalp")....he took every lady's hand that was laid upon his naked arm or his
shoulder as a challenge, and he said that he kissed every woman that he
passed....one thing was certain, that many there were in the room that evening
who went home to their husbands and mothers with streaks of red and black paint
upon their cheeks,...these (excitements) were now become of nightly
occurrence....*

– George Catlin, *Adventures of the Ojibbeway and Ioway Indians in
England, France, and Belgium: Being Notes of Eight Years' Travels and
Residence in Europe with his North American Indian Collection*

In the American Indian language of sign, Blue Thunder asked his
friend, "Have you yet discovered the trickster's true intentions?"

"I have not," answered Wind Eagle utilizing the language of sign,
"although this is only our first practice."

Both Blue Thunder and Iron Wolf nodded.

"Now, what are you boys talking about so seriously," asked one of
their entourage, a woman who was a pale, but beautiful, dark-haired
beauty.

"We are arguing over which one of you is the prettiest," answered
Iron Wolf.

The air around them filled with feminine giggles.

"And what have you determined?" asked a blonde.

Blue Thunder smiled at her, then at each woman present. "We each disagree. I fear, young ladies, that you are all equally charming."

While delightful, high-pitched laughter answered this statement, Wind Eagle came up to his feet and addressed the beauties, saying, "And now, I fear I must leave you, for my new partner has returned from his meal, and is awaiting me."

"Do you really have to go?" asked the blonde.

"I fear that I must. But please return here after dark, when our practice will be at an end. Perhaps we can all exchange words — and maybe more — then."

Three of the young women sighed, and, smiling happily because of the prospect of more fun to come, he turned away to pace back toward his new "partner."

But the frown on that partner's face indicated that she might not be in a good frame of mind after her meal, and Wind Eagle could only wonder what sort of food the attendants had served. As he came up to stand beside this girl/boy person, he watched her closely as "Miss Louie" blew out her breath in disgust. Then, without missing a beat, she asked, "What are all those girls doing over there, watching us?"

"They are looking at me," Wind Eagle clarified.

"Why?"

He shrugged. "Why not?" In truth, he wanted to laugh aloud, but he cautioned himself to merely show his humor by tone of voice.

"That's not fair, now," she said. "You answered my question with one of your own."

"And why shouldn't I?" he asked, his expression as deadpan as he could make it.

"Will you stop laughing at me?"

"I?" Feigning surprise, he asked, "Laughing at you?"

"Oh, stop it. You know that you are. Now let's get down to the business at hand. You're supposed to be showing me your own ability to shoot."

"So I am," he agreed, as he stood before this woman whom he had recently named Wíŋyaŋ Gnáyaŋ, Deceiving Woman. His look at her, although brief, took in her boyish disguise: from her baggy, brown pants that fell down to the top of her dirty, brown boots, to the red-checked shirt that she wore tucked into her loosely-fitted trousers. The suspenders that held up those pants allowed them to rise up above what was probably her natural waistline. And what was this? A long strip of material tied securely around what should have been her breasts? He did not allow his vision to remain on this area of her body, however.

A soiled and brown, wide-brimmed hat with stampede strings tied under her chin, sat atop her hair, effectively hiding any length of her mane, as well as the top of her face. Her eyebrows and eyelashes, however, were a shade of orange-red, a hair color he had rarely beheld on a human being, and he wondered if she had performed the ultimate in destroying her femininity by cutting her hair and styling it as a white boy might wear — short and ugly. Ugly, that is, according to his point of view.

She wore a holster around those baggy pants, which served to hide her womanly curves. Briefly, he speculated on what her figure might look like were she to dress herself as she should, but he abandoned that vision, realizing that his mind had produced an undressed and womanly image of this girl.

That would not do. He did not ever wish to think of Wíŋyaŋ Gnáyaŋ in this manner. Never. Girls who dressed themselves as boys were best left alone. Teased perhaps, because of their attempt at deception, but avoided if possible, for they could be as dangerous to a man's heart as a rattlesnake. His own personal experience knew this as fact.

He inhaled deeply before he gazed down at her, and said, "We will test our skills against each other now."

"Wait! You're supposed to be proving yourself to me. Didn't I have to do that earlier with you?"

"Ah-h-h," he murmured, drawing out the word. "I have already proved myself to the Showman."

"But not to me."

"Then let us begin. We should start as we mean to go. I have asked my friend, Iron Wolf, to throw two clay pigeons into the air. You will shoot the one on the right, I will shoot the one on the left."

"But I don't have that bow and arrow made."

He shrugged. "We will pit my bow and arrows against your gun and we will see who is the fastest and who shoots without a miss."

"That's ridiculous. Of course I'll win."

"Will you?"

She laughed. "You can't honestly believe that you — "

"Shall we shoot?"

"It's your loss, I guess."

"We will see," he uttered. "We will see."

***

Goodness! This man was as fast, and sometimes faster, with a handmade bow than she was with a ready-made pistol. How could that be?

It seemed impossible, and yet, shot after shot, he never missed; an odd element about his shooting was that he was both right-handed and left-handed, appearing to use either to his best advantage. Before now, she couldn't remember meeting a man who could shoot as well with his left hand as he could with his right.

After performing against him for what must have been an hour or more, she sent him a weary glance, and asked, "Where did you learn to shoot bow and arrows as fast as you do?"

"One does as he must," he answered. "A man is expected, after all, to bring in game for his family. He learns early in life what is needed from him, and he perfects his trade so that his family and those of his tribe never go hungry."

"That must be a good taskmaster, for I've never seen a man send off so many arrows as accurately as you do. I had no idea that a bow and a few arrows could be as fast, or even faster than a gun."

"And yet, we will do more than this, I think."

"What do you mean?"

"I mean that we have only begun."

"I don't understand."

"I think," he continued, "that the Showman wants us to compete first with your gun against my bow and arrows, as we have done here this day. But, while that may be the first of our competitions, we will then compete by use of bow and arrows, and then guns. It is to be a match with all three methods, and then we shall see who is the top performer."

"Wait. Let me ensure I understand you. First we'll compete with your bow and arrows against my gun, then we'll advance to both of us shooting bows and arrows, then the same with guns?"

"*Hau, hau,* and more, I think."

"More? More of what?"

"We will shoot at targets while we ride horseback; we will shoot with accuracy while jumping off a cliff, or fighting off a foe. We will compete in these feats of showmanship."

"But I've never ridden a horse as you have. I come from the city, where we travel in carriages and not necessarily by riding horseback. But you, you've probably ridden and performed trick shots off one of those ponies since before you could even walk. That's hardly fair, is it?"

"Did I say this was to be fair? This is what the Showman expects us to do. Being a boy…" He paused, raising an eyebrow at her. "You must assume that Buffalo Bill expects you to be as excellent a horseman as you are a marksman."

Did she detect sarcasm in his voice? Perhaps, but she chose to ignore it as she said, "Then we should tell him differently. I've never ridden a horse in this manner, and I don't know how to do it."

He brought a finger up next to his nose and shook it at her. "Do not say this word, 'never.' I will teach you."

"But I…this is so unfair, and unevenly matched. I will tell Buffalo Bill at once."

"Do not," was all he said.

"And why not?"

"Because," he lowered his voice, "if you wish to remain with the show, you must do as he says. He wants us to compete on every level that we can. Therefore, we will. I will show you."

"I can't believe this."

"Believe it. Now, do we practice the harder skills?"

She sighed. This was going to be more difficult, much more difficult, than she had ever anticipated. She would be required to practice all day and night, to even get into a frame of expertise that this man already possessed.

He raised a solitary eyebrow at her, as he lifted that right corner of his mouth into a smile. He was daring her…he was actually daring her. Suddenly, she saw red.

"Lead the way, oh master."

That's when he laughed. "Come, don't look so downhearted. You will learn. And do not call me that again. I am not your master. No man is master over another. Never forget it."

Her answer to this piece of wisdom was a frown, for, truth be known, she would have never guessed good sense to be a part of this man's nature. That he was also skilled in what he did lent her another lesson. She was going to have to practice, and practice hard, in order to become even a fraction as able as he.

But she would try. She would train in this manner of archery until her fingers bled and her legs would no longer walk, if need be. This she promised to herself.

***

An Indian, therefore, mounted on a fleet and well-trained horse, with his bow in his hand, and his quiver slung on his back containing a hundred arrows, of which he can throw fifteen or twenty in a minute, is a formidable and dangerous enemy.

— George Catlin, *My Life Among the Indians*

This afternoon of May 30th was to be the first performance of the Wild West Show since its return from abroad. The show had toured

The Eagle and the Flame

England and the European continent during the spring and summer months of last year; it had only sailed back to New York, arriving very recently, in May. She wasn't yet scheduled to perform with Charles Wind Eagle, which was good, for it allowed her the opportunity to watch the show in its entirety. Wind Eagle would be performing stunts, certainly, for she had come to learn that he and a few of his friends were considered to be the show's most popular act.

What was unbelievable to her was the amount of women who sat in the first-row seats. Their giggling and shrill, high-pitched laughter filled the atmosphere with cheer, and a good degree of expectation. Glancing around the stands, she saw that the tiered bleaching boards were packed, and Luci could find no seat that was unoccupied.

Buffalo Bill headed up the show's entrance into the arena, or the Grand Review, as Cody called it. Rough riders of the world, including cowboys and Indians, Mexicans, Cossacks, even the US Sixth Cavalry, and, even more men of particular skills, paraded into the grounds. Many of the performers walked beside those men and women who were mounted. All took off their cowboy hats or helmets, and waved them to the rounds of cheers and applause from the audience.

Last to enter the arena were the American Indian sharpshooters, the trick riders, the war dancers and the Indian drummers and musicians. Some of these rode and waved their bows and spears to the crowd, some walked. Charles Wind Eagle and his two friends were among this latter bunch, and were the last to enter the arena. They rode onto the grounds calmly enough, their ponies ambling side by side. But their appearance in the parade, although they were the last to enter, was followed by screams of rapture from the many young women who were seated in the front row seats.

Screaming?… Shouting?… What was going on here? Luci's question, however, would have to wait until the entire four hours of the show was almost finished before she and her sister were to discover what this feminine fuss was all about.

The three men entered on horseback and without saddles. They galloped back and forth, darting past one another at terrific speeds, and, whilst doing all this, they guided their ponies to weave patterns in and around each other. At the same time, each of the men jumped from one side of the animal to the other, over and over. Then, still at a fast gallop, they each one stood up on their mounts. At one point, as though in unison, they all appeared to fall from their seats, but they only disappeared on the other side of their horse.

Swoons from those of the feminine gender in the audience swept through the crowd when it appeared that one of three had fallen from his mount. But he hadn't; it was all for show. 'Round and 'round they galloped, and Luci was feeling more than a little sick to her stomach, simply watching them.

At one point, two of them dismounted and only Wind Eagle remained astride, riding at a fast clip around the arena. Within minutes, the other two men threw clay pigeons into the air. Wind Eagle, with his pony still at a run, hit each and every target, utilizing no more than his short bow and arrows. Too soon, Wind Eagle appeared to fall from his mount, making a clear shot at one of those targets as he fell. Screams of concern, as well as rapture, escaped from the lips of those women up front.

I am supposed to compete with this man? Am I expected to fall from a horse, while shooting expertly?

It wasn't long before the riding came to an end, and, while Luci was feeling more and more nauseated, the three young warriors disappeared, only to reappear again, this time carrying a large drum between them. Having set the drum on the hard ground in the middle of the arena, they seated themselves around it. Other Indians, men and women, filtered onto the field, and stood behind the three of them. In fact, several of the women in the front-row seats came up to their feet and filtered onto the grounds of the arena, also crowding around the three young men.

Then it started: the drumming, the singing. Several of the Indian men commenced dancing to the beat of the drum, while the native women bobbed up and down to the same rhythm. Even the young women from the audience, who had stepped onto the field, began to keep time to the beat.

"What do you think is going on there?" Luci asked her sister.

"I'm sure I don't know," Jane answered. "But it's intriguing, isn't it?"

"Intriguing? I don't think so. Why do you believe all these women are swooning over those young men?"

Jane shrugged. "Maybe because they're handsome? I don't know, but I'm beginning to wonder if Father was right about the native people."

"I am, too, but really, there's many a handsome man in this show. We've had a four-hour display of looking at these men and watching them, with their skill and brawn. They are some of the most handsome species of male that I've ever seen. Why these three in particular?"

"I don't know. Why don't we go down there and ask the women?"

Luci sighed. "Not this afternoon, Jane. I think I've had more than enough entertainment for one day."

Jane glanced at Luci, and Luci saw that her sister was smiling. After a moment, Jane commented, "You're going to have to practice pretty hard to compete with Charles Wind Eagle, I think." As Jane gazed out at the spectacle taking place on the grounds in front of them, she added, "I suppose I'll have to come with you to watch you and that man practice."

Luci frowned. "Why? We've talked about this already. I am in no danger from him."

"I know but… Maybe I have other reasons now. Truly, I'm beginning to think you might need a chaperone."

"Not you, too? Janie, don't become one of those women."

"Me? Are you insinuating that I might be romantically interested in one of those men? Never. I remember our father's warnings too well. No, I think that I'm merely curious to see how you match up with Mr. Eagle, and, perhaps I should be on hand to prevent you from swinging that hat off your head, showing that young man your long, beautiful red hair, as well as your gender. I'd hate to find out what he might do if he discovered —"

"Sh-h-h. Are you trying to cause trouble?" Luci stood up and made a show of helping her sister to her feet, as any well-brought-up brother might do. As they left the seating arrangements, Luci commented to Jane, "Don't say that again. I can never let my guard down on my disguise.

Please, have a caution. We have trouble enough. We don't need to add to it."

"Why, I would never do that."

Luci groaned as the two of them exited the park. If Jane had it in mind to flirt with any one of those three men, heaven help them. Jane simply didn't realize the appeal of her charm.

CHAPTER SEVEN

"*If* you desire to shoot fast with a bow and arrow, you must learn to hold your arrows in your right hand, since you are right-handed. Never grab from a quiver."

"Okay," she agreed, keeping the bow held as he had instructed her to do. She hadn't made this new bow that she now used; he had fashioned it for her and had presented it to her as a gift. True enough, she had tried to craft one. But all her bows, her bowstrings and her pathetic arrows broke. After she had taken several tries at perfecting the skill, he had seemed to take pity on her and had presented her with a bow and some arrows that he had recently made.

"What do you want as a good payment for this bow and these arrows?" she had asked him after he had presented the gift to her. "I should tell you that until I start performing, I have little money."

"I did not make this to cause you to have a debt to me," he had replied. "It is freely given."

"But—"

"If you insist, a good show would be payment enough." That had been all he'd told her, adding that ever-present wink of his to the reply. "It's what the Showman expects from us."

This exchange between them had happened several days ago. Currently, they stood side by side in the woods that they used for training, which was near to the show's Indian encampment. It was still early morning, with only a grayish tinge of light in the eastern sky and the chatter of songbirds, who, after awakening to the new day, enhanced the atmosphere with nature's most welcome songs. "I don't know why he teams me with you," she muttered in a sulky tone of voice. "After all, you're a good one-man show, all on your own. I mean, yours is one of the most popular acts — at least with the women."

He grinned. "So it is. But the Showman has a good idea. Take what is already well-liked, and make more of it, to bring in even more money."

"But I've never shot a bow. My skill is with a gun. How can I possibly compete with you?"

"Because I will teach you how to do it, and I will help you. Your skill with a gun is unusual, and your eye is already trained to hit a target, even at great disadvantage. With a little practice, adding this skill will come easy to you."

Her reply had been a snicker. All the same, they trained hard each day, starting early in the morning before the sun even had a chance to peep up in the eastern sky. Often, they took up practice again after his afternoon performances, shooting at targets until it was too dark to see well. But occasionally, when the moon was full, they drilled vigorously, well into the night.

Her arms hurt; her whole body hurt. But early on, she had promised herself that she would never let him know, if only to prove to herself that her father was right, and that she was superior to Mr. Eagle. And so it continued, each and every day.

But it wasn't simply target practice that she learned. Wind Eagle demanded that she become more physically fit, challenging her to wrestle and to lift stacks of wood, always ending the exercises by adding on more repetitions every day.

He even held foot races with her, increasing the challenge by asking several of the Indian boys in camp to compete with her. She always lost, but this didn't seem to deter Wind Eagle. Over and over, he ensured that she raced with the boys.

Eventually, she and Wind Eagle went hunting together, a practice dear to her heart. But when he'd teased her about her strength, adding a challenge to take a young deer recently shot upon her shoulders and carry it back to their camp, she had accepted the dare, even though it had meant that she could barely move afterward.

Always he laughed at her, that teasing glint of humor continuously gracing his handsome image. And, his was definitely a handsome face. If only all those women had an idea of what a hard taskmaster he was, they might not be so anxious to compete for his company.

Always, whenever he wasn't practicing, there were women around him, bringing him food or other amusements, vying for his attention. Indeed, one morning, when he hadn't shown up for practice, Buffalo Bill had sent her to find him. She had found him, all right; he'd been entertaining a woman within his own tepee. Embarrassed, she had turned away and had retraced her steps to the field where they practiced.

He had joined her sometime later, and she had ignored him. Frustrated, she had found herself shooting one arrow after another at several different targets she had set up earlier. It was fast work, it was furious. It was also accurately accomplished.

"You are doing this very well," he'd told her as he had come to stand at her side. "I see that you're shooting the arrows from the right side of the bow. It makes it easier to be fast, does it not?"

"It's the way you shoot 'em." She hadn't said the words in a nice manner, and she was glad that she hadn't.

"You jealous?

"Of course not," she'd replied, not even pretending ignorance of why he would ask her that question. Of course he was referring to the women, the girls who poured themselves all over him. Jealous? Her? What she couldn't understand was, why did they do it? Did these young ladies not realize that this man might be taking advantage of their somewhat open offers of entertainment?

"Of course not," he had mocked her. "Grow a little. You'll see. They'll like you, too."

"I don't care."

"I know," had been all he'd said.

"I know? What's that supposed to mean?" she'd asked, glancing up at him, only to be met again by the twinkle in his eye.

"Just that." He had grinned at her. "Simply, I know."

That exchange between them had happened several days ago. With her new skills in place, she and Wind Eagle were now expected to become a part of the show. In addition to his own acts, Wind Eagle was now to compete with her in duels of skill. There would be no quarter given, for it was a win or lose tournament.

Luckily, there was to be no horsemanship in their act—at least for now. Instead, they would walk forward and backward, always aiming to hit the targets placed along the way. They would compete in the fast draw; she, with her gun, and he, with his bow and arrows. Amazingly, although she had taught him the art of the fast draw, he was always quicker and better with the bow and arrow.

Their act was only one day away from its premiere, when it had happened:

As usual, Wind Eagle had been pushing her to do more, to run faster, to carry more upon her shoulders. They had pressed onward, away from the show's encampment, and had run to a forested and secluded spot. The ferns, trees and forested grounds they had found in this place grew around a magnificent pond.

Briefly she had paused to admire the glistening water that mirrored the surrounding trees and shrubs. Beautiful and serene, it had yet smelled oddly, both swampy and salty, which should have served to warn her. But it didn't.

Wind Eagle had come up behind her and said, "Indian boys your age can catch a fish with their bare hands. Can you?" He had grinned at her.

"Is that a challenge?"

Wind Eagle had shrugged. "Could be, but don't do it if you don't feel up to it." He had grinned at her, and that teasing light was in his eye.

"Why are you always poking fun at me?"

"Me?" His smile had been mischievous. "If I have done this, I apologize."

She had frowned and glared at him, wondering if he really meant it. After a moment, she'd decided to give him the benefit of the doubt, and she'd uttered, "Well, okay, I guess."

"You catch the fish and I will set about finding wood and tinder, enough to start a fire. We will have ourselves a good midday dinner."

"All right," she had agreed, as she watched him turn away from her and disappear into the thick woods that surrounded this place. She sighed. The man was far too handsome for his own good. To be sure, however, even if she were to dress as she should and present her true, feminine image, she would never seek to keep company with a man who enjoyed entertaining a different feminine personage each and every night.

Indeed not. Everlasting love—that's what she desired and what she ultimately sought out in a man. Besides, handsome though he was, Wind Eagle was from an entirely different and inferior culture than she, at least according to her father. If her father were here, he'd say that Wind Eagle's values in life were too far apart from her own, and his philosophy of how life was to be lived was fated to be a mystery to her. This alone would cause problems for any relationship. Not for her. Definitely not for her.

Besides, she knew that her father would never consent to or allow her to keep company with such a man as this; her father's viewpoint toward the American Indian in general would never allow it. Also, in the past, her Army General father had literally scared off any man whose occupation was not strictly military. And, if she were to be truthful, she would admit that early on in life, she had responded favorably to her father's constant drilling that she must marry no one other than a military man—indeed, a wartime genius. She couldn't recall a time when she had ever objected to this, if only because, from the time she could comprehend the meanings of words and sentences, her father had let her know that it was her duty to the memory of her mother, and to their family, to marry well, and to marry military…always….

She might protest and rebel against many of her father's other viewpoints and requirements, but in this, she knew there would be no quarter given. Thank the good Lord that there were many handsome, kind and intelligent men who were military. She simply hadn't met that special one yet.

So, she would remain friends with Wind Eagle, an easy matter to accomplish, especially since she was disguised as a boy. But never would she divulge her true identity to him. Those poor girls who ogled him...imagine, having to worry over what other women were attempting to do to him and for him? Not for her. Never for her.

***

It had started out well enough. Keeping on her boots, she had slowly waded past the ferns and tall grasses growing in the water. She'd been looking forward, out into the water to try to espy a fish, and she'd thought she had seen one.

Good. She'd catch that fish—if only to prove to him that she could do it. What a task. Why was he always challenging her?

That's when it happened.

She tried to raise her foot to take another step forward. She couldn't pull it up. She tried to raise up her other foot. It wouldn't budge, either. Both her feet were stuck.

She didn't panic; after all, she had been wading in all kinds of water since she was toddler. She simply hadn't tried hard enough.

With this thought in mind, she put all her strength into the effort of moving forward, but she couldn't budge. Surely this wasn't quicksand, was it? She breathed in deeply, gaining her composure before giving it another try. She strained at doing the simple act of pulling up one or the other of her feet.. Nothing. Actually, it was worse than nothing, as now, not only couldn't she move forward or backward, she was sinking. And, with every struggle she took to free herself, she sank farther down into the muck.

Indeed, she had sunk all the way up to her waist when panic at last came to roost within her, and she shouted out, "Wind Eagle!"

No answer.

"Ah, Wind Eagle, I need your help! Please! Can you hear me? Wind Eagle?"

Still no answer.

"Wind Eagle!"

"I am here," came his reply at last as he stepped out of the woods. "What are you doing so far out in the pond?"

"I...I..." She sighed, realizing it was a wasted effort to answer his question and tell him that she had discounted the possible danger of the mud at her feet. Instead, she told him the obvious, stating, "Wind Eagle, I'm stuck and I'm sinking far faster than is good for my continued health, I fear."

Clear understanding shone upon his countenance, as, suddenly and quickly, he went into action, removing his leggings and his shirt. She watched as he fashioned those clothes into a rope in a matter of minutes. Then he waded out in her direction.

"Don't come too close in case we both start to sink," she warned.

"I will not. Sorry I am for us both that I left my pony and my ropes back in camp, and it is several miles and a long run to my lodge. Maybe I could get there and back in time, maybe not. We will have to rescue you between the two of us."

"I have already tried to move. I cannot budge."

"Understood. Now, listen. Quicksand is made of sand, clay and water. Never fear that you will sink too deeply."

"Easy for you to say."

"Wiggle the toes of one of your feet."

"But—"

"If you do this, water will come into this area, and will help to loosen the sand's hold on you."

"All right."

"*Wašté*. Now wiggle the toes of your other foot."

"All right."

"Does it feel that the sand has loosened a little?"

"Yes, a little."

"Keep wiggling your toes as I come close enough to throw this rope to you. When I throw it at you, catch it."

"All right, I will."

He threw her the line he'd made, and she reached out for it, but it sank into the water and out of sight. He reeled in the rope, and again flung it to her. This time his aim was perfect, and the cord he'd made came within reach of her arms.

Quickly, she grabbed hold of it.

"Do not release your grip on the rope," he told her calmly enough, as though she might.

"I won't."

"Now, ever so slightly wiggle one of your legs. Do not let go of the rope as you do this."

"All right." Amazingly, her body floated up a fraction of an inch. It wasn't much, but it was enough to give her hope.

"*Hau, hau*," he told her. "You did well. Now wiggle the other leg, very slightly."

She did. Her body floated up perhaps an inch this time.

"*Hau, hau*. Gently repeat this, and tell me if you continue to rise up, even if it is only a little. If you sink farther, let me know that, too."

"Okay."]She stared at him urgently. "Am I going to die here?"

His dark eyes met hers, and, even as she sank deeper into the muck, she beheld an intense look of…was that admiration that shone there within his gaze? It was centered on her. Could it be? Did he like her? Perhaps admire her? Simply thinking this, she felt as though her heart expanded.

She'd never before witnessed an emotion that could be related to love, which could be so clearly seen upon a man's countenance. The fact that this was meant for her almost shocked her. He said softly, "You will not die here. Together we will ensure it."

She swallowed hard. Did her gaze back at him mirror the same emotion? Did she feel an affinity for this American Indian Casanova? Perhaps it was the intensity of her problem that caused a glimmer of truth to expose itself to her. But, the moment was quickly gone. She was simply too scared to consider the truths or lies of life right now.

As the minutes flew by, quickly turning into what must have been an hour or more, he talked her into wiggling her feet and her legs, when she might have given up. It was hard work, and she held tightly to the rope he had fashioned from his clothes. But, as the sun rose slowly to a noon-day sky, she was still stuck fast. Tears gathered in her eyes, for it seemed to her that for every inch she floated upward, she fell back half an inch. She bit down hard on her lip, tasting blood.

"You are doing well. Keep moving those legs and feet," he encouraged.

At last, perhaps after two hours or more, she had floated upward so that the water now came up lower than her waist.

"Look at what you have accomplished." His words heartened her. "Do you see that you are no longer sinking?"

"Yes."

"And now, I will pull you out."

"But I've heard that this is impossible to do."

"And yet, we will do it, I think. Continue to wiggle your feet and your legs. When I say 'now,' you are to twist your feet and legs as you are now, while I pull you out." Slowly, he positioned himself so that he was kneeling in the water, one leg bent and his arms outstretched toward her. "Are you ready?"

"Yes."

"Now!"

She moved gently, squirming, and she felt herself come a little loose as he pulled back hard. Looking up at him, she saw that veins stood out all along his naked torso and his arms, and that the muscles in both his biceps were flexed to their fullest extent.

She floated upward so that she was only thigh deep now.

"We break for only a moment. When I say 'now' again, you are to do as before. Do you understand?"

"I do."

"Now!"

Again, she wiggled back and forth, both legs, both of her feet. She felt the weight of his pull, and she was only stuck now up to her knees.

"Again, we break. Continue to move your toes, your feet and your legs."

"I am."

"*Hau, hau.* Now!"

She moved ever so slightly, while he pulled. Soon, she was only calf-deep in the mud, then ankle-deep, and that's when he reached out for her arm pits, and he pulled her the rest of the way out of the quicksand.

Breathing hard, he fell back into the water and swam backward toward the shore, but he never let go of her, so that her body lay flat against his chest, belly and the hard contours of his legs. Her head rested against his shoulder. He paused when he came to the shallow water, and she could feel him breathing hard.

She felt close to him, and she was; physically, of course. But more. She felt as though the essence of who she was had touched that which he was. Had this near brush with death caused them to become attuned to one another spiritually? Did he feel the same as she? Suddenly, she realized that she was shaking, but was it from the cold and shock, or was it from the experience of recognizing the truth and beauty of another being?

"Come," he urged, obviously aware of her trembling. "Let us return to the shore, where we will rest for a while, I think."

"Yes."

With his arms still firmly clasped around her, he came up to his knees, then, taking her into his arms, he stood to his feet. Slowly, he trod onto firmer ground.

"You saved me." She was crying. But was it from shock, from fear, or the realization that she felt deeply connected to this man?

"Of course I saved you. You didn't expect me to leave you, did you?"

She brought up a hand to swipe at her hat, but it was gone. Her cries increased, and the reality of what might happen because of its loss struck her. "I've lost my hat."

"That is true."

She gulped, and her voice, as well as her body, now shuddered as she added, "No! Oh, no. There is no hiding my secret from you now."

"*Hau, hau*, it is true, but—"

"You'll tell *him* won't you?" There was no need to explain who "him" was or what secret she was asking Wind Eagle to keep.

"Why would I do that, when I haven't done so in all this—"

"Because I've heard that Indians never lie."

"It is true that they never lie to their friends."

She screeched. "I am done for, because if there is one thing we are not, it is friends."

He took a deep breath, then said, "I have known the truth of your gender all along. It was never a mystery to me. And what you say is not true. We are partners." He sat down on the more secure ground, bringing her with him, still holding her closely within his arms.

"Being partners is not the same as being friends. And, what do you mean," she asked, "all along'?"

"From the first moment when we met and shook hands—from that time onward, I have always known. But come, we talk when perhaps we should be quiet. We have both had a scare. Be patient while I build a temporary stick and leaf shelter for us. There you can remove your wet clothing."

"Oh. A shelter. Yes, I suppose you must do that if I am to remove my clothing."

He nodded and let go of her, while he rose up to leave. Violently, she shivered.

He appeared to have noticed the reaction; at once he sat down again and took her back into his arms. He said, "Perhaps I dare not build that shelter yet. But then you will have to remove your clothing here, where we sit, for you are trembling from the cold and from shock. I fear that your wet clothing must go."

"I can't take my clothing off. Not in front of you."

"Understood. Then, I must make that refuge for you." Again, he stood up away from her. Once more, she shook so fiercely, the entire frame of her body convulsed and her teeth clattered.

As he gazed at her, it seemed to her as though he made a decision, for he bent over suddenly and picked her up, holding her in one of his arms as he explained, "I have nothing to warm you with except my body heat, for my clothing, too, is wet. You will have to let me hold you, then, while I gather some sticks and leaves and moss to make a temporary place where you can become warm again."

"You can do that? Carry me while you construct some sort of cover for us?"

"*Hau, hau*," he said. "You are not heavier than a deer. Besides, what I intend to do is light in weight and easy to do."

"I—" She gulped. "I thank you."

How he ever managed to do it, she might never understand, but, carrying her in one arm and pressing her next to his chest, he utilized his other hand and arm to begin the task of gathering sticks, moss, mud and leaves and putting these together until all these parts of nature started to make a form. Gradually, a weird-looking, low-to-the-ground shelter began to appear. Lastly, he waded into the woods until he found a large pine bough and carried that back to their new lodging, placing the fragrant branch within the quickly built, little hut.

His voice was low, almost a whisper, when he uttered, "You must remove your clothing now, for you are shivering, even as I hold you."

She nodded.

"I will put you inside the protection of this lean-to, and I will bring you two or more pine boughs, as well as leaves to place over you for warmth. Then, when you are ready, I will run back to my lodge and retrieve many blankets and a change of clothing for us both. Do you think you can do this?"

"I…" What could she say? She didn't want to be left alone right now, not for perhaps an hour or more. She couldn't explain why, and she really didn't understand why, except that maybe she wasn't ready to put distance between them yet. She couldn't tell him that. However, she did manage to stammer the words, "I...guess I ...can do...that."

She stared up at him, and, within her eyes, she tried to erase the fear that she felt inside. Alas, it seemed that she had been unsuccessful in that attempt, for, as his deep brown eyes met her own, he sighed, and he said very softly, "You need warmth. I have no way to give it to you, except to hold you close to me. Would you rather I do that, than leave you here while I run back to camp?"

She nodded.

"You realize that we would neither one of us be wearing much clothing? And, although I mean you no harm and no seduction, we are yet male and female, and of age. I must ensure you know this."

Again, she nodded. "I know." She couldn't look at him.

He was silent for several heart-stopping moments, until at last he muttered, "*Hau, hau.* I understand. Now, if I set you within this tiny shelter, do you think you could remove your clothing and give the garments to me through the entryway so that I might set your things out in the sun to dry?"

"I will try. Have you decided to stay, then?"

"I have. I will not leave you while you need me to remain here," he replied calmly as he carried her to their new shelter. Still holding her against his chest, he bent down onto his knees, and, leaning forward, he placed her within the darkened interior of their little stick and grass retreat. "I will turn my back now while you remove your gear and hand it out to me."

"You won't look?"

"I won't look."

Article by article, she stripped, carefully passing him each piece of her boy's clothing until she sat nude within the low-to-the-ground shelter. Unfortunately for her, all of her clothing had been wet, and she now sat, alone, cold, and also as naked as the day she had been born. She shivered, and her teeth chattered.

"I am going to look for firewood now."

Her lips quivered as she said, "All right."

However, the rattling of her teeth must have been loud, for he asked, "You are so very cold?"

"I...I..." *Click, click, click* went her teeth.

She heard him take another breath, and then she looked on as he bent down and squeezed himself through the lodging's tiny opening. Then, lying down at her side, he positioned her into a place next to him, and at last he took her into his arms. "I will give you what warmth I have to give. And, when you feel well enough, I will hunt for that firewood."

Her lips shook and her teeth continued to rattle on noisily as she replied, "Yes, all right."

And then he pulled her in so closely to him that she could feel each hard contour of his body, and, as his warmth filled her system, she thought that his body temperature was as good as, and perhaps better than, a fire. Feeling temporarily secure, she closed her eyes. Sleep was close to hand, and the last thought that she had before she passed into unconsciousness was that this man's scent was as pleasant as was his handsome face....

CHAPTER EIGHT

*O*dd, he thought, that he had not noticed how deeply gray were her eyes until they had stared at one another, there in the depths of the pond. Of course, he had long ago committed their unusual hue to memory, but not until then had he noticed how intense was that shade when set against the golden-red color of her hair, which now lay around her in all its glory. Her beauty was an odd sight to his eye. Yet, he couldn't deny that she was beautiful.

But she was not for him…ever. Still, a thing had happened between them in that life-and-death struggle. They had…become close. He could not explain it except that, for a moment caught in time, she had slipped into his heart.

He didn't like it. He didn't want her there. And, as surely as he loved the Creator of all, he would fight this feeling, and he would remove her from his affections.

Yet, here he was with this nude woman in his arms, and, as he held her closely to him, he was aware that his body was ready to do more than simply embrace the shivering, lovely woman next to him, she as naked as nature had intended her to be. Lying here next to her might be the utmost in masculine discomfort, for he was clothed in only his breechcloth and moccasins, and there was nothing left to ponder about the extent of the hills and valleys of her figure.

His clothing had also been wet, having been used as the rope to pull her out of danger. But he had unloosened the tie of his clothing and had placed his own things next to hers. Both sets of apparel lay atop their shelter now, serving as an extra roof, as well as a place where the sun could dry them. Was it his imagination, or did their clothing now mirror the closeness of their nearly naked bodies — the closeness of themselves in spirit?

In resignation, he drew in a deep breath. She was not for him, would never be for him, and he reminded his body to calm down. Nothing would happen here, and not simply because she required care. As close as he might feel to her, this woman, with her trickster-like boy's clothing, was as unwelcome to him as was a bed of thorny bushes.

Her presence here, as well as her deception, reminded him that his mother and sister had been of a similar nature as she, that both had once dressed as a boy. He shivered. He didn't wish to recall it, for those were bad memories.

As the woman trembled again in his arms, he brought up his hands to rub them down and up over her back — not to caress her — no, not that. But to try to bring warmth back into her physical self. He hoped that she would eventually sleep, and, if she did, he would use that time to build a fire. For now, he abandoned the idea of returning to his lodge for blankets and a change of clothing. What if she awoke to find him gone?

It would alarm her at a time when she was already in a state of shock. No, he would stay close by her until she awoke and was in a better frame of mind. Eventually, they would both need sustenance, but that was still several more hours away.

For now, he thought it best that he, too, lie against her and seek to forget his cares, if only for a mere breath in time. Indeed, he had been as afraid for her life as she. But a stray thought occurred to him over and over: why had the incident caused them to reach into one another's souls?

He couldn't answer his own question, and, on this thought, he closed his eyes and inhaled the sweet, womanly fragrance of her, content for the time being to do nothing more than rest.

***

She sat up, screaming. She had dreamed that...

Suddenly she was cold, and she glanced down to behold the reason why. She was naked from head to foot. Glancing to the side, she noted that Wind Eagle was awake, and that he had come up slightly to hold his head in his palm, his arm bent at the elbow. He looked endearingly handsome, and she glanced down, away from him, only to see that the warmth of his arm still embraced her, and it was close to her...

Quickly, she threw her arms over her breasts.

"It is too late for that, I fear," he observed.

"It's never too late."

For answer, he merely grinned at her. After a while, he asked, "Are you hungry?"

"No. Are you?"

"A little," he seemed to answer honestly. "But it will keep."

"What time is it? How long did I sleep?"

"It is mid-afternoon, and you have been resting for a few hours."

"Oh," she replied, glancing down at her nudity. "Thank you for coming to my rescue."

He nodded.

A shiver of cold shook her whole body.

"Here," he said, "come and lie down again. I will hold you until you are warm again."

"Ah, no, thank you."

"You are safe with me. I will tell you now that I have no interest in girls who dress themselves as boys, so do not fear that I might have it in mind to sweet-talk you into passion. I promise that you are safe with me."

But, am I safe from myself where you are concerned?

The thought, though brief, was unwelcome, and it reminded her of their sharing of themselves spiritually, only hours earlier, there, within that swampy pond. She drew in a deep breath, willing herself to consider other matters. "What do we do now?"

"We wait until our clothes are dry, and then we should dress and return to camp."

"Yes, of course."

Silence fell between them.

"What's it all about?" he asked after a moment.

"What? "She glanced down at him.

"Why do you seek to deceive others as to the true nature of your being?"

"I'm not trying to deceive others."

His silence was deafening, and, as she glanced down at him, she was met with his much-too-common and dreaded smile.

"Why are you always laughing at me?" she asked.

"Am I doing that now?"

"Yes, you are, and you know it."

"Then I apologize." Yet, he still grinned at her.

"If you have known about my disguise all along, why have you taunted me with boy chores? With running and racing until I can barely stand, with carrying a deer on my shoulders all the way back to camp? Were you aware of how greatly I was tasked at doing that?"

He laughed, and it was not a pleasant observation to note that his amusement was infectious, even when it was given at her expense.

"You've been having some fun all to my detriment, haven't you?"

Her question was met by a roar of such delight, even her own lips twitched upward.

She scolded, "It's not nice to make fun of other people, you know."

"*Hiyá*, that is true. And yet, you must admit that the circumstances merited a great deal of teasing. So come now, tell me what this is all about."

She glanced down, too well aware that she was sitting beside a man who was barely clothed, and that she, herself, was naked. nstead of answering, she asked, "Are our clothes dry yet?"

"I do not believe that they are, but I can look outside to see. Shall I?"

"Yes, please."

He came up onto his hands and knees, and, bending, he scooted out of their little hut. "I fear that they are still wet." His words and his voice came from outside. "But," he continued, as he peeked back into their refuge, "I can run back to camp and gather up blankets and extra clothing for us both. Do you feel well enough to wait for me here?"

She was too well aware that her lack of clothing gave her a feeling of vulnerability, and this would never do. After all, it was she, who, in this life, was more commonly the aggressor. To feel weak and needy did not suit her well. And so, squaring her shoulders, she said softly, "I...I guess that I am."

He peeped his head back into the shelter. "I did not hear that."

She cleared her throat. "I said that I suppose that I am feeling well enough."

"*Wašté.* I will hurry, for I do not wish you to catch a chill."

She nodded, then, realizing he was no longer looking back at her, she voiced, "Yes, your attention to this matter would be quite in order." Drat. She did not like this feeling—as though she were helpless, vulnerable.

He had squatted down in front of their meager shelter, and, as he looked inside, he winked at her, adding, "I will build a small fire to warm you until I return. It must be very small and left alone, for I do not wish it to burn this small lodge. Kick dirt on it if it starts to catch fire too greatly. Do you understand?"

"I do."

As she listened to his movements outside the tiny shelter, she realized that he must be an expert at building fires from nothing, for he accomplished the task rather quickly, considering that he had no matches.

"Watch it, but do not stoke it. It should help to warm you until I return."

She acknowledged him with a quick nod of her head.

Then, with nothing else to be said at this moment, he was gone.

***

He had brought her back a dress. A dress, of all things. As soon as he had laid the feminine clothing before her, she asked, "*This* is what my sister gave you as a change of clothing?"

"*Hau, hau.*"

"I can't believe it." Luci was glad that Wind Eagle hadn't tried to scoot into their rather tiny shelter. Instead, he had squatted down in front of it, keeping the flap of his shirt, which was the little hut's entrance, between them. She could see him through the cracks in the sticks and leaves that held the overlap in place.

He answered, "Maybe I convinced her."

"Convinced her? Jane? Are we talking about my sister?"

"She gave me the dress willingly, especially after I told her that you were sitting within my camp, naked."

"Wind Eagle! How could you have said that to her? She will think that you and I… I mean, she'll believe that we, that I—"

He laughed. The man was actually enjoying another joke at her expense. After a moment, however, he said, "I did not know that she was with child. It is starting to show."

"Hmmm. You are avoiding my question. How could you have said that to her?"

He winked. "In truth, I told her of your adventure, and my discovery of you. It was she who decided what manner and style of clothing that she would send you."

Luci sighed. "Never mind. I will wear my boy clothes, then, dry or wet."

"Why? Are you that kind of woman who wishes she were a man?"

"Ah…no."

"Then why do you choose to deceive others?"

"I…" she hesitated. Dare she tell him? After all, he had known of her disguise all this time, and yet, he had not said a word of it to Buffalo Bill. Plus, she now felt as though she knew his heart, the essence of who and what he was. And, she believed that he was not only trustworthy, he was also a man inclined toward moral qualities.

Still, she argued silently, were she and Jane safe from the law and the lies of the formidable Hall family? What if she related their problem to him, and he spoke of it casually to another within hearing distance of an enemy? Should she risk it? No. Quickly, making up her mind, she murmured, "I cannot speak of it."

He nodded. "It is a secret?"

"Indeed, yes. It is a secret."

"Then, come, dress yourself in whatever clothing you wish, and we shall share a meal before we go back to camp. I have brought us both our supper."

"Thank you. Hmmm, could you please gather up the boy's clothing for me? It matters not to me if it is wet or dry."

"I could," he agreed. "However, I should warn you that, although I do not wish romance with girls who dress as boys, I do appreciate the feminine form. Perhaps I might like to watch you as you crawl out from this shelter and obtain that clothing yourself."

"What?"

Again, he laughed and she saw that he gave her that irritating wink as he produced the clothing she had asked for, and passed it through the entrance flap. "I had already guessed that you would prefer to dress as a boy."

Still chuckling, he stood to his feet and she could hear his footsteps going away. *Drat the man.* Suddenly, she came to a knowledge she wished she didn't have, considering what had happened here between them. Yet, she couldn't deny it: Her father was wrong, very wrong about the American Indians. If this man were a representative of the ways of his people, they were not only clever and smart, they were handsome—much too handsome to be of any good for a woman's heart.

***

Except for that amusement in his eye, Wind Eagle looked the part of a deadly warrior, ready to take to the warpath. He had painted his cheeks red, and, on both his nose and his chin, he had dabbed on a red streak. His hair was pulled back from his face, as he usually wore it, while a section of his bangs hung low on his forehead. His clothing looked much the same: cloth pants, breechcloth, a shirt with metal arm guards and a beaded, embroidered vest. He held a bow in his left hand, and across his back hung a leather, beaded quiver.

She caught his eye, and he showered her with yet another of those exasperating winks, but her reaction back at him was an angry scowl. And why not? Lucinda was furious with Wind Eagle.

How dared he rig their first exhibition? He was letting her win too many of these shots in this, their first performance in front of an audience. Did he think that she didn't know it?

"You're deliberately missing some of these targets," she scolded him as they passed one another along their path, both of them shooting at the marks they had set up earlier. It was their first, and probably their easiest act. "If I am to win, I would do so with you at least trying your best."

He grinned at her, then said, "Perhaps I am not on my game at present."

"You're always on your game. You're doing this because of what happened yesterday, aren't you?"

He didn't answer.

She blasted off a shot, waited for him to take his, then said, "You were as tasked as I was."

"My body did not go into shock. I told you when we returned to camp after our adventure, that you should not perform today."

He shot off another arrow, and she waited until it was done before she stated emphatically, "But don't you see, if I am to keep my position with the show, I must perform regardless of what has gone on in my life personally. The truth is that, if I am to win, I would like to win on my own merit, and without you pitying me, if you please."

He didn't answer as they changed positions, darting in and around each other quickly, taking their shots as they had done in practice.

"You won't fool me. I know what you are capable of, and if you are holding yourself back, I will know. I mean, after all, I won't break if you beat me at this. It simply means that I have to practice harder."

They switched their positions again, then, turning around, they walked backward, both of them firing at their targets.

Oddly, as they talked, neither of them missed their staged posts, she utilizing her gun, he with his bow and arrows. This part of their act resembled a dance as they wove in and out between each other, each firing off a shot; then switching positions, fire; walking forward, take another shot; then walking backward, shoot. This, they had choreographed. The rest of their performance would consist of the standard clay pigeon gallery act, first pitting his bow against her gun; then they would compete with both of them firing at marks with guns, then they would contest utilizing the bow and arrows.

Their last act would be performed from the back of a wagon, where they would aim at a target as they jumped off the cart. He usually won this contest, mostly because she didn't like the idea of falling off a moving vehicle, regardless of how low it was to the ground. It wasn't that her eye for the target was inaccurate while she was mid-air, it was more the notion of falling that bothered her. It seemed to her as though she always landed in awkward positions, and once, in practice, she had twisted her ankle on a fall. He, of course, had noticed and had required her to do this particular stunt over and over until she "knew" she could accomplish it without injuring herself.

Fair enough. She had done it, and she would continue doing it. Didn't mean she liked it.

It was then that it occurred to her. Why was he giving her quarter? He had never done so in the past. Was it because of what they had shared yesterday? Did he now see her as a woman, instead of a girl pretending to be a boy?

Well, if that were the case, she, too, knew how to tease, and she announced to him after he had taken a shot, "It's because I'm female, isn't it?"

"I have been aware of this all along," he replied to her after she had fired at a target. "That you now know that I know changes nothing."

"Except that maybe the fact that you held me in your arms has made a difference to you?" She grinned at him as she passed him in this, their first act, and she baited him further, saying, "You never showed me quarter before. Did rescuing me and seeing me naked cause you a problem, is that it? Have you discovered suddenly that you love me?"

"I don't fall in love with girls who pretend to be boys."

"Hmmm. Then you tell me the reason why you're treating me differently."

"I am attempting to show you kindness. After all, you are a friend."

"Am I? Up until yesterday and today, you could have fooled me."

He frowned at her, his look, with all the paint covering his face, fierce. But she grinned. He obviously did not like this line of thought, and she realized that it felt good to turn the tables on him, at least this once.

Their first enactment had come to a close, and, as they stood together, she figured she'd press the point, and she teased further, smirking. "Personally I think you'd like to make love to me and kiss me, and that's why suddenly you're acting so differently toward me."

She laughed when he turned toward her and gazed at her as though she had taken leave of her senses. But he said nothing; he did nothing except turn quickly away from her. Then he stalked off, heading toward the shooting gallery and their next match.

Well, she surmised, perhaps her impish bantering with him held some merit? Or was his reaction to her flirtation no more than the manner by which he demonstrated his anger and frustration at her? Maybe…

CHAPTER NINE

The rest of their performance had come and gone, and had been accomplished without further incident. After the initial exchange between them during that first act, Wind Eagle had gone on to amend his attitude toward her, becoming again that teasing, amusing man that she had come to know these past several weeks. Thereafter, he had gone on to win each match between them.

Not that she hadn't given him plenty of competition; she had. But he had won those matches fairly, many times beating her by one point only. She hadn't really lost; it was encouraging that she had done as well as she had against this master. She would practice harder, try harder.

It was evening now; the show, although long, was at an end, and the performers were congregated beneath a large, oversized tent. Because several new acts had seen their opening debut this day, and, because ticket sales were high, Buffalo Bill had decided to throw a party. All were invited, including many of the New York elect.

The canvas tent chosen for this event was huge; it must have stood about twenty feet tall and a hundred feet in diameter. The atmosphere within this enclosure was warm and lit by several torches, causing the interior to appear almost as light as day. However, the smell of kerosene and gas from the illumination was heavy in the air, which caused many of the performers to temporarily step out into the open air, where they might gain a moment to catch their breath.

Still, red wine flowed freely among the partakers of this celebration and many a tongue was slightly slurred. Several couples were dancing; there were even a few men who stood on the sidelines of the dance floor, tapping out the steps of a jig. The conversation was loud in this place, appearing as though it were an entity that competed with the band for dominance, and laughter shook the canvas sides of the pavilion, giving the tent an appearance of being alive.

Since the atmosphere within this large space was warm, and the air outside was cool, many of the dancers were choosing to step outside. Luci had tired quickly of the heavy air inside the tent, and she, too, had trod outside temporarily, inhaling deeply. The moon was full and bright tonight, giving brilliance to the several married couples and lovers who were pacing along the many paths that led up to and around this place.

Luci had learned that Buffalo Bill loved parties, and these gatherings usually came complete with music provided by the Wild West's band, free drinks and a generous selection of food. Tonight was no different than the show's other get-togethers, and, as Luci slipped back inside the pavilion, she watched from the sidelines as more and more couples took to the dance floor, matching their steps to the three-quarter time of a waltz.

How she wished she could be one of those dancers; at least it appeared that Jane was enjoying herself, for her face glowed as her partner twirled her around the dance floor. Fate had been good to them in this regard, since Jane, who had feared that she and Luci might have to flee their home, had wisely packed a trunk and had filled it with many dresses. Her attention to that detail had been a blessing, because it allowed Jane to change her outfit every day.

Luckily, Jane's condition was showing only a little, and she wore one of Luci's dresses — her favorite, the amber and cream-colored creation, with a low bodice, a nipped-in waist and a long amber-hued train, which Jane had scooped up and flung over one of her arms. Jane's partner was a handsome young cowboy who rode bucking broncos. His name was Will Granger, and he was not only good-looking and rugged, he was also the Wild West's best at the bucking event. As the couple waltzed quickly past her, the sound of their laughter brightened her mood a little, for Luci had always loved to dress up in her best dresses.

She adored arranging her hair in the latest style and showering herself in perfume, and then, putting her best foot forward, she had been known to dance and dance until her feet were red and raw from the exertion. Indeed, it was a rarity, that, given the opportunity, she sat out a single song.

Looking toward the other side of this large space, she beheld Wind Eagle and his two friends, each one of them appearing to be deep in conversation with various, and attractive, young women. As though Wind Eagle suddenly became aware of Luci's stare, he looked up and caught her gaze. He nodded and winked at her before he turned his back on her and gave his full attention once more to one of the girls who surrounded him.

An unwelcome emotion took hold of her, and she wished for a moment that she could be that young woman who had captured his attention. Was she jealous?

Never… Yet, perhaps she was, if one considered their closeness to one another yesterday.

Still, she refused to admit to the green emotion of envy. How many times had this man admitted to her that he had no attraction toward her as a female? Even yesterday, holding her naked within his arms hadn't caused him a stirring of lust, not even a little. She might tease him that he had been moved by her, but she knew the facts were likely different.

Or were they? She hadn't dreamed that look of admiration given to her during a moment of stress, there in the forested swamp. However, she might have put the wrong interpretation on it.

Indeed, that might be true; she could be making more of their closeness than was factual. But even if their affinity for one another were genuine, there would be little chance for a happy relationship with him, considering his popularity with women. He might be handsome, congenial, as well as a sure shot, but she realized that if she were to fall in love with him, she would have unquestionable and varied competition from a fair amount of feminine hearts.

Besides, any attraction to him might create problems in their working relationship. That this could endanger her place here with the show did not bear consideration; she might be fired.

And, if that were to happen, what would she and Jane do? They couldn't go home; at least not until their father returned from Hawaii. She sighed as she considered what her father's reaction would surely be if he were to discover that she was keeping a close working association with Wind Eagle.

True, her father might understand that she'd had no other choice, but she couldn't be certain. However, imagine what her father might think, what he might do, if she were to harbor feelings of attraction for Wind Eagle, even love him?

But she worried for nothing. They had shared an intense moment. That was all. She could not really be in love with Wind Eagle, and, for his part, he appeared to be as fascinated with her as he might be with a stone in his shoe.

However, gazing outward again, toward the other side of the dance floor, Lucinda picked Wind Eagle out of the throng of women. He was smiling at the young, beautiful creature he was speaking with, and Luci cringed.

What would it feel like if he were to gaze at me with the same, steady attention?

The thought startled her, for she realized, that, despite it all, she *was* jealous, and that this would never do. Worse, she couldn't quite shake off the notion that Wind Eagle should be hers, that somehow he belonged to her, not to some beautiful and devoted fan.

Perhaps, she thought, Wind Eagle wasn't the only one who had changed because of what had happened between them yesterday. She thought she had settled her feelings for this man weeks ago, and they were negative. But, maybe his saving her had brought him into her life in ways that she didn't fully realize and didn't understand.

Well, she didn't have to stand here, gaping at them. Certain that she needed a breath of the cool, night air, she turned her back on Wind Eagle and his entourage, and, pacing forward, she fought her way through the crowd, heading toward the tent's entrance.

As she stepped outside, she wondered where she might go. She didn't wish to return to her quarters. Not yet. She needed to think.

And, so it was that she directed her course toward the belly of the woods. There she could be alone to come to terms with herself. What had really happened between her and Wind Eagle yesterday? Had she pledged her heart to him without being fully aware of it?

She shook her head. This line of thinking would not do.

As she paced farther and farther away from the party, the music from the pavilion gave her steps rhythm, and she found herself waltzing along the path instead of walking. It gave her an idea.

She loved to dance. Why not create a party of her own making, here in the woods, away from the rest? After all, the music carried well into the timbered forest, and she could pretend for a few moments that some beau, perhaps Wind Eagle, was desperately in love with her. She could even make believe that Wind Eagle liked her best of all, and had followed her so as to dance with her.

She smiled. It would be a good make-believe. Why not do it? No one would see her, no one would know that for a few precious moments, she had imagined herself to be the true love of this man.

Feeling as though she had stepped into the role of a misfit sort of Cinderella, she danced more lively along her path, keeping to the three-quarter time, until at last she came to a clearing in the woods. The air in this place seemed warmer than outside of it; perfect for a young woman to fantasize. Later tonight and tomorrow, the pretense would end, but for now, tomorrow seemed far away.

***

Wind Eagle watched her go. Although it was true that he enjoyed these gatherings as much as any of the other performers, and, although he commonly took part in the merriment, tonight he didn't. For a reason he couldn't fathom, he was not interested in the merrymaking or the usual crowd which commonly grouped around him and his friends.

In truth, his attention was introspective as he recalled again what Miss Deceiving Woman had accused him of: that he had wanted to kiss her, to make love to her. It was a lie. It had to be a lie. He would never be interested in a girl such as she.

Still, it was one matter to be aware that she was a woman, not a boy, and quite another to be presented with the evidence of her gender. He recalled again that her curves had fit the contours of his body as though she had been made especially for him. He let out a disgusted breath.

Never would he exercise any romantic interest in such a person, and he had no more than envisioned this adverse thought, than an image of Miss Deceiving Woman crowded into his mind's eye. There, in that pond, it had happened; he had feared he might lose her. And, as he had looked deeply into her eyes, he had experienced the essence of who she really was. And worse, he had found her to be beautiful.

He reined in his thoughts. This would not do. Looking up, he caught sight of her briefly, before she stepped out into the night.

Why was she leaving? Where was she was going, why, and what was he to do about her?

Perhaps it wouldn't hurt to follow her, if only to discover if she might be up to some mischief. After all, close as he had felt to her yesterday, he could never forget that she was deceiving others, and that he owed it to himself and to his tribe to discover as much about her intentions as he could.

This decided it, and, making his excuses, he, too, left the ballroom. Silently, he stepped out into a moonlit night.

***

Trailing a person was a simple task for a scout, yet, still, by the time he had caught up to her, she had wandered into an open clearing, where the silvery luminescence cast by the moon created such a misty and enchanting atmosphere, he would not have been surprised to see little people dancing merrily around her. But none were there.

He watched as she bent and picked up a long stick. Was she fashioning it into a weapon? If she were, why was she doing that? Would this be the time and the place where she would play her hand, demonstrating the reason behind her deception?

He wasn't left long to speculate. She held that tree branch out in front of her, and, as he watched her curtsy to the thing, he heard her giggle.

Giggle?

"Me?" she whispered. "You wish to dance with silly me?" Again, she chuckled.

And then, she began to move to the three-quarter-timed beat of the music that wafted into this place. She even hummed to the melody. Me?" she asked again. "You consider that I am beautiful?" She gasped. "You wish to kiss me? Will I let you? Shame on you for trying to capture a young girl's heart. But... Yes, please do kiss me."

In less time than it takes to think it, he realized that this would not be the hour or the place where he would come to know her secrets; in truth, he grasped that she had come here not to misbehave, but to enjoy the merriment of the ball in her own way. Dared he play along with her and become her invisible partner?

No. There was danger in that direction. Until he discovered more about her intentions —

All at once, his attention was caught by another of her chuckles, as she whispered to the stick she was holding, "Oh, what a marvelous kiss that was. But then, I expect you have more experience than I do. What? You would like to do it again?"

Was it because he had become accustomed to play-acting with her in these shooting matches, or was it because of what had happened to them yesterday? Whatever was to account for it, he found himself wishing to reach out to her, to take the place of that ridiculous stick in her hand.

Resigning himself to enacting his desire to be a part of her fantasy, he found his voice and uttered softly, "I will."

He let those simple words alert her to the fact that he was here, watching her. "It is I, your partner," he told her unnecessarily as he stepped up behind her, and, tapping her on the shoulder, he quickly pressed a kiss to her cheek. Then he turned her toward him.

Her eyes had opened wide at his words, and, as she stared up at him, he realized that he had surprised her too greatly; shock was mirrored in the depths of her eyes. He smiled at her as he murmured, "I saw you leave the party, and decided to follow you — see what this deceiving woman was planning to do."

"Deceiving woman?" she questioned. "You don't like me very much, do you?"

"I like you well enough, but I don't trust you, for you try to trick others into believing you are a person you are not."

"But can you deny that you are attracted to me now because of our adventure yesterday?"

Quickly he burst that bubble, and he said, "I am not interested in the way you suggest, for I will never again hold in my heart a woman who pretends to be boy."

"Never again?"

He sighed. Had he truly shared that part of his early life with her? He would have to beware the words that fell too easily from his tongue when he was in the presence of this woman. "I do not speak of it," was his answer to her.

He was about to turn away from her when she asked, "Will you dance with me?"

His answer was honestly blunt, as he said, "I do not make it a practice to dance with girls who look like boys."

She glanced away from him. "Oh, I see," she replied, with a note of melancholy in her voice. But then, her tone brightened as she suggested, "But if I were to stand before you as a woman, fully dressed as a woman, would you dance with me then?"

He sighed. He shouldn't agree. He knew he shouldn't, for already his body was more than aware of her feminine gender, and even now he wished to touch her. Still, when he gazed down into her eyes, he was aware that she was not simply asking him, she was pleading with him.

Knowing that he should ignore her, however, was not as easy as it might seem, and he found himself replying to her, even though it was against his inclination, "I will."

"You promise? If I run home to gather a change in clothing, will you still be here when I return?"

He let out his breath in an acknowledgment of a temporary truce, and he vowed, "I promise."

"Don't leave. I will return here shortly."

And, with this said, she was gone.

She returned, however, within what seemed to be only a few moments later, and she was holding a dress in her hands. "I didn't dare change in my own quarters, for I might be seen there. So please turn around; I intend to get into this dress now, and there is little cover that I can retreat to where you cannot see me."

"I will do as you ask, but you must realize that I have already beheld you in your most vulnerable state. Your body holds no secrets from me."

"Sir, be that as it may, I still ask you to turn your back."

He did so, but he chuckled, nonetheless.

It was only a short time later when she murmured, "You may turn around now."

He did as she bid, and he congratulated himself for his wisdom in retreating into the shadows, for the darkness might surely hide his first reaction to her. She was, indeed, a vision of loveliness. Admittedly, the silvery light from the moon cast shadows over her figure, making her appear perhaps more beautiful than she might look under a bright sun. But he also recalled unwillingly how she had appeared in the light of day and how she had felt in his arms. Even then, with mud splattered on her face and figure, she had seemed comely.

At present, she had loosened her red hair, and it shimmered down her back. Her dress looked to be a light shade of green, and it accented every curve of her stunningly rounded woman's body.

He swallowed. Hard. The realization that he was, indeed, attracted to her was not a pleasant insight for him, and he tried to harden his heart against her.

She grinned at him as she stepped closer to him, and he couldn't help admitting the truth as he said, "You do yourself a disfavor when you clothe yourself as a boy, Wíŋyaŋ Gnáyaŋ, for, dressed as you are now, you are the most beautiful woman I have ever seen."

He heard her intake of breath before she whispered, "Did I hear you right? Did you actually mention me and the word, "beautiful," together, in the same sentence?"

He chuckled a little. "That I did, Wíŋyaŋ Gnáyaŋ."

"Wíŋyaŋ Gnáyaŋ? I forget. What does that mean?"

"It is the Nakoda way for saying Deceiving Woman."

"Oh. You have called me that now too many times. I think I don't like that name."

"And so you shouldn't. But do not despair. It is a custom of my people that a relative might select a negative trait to call a person, hoping that he or she will fight to change it, for among my people, what title a man or woman is known by may often change. Perhaps you might try to sway me to amend yours?"

Her response was merely to shake her head in the negative. She countered, "To do that, one would have to care about your good opinion, and I'm not certain that I should."

He sighed as he took a step toward her. "Come, let us not argue about affairs that we cannot change, not tonight. You have told me that you wish to dance, and I have consented to be your partner." He backed up slightly from her and offered his arms to her in the style and in the position of the waltz.

She questioned, "Do you know how to dance to this music?"

He grinned at her, then added, "Do birds sing gaily as they greet the sun?"

"You didn't answer my question."

"I have returned from a tour of Europe, where there were many balls and welcoming parties. Do you honestly believe I would not take the time to learn the steps of a dance that allows a man to hold a woman in his arms, a woman who is not his wife?"

Her laugh was strained as she observed aloud, "You are a rogue, aren't you?"

He shrugged. "I do not ask these girls to bring me presents. Do you know of a man who would turn away from that which is so sweetly offered?"

"A husband, perhaps," she replied without hesitation. "I would hope a husband would be such a man."

"Ah, you are right, for a man who promises a woman that she will be his in marriage should remain true to her, and to his word of honor, for all his life. But come, we continue to bicker when we might be dancing." He smiled at her, and held his hand out to her. "May I have this dance?"

"Yes. Indeed, I would be honored," she murmured as she took his proffered hand. Then he placed her left hand on his shoulder, and, still holding her right, he took possession of her around her waist. She sighed a little, then said, "We are lucky that the band is playing another waltz."

He didn't answer, for the feel of her in his arms was an exquisite pleasure, and he kept his body's reaction to her, to her scent and to her beauty, under his firm control. And they danced, there in a wooded clearing, where the only light to be seen was that of a multitude of stars and glimmering beams of moonlight. They twirled around the little clearing, he watching her, and she staring up at him. It was a moment of magic, as though this instant were not happening within the agreed-upon stream of time.

They didn't speak. There was no need to do so, for their bodies were perfectly attuned. And still the music played.

He desired to hold her closer. Yet, he retained his caution toward her, knowing well that he mustn't bring the essence of her femininity in too closely to him. She was not for him. Indeed, in a world where he could easily have his choice in a woman, he told himself that he didn't need her. He held onto this bit of information as though it were important and a truth, for, as he gazed down into her most lovely face, he panicked. She was that beautiful.

The music stopped, and so did they cease to dance, but he did not relinquish his hold upon her, and, when she tilted her face up toward his, he leaned down, ready to receive her kiss; wanting it, desiring it, even against his will. But the caress never came.

At that last moment, he reined in his sense of urgency, and, although he didn't back away from her, he nevertheless did not kiss her. He dared not.

Her voice was soft as she asked, "Didn't you say you would kiss me?"

"I already did," he answered.

"No, you didn't," she contradicted. "That was a mere peck on my cheek."

"It was a kiss."

"When I asked my invisible friend to kiss me, I meant on the lips. And, since you are and have become that invisible partner, will you do it?"

"No."

"Why not?" It was more than her tone of voice that had laced her question with disappointment.

He sighed. "Because," he said, "you are my ally in the show, and there must be no hint of your womanhood allowed into our relationship. Besides, although you stand before me in all your womanly beauty now, I know that on the morrow when we have our next performance, I will behold a woman pretending to be a boy. I do not kiss such women."

She sighed. "Then I guess I will remain nineteen, and ne'er be kissed." There was a twinkle in her eyes as she looked up toward him.

He stated a warning, saying, "Do not tease me, and do not dare me to do it."

"I am not. I am stating a truth. I have never been kissed. Not by anybody."

He blew out his breath in a hiss. "What is wrong with the men of your acquaintance?"

She laughed a little. "I think, Mr. Eagle, that they are afraid of me. But I don't believe that you are." She smiled up at him.

He bent toward her, and, despite himself, he was well aware of his body's readiness for her. But this was all wrong. Terribly wrong, for he was still unaware of the reason for her deceit. And, in self-defense, he uttered, "I must go."

"Will we have no more dances, then?"

"Not tonight." He dropped his arms from around her. He needed to get away from her. In truth, he was in great need of a long, cold swim, followed by intense soul-searching. What was he going to do about this beautiful, deceiving woman?

And then she did it. Rising up to tiptoe, she brought her face up to his and urged her lips to his. It was nothing, really. Just her bare lips against his own; no lip pressure in the gesture.

Yet, it was as though a light flashed brightly within him. Indeed, the simple kiss provided him with such a perfect carnality, he felt himself ready to make love to her now, and to the devil with the consequences. But he mustn't, he argued with himself. Despite the swirling world of sexual stimulation that enveloped him, he realized he must remain immune to her. All the same, he whispered, "You call that a kiss?"

"Well...yes, I believe that I do."

"You are truly innocent, I fear." And with nothing else said, he threw away all his reasonable arguments against her, and took control of the kiss, opening her mouth and tracing its inner recess with his tongue, kissing her as a lover might, discovering the taste of her, playing tag with her tongue. He felt her surrender to him, and, without thinking, he broke off the kiss on her lips to trail wet caresses over to her ear, down her neck; he even pulled at the bodice of her gown to expose her breasts, and he was quick to kiss the lusciousness of each one. It was with the barest of grips on himself that he drew back and brought his head up to a level with hers, placing his forehead against hers. Then he whispered, "That, Miss Deceiving Woman, is a kiss."

She seemed to be speechless, and when he drew back to gaze at her, he realized he had again stunned her. He said, "And this is why we must never again kiss, for I feel it only fair to warn you that I can barely hold myself back from you and exploring more of your body, and that will never do. Know this: I might admire you, I might like you even against my will, but I shall never marry you. Never. And to do more than what I have already done is an act of dishonor to you. Do you understand?"

She nodded. "I do. Perhaps you should also know that I do not wish to marry you, either. Still, I thank you for that very real kiss. I am no longer nineteen and ne'er been kissed, nor fondled."

Did she tease him? For he certainly felt baited. Yet, he had spoken wisely, and, although he longed to experience much more with her, he kept his desire firmly in check, adhering to his own code of morality. He forced himself to step back from her.

In truth, he had never intended kissing her in such a sexual way. He realized all at once the hypocrisy of his words and his deeds; he spoke of lofty intentions while he had, only moments ago, seduced her.

He needed to think. That's what he needed to do, and so he turned away from her and trod swiftly toward a darkened corner of the clearing. He turned back to face her once he had settled himself within the shadows, and he said, "I will wait here while you change."

"That's not necessary."

"I believe that it is. I will see you safely back to the party or to your own quarters."

"Why? You know I can take care of myself."

He sighed. Why, indeed? He knew the answer, of course. He was now more than aware of her femininity, and, because of this, he could not let her step out into the night unescorted. To do so would be as to humiliate her.

However, he couldn't tell her this. In the end, he simply remained silent, as, beside himself, he watched her undress. He told himself that it was right that he peer at her in this way because she hadn't asked him to look elsewhere, and he was, after all, a man….

CHAPTER TEN

*S*he watched him slip into the shadows. She should ask him to turn his head away from her, knowing that he would do so. But she didn't. Why she did not require that of him she wasn't certain. She only knew that she was burning up with a need spurred on from that brief, but soul-stirring embrace. She wanted more of that.

No wonder people married in order to attain such pleasures, for the heady, joyful feeling he aroused in her was like none other of her experiences. Indeed, it was an exquisite indulgence. Why was it so?

Innocent she might be, but she was also nobody's fool. Instinctively, she was more than aware that not every man's kiss would cause the very foundation of her world to sway upon its axis.

Trouble was, it was a point in his favor. Still, he was not a man she could ever marry, and her father's certain censure of an affair with him was not the only reason; they each came from different cultures, held dissimilar values, and Wind Eagle's own reluctance and stance against her personally could not be forgotten.

Thus, she should end her fascination with him. Yet, how could she, when she yearned for another sampling of his embrace?

It had been an odd sensation to have pretended his presence in a simple dance, only to have the real person materialize before her. Strangely, she had at first wondered if her imagination were playing tricks on her. It had taken her several moments to realize that he truly was in her arms.

Momentarily, she waged a war internally, at odds with herself. It was puzzling. He spoke about her as though he couldn't wait to get away from her. Yet, he had kissed her so sensuously…and she had liked it. He had seemed to enjoy it, too.

She sighed. She knew what she should do: get dressed and go home. But she ached with feelings she had never known existed. And there he was, watching her; and here she was looking back at him.

In the end, it was the desire for more of the same that won, and so it came to be that she stripped off her gown in front of him, more than aware that he would be hard-pressed not to stare at her. It was a bold act she attempted, yet it seemed the right thing to do. And, as she stepped out of her clothes to stand fully nude under the moonlight, she deliberately goaded him, striking a feminine pose for him, tucking in her stomach.

She heard his voice from the shadows as he asked, "Do you think to taunt me?"

"I? Why would I presume to torment a man who has, himself, baited and laughed at me for many weeks? Would I dare to try to change his mind about me?"

"Do you not realize that you play with fire? I am but a man, and I warn you that after what we have already done, I am barely able to hold myself away from you. Should I educate you and remind you that I would ruin you for another, if I did to you what you seem to be begging me to do?"

"I? Begging you?"

She heard him sigh. He said, "Do not do this."

How dare the man. How dare he give her a sampling of what could be, and then, not only withhold it from her, but caution her about its use.

She deliberately struck another pose, throwing the long mane of her hair over her shoulder, more than aware that her naked body shimmered beneath the softened, silver-like beams. She had been looking upward and in another direction, so she was a little startled to learn that he had come up behind her, and that he had pressed his hardened figure against hers.

He warned her again, saying, "Do you wish me to enlighten you more into the ways of men and women? If you do not, I warn you again that your flirtation might end in only one way."

"I…"

"Do you wish me to touch you here?" He trailed his fingers down one of her breasts.

Like chocolate under a summer sun, her body melted as her knees buckled under her.

"Or here?" He slid his hand over to her other breast and caressed it, tantalizing her. She leaned back against him. *Oh my, what glorious ecstasy this was.*

She whispered, "Why does that feel so good?"

"Because it is the way it should be between a man and a woman," he answered. "If I trace a path down here," he pressed his hands down lower, over her stomach, "you might yearn for my touch upon you here." He pressed his palm over the mound of her short hairs.

"Yes," she responded.

"Here?" With a single finger, he touched her core, there between her legs.

"Oh, dear." She slumped and would have fallen, for her legs would no longer hold her. Luckily, he caught her.

He proceeded to kiss her neck and she shivered, pushing her head against his shoulder and surrendering to him. As though this were the pose he had been awaiting, he reached down lower to fondle her there, and she thought she might surely faint from the pleasure, which even now felt like liquid fire shooting over her limbs, flaming through her body.

"And now," he whispered against her ear, "do you understand why you should not bait a man such as myself?"

She let out her breath in a sigh. "Wind Eagle, I fear that you teach me the opposite. Now I understand why these young women flirt with you as they do. If this pleasure is the result, I surely do not blame them anymore."

"Come." He turned her around and picked her up in his arms, then he trod toward a patch of grass that grew beneath a tree, the weeping willow that sheltered this place. He sat down beneath its branches, effectively hiding their figures from the moonlight above, bringing her with him and positioning her over him and facing him so that she straddled him. And then, seeing to her comfort, he again used his fingers to ignite the blaze within her core.

The pleasure was unlike any other she had ever experienced, and yet, instinctively, she was soon meeting the rhythm of his fingers, swaying her hips and twisting against him. She wanted more. But what? What was she struggling toward?

"Forgive me," he whispered, "for I cannot allow my touch to become too deep, because if I did, then I would surely ruin you for another," he murmured against one of her breasts, which she, in this position, couldn't help but display before him. The feel of his breath, against her down there seemed to stir her in an entirely different way, and, as she reeled against him, she suddenly felt a pleasure that was building and building there, until…

Gratification and fire unexpectedly rocked her body. Over and over, wave after wave of excruciating uproar washed through her, body and soul, until, all at once, a peak of pure pleasure raced over her there, where he caressed her, and everywhere. Then, with his fingers still within her, she sank down against him, her breathing fast, and her heart pounding against his.

For the space of a single beat, she again experienced that feeling of being one with this man. So close was she to him that she was certain she knew his thoughts, and it seemed to her that his were as jumbled as her own. They were partners, they were antagonists, and yet here they were holding on to one another. What did one say at a moment like this? She could think of nothing, and so she decided to be honest, and she whispered, "I do believe, Mr. Eagle, that whether you pressed against me too deeply or not, you have surely ruined me for another, for I do not think I could ever experience the same thrill this has caused me with anyone but you. Only you, and I fear this is not good, for just as you say you must not and will not marry me, that is echoed within my own heart: I cannot marry you."

He didn't respond for what seemed to be a very long time, and, when he did speak, his voice was soft and low as he whispered, "I know of that which you speak, for I was moved by you, also, as I never expected I would be."

"I don't understand."

He gathered her in close to him with his other arm around her, saying, once again, "I know."

***

He didn't sleep this night; he knew it was useless to try. He had escorted Oi'le Kitaŋla back to her quarters. Oi'le Kitaŋla: it was her new name, Little Flame. Flame, because her hair color reminded him of fire; Flame, also, because he was now aware of her deep-seated passion, not only for life and her endeavors, but in the heat of seduction. He might not ever love her or marry her, but he would never forget her.

Indeed, even after a long, two-hour swim in the coldest part of the lake, he found himself still moved by her: the feel of her, the scent of her, the taste of her. No, he would never forget.

Shivering in the cool night air, he welcomed the effect of the chilly water slowly evaporating on his skin, for he required a return to sanity. He knew, better than most, that there were other incidents from his past that he could never disregard, and, even though he rarely allowed himself the time or the space to recall them, tonight, the memories would not stay at bay.

He had been no more than seven years of age when it had happened.

It was a time of war; the Lakota in the south and the Dakota to the east were engaged in life or death wars with the Blue coats in this country. These men, who wore the blue coats, were young and womanless, and they appeared to be here to steal the country of the Lakota. Though his own tribe was a traditional enemy of the Lakota, members of the Húŋkpapha band of the Lakota had sought help from his own people, the Nakoda, who, after all, had once been of the same tribal heritage.

His father had answered that call.

Wíŋyaŋ Zintkála, Bird Woman, was his mother, and, upon learning that her husband had set out upon the war path without informing or consulting her, had collapsed. Later, as she'd awakened, Wind Eagle had watched from the corner of their lodge as she had donned the clothes of a boy.

Although among his people a youngster is taught early in life that he should not voluntarily begin a conversation with an elder, he found he was unable to resist asking his mother, "Why are you putting on those clothes? They do not suit you."

His mother had gasped her surprise, then, espying her son, she had answered, "Excuse me, my son, I did not know that you were here in the lodge with me, but now that I am aware of it, let me answer your question. I mean to follow and protect your father from harm."

Wind Eagle had digested this piece of information with a distinct impact of alarm, and he found himself speaking out, saying, "Could you not send my older brother to do this for you? I am certain that he would take your place willingly, for he knows the danger of warfare."

"My son, he has already gone with your father. May I speak plainly to you?"

Wind Eagle had nodded, muttering, "Hau, hau."

"The truth is that I fear that if I do not also set out upon the path they have both taken, that I might never again see either my husband or my eldest son. Please try to understand why I do as I feel I must. Neither of these men, whom I love, bade me farewell, for they know my heart is hardened against war, and I am told that neither wished to argue with me. Yet, there is urgency within me, for I know their lives are in danger. Do you understand? I must go. If I don't follow them, I am certain that I will never forgive myself for staying behind."

Wind Eagle's response was swift. "No, my mother," he countered, "I will go in your place. Since both my father and my brother have gone, this leaves me as the man in our family. And so, my will should not be ignored. All of these seven years of my life have I played at war, and I have trained well to protect my family. You have not done so. So it is I who will go to them for you, and I, who will protect them."

"My son." His mother had stepped to where Wind Eagle sat, and had reached out for him, taking him into her arms. "I cannot permit you to do this. You are only seven winters old, and you have your life ahead of you."

"As do you." He had shrugged off her hold on him, and had stood up to his feet. Then he'd ordered, "You stay here. I will go."

She had bent forward to press a kiss on his forehead.

"Please, let me go," he'd begged.

She had smiled as she had run her hands gently down the two braids of his hair, which he wore at the side of his face, then she had bent over to again press a kiss on his forehead. She'd whispered, "I will ponder your words, my son. Come now, let me take you to your grandmother's lodge, and, while you sleep, I will decide whether you shall go in my place. In the morning, you will know of my decision."

He had nodded. How he wished now that he had not let her escort him to his grandmother's tepee. He should have stayed with his mother throughout the night, for when he had awakened, she had gone.

He had cried, so young had he been, but then realizing that he had never seen warriors cry, he had dried his tears, and had, instead, prayed, offering the Creator his most prized possessions, his bow and his arrows and his clothing; he had begged for the safe return of his mother, his father and his brother.

But it was only his father and his brother who had returned to camp with their life's blood still flowing through their bodies. His mother had died saving her husband and son. Not until she had come between him and the enemy had his father even known that she had followed him.

His father had never been the same after that. As though his wife's loss had cut a deep crevasse within his soul, he had never smiled again and the joy had gone out of his life. Later, Wind Eagle had come to understand that his father blamed himself for her sacrifice; indeed, he had thereafter mourned the day when he had left camp without speaking to her first.

Although his father still lived, he had never truly recovered from the loss of his wife, and, if Wind Eagle were to be honest, he would admit that he, too, had never healed from that same loss. Always he blamed himself. If he had only stayed with her that night…

Worse, only one year later, his older sister had followed in the footsteps of her mother, and had trailed her sweetheart onto the battlefield; she, too, had disguised herself as a boy. That her adventure had ended in a similar manner was more than Wind Eagle could readily face, and he had gone into years of mourning.

His sister's sweetheart had grieved openly, and, deciding he could not live without his true love, had mounted his favorite pony, and had ridden out onto the prairie. There he had picked a fight with a buffalo bull. The bull had won.

Learning what had happened, Wind Eagle had sought out that bull and had killed it. But even in this act of vengeance, his heart had not healed. And, so it was that Wind Eagle, standing alone over the bull he had slaughtered, vowed to himself that he would never forget his mother or his sister, and what had caused their end.

In time, he had learned that other women sometimes dressed themselves as boys in order to be near their husbands during periods of danger. ot always did these acts end in loss.

Nevertheless, Wind Eagle had pledged that he would never entrust his heart to such a woman, for a man's affection, once given and pledged, could not be healed. No, he had determined that he would remain firm in matters of love and marriage. Never would he let a headstrong woman into his life or into his heart. Not for any reason.

Yet, he had nearly lost himself tonight to the charm of Little Flame. Indeed, his body still ached with frustration, urging him to seek her out and complete his carnal knowledge of her.

It would not happen. He would ensure that it did not.

Still, he understood that he would have to exercise great caution when she was near. An attachment he could little explain had sprung up between them, there at the forested swamp; somehow, in some way, their hearts had touched. Worse, tonight he had strengthened that intrinsic knowledge of each other, for, in seducing her, he had seen deeply into her soul, and he had found her spirit to be beautiful.

It has been said that when one person saves another's life, they are, from that point forward, forever entwined. Belatedly, he realized that his act of becoming the hero had come with a price. It was also a cost he was unwilling to pay, for to become too close to her would be as to betray himself and the memory of his mother, as well as that of his sister.

Besides, he still didn't know Little Flame's intentions: was she the deceiver who would cause the children of his tribe to die? And, if she were the one, was he not required to thwart her? To banish her activities from the face of the earth?

He felt at war with himself. Was he so cursed as to be attracted to a woman who was not only headstrong, but a woman whose intentions could be disastrous for his people?

Briefly, he recalled his vision's message: "*Trust your heart.*" But how could he? If she were *the one* who would ruin his people, trust was not possible.

But of this he was certain: until he learned more about her, he must avoid any impulse to touch her or gaze at her too deeply. Therein was danger.

Still, he could not avoid being in her company; how, then, should he do it? They were partners and they were, of necessity, together for many hours each day.

Perhaps his only course of action might be to take none; to pretend that nothing of importance had happened between them. This thought, although it harbored a lie, still produced a calming effect on him, as he recalled that she, too, did not wish a more permanent place within his heart. If he were to deny air to the fire they had lit, would it, given time, burn out?

Perhaps. The problem was, that, while he might compare their passion to a fire, he was well aware that a flame and sexual desire were not the same, and that his plan to ignore what had taken place between them might cause the blaze to be fanned into a bonfire.

Yet, he couldn't make love to her, not again. Particularly he could not do it while he was uncertain if she were to be a good influence upon his people, or bad.

Realizing that his thoughts were spinning around in circles, he reined them in. Admittedly, his decision to ignore the passion between them might not be the best plan, but he had none other at the moment. Thus, he vowed to himself that he would put distance between himself and Little Flame, and, if possible, he would discover the reason behind her deception, thus enabling him to bring it to an end.

CHAPTER ELEVEN

 General Benjamin Glenforest returned Sergeant Anthony Smyth's salute, motioning Smyth to his ease, then inviting him to unwind his tall frame in the chair that sat directly across from the general's desk. At present, the general sat within his office in the south wing of the newly built State Department Building. It was a grandiose building, quickly winning the reputation of the biggest and best-built structure of its kind in the Nation's Capital. It boasted exquisite granite stairs and corridors that spanned one and three-quarter miles, lined with white marble and black granite.

Personally, the general thought that the money which had been spent on the building would have been better served by improving the lot of each soldier. But he was not in charge of such matters. Still, all things considered, it was a beautiful building, and one that he could call home.

"In your report regarding the duel between my daughter and Captain Hall," began the general, once Smyth had seated himself, "you mention that you instructed both my daughters to lose themselves in the west?"

"Yes, sir."

"Do you know where they went?"

"I do not, sir. I stayed behind to guard your home from the lynching mob. I did, however, urge them to go by train and to leave at once, for I feared what might happen to them if the "hanging" posse should find them."

"Ah, yes, the Hall family newspaper clique. I have seen their articles on the affair, and I assume that, as usual, what the newspaper prints is nothing but lies?"

"Yes, sir, there is not a single speck of truth in those papers."

"Indeed. I see from your report that you were only able to bring order to the crowd by firing a few shots into the lynching mob. You also mention that no one was injured. Is that correct?"

"Yes, sir."

"Here before me," he shuffled some papers, "are your reports, yours and Lieutenant Quinten Michaels, the medical doctor."

"Yes, sir. I sent you word of the affair at once, and followed it up with full reports. Both I and Lieutenant Michaels wrote the exact details of the match, and what really happened, so that there would be no doubt as to what the truth was of the duel."

"Yes, and you are both thanked. Am I to understand that Captain Timothy Hall is still at large within the army, and that no court-martial taints his name?"

"Yes, sir, as you know, the Hall family has much influence in the politics of Washington and with the President, in particular. I believe the general feeling of the government is a certain fear in bringing a suit against him, for he is, after all, a Hall. Perhaps it is hoped that the incident will be forgotten."

"Yes, perhaps. I see from these newspaper clippings that the Hall family is attempting to cast doubt upon the parentage of my younger daughter's baby. Do you know if there are any witnesses to the affair between my daughter and Captain Hall?"

"I do not know, sir, as Hall's position is great within his area of control. I have asked for gossip among the enlisted men, but I have not attained any. Still, I have not yet attempted to find someone within his peers who might bring forward information concerning Captain Hall and his family. Perhaps there, within his own camp, I will find witnesses. And, if there are people who know of the romance between himself and Jane, and if those people are military, we might have a chance to build a case."

"That is my hope. Now, Sergeant Smyth, I charge you with the task of determining if any of Captain Hall's friends or acquaintances were witness to their affair. Meanwhile, I will send out as many army intelligence men as can be spared, to try to find my daughters. They can't have much money, for I assume that their departure from our home prevented them from taking what was in the safe."

"That is not entirely true, sir. Jane did withdraw a few gold coins from the safe. I even loaned Luci and Jane some of my own silver."

"Good. Thank you. How much did you give them?"

"No more than two dollars."

The general reached into his pocket and took out four silver dollars, placing them on his desk in front of Sergeant Smyth. "The extra is for your trouble."

"Thank you."

"Now, I believe," said the general, "that their money will have run out by now. It is therefore to be assumed that they might be working somewhere in some city — perhaps to earn enough cash to go farther west. There aren't many positions to be had for a young woman, for I am assuming that my oldest daughter will be caring for her sister. And what do you know of her skills?"

"She is a crack shot, sir."

"Exactly. Perhaps that is where we should start looking. Maybe we will find my daughters in some circus or some other form of amusement, where Lucinda's prowess might be ably utilized. But above all else, no one is to know that we search for my two daughters, do you understand?"

"Yes, sir. If Captain Hall were to discover that we are looking for them, he might do something unforeseen."

"Yes, he might." The general hesitated, as he glanced through the many papers on his desk. "But I can't help wondering, why did Hall do it? Why did he agree to the duel? Even though Lucinda can be intimidating when roused, why did he engage in a shooting match with her?"

"I believe she threw his manhood into question, sir."

"Not a good enough reason."

"Perhaps with you out of the country, he had hoped to frighten her into fleeing, along with Jane, and without the duel taking place. I don't believe he ever thought she would go through with it, and, if he could cause the two of them to leave, his misdeeds might remain hidden."

"He doesn't know Lucinda very well, then, does he?"

Smyth grinned. "Indeed, sir, he does not. And that, I think, is to your daughter's advantage."

The general sat back, and, with one hand on his forehead, he fell into deep thought. He couldn't help but wish, as he had often done in the past, that his blond and beautiful wife were here to help him. There was not a day that passed when he didn't miss her. At last, he looked up at Sergeant Smyth, and said, "You have your orders. Interview at least ten soldiers who know him well. Let me know the results."

"Yes, sir."

General Glenforest nodded. "You may go."

Sergeant Smyth arose from his chair, giving his superior officer a smart salute.

"At your ease, soldier. We will find them. Let us now get to work."

***

"You are late," Jane accused. "The party ended hours ago, and I thought that I would find you here when I returned to our quarters. I was wrong. What's that you are carrying?"

Luci shrugged. "One of my dresses."

"One of your…? Where have you been?"

Luci frowned. Jane sounded like a mother instead of a sister, prompting Luci to wonder if this role shift were part of Jane's changing emotions of late. Always in the past, Luci had been the sister to take on the responsibility of being the mother.

"Well?" Jane inquired, tapping her foot against the woolen rug, recently bought, which covered the ground of their tent. "You were with him, weren't you? And you wore a dress around him? Oh, Luci, did he take advantage of you after he had saved your life yesterday?"

"Of course not."

"Of course not…what? Of course he didn't take advantage of you? Or of course you were with him tonight?"

"What is this? An inquisition?"

"Yes."

"Oh, Jane. Yes, I was with him. And yes, I wore this dress with him, but only because he wouldn't dance with me if I looked like a boy."

"You *danced* with him? Where? I didn't see you and Wind Eagle together at the party."

Luci inhaled deeply. "We danced in the woods. I had gone there to enjoy the music in my own way. Wind Eagle followed me there."

"I thought so. I saw him leave after you did."

"There is nothing to be concerned about. We were dancing as part of our practice."

Jane frowned. "A part of your practice? I don't believe you. Now tell me, did he seduce you?"

"What is this? Are you my mother or my younger sister?"

"Both. Tell me what happened. Do I need to remind you that I am well aware that you have never had a boyfriend, and I fear that you might let a man take too much advantage of you, especially a man who looks like Mr. Eagle. Do I need to warn you that he could have his pick of women to devour?"

"No, you don't. I am well aware of that. Now Jane, calm down. He calls me 'Deceiving Woman' because he has known all along that I am not a boy, but a woman. He is not interested in me in that way…" …*very much*, she added to herself. "He followed me to find out why I am dressing as a boy."

"And did you tell him?"

No, how could I do so when I fear for our safety?"

Jane frowned. "So, if I understand this correctly, he followed you to find out why you are trying to deceive others? And he ended up dancing with you?"

"Yes."

"Oh, Luci. 'm afraid you are out of your depth. Have you considered what our father would say if he were to learn that you spend every waking moment of your day with this man?"

"We train for our performances. That's all."

"And yet, you were naked in his arms when he rescued you."

"He told you that?"

Jane grinned. "No, he didn't. But you just did."

"I did not."

Jane laughed. "It's too late. You have now admitted as much to me. Did he seduce you tonight?"

Luci turned her back on her sister, saying, "I've had enough of this. I'm tired. I'm going to bed."

"He did, didn't he?"

Luci groaned. "No. It is I who seduced him, I fear. He was a perfect gentleman."

"What?"

"Don't worry, Jane. I promise you that it is impossible for me to become impregnated because of what happened between us tonight."

"My dear sister, I hadn't even considered that. What did go on between the two of you?"

"I'm going to bed. I have to get up early for rehearsal tomorrow before the show."

"I'm coming with you."

"No, you need your sleep in the morning."

"One day will not hurt me. I'm coming with you to this run-through of the program."

"All right. Suit yourself. But I think, come morning, you will still be here sound asleep."

"I will be ready and waiting."

Luci couldn't give up her objections, however, and she tried one more time, saying, "This isn't necessary, Jane. I am, after all, nineteen years old and able to take care of myself."

"True," Jane admitted. "Still, I'm coming with you."

On a deep sigh, Luci gave in, and, dressing herself in her boy's pajamas, she settled down for a much-needed sleep. She only wished that upon the morrow, Jane would have changed her mind and would decide that she preferred sleeping through the morning hours, instead of becoming a chaperone.

However, as it turned out, Luci was wrong about her sister. Bright and early in the morning, Jane was awake, dressed and ready to go.

CHAPTER TWELVE

It was the deepest, darkest part of the morning when Luci and Jane stepped out from their lodging, pacing toward the clearing in the woods where Wind Eagle and Luci usually practiced. The air felt chilly this morning, but Luci welcomed its temperature, knowing that soon her exertions would cause her body temperature to rise. Most often, when she was hot, she had no means to cool off, except for a quick dip in the lake, an option she never took. But this morning was different; the chilling dew covered the grass here, its moisture wetting the leather of her rather ugly brown boots, and Luci glanced to the side to see that the bottom of her sister's skirt was damp.

Luci sighed, for she realized that she and Jane would be required to do laundry and other personal chores soon. Glancing up, she noted that the moon had set long ago, which was common for such an early time in the morning. Overhead, she noted that the few remaining stars in the sky twinkled and appeared to dance in a blackened sky that seemed as though it served as a mere backdrop for the brilliant and jewel-like, sparkling lights. Were the stars dancing…like she and Wind Eagle last night…?

She sighed. It was a beautiful morning; the sky was a perfect spectacle, and, for a moment, a sense of peace fell over her. But such a feeling would soon dissipate, she was certain, if only because she didn't know what to expect from Wind Eagle. Something wonderful had happened to them last night…yet not….

When he had kissed her, there in the enchanted woods, she had thought she might faint from the pure pleasure of it, and when he had encouraged the fire in her to build into an exquisite fulfillment, she had felt so close to him that she had wondered if they had again touched one another's souls.

But he had not sought his own pleasure, and, although she wasn't certain of the exact mechanics involved in the marriage bed, she knew enough to realize that he needed to fit himself to her — and he hadn't done that with her. Why hadn't he?

Worse, he had withdrawn from her afterward. Yes, he had helped her to dress, had escorted her out of the woods, but he hadn't said a word to her. She had expected more loving, perhaps some laughter, even a strong sampling of his usual teasing; she had yearned for it. But he had given her none of that. He had drawn inward and had become a silent partner, and, in keeping with his word, he had accompanied her safely to her own quarters, but with no conversation at all.

Glancing up at the jeweled, black sky once more, Luci felt confused, and she shivered as she brought her attention again to the side. Only then did she notice it. Jane wasn't wearing her dark-haired wig. Instead, her long, blond hair fell in curls and waves down her back. She looked serene and beautiful, but hardly the same image that Wind Eagle had witnessed several weeks ago when the three of them had first met, and more recently, when Wind Eagle had been tasked to ask Jane for Luci's clothing.

Of course he would notice the difference. Even a child would do so. What should she tell him?

She could think of no logical explanation that she might share with him, and, realizing it was probably best to discount it, she shrugged. He called her Deceiving Woman. Perhaps that description would now include Jane.

Jane was silent this morning, but it didn't matter to Luci. She had changed her mind about her sister accompanying her, and was glad that Jane had awakened and dressed. Indeed, Luci was feeling more and more self-consciousness, an unusual occurrence for her.

She wondered, was Wind Eagle disappointed in what had happened between them? Is that why he had withdrawn into himself? And, though it pained her to think about it, she recalled that she had practically begged him for his embrace. That he had accommodated her had elated her at the time. The only problem now was that they had both committed actions that were not sanctioned between unmarried individuals, and, not only was she not committed to him, she was well aware that he, too, did not intend a lifelong allegiance with her.

What did that say about her? About him?

She didn't blame Wind Eagle; he had warned her against the consequences of her actions. Once more she considered the fact that he had not reached his own satisfaction.

Why hadn't he carried their lovemaking to its ultimate end, including his own elation? Perhaps she should have ensured that he, too, had experienced the joy that she had, but she had no knowledge of what else she could have done to bring that about.

Maybe she should have confided in Jane, for her sister might know what Luci could have done differently; also, it was possible that Jane could have coached her through what to say to Wind Eagle today, and how to act. But Luci hesitated to discharge her burden with Jane, if only because Luci could not give up her role as being the mother that Jane had never had.

Looking down at herself, at her boy's ugly clothing, she wished she could meet Wind Eagle this morning looking like the feminine personage she would like to present. He disliked this boy-like image of her; he had stated his opinion on this matter many times. But life, at present, would not allow her to be and to dress as she…and he, would like.

Plus—and she could never forget this—she had terrific competition for Wind Eagle's attention. She didn't need any imagination to recall the images of the comely women who flaunted themselves at Wind Eagle and his friends, which brought on another question: why had he followed her, singling her out?

He called her Deceiving Woman. Besides their partnership in this show, was there another reason why he had shadowed her last night, when he could have been with any one of those young lovelies?

These were questions she couldn't answer, and she dragged her steps as she and Jane approached the point of rendezvous. Should she speak to Wind Eagle about this? Perhaps. She tried to envision what he might say and what his reaction might be. It seemed useless, however, to try to conceive of it. But, of one fact she was certain: she was, indeed, glad that Jane had made good on her threat to accompany her.

***

Not only was Wind Eagle already awake and awaiting her at their rendezvous point, but his two friends were also in attendance. Why? Were they, too, concerned and determined to chaperone her and Wind Eagle?

Not likely. Men didn't really care about that sort of thing, did they? Yet, the reality could not be ignored. There they sat, and here, beside her, was Jane.

Momentarily, Luci closed her eyes, her only means of hiding how surprised she was at their appearance here. And, as dew surrenders to a warm, summer sun, so, too, dissolved her aspiration to have a private conversation with Wind Eagle.

Opening her eyes and shaking her head, she whispered to Jane, "Wind Eagle's friends have never been here for a practice. Why do you suppose that they are here now?"

"I don't know, except that maybe they are also aware that you and Wind Eagle have become more than simple partners."

"You don't know that. I didn't tell you that."

"It's evident, dear sister. If *they* are here, it means that something of worth really did happen between the two of you last evening."

"But nothing did," Luci declared, although she did add to herself, *nothing much.*

Luci gazed at the three men. Each one of them, utilizing a piece of wood and a knife, was busy whittling what must have been some masterpiece, if their attention to it were any indication. Only Wind Eagle looked up when the two women made their presence known.

Slowly, he set the wood and knife to the side and rose up to his feet; and, he ambled toward them. At once, the mere act of coming face to face with him again caused a fire-like sensation to cascade over her nerve endings, making Luci stumble. He, however, appeared not to notice, and gave Luci that infernal wink as he approached them, yet he didn't step in closely to her as he greeted her and Jane.

Addressing Luci, he announced, "Our schedule has changed. My two friends and I are to add a new war skill to our routine, and it will require practice, which we will do at this time of day." He looked at Jane and nodded at her, as though there were nothing out of the ordinary with her appearance.

"Oh," was all Luci said. Then it occurred to her, "Will our routine change?"

"*Hau, hau*, a little. The Showman spoke to me when I returned to the party last night. He told me he likes our performance, yours and mine, but he has asked that you and I compete on horseback. We may shoot as we have practiced, but mounted."

"But I...I...don't think...I mean..." Rather than continue to trip over her words, she swallowed hard and looked away.

He murmured, "Do not be afraid."

"I am not afraid, Mr. Eagle. It's only that I am not the horseman that you are."

"You will learn."

"Yes, I suspect that I will." Then, remembering her manners, she continued, "You know my sister, Jane, of course? She has decided that she would like to accompany me here when we practice. Jane, this is Mr. Eagle."

Jane smiled prettily at him and stated pleasantly, "Pleased."

Once again, Wind Eagle nodded in her direction. To his credit, he continued to remain silent as to Jane's changed appearance.

Luci had brought a blanket for Jane to sit upon, and, murmuring a quick, "Excuse me," she strode to the far side of the clearing—away from Wind Eagle and his two friends. Finding a level spot, she opened the blanket and set out Jane's darning. Jane followed her, and Luci noted that both of Wind Eagle's friends watched Jane's progress across the clearing.

Did Luci need to be worried in that direction? No, she answered to herself. Soon, Jane's condition would be evident, and then, Luci assured herself, neither of those men would pass the time of day with her sister.

Breathing in deeply, she settled Jane upon the blanket, like any good "brother" would do, and then, rising up to her feet, she walked in Wind Eagle's direction. She gazed at him as she stepped back toward him, and, although her senses were alerted to his presence and her heartbeat had picked up speed, she became aware that he was holding himself distant from her.

But, she didn't know what to expect. Prior to last evening, she had never experienced a romantic encounter with a man. Had she given it any thought, she would have assumed that he might smile at her as he had done last night or at least he might reach out to touch her hand. He did neither.

He had positioned himself next to his friends, and, as she stepped back toward him, he squatted down before them, and, with a hand signal, he indicated that she should do the same. She did.

He pointed at one of the men and introduced him, saying, "This is Macá Mazasapa, whose name in English means Iron Wolf. He also has chosen the name, Michael, and so he is known here as Michael Iron Wolf."

Luci gave him a brief nod.

"And this man," he pointed to the other, "is called Wakiŋyan Paza Tosaŋ, and that name means Blue Thunder Striking, although he is known merely as Blue Thunder here at the Show. His English name is Luke. Therefore, many people call him Luke Blue Thunder, as you may do, also, as you please."

"Howdy do," Luci responded in a tone as low-pitched as possible.

Blue Thunder gave her a brief nod, then returned his attention once more to his whittling with wood and knife.

But Wind Eagle hadn't finished, and he continued the introductions, saying, "Iron Wolf and Blue Thunder, this is Oi'le Kitaŋla."

Except for a brief, "*Hau, hau,*" from the young man known as Iron Wolf, there was no other acknowledgement.

Wind Eagle stood up to his feet, and gave her a motion to indicate that she should do the same. He said, "While my friends and I practice the stunts that the Showman has said he would like us to add, he also told me that he would like you to perfect your skill in riding. You will learn to do this utilizing my horse for your training, for he is a gentle animal and he will ensure you get through many performances. If needed, I can always train the other pony that I brought with me, for, as you have said, I have been riding since before I could walk."

"Come," he ordered, as he took the lead, and trod toward the side of the clearing, where several horses were munching happily on the grass. Wind Eagle glanced over his shoulder to ensure that she followed, and when he saw that she had, he added, "And now I will introduce you to the gentlest soul that I know. Soon, the two of you will be good friends."

And so it was that Luci came to meet Sure Foot, the little Cayuse pony whom, if Luci were to have christened him, would have been named, "My Love, the Show Horse."

***

Jane glanced nervously to her right side, her look quick so as to hide her curiosity about the two men, who sat on the ground less than seven feet away from her. Both were slender, and, if Jane recalled it exactly, they were about the same height as Wind Eagle. Both of these men looked foreign, alien…and perhaps deadly?

Nervously, she shifted her gaze and watched Luci and Wind Eagle as they approached the horses, which stood off to the left side of her. At least Luci was within sight.

"They are all liars, thieves and murderers…." One of her father's many warnings drifted through Jane's mind. Was it true? Were these young men liars? Thieves or murderers? Was she safe here?

She sighed, remembering that only a few days earlier, Wind Eagle had saved Luci's life. Would a man, who might be little more than a killer, have risked his own life for another?

Doubtful.

Glancing again at the two men who reclined near to her, she was struck by their masculine silhouette: they were broad of shoulder, slim in the waist, and, although they sat with ankles crossed and knees apart, it was easy to see that they were both long of leg. Even though their facial features were faint, given the darkness of the hour, she could observe that both of them were clean-shaven and that they each one showed strong jaw lines and high cheekbones.

The men had arranged their hair in a similar manner as Wind Eagle. Each had cut his mane's forelocks and had brought that part of his hair front and center, over the forehead. The rest of their hair was long, but braided and pulled back behind their head, being held together by a beaded clip or a feather.

It must be the style of their particular tribe, she thought.

They were each fully clothed, with what appeared to be cotton trousers, and a cotton shirt overlaid with a beaded vest. Metal wrist guards at the elbow and wrist of their shirts completed their look. Leather moccasins graced their feet and the ever-present breechcloth fell down between their legs as they sat cross-legged.

Her father hadn't mentioned the handsome image of the American Indian race, although in fairness, it would probably not have occurred to him to notice this or to admire them in any way, his duty being to kill or to subjugate them.

Still, she might as well have been poison ivy, for they both ignored her, as though she were not even present. Of course the two men hadn't been formally introduced to her, and so perhaps this was reason enough for their reticence. Did the American Indian stand on courtesy and manners?

Maybe.

"*Ouch!*" Her scream was high-pitched, short and loud, an instinctive reaction. The needle she'd been threading had pricked her finger more deeply than usual, and, as it fell from her hands, she put her finger in her mouth. She shouldn't have been threading a needle in the dark, anyway.

However, wanted or not, her exclamation brought on some attention, as one of the young men jumped to his feet and stepped toward her. Bending, he knelt on one knee before her.

She didn't have a moment to be afraid of him, however, for he immediately asked, "Did you hurt yourself?" His voice, she noted was deep and ringing of a bass tone.

"Yes, a little," she answered. "It's my own fault, though. I shouldn't have been trying to mend these clothes in the dark."

"*Hau, hau,* that might be true, but let me take a look at it."

She nodded her assent, and extended the finger that she'd pricked toward him.

He accepted the gesture and took her hand in his own, and, bending down, he examined the wound. Without releasing her hand, he dug into a leather bag that he wore over his shoulder, and pulled out another, smaller container that looked to be filled with an oily substance. He set her hand down on the blanket where she sat while he scooped out a finger-full of the salve. Picking up her hand once more, he dabbed a bit of the balm on her finger.

With her hand still remaining grasped within his own, he gazed up at her and asked, "Does that feel better?"

"Yes, I believe that it does."

His smile at her was incredibly winsome, pulling up only one corner of his mouth. After a moment, he replied, "I am glad."

When he didn't release her hand at once, her fingers began to tingle with renewed feeling, as though that part of her body enjoyed being held by his. To counter the sensitivity, she gradually drew her hand back from his grasp and set it in her lap. Strangely, she missed his touch.

He sat back on his haunches and said not another word to her; however, he also didn't leave. After a while, Jane asked, "You are friends with Mr. Eagle?"

"*Hau, hau.*"

"What does that word mean?"

"Yes, it means yes."

Jane smiled at him, and she noticed that his look at her lips was long until he, at length, averted his gaze. Another moment passed before he asked, "You are sister to Mr. Louis?"

"Mr. Louis? Oh, yes, yes, indeed, I am."

With a quick nod, he started to rise, but she held him back with a simple graze of her fingers on his wrist. "Please," she murmured, "if you would be so kind as to allow me a moment of your time, I would ask you a few questions, for I do not know your customs well, and I have a concern."

He sat back onto his hips and crossed his legs. He nodded. "I am here. I will listen."

"Good," she answered, but she said no more at first, letting several minutes pass by as she assembled her thoughts. She had spoken truthfully; there were concerns she needed to voice aloud, but she desired to do it in a way that would not put both her and Luci at risk. She paused for a few moments before asking again, "You are friends with Mr. Eagle?"

"I am. He is my *ǩóla*."

"Oh? What does that word mean?"

"We are good friends," he explained. "We know each other's hearts."

Jane dipped her head briefly in acknowledgement. "I worry about my…" she hesitated before continuing, "…brother. He can be difficult at times and stubborn, but he is a good boy. Do you believe that Mr. Eagle will instruct my…brother in ways so that he does not get hurt?"

"*Hau, hau.*"

"Truly?"

He nodded.

"I am concerned," she admitted. "I see so many women who flock around the three of you men, that I fear Mr. Eagle may be a bad influence on my…brother."

Iron Wolf paused, and, seeming to put thought into what he might say in reply, he took several minutes before he spoke. "Do not be fooled by what seems to be our fame," he began. "We know well why these women show us strong admiration."

"You do?"

"*Hau, hau.* We are different from what is familiar to them. We are skilled in what we do, for we have long practiced our shooting and riding and other skills. In our country, whether our people starve or enjoy a good life depends upon a man's ability to provide food, clothing and shelter for those he loves. He learns as soon as he can walk what is his duty to his people, and his play consists of learning well the skills that he will need throughout his life in order that—"

"But I thought that—"

He held up his hand. Gently, he murmured, "In the Nakoda tribe, both men and women are permitted to speak fully until he or she decides that there is no more to be said."

"Oh, I didn't know." Jane felt immediately contrite. "I'm sorry."

"I mean no criticism," he clarified. "Our customs are different in many ways from yours. I only tell you this because I am used to speaking wholly what is in my mind without another interrupting me. It allows me to remember my thoughts more easily so that I do not leave an idea unsaid. I have learned that it is different in your society."

"Indeed, it is."

He nodded. "Let me continue in the same line of thought in which I began. I tell you true, that we like the attention from these women, and we realize it is only natural that they would be curious about us."

She nodded.

"But what would happen," he continued, "if we were to make more of it, and, as these women grow in age, they discover that their ideas and ours are as different as a robin is to a squirrel? While interesting at first, these disparities are not qualities that provide a good home for children. A man must always consider what end is in mind when fostering exchanges of ideas between a man and a woman, and, if that end does not include providing a calm and safe upbringing for one's children, is it wise to nurture it?" He hesitated, as if he were again choosing his words cautiously. "So do not be fooled. We like that the women admire us. What man would not? But we know the reasons why they do, and, without being critical, we do not become entrapped in a bad way by the pleasure of their company."

Jane sat in silence, simply gazing at him. Was her father really right about these people? What this young man had related to her was not only wise, but, even in the state of her own youth, she was well aware that his observations were astute.

She gazed away from him, and, in doing so, saw that the sun, which was directly in back of her, was throwing her own shadow, though faint, onto the blanket. More importantly, gazing back at him, she saw that the sun's dim light threw this man's features into a misty prominence, and she thought at this moment that she had never witnessed a more handsome man.

She sighed. Apparently, she, too, was not immune to his charm. She swallowed hard and gazed away from him. "I think," she began, "that we should introduce ourselves to one another. My name is Jane, and you are?..."

"Pardon," he grinned that masculine half-smile at her, and, in response, her heart seemed to flip over in her chest. "Another difference. A Nakoda man does not say or tell his own name. To do so is considered conceited."

"Oh, but how, then, shall I address you?"

"You may call me whatever you like. Friend, perhaps. Or you might ask your brother, for he and I shared each other's names earlier this morning."

Jane nodded. "Thank you…Mr. Friend. I shall ask my si…brother when next I have the opportunity."

He smiled at her again, and Jane was once more captivated by him. She asked, "Will you be coming here to practice with Mr. Eagle and my brother?"

"*Hau, hau,*" he answered. "We are to introduce a new war stunt into our performance, and so my friends and I will be here each morning."

"And so will I," she replied. "So will I…"

Looking up at him, she shared another happy grin with him, and, in doing so, Jane couldn't help but question her father's opinions. Was he wrong about the American Indian people? Quite possibly, he was.

***

Wind Eagle singled out his pony, and, stepping to its side, he petted Sure Foot on the neck. He asked Luci, as she came to stand beside him, "Have you knowledge of how to care for a pony?"

"A little, but my father holds a command in the army, and because of that, others — usually soldiers — have always taken care of our animals, as well as doing the work to hitch up the horses to our carriage. Though I have learned to ride, of course, it is not often that I do so, for it is easier to take a coach into town, especially when someone else is required to furnish the animals and the gig for you."

He shot back a question at her as quick as one of his arrows, and he asked, "Your father is in command of soldiers? Are those the men my people call the Blue Coats?"

She hesitated a moment before she answered. Had Wind Eagle fought in the wars? And, if he had, did he, like her father, have an ill opinion of his former enemy? Perhaps a bad experience? After a rather long pause, she replied, "Yes."

She noted that his hand, which had been petting Sure Foot, stilled, and that Wind Eagle jerked his chin to the left as though her words packed a punch. He said nothing, however, nor did he move.

She asked, "Did you fight in those wars?"

"I was too young at that time to go to war."

"Oh." She didn't know what else to say. After several moments of uncomfortable silence, she murmured, "I can only think that, even if you didn't fight in the wars, the experience must have been bad for a young boy. I am sorry that our people were once at war."

"It is not your fault."

"No, it isn't. But that doesn't mean that I am unaware that you might have lost friends, perhaps even family, to those wars."

He turned away from her so quickly, he practically left her gaping. He might have left her without another word, too. But she wasn't going to let him leave so easily, and she touched his hand before he could take a step away.

As though her fingers contained more magic than flesh and blood, her touch stopped him, but he didn't look at her, and, she thought, he seemed anxious to be away.

"Did you lose someone close to you?" she asked.

"*Hau.*"

"I see. Do you hate me, then, after learning that my father once led the men you call the Blue Coats?"

"*Hiyá.*"

"What does that word mean?"

"No," he answered curtly. He paused for a moment, then said, without looking at her, "I must go now. The others await me so that we can practice."

"Please, don't go away yet." They were both standing together, on the same side of the horse, and she took a step toward him. "Please, stay with me for a moment longer. I...I don't know who else to speak to about last night except you, and I must talk to someone."

He gave her a brief nod, but, outside of that gesture, he remained silent.

"I am uncertain what we do from here. While it may be true that I should keep my thoughts to myself, I am distraught and confused about me and about you, and it seems that because what took place was between you and me, that you might be the person whom I might persuade to listen to me. Please forgive me if this is a conversation you would rather not have."

He caught her eye, and they stared at one another for the precious sixty seconds that are required to become a minute. Gently, another minute transpired between them until at last, he admitted, "I am sorry about last night."

She gasped. "You are?"

He shook his head quickly. "I should have left before you began to change clothes. Perhaps, also, I should not have followed you into the woods."

"You regret what happened between us, then?"

"*Hiyá*. No. Not that."

"I must admit that I am glad to hear that, but if not that, then...what?"

The breath he took in was deep, and he let it out slowly before he asked, "May I speak freely to you of my thoughts?

I warn you that they may not be what you wish to hear."

"Yes, please. Whether pleasant or not, I think it only fair that you tell me what is in your mind, since we engaged in actions last night that... Well, I don't need to tell you what happened."

He gave her a short bob of his head, saying, "I understand. I do not regret what took place between us. It was natural and it was good. But I fear that the experience might affect our work together in a bad way."

She started to interrupt him, but he held up his hand, and she became quiet.

He continued, "Were we to pledge ourselves to one another in marriage, then last night would have been the beginning of our life together. But I have been honest with you when I have told you that I do not wish to become too close to you, a woman who dresses herself as a boy. I have been truthful with you, also, when I tell you that I will not marry you, and yet, I led you into a passion last night that is reserved for those who are married. The fault is mine, not yours."

"Oh. I see. But I believe that I must disagree. The fault is both of ours. I am sorry, too, because...because... May I also speak plainly to you?"

"*Hau, hau,*" he murmured, looking away from her.

She gulped, then whispered, "I am aware that you didn't reach your own enjoyment last night, and I don't know what I could have done differently. You see, Mr. Eagle, I feel that I failed you."

He let out his breath in a deep sigh, as he divulged, "You did nothing wrong and you did not fail me. It was I who brought our time together to a close."

"But why?"

"Because it is well known amongst my people that a woman pushed too far into the excitement of first lust cannot pull back. It is up to the man to call a stop to it, and, since I do not intend to marry you, and, because we have become friends, then I should not have let it go as far as it did."

"Oh," was all she said in acknowledgment, that word sounding sad, even to her own ears. "But don't you have these kinds of relationships with the women who flock around you?"

"Not as often as you might think."

"But still, I know that there are some, and I can't believe that you would feel this same way with them? Do you?"

"*Hiyá.*"

"Then why with me?"

"Because we must work together, and because those other women know what they do. You are different. You are innocent, and do not yet know the ways of men and women. However, it is not my right to educate you about what is shared between married people."

"Oh, yes, of course you are right."

"It might be difficult to do, but I believe that we must try to forget what happened between us. It is in my mind to ask if you think it possible that we ignore what took place between us last night, and try to go back to how we viewed each other before we kissed."

"Do you really think that's possible?"

"I hope that it is. Do you agree that we should try?"

She hesitated. Somehow, although she knew that in the end, she would agree with what he asked, it didn't seem right. At last, however, she uttered, "Yes."

"*Hau, hau.* And now, might I ask you a question that may be a difficult one for you to answer?"

"Of course."

"Does your father, who is a chief of the Blue Coats, know that you are spending most of your days with me?"

"No."

"If he has fought my people, might he be angry if he learns that we are working together?"

"Yes, he might."

"Is he the reason why you are trying to be someone you are not?"

"No, he isn't."

"Are you and your sister running away from someone, perhaps your father? Is he the reason why you are both in disguise?"

"No, my father is not the reason for our disguise."

"Is he or perhaps another demanding that one of you marry a man you don't love?"

She inhaled deeply. "No," she answered. "Our father is not in the country at present, so he knows none of this. Were he here… But then he is not, and so Jane and I must do what we must."

"And the reason you and your sister must do as you must'?"

She glanced away from him.

With softness of voice, he continued, "When my people engaged in fighting yours, we Nakoda learned that men and women are sometimes put in cages for reasons that my people cannot comprehend, for many of those put in cages committed no crime as we know it. So, when I ask you this question, do not feel that I am accusing you or your sister of wrongdoing."

"All right. I will try."

"Have either you or your sister committed a misdeed that you feel might be punished by a desire on others' part to put either of you in a cage?"

"Excuse me, although I understand how you might think this is so, my society does not put people in cages."

"Indeed, they do. In both Europe and here at home, I have seen these enclosures and the men or women who suffer in them."

"Oh, I see." She paused.

"I know that you call them 'jails'. It is the same thing. Cages, jails. In both, freedom is impossible." He hesitated, and, after a moment, his gaze sought out hers. "Is this what you fear?"

"Please, Wind Eagle, although I can appreciate your curiosity as to why I must dress myself as a boy, I would ask that you not continue this line of questioning, for I cannot speak of our reasons for being in disguise. Do you understand?"

"*Hiyá*, I do not."

She drew oxygen into her lungs, letting it out slowly, as she murmured, "Harm might come of it, and that's all I can say, so please do not continue to ask me questions about this matter, for I will say no more."

He nodded once, concisely. "Come, then," he urged, "and let us continue our work. Before I leave to practice with my friends, I will show you how I care for this pony. I believe you and Sure Foot will become good friends."

She nodded. "Yes. Good."

CHAPTER THIRTEEN

*L*uci brought the curry comb down the flanks of Sure Foot. The horse whinnied in response.

"Do you like that, boy?"

He answered by looking back at her. She smiled at him, and, reaching up to his neck, she hugged and kissed him.

It was early morning, five o'clock to be exact; time to exercise and practice riding Sure Foot. Was it only a few weeks since she had been introduced to this pony? In some ways it seemed as if she had known this calm, gentle animal all her life. Sometimes she wondered how she had come to live her life up until now without becoming friends with at least one of these wonderful creatures.

As she stood in the pasture beside the animal, she asked, "Would you like to hear about the three pigs this morning?"

Sure Foot switched his tail and stomped a foot in answer; a clear "yes."

"Good. Well, the fairytale goes like this: Once upon a time, there were three little pigs who were trying to discourage a big, bad wolf from eating them. I'm sure you would understand about that."

Sure Foot neighed.

"Now it happened that they needed to escape from the wolf, and so the first little pig built a house of straw...." Luci's voiced droned on and on as she told the story of the pigs. She had noticed about a week ago that Sure Foot would often refuse to eat this early in the morning, which was hardly good or healthy for him if they were to practice for several hours, and they did need to practice. Then, one morning, as she had brought out the usual hay and water for him, she had discovered that if she talked to him and told him stories, he calmed down enough so that often by the end of her story, he might accept the food.

"'Let me in. Let me in,' said the big, bad wolf.

"'Not by the hair on our chinny-chin-chins,' came the pigs' retort.

"'Then I'll huff and I'll puff and I'll bl-o-o-o-w your house in…' said the wolf, and he huffed and he puffed, but he couldn't blow down that house of bricks. And do you know what the wolf did, then? He climbed up on the roof of the house and came down the chimney, landing in a pot of boiling water. That was the end of the wolf and the three little pigs lived happily ever after. And that is the end of that story. Did you like it?"

Another neigh from Sure Foot was her answer.

"Good, well, then I hope you are ready for your grooming and these oats that I have brought you." She steadied the bag of oats in front of him, then reached over for a brush, but, using his nose, Sure Foot caused it to drop to the ground.

"What are you trying to tell me? That you're wanting me to use the soft brush already?"

Sure Foot neighed in answer to her question, and stamped his foot once. Another definite "yes."

"Don't worry, fellow, I'm only beginning my grooming of you for today. We'll get to that soft brushing that you like so well, but first I have to make sure there's no debris on you before we go out for our ride. You know that if there were anything between you and the saddle I use, it could be mighty uncomfortable."

Sure Foot neighed softly.

Luci smiled, and silently thanked Wind Eagle for his instructions to her. That first day, Wind Eagle had kept his word, and had taught her the basics of horse care, instructing her that one must groom the pony before and after every ride, that one must provide plenty of water and food for Sure Foot, in this case hay and oats. Another daily necessity was that she must be attentive while brushing the animal to look for any possible scrapes, cuts or puncture wounds the little Cayuse horse might have obtained. He had also shown her the natural remedies for these.

Although there were more than these simple chores that would ensure the care of the animal, there were men who traveled with the show who provided food and water to all the animals. But, according to Wind Eagle, it was up to her to ensure that it was done properly.

"Here we go, my handsome, young fellow," she said to the pony. "Time for the soft brush, the one I know you love so well."

Sure Foot whinnied softly, and Luci smiled. "It occurs to me that you might be missing Mr. Eagle, who usually sees to your needs. I must admit that I do, also, although I would never confess that to him. He now practices in the morning with his two friends, and I see him only when we are performing in public. It's odd, too, that I should miss him, for he seems to do little more than irritate and tease me, but there you go. I miss him, too. But perhaps not as much as you do."

The pony shifted his weight as Luci came around to bring the brush down the other side of him. "However, Mr. Eagle tells me that soon he will be teaching me how to ride you properly while shooting at targets. I am curious as to how it is done, although I'm certain you know your part in it, since you are Mr. Eagle's favorite mount. Many times now I have seen him shoot his arrows while you are running at top speed. I have even seen him drop to your side, while firing an arrow at a clay pigeon. Do you know that I have never seen him miss any of those shots? Well, soon he will be teaching this to me."

"Are you telling my pony stories about me, now, instead of the terrible legend of the pigs?"

Luci jumped. One would think that she might have become used to Wind Eagle coming upon her silently, but this was not so.

She gasped. "I do wish, Mr. Eagle, that you would please make some noise when you sneak up on me from the rear." She spun around to face him, and smiled at him. Her glance took in his tall and handsome silhouette, for it was still too dark to discern details. Yet, she could tell that he had only recently engaged in his usual morning swim, for his long hair, beneath the dim light, was still wet. She finished her thought, saying, "I am often startled to learn that you have come to stand right behind me."

"I will try to remember to make more noise, then," he replied. "Have you inspected Sure Foot's hooves to clean out any debris?"

"Not yet," she replied. "I usually leave doing that until the end of his grooming."

"Then I will do it for you," he offered, and, bending down into a squat, he took one of Sure Foot's hooves into his hand.

"Do you need a horse pick to clean out any grasses and dirt? If so, I have one right here." She reached to grab hold of the tool that was supposed to be on top of the corral's fence, but Wind Eagle looked up at her, and, opening his hand, he showed her that he had already selected it out.

They worked over the horse's grooming in silence for several moments, until at length, she asked, "Are you practicing with me this morning or your friends?"

"With you."

"Oh?"

"*Hau, hau.* The Showman has spoken to me and has told me that he wishes you to be ready to compete with me on horseback by next week. We have only a little time left of the show here in this harbor before we move on to another location, which he said was a village called Philadelphia. He would like our act to be ready by the last week of the show that we do here in this harbor."

She nodded. "I think I am ready to learn more, because I have been practicing my riding, the kind that you showed me."

"Yes, I have seen you doing this."

"Have you?" She glanced down at him as he worked over one of Sure Foot's hooves, and, smiling at him, she did her best to sugarcoat her words, as she added, "I wouldn't have known that you have seen me doing this, for you rarely speak to me anymore."

He grinned up at her and then winked. "Of course you have not observed me watching you. I have ensured that I am…what is the English word?…discreet. I believe, also, that we agreed to keep our distance from each other."

"Did we?"

"How else can we ignore one another?"

"Yes, indeed, how else? Well, it doesn't matter. I think that I am ready to learn how to shoot from horseback, especially since I believe that Mr. Sure Foot is a very trustworthy mount, and that he will do all he can to ensure my safety."

"*Hau, hau.* That is why you now ride him."

"I'm sorry. It sounds as if I am a bother. Have you another pony that will do as well as Sure Foot?"

"*Hau,* I do. Iron Wolf has volunteered his own mount to me until I can train my other Cayuse."

"Have you begun your work with your other pony, then?"

"Not yet," he responded. "It takes much time and patience to prepare a horse for his job in the show; he must be gently encouraged to learn, using kindness and understanding, and never dominated, for to overwhelm his decisions does his training wrong, and he may not be calm enough to think through many of the different emergencies that might happen in a performance. One's life is dependent not only upon your mount's instruction, but upon the pony's intelligence and his strength, and therefore my teaching him must be done in such a way as to not overwhelm his own natural inclination. It will take time."

Wind Eagle had come up to his feet, and, with careful positioning, placed Sure Foot's body between the two of them. As he gazed down into her eyes, Wind Eagle said, "I prefer the ponies trained by the Cayuse," he explained, "for they are known to use kindness with their breeds, and the Cayuse show unusual horsemanship, which I have seldom seen elsewhere, even considering the skill of the Russian Cossacks."

"Really? Even considering them?"

"*Hau, hau,* it is true. Lucky I am that Iron Wolf's horse is also Cayuse-bred, for the Cayuse live a great distance from here, and so their breeds are not easily obtained," he said, then he asked, "Have you combed Sure Foot's mane and tail?"

"Not yet. I am only now finishing brushing him. Do you not notice how his coat shines now?"

"I do." He smiled at her, and, as their eyes met, a feeling, not unlike the intensity of a live spark, awoke within her. What sort of power did this man hold over her, that such a simple gesture should produce an excitement that had her remembering that night in the woods?

She gulped and suppressed the feeling. After all, she had given her word to him to try to ignore the flicker of passion between them. She would do her best.

Glancing up at him, she asked as demurely as possible, "Could you hand me the comb for his mane and tail? It is closest to you."

He did as she asked, but she noticed that he took pains to avoid touching her. Indeed, he had no more than released the comb to her when he glanced away and frowned.

He took a few steps back from her, which put his back directly in front of the fencing that encircled the corral. Leaning his weight against the fence, he seemed content to watch as she completed the necessary combing of Sure Foot's mane and tail. As soon as she was done, he muttered, "It is getting late. Let us place blanket and saddle on this little pony and settle into our work, for this stunt is dangerous and must be done exactly as I teach you. Do you understand?"

"I do," she agreed, adding to herself that she understood much more than this. But this thought she kept to herself.

Wind Eagle had already grabbed hold of Sure Foot's lead and was guiding him out of the corral, and, as she followed both master and friend, she admired the gait of them both as they ambled and strutted in front of her.

***

As Wind Eagle stepped into the clearing they used for training, he could sense the unsteady vibrations in the air that announced that she was already here, that she had even now groomed and saddled Sure Foot, and that she had done this long before he had awakened — and he, a man who was not prone to sleep in late. He realized it was very good that she was already at work, and, even though it was against his will, he did admire her for it.

He saw her in the distance, and, as he assessed her skill, his respect for her flowed over with good opinion. Not even a man, given her situation, would do as well as she. And, she was doing all this work with good cheer and appreciation. No complaints.

Was he right to doubt her? Perhaps, but until he could discover the reasons for her disguise and unmask her to the world, he could not allow himself to like her too much. Seeing her dressed as a boy reminded him, also, that whatever else she might be, she was a deceiver, even if she might not be *the* trickster he sought.

It was now several days since he had begun her indoctrination into the sport of mounted shooting, and, not wishing to announce himself yet, he watched her carefully, so that he might judge her proficiency. Because there was so little time left to rehearse this stunt, he felt lucky that she appeared to know naturally the needs and subtle communications of her horse.

She had easily learned the nature of the animal, and that a horse understands that he is the hunted, not the hunter. Therefore, she had discovered early that the pony has a great and inherent need to have and to trust a leader. It was a bond between human and steed that must never be betrayed.

Also, in these last few days, he had observed that when she wasn't riding Sure Foot, she was grooming him, telling him fairytales or spending time with him in other ways. It was also easy to see that, although she continued to practice her shooting daily, with the advent of Sure Foot into her life, she had arranged her schedule so that Sure Foot was the uppermost part of her workday.

He watched as she maneuvered the little Cayuse around and through the many targets that both he and she had placed strategically, which would be a part of their opening act. Similar to their original performance, where they had walked in and around each other in a choreographed "dance," this part of their program was also strictly planned and organized. The danger of the sport allowed no room for error.

Her gun held no ammunition, for when she shot at the targets, the weapon simply clicked. He was well aware that this was little more than exercise, which was done in order to acquaint Sure Foot into the steps of their opening "dance."

Soon, Wind Eagle would mount his own pony and join her in these drills, so that both human and horse had committed the moves to memory. But for now, he enjoyed the pleasure of simply watching her guide the little Cayuse through their planned turns.

She had completed one run-through around the targets when she dismounted, and, stepping to the front of Sure Foot, she bent down to inspect one of his front hooves. She brushed a piece of debris from that hoof, then rose up so that she was standing before Sure Foot. Wind Eagle smiled, for he was touched by her show of good care, witnessing the love that was shared between human and animal. Yes, it was true; not only did Little Flame love and admire Sure Foot, the emotion was returned.

All at once a moment of great import happened, and Wind Eagle caught his breath at the sight. What was this? A vision? Or a dreaded omen?

As he stood here now, he saw in front of him a future time: there he was, casually posturing beside her, and there were their three children crowded around them, each little one looking to be representations of their parents. Moreover, much happiness could be witnessed in this scene, for they were all laughing, and he saw himself teasing not only her, but their children.

No! To say that the vision shocked him would have been greatly understated; what he could see here before him could not be. Had he not sworn to himself that he would never marry a woman such as she? Hadn't he realized long ago that great unhappiness lay in that direction? Weren't his father and his mother, as well as his sister, proof of that?

However, there was more wrong with this look into the future, for there was another objection he must consider, one that was deep and overpowering: She might be the deceiving one.

Although sanity might have ruled out this possibility, he reminded himself that he still did not know her and her sister's reasons for disguising themselves. Were they not, in fact, living a lie? How could he possibly contemplate aligning himself with a woman who could not live with the truth of who she was?

Further, what of her family? He knew now that her father was a man who had led men, the Blue Coats, to kill the Lakota and the Assiniboine people. Surely, this was a bad man; one, also, who would not likely allow his daughter to marry an Assiniboine. And, conversely, *he* could not permit himself to marry her because of this same reason.

He shook his head, as if this simple action might dislodge the vision and return him back to the world of the present, where sanity reigned. The attempt didn't work. The vision remained.

Was his only choice, then, to ignore this look into what could be a possible vision given to him by the Creator? Dare he? Or did he do the opposite and court the daughter of the enemy, possibly flaunting his own people?

These thoughts, extremely opposite in nature, must have held great power over him, because instantaneously the future images faded, until what he saw before him was again the real universe as represented at this moment in time. But he did wonder, was he, as well as his pony, enchanted with her? Had he fallen in love her? Was this a truth he dare not face?

Unwanted tears gathered in his eyes, and he longed to walk away from the knowledge shown him and ignore it. Yet, he was wise enough to realize he could not pretend that the Creator had not spoken to him.

As he choked back the tears, he thought he could not recall a time when he had been so emotionally conflicted. Either he was wrong, or the vision was. He knew now that he could not face her or talk to her.

He would leave her and Sure Foot this morning, if only for the moment. He would seek out a place where he might be alone, where he could try to speak to his Maker, since it was He who had shown this to him. Perhaps the Creator might speak with him and encourage him to understand.

So deciding, he silently trod away from the field of their daily practice. He would take the morning to bathe himself with the herbs and the smoke of a small fire, and perhaps, if he were fortunate, the Creator would give him insight into what he had seen. For the moment, he could only hope that it would be.

***

Tonight was to be the last show performed in the New York harbor, at least for this season. As Luci sat forward on Sure Foot, she checked the holsters that she had positioned directly in front of her. Each holster contained a .45 single action gun with five black powder leather blanks already loaded into each gun. She glanced nervously toward Wind Eagle, who sat mounted to her right. He was riding Stormy Boy, the little Cayuse that belonged to Iron Wolf. Although Wind Eagle had only been able to put the little pony through a week of rehearsal, he had assured Luci that Stormy Boy knew his part in this, their mounted debut.

At the conclusion of the presentation today, the show would move onward, journeying to Philadelphia. At least in traveling, there would be several weeks where Wind Eagle would have the opportunity to work over Stormy Boy's training.

She was a little unnerved about this, their opening act, if only because Stormy Boy really needed more practice. But Wind Eagle had assured her that he was horseman enough to control the animal and keep his seat, if the need even arose.

Their new act was similar to the one they had originally performed afoot, but it was now to be accomplished mounted, and it was also to be executed with a dizzying speed. Because the horses were trained at a run, and, because they weaved in and out and around each other, every movement was strictly choreographed. It had to be, for their own safety and for that of their animals.

But there was a further difference between their original representation and this one: Wind Eagle would be accomplishing the performance utilizing the same type of weapon as she, the single action .45; it was simply too dangerous an act to attempt this using bow and arrow.

Also, their targets were no longer to be buckskin or paper. On Buffalo Bill's suggestion, they had changed their targets to the new rubber balloons that had become so popular. The balloons would pop when hit with the black powder. Thus, it would be easy for the audience to see immediately if their aim were true.

"Stay your seat and concentrate on shooting accurately," Wind Eagle advised. "Sure Foot knows his part and he will guide you through the act without your having to lead him too greatly. Grip your reins tightly with one hand without worry, for our horses know the routine as well as we do."

Luci nodded. Soon it was time. Buffalo Bill was already riding into the middle of the arena, announcing their new act of daring.

"Here we go," Wind Eagle announced as he winked at her. Together, as one, they waved to the audience. At once, screams of the feminine gender arose from the front seats, and, to this high-pitched whine, they set their ponies into a run. Weaving back and forth and around each other, they shot at the balloons they'd set up earlier.

No misses; it went off without a hitch. They waited as a few of the men with the show set up more balloons as targets.

Only two more rounds of the same, she thought, and they were done with this, the hardest part of their full act. The second run was done at an even faster clip than the first, and Luci laughed along with Wind Eagle as they completed that run.

"That was fun!" she couldn't help observing. "Once more around and we're done!"

He grinned at her and winked. "Here we go! Let's make the last one the best!"

With their horses galloping at top speed, in and around each other, the further difficulty of shooting at targets added an explosive element to their act. Indeed, when this new enactment was done correctly, it was exhilarating, and, after the last two runs, this third and last run seemed to lift Luci's spirits.

It seemed as if all would be well, and that they had accomplished the entirety of their exhibition when a stray spark hit Stormy Boy in his flanks. He reared!

Wind Eagle appeared to control the pony and calm him, but it was only for a moment. The little Cayuse reared again, then without warning, he set off into a fast run around the arena, and when Wind Eagle reined him in to a stop, Stormy Boy reared again, then he bucked, over and over.

The accident and its immediate danger happened so quickly that Luci was caught off guard, and her reaction was too slow to try to prevent it. She could only watch in horror as the pony reared, then ran to the other side of the arena. Helplessly, she watched as Wind Eagle struggled to bring the little steed under control.

Dismounting, she dropped Sure Foot's reins to the ground and dashed forward as fast as she could. Ahead of her were Wind Eagle's friends, Iron Wolf and Blue Thunder, who sprinted toward the spooked pony. But, although they reached the animal within minutes, even they could not come near the frightened horse.

It was then that it hit her. Wind Eagle could be killed. Good horsemanship or not, accidents were always possible, and sometimes they were fatal.

"No!" she shouted as she ran toward the spot where Wind Eagle struggled with the pony. "Don't you dare get yourself killed. Because I don't want to live without you! Do you hear me? I don't want to live without you!"

All at once she realized that her shouted words were true. Indeed, it is said that there are times when a truth needs only adversity to cause it to appear full-fledged into the light. Perhaps there was some basic wisdom to this saying, for she realized it had certainly happened now, and to her. She loved Wind Eagle.

Truly, she loved him. And, he was in danger. She quickened her sprint into a dead run.

At last, she came within shouting distance of the drama being played out at the side of the arena, and, as she came in closer, she yelled out,

"Don't you dare die, Wind Eagle, because I love you! Do you hear me? I love you!"

In the pulse of an instant, he caught her eye and at that same moment he bent forward to place his arms around Stormy Boy's neck. It seemed to help, for she could see that Wind Eagle had been trying to control the animal using reins only, and, although he was holding tightly to Stormy Boy's neck, the pony responded positively to the embrace. Luci watched as Wind Eagle spoke words into the steed's ear.

Stormy Boy calmed, neighing softly, as he shifted his weight from one foot to the other. It seemed as if this was all that was needed to allow Iron Wolf and Blue Thunder to approach the animal and take control of the reins, steadying the little Cayuse. She watched as Iron Wolf went further and took Stormy Boy's head into his hands, where he breathed into the animal's nostrils. It was with a great degree of respect that Luci watched as the pony settled down under Iron Wolf's control.

It was at that moment that Wind Eagle slid off the little cayuse, and, as he did so, he took a few steps in Luci's direction. And then, to Luci's amazement, Wind Eagle smiled at her, and there was a half grin on his face as he admitted, "I, too." To this he added his infuriating, yet endearing wink.

CHAPTER FOURTEEN

*L*uci tenderly laid out two of her favorite dresses on her cot: the orchid and the delicate green. Lovingly, she slid her fingers over the soft, silky material of the orchid's chiffon and then the lacy material of the green. The bodice of the green gown tended lower and was rounded, whereas the orchid's neckline formed a "V."

She supposed she favored the green, and her touch traced over the trimmings of lace at the front of the skirt, which created a flattering "V" shape over the upper hips. Many volumes of swathed material in front and in back of the skirt draped loosely to the floor. The gown was made with a train; it was plain, yet silky and overlaid with lace, and was gathered to the lower end of the bodice in back.

Opening her trunk, she removed her satin, ivory-colored slippers. They were simple, yet pretty, and they would match either dress. Dared she do it? Dared she dress up in her most beloved feminine clothing tonight?

It would certainly complement the style of the evening planned ahead, for Buffalo Bill had announced that in addition to entertaining many of New York's elect, there was to be a sit-down supper, given to celebrate the closing of the last show here in the New York harbor. A ball would follow as soon as dessert and coffee were served, and Luci, as feminine as any other woman, wished with all her heart to attend that ball; she, dressed as Jane's "sister."

"What are you doing, Lucinda?"

Luci jumped, and turned quickly to see that Jane had come to stand behind her. Pressing her hand to her heart, she admitted, "Goodness, you scared me. I had seen you with the very handsome and talented Will

Granger after our last performance this afternoon. I thought you were still with him."

"Yes, I was. But a few of his friends soon joined him, and I felt…" Jane's words trailed off. "There are one or two of the men he keeps company with that scare me a little. One of them in particular looks at me as though…as though…" Jane shrugged. "I don't know, Luci. Sometimes I feel uncomfortable when I'm with Will and his friends."

"Then you shouldn't have to be with them. You were wise to walk away."

"I suppose you're right. By the way, what are you doing?"

Luci turned her back on her sister, and mumbled softly, barely audible, "I'm thinking of dressing as myself tonight."

"I'm sorry, Luci, I didn't hear what you said."

Luci turned around slowly, facing her sister. She put her hands behind her back, and, looking down at their recently purchased woolen rug which covered the hard ground of their shared bedroom, she answered softly, "I'm considering attending the dinner and ball tonight as your sister, who has only recently come to visit."

Glancing upward, Luci saw that Jane looked at her oddly before tendering an opinion, and, even then, it was after some minutes that she said, "I think that's a splendid idea. Brilliant, really. But what will we do about our 'brother'?"

"Well, I intend to have your 'sister' return to the DC area in less than a few days. When she leaves, we'll again see more of our 'brother,' as I once again become him."

"I love the idea, Luci. You realize, of course that Wind Eagle and his friends will be a part of the celebration tonight?"

"Yes, I do, and perhaps it's why I've decided to do this, for I have discovered that I have…feelings for Wind Eagle."

"Well, it's about time you admitted it," Jane said as she reached down for one of the dresses. "I've been watching the two of you together in the mornings as you practice, and it's abundantly clear to see that the two of you hold great respect for each other."

"Truly? You have realized this? And you don't object?"

"Of course not."

"I didn't know that you felt that way."

Jane shrugged. "It seems to me that he and his friends have now become a part of our culture by participating in Buffalo Bill's shows. Indeed, Luci, I begin to wonder about the truth of our father's opinions about these Indian people. Do you suppose his views are nothing more than tainted?"

"They might be. His job was, after all, war. It meant that he had to subjugate the Indian tribes, and, when he couldn't subdue them, to kill them. How could he hold a good opinion of them and still do his duty to his command?"

"Indeed." Jane dropped her gaze to the floor. "Perhaps you've noticed that I've come to know Iron Wolf a little, since I, of course, accompany you to your practices, and I think that — "

"Iron Wolf? Yes, I have seen the two of you talking, of course, but I hadn't realized that you might hold him in good esteem."

Jane looked away from her. "Yes, I admit that I do. Mr. Wolf and I have spoken often now, and I do believe that he is a good and honorable young man."

"I see. You do realize, don't you, that he has a goodly amount of women who hang upon his every word?"

"As does Wind Eagle."

"Yes, indeed," Luci agreed. "Which brings our conversation back to the dinner and the dance we'll be attending tonight. Whether for better or worse, I wish to appear in a flattering light, and perhaps, by doing this, to gain Wind Eagle's approval of me."

"Dear sister, you already have it, I believe."

"Are you speaking true?"

Jane nodded.

"Yet, Wind Eagle says that he cannot ever become too close to me. Indeed, he has told me often that because I dress as a boy, I am deceiving others, and for this, he does not wish to know me more intimately. I fear that I might never be able to cause him to give up his prejudice toward me. And," Luci raised her gaze to Jane's, "I do believe that I wish for his good opinion, and that he might look upon me as the woman that I really am...if only for tonight."

Jane grinned at her. "Then let me help you to into your clothes. Perhaps together we can dress you up so that he will not be able to ignore the facts presented so clearly to him."

Luci chuckled. "I fear that may never happen. But..." her smile widened, "I admit that I like your idea very much."

***

Accompanied by Jane, Luci stepped into the brightly lit tent that had been set up for dancing. Night had fallen during the dinner hour, which placed the present time at about eight o'clock, and, with the wonders of Edison's genius, a new form of lighting, the incandescent light bulb, had replaced the kerosene and gas illumination that had previously lit this large and oversized tent. The new fixtures were attached to poles, which were positioned throughout the pavilion, and the luster of the bulb was, even now, throwing a soft, yellow-tinted glow onto the wooden platform that had been specifically built to be used as a dance floor.

The musicians in the orchestra had already taken their seats at the head of the exhibition area, and an eerie sort of tune filled the hall as the performers tuned their instruments. The room was warm and welcoming, and Luci felt her spirits lift as a spark of hope filled her being.

Would her ploy work? Would this be the night when Wind Eagle acknowledged her womanly inclinations? She prayed that it would be so, especially since the supper hour had proved to be less than satisfying.

Next to this particular pavilion sat another, where many of the performers and several of the New York elite still lingered over their coffee and dessert. The supper had been served by the several cooks who were attached to the show. The menu, being mainly of Western origin, had consisted of buffalo and beef steaks, complemented with potatoes, turnips and greens. The many tables of their dining hall had been decorated with red, white and blue tablecloths, which had set off the brilliance of the silver plates and silverware. Oil lamp posts, positioned every few feet within the tent, had thrown a flattering radiance over the entire company, adding to the cozy feel of what the cowboys humorously called their chuck wagon.

Wind Eagle hadn't attended the dinner, however, and Luci had found it difficult to quash her feeling of disappointment. Because she and he worked together so closely, their schedules were similar, and they usually shared their meals. Truth was, she had missed him.

It wasn't as though she had suffered from lack of attention during the meal. Many of the show's performers had paid her especial notice, and she had enjoyed the feast and the conversation. But in the end, she'd realized that it wasn't the same without Wind Eagle; she had wished for his companionship, then and now.

At present, drums beat across the camp in the Indian village, announcing that those people were celebrating the end of the New York season in their own way. Was that where he was now? Most likely, she decided.

Would he stay away from the ball, as well? More importantly, would the rest of the evening prove that the time she had spent in dressing in this elegant dress had been wasted?

Indeed, it was true. Even her toiletry tonight had been laborious, as both she and Jane had consumed the better part of an hour slaving over her hair; fashioning it into the latest coiffure, tying ribbons through her several loops of curls; curls that now fell low onto her neck. Her waist was nipped in tightly, and the femininity of her upper body was supported by the latest style of corset. The mountainous yards of material in her skirt draped softly to the floor, as though it were made of liquid, instead of satin and silk. Dressed as she was, she felt feminine and pretty, and she realized that this was the image she longed for Wind Eagle to see, and, hopefully to appreciate.

Surely, Wind Eagle would attend the dance. After all, the women who so admired Wind Eagle and his friends would be in attendance at this ball. Would Buffalo Bill encourage the three men who formed his most popular act to be present here tonight? It did seem likely.

Does he love me?

The thought came out of nowhere. Did Wind Eagle love her? Perhaps. After all, he had uttered, "I, too," directly to her. Of course, it had been said under the greatest degree of danger that a man could face.

He'd said, "I, too." But what had he meant by those words?

Had the threat of death caused him to plummet into a realization of everlasting love for her? Or was there another, less romantic meaning to those few words? Had he implied, perhaps, that he, too, had been concerned for his life?

She didn't know the answer to these uncertainties, and she'd been unable to ask him about it further, because the rest of their performance, which was an open and direct competition between them, had been accomplished in silence. Luci had hoped to carve out a moment and question him about it further after their very last performance. But the opportunity hadn't presented itself.

He hadn't helped, either. He'd been his usual self, of course, smiling and winking at her now and again, but he had seemed distracted and cut off from her.

She had searched for him after that last performance; she'd found him easily enough — surrounded by his usual crowd of young women. At the time, she'd thought about becoming part of that admiring crowd, but upon glancing down at the state of her dirty boy's clothing and the less-than-appealing image she presented, she'd decided against it.

Was she fooling herself that he could ever love her? She turned that question over in her mind now, and, as she continued to think about it, it appeared less likely that he might really care for her in that manner.

She, however, was no longer left in an unknowing state as to her true feelings toward him. She loved him, sincerely loved the man, infuriating though he might be. Yes, she admitted, if they did become a romantic couple, there would be many future problems they would face, including her father's wrath, but those unknowns could wait for a moment or two.

Luci shook her head. What was she thinking? A romantic couple? Since when had she taken to daydreaming?

And yet, he had kissed her, had given her the ultimate in carnal stimulation, and he had done it without seeking his own pleasure. Surely, that counted for something, didn't it?

Problem was, he could have his pick of women. Worse, because she looked like an unkempt little boy each day, she was more than aware that she reminded him of that within him which drove him to repulse her.

Her sigh was deep and troubled. Looking outward, however, she saw that two of the men who worked for the show were approaching her. Perhaps they wished a dance with her? Would the opportunity to dance help to ease her inner tension?

Perhaps. Smiling kindly at the two men, she hoped that one of them might ask for her hand in a stimulating whirl around the tented ballroom. Yes, indeed. A waltz or even a fast-paced Irish jig might surely relieve her of the fear and nervousness which currently plagued her.

"May I have this dance, pretty lady?" asked a bronco.

Lucinda laughed. "I would be honored, sir. Truly honored." And, accepting his hand, she allowed the gentleman to guide her out onto the special platform, which had been built and set aside for this special activity.

Ah, how she loved to dance.

CHAPTER FIFTEEN

How had it happened?

Smoke wafted and curled through the evening's warm, humid air.
Drums beat out a steady, magnetic rhythm that invited both men and
women of all races to be a part of the welcoming round dance — and they
were dancing, visitors and Indians alike. Vivid colors of red, blue, yellow,
orange and deep green flashed before Wind Eagle's eyes, as the
participants flicked their regalia, their arms and feet, keeping time to the
pulse of those drums.

Tonight Wind Eagle had chosen to remain apart from that "drum,"
which was a group of men who sat around the large drum and provided
the music and rhythm for the dancing. The round dance song was an old
one, purposely composed and sung in a soothing, minor key, the melody
and rhythm aiding and encouraging the people to forget their cares and
dance.

He listened to the deep voices that contrasted with the high-pitched
notes of the tenor solo that would soon be repeated by each man within
the drum group. He knew the song they were singing, and his spirits
lifted, allowing him a moment of freedom from his heavy and consuming
thoughts. But it was a short-lived instant.

He could have been a part of these goings-on tonight. After all, he
and his friends usually joined in with the singing. But he had chosen to
remain apart from them. He was too conflicted, and he was well aware of
the reasons for his disquiet and the heaviness within his mind. Even his
stance over the ground felt weighty, the gravity beneath him pulling him
down.

The truth was that he could no longer pretend ignorance of his
devotion for Little Flame. He had heard her impassioned declaration of

love, which had been shouted to him above the noise of the crowd and amidst the danger of Stormy Boy's frightened run for freedom. In fact, Little Flame's avowal had created a calming effect upon him, and it had come at a time when he had needed it most. Because of her, he had remembered how easily the little Cayuse responded to whispered words of adoration. That memory had set him free, and he had been able to more easily bring comfort to the frightened horse.

Why that piece of insight as to the animal's nature had remained hidden to him when he'd needed it most, he didn't know. But of this he was certain: it was because of Little Flame that he had summoned it up. *Hau, hau,* it was because of Little Flame, his beautiful, but not-so-easily-understood partner. When he had told her, "I, too," he had meant it.

Indeed, in that time, he had faced a true, but reluctant reality: he loved her, too. Now what? Where did he go from here?

Did he run to her? No. He had promised himself that he would never allow a woman such as she was into his life.

And yet, it would appear that his best efforts to keep Little Flame out of his heart had been for naught. Worse, despite his newly admitted love for her, he still doubted her: was she the deceiver or not?

He couldn't answer that important question, and yet, he could no longer pretend to himself that he felt nothing for her.

What should he do now? Continue to remain distant from her? Pretend that this recent event held little importance? Persist in doing the same as before?

Could he? Could she?

"*Hiyá,* no."

He muttered the words aloud. He was in love with her; he wanted to make love to her. Yet, given their situations, that gigantic step would involve marriage, a commitment he was certain he dare not make.

Perhaps, as he had done in the past, he should do so now, which was to take no action and make no vows. But was that right?

Reluctant though he was to admit it, he fell headlong into another truth: doing nothing was no longer possible. Not now. This time they had met one another on a level for which there was no going back.

Suddenly, within the words of the song of the drum group, came a familiar feminine voice from out of his past: "In matters of the heart, a man must share his thoughts with his wife and his children. Do not refrain from speaking to those you love, my grandson, no matter how hard it might seem to be."

So had his beloved grandmother said. In spirit, these remembered words gave him courage. Certainly, Wind Eagle knew the reasons for his grandmother's command: had his father sought out his wife and told her his intentions, Wind Eagle's mother, and perhaps even his sister, might yet be alive in the flesh. There was no doubt in his mind that his father was now burdened by his failure to speak to her.

Should he learn from his elders? As troublesome as it might be to bare his heart to Little Flame, should he take the chance and do so?

Perhaps, yet it seemed to him that it might be easier to go to war with an enemy than to seek out Little Flame and simply talk to her. However, he also realized there was no substitute for doing the right thing. Sighing deeply, as though a needed breath could decide his next course of action, he made his resolve: He would talk to her, he would tell her of the depth of his admiration for her, and he would let nature have its way.

This decided, he wondered where she would be. In the woods? If he did go there, and if they did speak to one another, what outcome might he expect? Lovemaking? The thought of that sent a jolt of sexual arousal toward his nether regions, and he became suddenly alert, making it difficult for him to think with his heart and not with his baser, fleshly instinct. It was that instinct, however, that rose up over all other thoughts, and seemed to be all he needed to make a resolve. He would make love to her; tonight, he would finish what he had once started.

Yet, cautioned a voice of reason, could he take that step irresponsibly, without marriage? Yes, he could. The culture that he had become a part of allowed this, if it were done discreetly. And a man, because he was a man, might do this.

But is it right? He closed his eyes, and shook his head. He would speak to her, he would make love to her, and he would let the future take care of itself.

Enough thinking. He had made his decision, and he intended to act on it. Turning away from the dancing and drumming, he stepped quietly toward his lodge, where he would find the blankets and the needed supplies he might require for the rest of the evening ahead. It was, after all, best to be prepared....

CHAPTER SIXTEEN

"*She* is at the Showman's ball, my brother." Blue Thunder's voice reached out to Wind Eagle even before his friend stepped out of the woods and into the clearing. Blue Thunder continued, "I fear she will not join you here tonight."

Wind Eagle rose up from where he had been sitting beneath the old weeping willow tree. He took the few steps necessary to bring him face-to-face with his *kóla*, Blue Thunder. He had expected him, having heard his steps along the path.

"At the Showman's ball? Why would she go there?" asked Wind Eagle aloud. "She loves to dance, which she cannot do when she is dressed as a boy."

It was too dark, really, to see the spark of humor that Blue Thunder quickly hid. But Wind Eagle did see it, and he asked, "Why do you laugh?"

"That is for you to determine, my friend. Come, we will go there together. The Showman found me at our own camp's celebration, and asked me to locate where you had gone to, and bring you to the place of the music. He has instructed me to tell you that he wishes the three of us to attend."

Wind Eagle drew in a deep breath and let it out slowly. Although he had already decided that he must tell Little Flame his thoughts and invite a discussion between them, deep within him was the knowledge that regardless of how their talk ended, he intended to seduce her.

With this in mind, he had prepared for their confrontation tonight in many different ways, but what he had not envisioned was that he might have need to revise his plans. However, it appeared that this was exactly what he must do.

What he couldn't understand was why she would be at the place of the music, and not here in this private spot in the woods. Was her presence required there? Had Buffalo Bill asked her to attend the party, as well as he?

Wind Eagle answered Blue Thunder in the only way he could, and he said, "I thank you, my brother, for coming here to find me. *Hau, hau,* let us make our way to the celebration."

"*Wašte,*" acknowledged Blue Thunder. "Let us go there together."

***

As Wind Eagle and Blue Thunder trod into the tent which had been especially set up as a ballroom, they both stopped short, temporarily blocking the entryway. It took Blue Thunder's nudge to cause Wind Eagle to move aside, thus allowing the others behind them to come farther into the tent.

Certainly, thought Wind Eagle, she was here tonight. Over there to his left, she stood, and she was surrounded by a circle of men. Many of those admirers were performers in the show, but not all. Some of the men he didn't recognize. However, they all appeared to have one trait in common: they were acting as though each one of them were enchanted with her.

And why not? She looked as though she had stepped out of a young man's dream. He didn't know what he had expected to see here, but it wasn't this, and, as he watched her accept an invitation to dance, an emotion that felt suspiciously like jealousy rose up within him.

He suppressed it.

Did her actions here tonight signify that she had impressed Buffalo Bill with the truth of who she was? Was her deception at an end?

As though reading his friend's thoughts, Blue Thunder murmured quietly, "I overheard others saying that she is the sister of Miss Jane and Mr. Louis, and that she has come here for a short visit."

Wind Eagle paused a moment before responding, using the language of sign, "Then the deception remains." It was no question.

Blue Thunder nodded.

Wind Eagle stared at her as if by heated glance alone, he could bring her to his side. But it was not to be. She was surrounded by too many men to see or to feel his intention.

Her dress tonight was a deep, green color, he noted, and it shimmered with her every movement. Its low-cut bodice showed off her ample breasts, and, unwillingly, he recalled the look and the taste of each one of those feminine mounds. A feeling of lust, deep within him, raised its ugly head, complementing his already wanton intentions.

The waist of that dress she wore accented how tiny she truly was. Her hair was worn down and coiled into curls that fell softly to her shoulders. On her feet, she wore white moccasins that might have been decorated with jewels.

As his scrutiny followed her out onto the dance floor, with her hand placed securely within that of her partner's, Wind Eagle felt as though he might burst into flame, and he knew he could not remain here and watch her being held by another, even if only in a dance. Briefly, she glanced up and her gaze at last caught onto his.

They stared at one another. Time sped by, and still they looked at each other. Neither of them smiled, nor was it necessary to speak. He knew in his heart that she meant to challenge him, and that he was, indeed, dared to action. Although lust and jealousy coursed through his veins, he also understood that if he wanted her, he had but to step forward and she would become his. However, he wasn't ready to face that particular event and the repercussions that would ensue from it. Not yet, not now.

Without waiting for another minute to tick by, he broke eye contact with her and turned around, deliberately stalking out of the tent. Let the Showman find another of the performers to attend that dance. He could not remain standing at the side of the tent and casually watch her in the arms of another man.

Knowing that his best course of action was to come to terms with this adverse turn of events, and also to cool the ugly resentment filling him, he acted wisely, before a "hot head" could cause him to engage in actions he might later regret.

In his heart was a certainty that she did not belong to another man. She was his; she would always be his, and he would not be a man if he did not feel the rush and the urgent need to force her into his arms and into his sleeping robes. Take her, and to the devil with the consequences.

Yet, it wasn't right, and, the problem was, he knew it wasn't right. Yes, he had intended to make love to her tonight, but he had not necessarily planned to lay claim to her. He couldn't. Still, the choice was his: take her or leave her.

But it wasn't that simple. For him, lovemaking did not have to require marriage, especially when his loyalty lay elsewhere; with his mother, his sister, his brother-in-law; indeed, the welfare of his tribe.

But now? He had a choice to make, and he had best come to that decision alone, within the presence of the Creator.

And, so it came to be that he took out his rage in the heavy steps that he took. He stomped out into the warmth of the summer night, with his direction heading unerringly back into the woods....

***

"Creator, I come before you in need.

Creator, I ask for your help,

I am torn.

Is she the deceiver?

Or is she the love that I have been searching for?

I love her.

I have seen that she is gentle and that she is kind.

Yet, she is a deceiver,

And I have sworn to myself

That I will not let a woman like she is into my life."

As Wind Eagle sang his song, he raised his face to the heavens. Because it was a cloudy night, there were no stars and no moon to witness his plea. Still, he would not be turned away. Intense and hostile emotion

175

coursed through his body, and he knew that he had best settle this now, tonight.

There was no answer to his prayer. He swallowed, hard, and he waited...and he waited.

After a moment, he began to think with his head instead of rage and his physical need of her. There was no doubt in his mind that she was challenging him: take her now or she might find another. Yet, putting his brand on her now, within the witness of others, demanded of him that he do it with honor and with respect, which meant marriage.

Yet, love aside, how could he contemplate marrying her, simply to ensure that all other men would know that she was his? She, a deceiver?

Or was she?

From out of the past came images of their recent encounters, and he saw again the love and the care she demonstrated for Sure Foot. The animal loved her, and she loved him. Also, as further witness, was the consideration and devotion she showed to her sister. Could he overlook these obvious acts of the truth and kindness that told of the wealth of love within her heart?

Memories of that one brief look into his future filled his vision now, in the present. It had happened only weeks ago, and had shown him a time that could be; it had included not only her, but three of their children. Despite the raging emotions filling his soul, he knew the happiness in that fleeting glimpse could not be turned aside.

The sudden sensation of being slapped in the face with an unwilling truth took hold of him, causing him to take a straight look at the honesty of his heart. Would he really be attracted to a woman who had sinister plans envisioned for others? The answer was obvious: no. He was not so unaware of the spiritual nature of life that he could be easily fooled.

Did this not prove that there could be a good reason for her deception? Did it, then, matter that he did not know it?

No, it did not, and the realization of this hit him as though with a blow. Trust; it had been long in coming, but it was unexpectedly here before him now.

Trust? Was it really that simple? Indeed it might be, for unexpectedly, he felt free at last to act in an honorable and true fashion toward her.

So it was that he made his decision without further hesitation. Yes, he would seduce her as he had planned, but he would also marry her in the process. It was right; it was good. He was not wrong about this; he knew in his heart that he wasn't. He belonged to her, and she belonged to him. It was time to become straightforward in his thinking and in his actions, and in hers, also.

She loved him. A woman such as she would never have given herself to him unless she had forever in mind, if unacknowledged. And he loved her. Had he done so almost from the start?

Perhaps.

Would she marry him willingly? He suspected that she might, even over her father's objections, and despite his and her own differences in ideas and culture.

Yes, the time had come to confront what had been here brewing between them all along. They were better together than left apart.

The sound of Little Flame's laughter, gay and beautiful, broke into his contemplations. He was too distant from the dancing tent to hear it, yet hear it, he did. It was in that moment that he knew what he would do—perhaps what he had always been meant to do. His decision, he knew, was good and it was right.

Turning, he stepped lively back toward the dancing tent, and, as he did so, he heard the wind whispering through the trees, repeating a message once given to him by the Creator, "Trust your heart, my son…trust your heart…."

He smiled.

CHAPTER SEVENTEEN

$\mathcal{L}$uci laughed merrily, as she turned to the young gentleman who had escorted her out of the pavilion and into the darkened night. Several couples were here already, speaking quietly to each other in this place that had been set aside for any of the dancers who might wish to catch their breath.

"Would you care for some wine, or perhaps some other brew to drink?" asked the gentleman whose name she couldn't remember, simply because he was a New Yorker whom she had never met until tonight.

She smiled up at him. "I would certainly appreciate a sip of wine, if you truly do not mind fetching it, sir," she answered. "I fear that the fast pace of the jig has left me quite without breath, and I am in need of this night air."

"Your wish is my command, dear lady, and I will get your refreshment at once."

Luci grinned. "That would be most welcome, sir; most welcome, indeed."

The young man smiled and turned away, and, as he did so, Luci revolved around in the opposite direction, staring out into the night. Although the dancing served as a means to quiet her fear, she couldn't help but wonder where Wind Eagle had gone. Why had he gone? In truth, it did appear that her ploy to cause Wind Eagle to take notice of her as a pretty and genuine female, had failed.

What did she do now? There was little she could do except enjoy the rest of the evening as best she could, and to set her sights upon another plan that might bring about a better result between herself and Wind Eagle.

She sighed as she glanced over her shoulder in the direction of the tent's entrance, wondering when that young gentleman might return. And, so it was that when someone grasped hold of her hand to pull her away from the pavilion, and to step out into the night, she gasped.

Looking forward, however, she saw at once that it was Wind Eagle. He didn't speak to her; he didn't even look back at her. He simply pulled her along with him and behind him, as he made their path into the forest.

Joyously, her heart leapt in her breast. He was here, presenting her with the attention she so desired. Perhaps he wasn't as immune to her as he might like her to believe, for she felt certain that she knew his plan. He meant to finish what they had started so many weeks ago.

Her spirits lifted. Did she dare to hope that he cared for her? Perhaps, that he might love her? Had she, after all, put the right interpretation to those two words, "I, too?"

Suddenly, an evening that had seemed so empty and devoid of him turned into a night that could be filled with hope and with promise. And, Luci simply couldn't help herself. She smiled.

***

As she had anticipated, he led her to the same open meadow that she had discovered weeks ago, it being surrounded by the wooded glen. As he stepped out onto the grassy openness, he stopped, turned toward her and opened his arms to her.

He murmured, "I have brought you here to dance."

She raised her face to his and smiled up at him. "I suspected as much."

"But there is more," he admitted as he turned her into his arms. "Let me tell you my true intentions, so that if you do not like them, you may leave. I intend to make you mine tonight."

"Yes," was her only reply.

"And if I do this, you do realize that this will cause us to become married—"

"But I thought that you could never do that."

"A man does not make a woman his own without consequences. Nor does he dishonor a friend. Know that if you stay here, you will be my wife."

She looked up at him and stared. The night was cloudy and dark, yet she could see him well enough, and his image was so handsome that she caught her breath.

Yes, she had meant to challenge him, but marriage? This turn of events was unexpected. Or was it? From the start, he had made his thoughts on the matter quite plain, and it was for this reason that their earlier descent into passion had been left unfulfilled…at least by him.

"Do you stay?" he asked, his voice sweet, low and baritone.

It took her a bit to answer, but when she did, she looked up at him, and, opening her eyes wide, she uttered, "Yes, I do, for you see, I love you. But know also that I cannot marry you. Indeed, I fear my father's actions were he to discover you and me together…and married."

"It matters not. If you stay, I will make love to you, and there will be marriage between us. Such is the way of my people that when there are objections to a union, a girl and a boy might steal away that they might commit themselves to one another in the most natural way that can be between a man and a woman. Their parents might still object, but usually there is no trouble about this. Know this, when at last your father and I meet, we will face each other, man to man. But let there be no mistake, you and I will marry if you decide to remain here with me. I will not allow you to let me dishonor you, and you, me. Do you understand?"

She took another long moment to answer him, for it was not a lie to say that she feared what her father's reaction might be. Would he try to dissolve the marriage, ending it with a divorce? And, if both she and Wind Eagle refused that, and, since her father was military, might he consider killing Wind Eagle?

"I do understand you," she said at last, "but…I can't discount what my father might do if he were to discover that I have married you."

"Better it is if he finds us married, than not."

"I'm not certain about that. He might take more kindly were we to have an affair than to actually discover that we have bound ourselves to one another."

He sighed, seeming to weigh his words before he asked, "Are you using your father as an excuse to refrain from marriage to me? Because if you are, you have only to say 'no' and I will go away."

"Would you? Go away?"

"I would," he said. "Do not think that it would be easy to do, and, because we work so closely together, that our performances might suffer because of it. But if you decide that we will not marry, know that you might never know what it feels like, if I were to do this to you."

He traced a path with his forefinger, from her chin to her breasts and followed that trail with his tongue. She moaned and swooned in toward him closer.

"Or this," he murmured, as he brought his hand down farther, over her stomach, down toward that place on her body most private. She shivered, but she didn't draw away.

"I could take you now, you realize, and force you into my life," he announced unnecessarily, as he massaged the back of her neck with one hand, while he drew her hips in so close to him, that she could feel the swell of his masculinity against her stomach.

"So you could," she acknowledged, "but I don't think that you will."

"Are you certain about that?"

She sighed, but she felt herself surrender to him. How could she not? She so loved this handsome, eye-winking, teasing man. "Just know," she murmured, "that when my father arrives—and he eventually will—that there will be trouble."

"I know," Wind Eagle acknowledged. "I know. It is decided, then."

"Yes, I do believe you are right. It is decided, for you see, Mr. Eagle, I love you dearly."

So close were they that she could feel the exact moment when he relaxed and when the tension that he had been holding within him found release. He laughed, and it was a good-hearted, vigorous laugh. "As I love you, Little Flame, as I love you."

"Little Flame?"

"It is your new name. Little, because you are greatly smaller than I am, and Flame because of your passionate nature."

"And my hair color?

"*Hau, hau.* And also because of the color of your hair."

"How do you say it in your language?"

"Oi'le Kitaŋla."

"Oi'le Kitaŋla," she repeated. "I like the sound of that so much better than Deceiving Woman."

He winked at her. "I, too."

She laughed.

"It is a better name."

She grinned up at him, and he took advantage of her open mouth, delivering a hungry caress to her lips. And they kissed, and they kissed. Barely audible, yet tender strains from the dancing tent sang out a three-quarter waltz, and gently, as though they only now heard it, they swayed to the beat of that music.

He whispered in her ear, "I will never forget our first dance together. Do you remember that it was a moonlit night, with many stars to light the heavens? Your skin felt as soft as the petal of a rose blossom. You looked even more beautiful and more precious than the golden eagle in flight. I think I was already in love with you, then."

"Yes. I was in love with you, too."

"Look at me."

She complied and raised her gaze to his, and, even though it was too dark to discern his features, she could still see a light in his eyes, as he whispered, "Do you feel the warmth in the air?"

"I do."

He continued, "And how dark it is, the moisture held within the heavens? Let us commit this moment to memory; let us recall always what our senses tell us are real; the feel of your body, its valleys and its curves that I hold within my arms, the sweet scent of who you are? Always, I will remember this time when we pledge to one another that we will become of one flesh."

Tears filled her eyes. "Yes," she answered, almost choking on the word.

"I love you," he whispered. "I will always love you. I vow this to you. Even in old age, when the passion between us might be a mere spark, I will love you. I promise you that from this moment on, there will be no other who will share the desires of my body so long as we are one."

Her next words escaped her lips before she could pull them back, and she hiccupped before she uttered, "But an Indian man is allowed more than one wife, and there are so many women — "

"But I love you, and I want only you in my life. Do you think I do not know that your God allows a man only one woman? And that this is the way in which you have been raised? I will not go against what you believe is right and true, so great is my respect for you."

A knot had formed in her throat, and she could barely utter the words, as she admitted, "I will tell you true that I don't think I deserve you, my dearest love. But I promise you that I will try to be all that you believe me to be. You have my heart…for all my life and forever. I will never stop loving you and I will do all I can to make our life together a good and happy one. You will be the father of our children, the man that I will love and adore with all my heart from this day forward. All this I promise you."

She heard him swallow, hard, and there was a catch in his voice, as he whispered, "I love you."

"And I, you."

***

He bent his head toward her to bring his forehead against hers, quelling, if only for a moment, the flood of diverse emotions that were coursing through him; love, passion, admiration, and yet a fear of her that he hoped was misplaced. He had put his heart in her hands, and he still did not understand her or what motivated her to act as she did. Would she hurt him, as two other women in his life had done?

But he'd meant every word, every vow he'd uttered. They would soon be of one flesh, one heart. He whispered, "Let us join our bodies together, as I have yearned to do, since that night so many weeks ago."

"As have I."

"Have you? And yet you agreed without protest to my plan to ignore that passion."

"Of course I did. It was what you wished, and loving you as I did, and as I still do, I would bow to your wisdom. But I wonder if you know that it has bothered me that I did not know how to cause you to reach the happiness and pleasure you brought to me. Still, I do not know how to bring about that joy for you. Realize, please, that I told you true: you are the man of my first kiss. I truly felt that I had failed you."

He sighed. "I am a lucky man. And I am glad that I will be the last man to receive your special kiss."

He felt her smile.

"Come." He gathered her up into his arms and trod toward that same weeping willow tree that had been witness to their passion only weeks earlier. He whispered, "A moment, please." Bending, he straightened a quilt that lay at the foot of the tree.

"There's a blanket here?"

He grimaced before he straightened up. Then, presenting her with a wink, he swept her off her feet, taking her into his arms, and, bending once again, he laid her down on that coverlet, following her onto it with one bended knee. "I fear," he admitted, "that I had come here earlier tonight, hoping to find you in this place. I had planned to sweet talk you into changing into a dress so that we could dance. Perhaps it was wrong of me, but I had planned for the evening to end with you in my arms, and with the satisfaction of lovemaking for us both."

"Without marriage?"

"*Hau, hau.* I admit that I did not desire marriage to you then, for I had hoped to follow in the white man's path, and share an affair with you."

"But?..."

He shook his head. "But seeing you with that man tonight urged me to change my mind about what you and I should be to each other."

She giggled.

"You laugh?"

"I wonder if I should tell you that this is what I intended. I wanted you to see me as a woman, not as a girl disguised as a boy."

"I know that you hoped for this."

"You know? But?—"

"I also realize that a good woman loves but one man. She may try to frustrate a man by pretending affection for another, but she loves only the one. Of course, I understood what you were doing, and your intention behind it." He smiled at her as he came to lie down beside her. "It did drive me to action, for I told you true: I do love you, but I had to realize also how much I am devoted to you, for, I fear there are ghosts in my past."

"I remember once that you said to me that you didn't wish to get involved *again* with a woman such as I am. Did someone like me once hurt you?"

He winced. He was not yet ready to have this conversation with her. Soon it would be necessary that they bare their hearts and their innermost secrets to one another. But not now. Now he wanted only to make love to this woman.

He told her simply, "I cannot speak of this yet. But we will talk of it, and soon. I promise you this, for there is much that we must discuss. It is my belief that we two have secrets from one another, and we must release each other from the burden of them. But in this present moment, I wish only to release this dress from your body."

She chuckled. "I could help you."

He sighed. "I would appreciate any aid you could give me, for I confess that the white woman's style of clothing baffles me."

She placed her arms around his neck, and brought him down to her, raining sweet kisses over his neck, his forehead, his cheeks. And then she grinned.

"Oh, my, how I love you," she declared. "Come, the dress unfastens in the back. There are hooks and eyes. I'll show you how to undo them." And, turning over, she proceeded to do exactly that.

CHAPTER EIGHTEEN

$\mathscr{S}$he trembled as his fingers fumbled over the fastenings of her dress. Though she wore both corset and chemise beneath her outer clothing, each touch of his fingers sent a frenzy of ecstasy racing through her bloodstream and over her nervous system. Never had she experienced such passion and hunger, as if every inch of her were attuned to this man's gaze and seduction. And, with his every touch—simple though it was—her body craved more. Even his scent, musky and masculine, enthralled her, and she drew in a deep breath that she might always remember this most dear perception.

"As seems to be the style of your people, there are many layers of clothing beneath your dress." His gentle breath filled her ear. It was no more than his lips and voice there, but the feel of his lips moving over her ear sent excited shivers careening through her.

"Yes," she uttered, as she turned over until she lay beneath him, and faced up at him. "It will take some time to remove all of my clothing. Forgive me, but I so long for you to kiss me now, instead of trying to remove the many layers of my clothing. Could we not skip ahead?"

He chuckled softly, then muttered, "My pleasure," as he bent his head toward hers, fondling her lips with his own. He slanted his lips over hers as he kissed her. Then he brushed the inside of her mouth with his tongue, his taste one of passion, and Luci thought she might expire from the pure desire of it.

He broke off the lush assault on her lips to trail wet caresses down her neck to her shoulders and over to her breasts. Pushing her gown down toward her waist as far as it would stretch, he adored her breasts with one kiss after another, ignoring the material of her chemise and corset which hid her womanly mounds.

She groaned, before she whispered, "Oh, my."

"Are you wearing drawers that will require me to remove them?" he asked.

"I am, but, as is the fashion of today, it is open at the crotch," she answered. Then she added, "There is nothing under my dress there to restrict you."

He came up onto one elbow as he leaned over her, and he smiled before he murmured, "Open your legs for me."

She complied at once, and he lifted the dress up, immediately reaching down to gift her with the touch of his fingers, there, at her core. At once, she sucked in her breath, but, as he continued to stroke her there, he kissed her as though he were a thirsty man, his tongue seeking out hers.

She moved her hips in unison with his touch, and was rewarded with a pleasure that rocked her to her core. As though he sensed this, he let his fingers create magic there, and she almost burst with sexual gratification, but her plateau wasn't to be reached yet.

Over and over he kissed her and fondled her as she struggled upward toward a pleasure that she remembered well from only a few weeks past. And then, she was there, twisting against him as the feeling of ecstasy washed over her. It went on and on, until at last, with one final surge of gratification, she collapsed in utter adoration of him.

He continued to kiss her, but as he had done once before, he withdrew his touch from her, although he didn't take his body away from her so completely, as he had done all those weeks ago. And, while he showered her lips, her cheeks, her eyes and even her ears with one kiss after another, she moaned, whimpering out the words, "And now, I fear that I do not know what to do."

"*Hau, hau,*" he groaned against her skin, there at her neck. "It is my honor and duty to teach you."

"Yes." It was all she could say at this moment.

He came up onto his knees and moved downward until he was kneeling, there at her core. Taking both of her legs, he placed each one of them over his shoulders, and then he untied his breechcloth, throwing it to the side. He pressed his swollen member at her junction as he bent toward her, until he could whisper, "The act of love is known to hurt a woman the first time."

"Yes, I have been told this."

He nodded. "I will try to be gentle, but forgive me if I am not as tender as I would like, for I am almost bursting with need. Are you ready to receive me?"

She smiled at him. "Indeed, I am." He joined himself with her then, and, as he had predicted, it hurt.

"We will proceed slowly, so we might make your pain less."

She nodded, and, as promised, he slowly, but regularly pressed upward, until at last he was fully joined with her. He stopped as soon as they were completely united, and she could feel him shivering against her. She knew without even asking, that he was holding himself back by the strength of a slender thread.

He murmured, "It is a man's way to move upward and downward, over and over. Do not fear to tell me of any hurt you might experience because of this."

"I will," she answered.

Then he pushed against her; he waited. He withdrew and waited, then he repeated the dance all over again, upward, outward, over and over. His voice was husky, as he asked, "Does it still hurt?"

"Not so much."

But she had no more than said those words, when he suddenly bore against her upward with more intention and force than before, and she felt his fullness there, as he spilled his seed within her. Over and over he bore against her, and despite herself, she felt that overwhelming sense of pleasure engulf her. In unison with him, then, she tripped over that same precipice as he thrust upward one more time. And, as she met him there, she experienced not only the pure ecstasy of love, but another, more profound realization hit her: she knew the essence, the raw beauty of this man's soul. Indeed, her body shuddered under the force of this recognition.

Was this what love was about? Was it a bringing together of two people in the most intimate manner possible, so that for all their life, they would be locked together in the happiness of their devotion?

Being held in his arms, with his spirit, as well as his body, joined so closely with hers, she felt an exquisite joy. And, he was beautiful; there was a goodness about him that was perhaps rare, and she realized in that moment that he would never willingly hurt her. Indeed, it was there, pronounced, in the essence of who he was; he would protect her as he would protect himself and their children.

Children. Had they made a child from this union? The thought was pleasing beyond comprehension. She prayed that their offspring would look like their father, but moreover, that together, their union would bring happiness for their children yet to be.

Together. How she loved the thought of that.

In the aftermath of their lovemaking, he did not remove himself from her, as he had done that other time. Instead, without retreating from her, he yet came down to lie atop her and against her, although he took most of his weight onto his forearms.

But she wanted all of him against her and she pressed him downward and against her until they lay breast to breast. She sighed. Obviously, she thought, this natural act between a husband and wife joined them together, as though of one body, unified. And, so it was upon this rather astute observation that she closed her eyes.

However, before she drifted off into a dream-like state, she heard him whisper, "With my body, I do thee adore. I love you, my wife."

She grinned, and sleepily kissed his shoulder. She breathed out the words, "And I love you, my husband. I love you. Now. Forever."

***

Luci wasn't certain what it was that had awakened her. Nor did she have any idea as to the time of day. Was it late at night? Or early morning?

Instinctively, she realized that whatever it was that had caused her to wake up was not dangerous. Perhaps it had been little more than the howling of the wind through the branches of the old, weeping willow tree. In his sleep, Wind Eagle had moved to the side of her, and had pressed his body up close to hers. Additionally, her head was nestled upon his outstretched arm.

Scooting as silently as possible onto her side, she positioned herself onto her elbows and brought her face upward toward his. He was a handsome man, yes, but he was also a kind man. The abundant evidence that this was so could not be ignored. Even with his suspicions and distrust of her, he had been a humorous and thoughtful companion. His male prowess and strength were more than displayed before her each day, and she was left in no doubt, that, in the beginning, had he the inclination to do so, he could have easily crushed her.

But he hadn't. Instead, he had teased her almost continually, and, it had been a good ploy, for his constant bantering had kept the knowledge and guilt of her deception always before her. There was more; he had never taken any tales of her duplicity, nor exposed her deception to Buffalo Bill, although Wind Eagle had been aware of her ruse from the beginning.

Reaching up, she ran a finger over his cheek closest to her, sweeping her touch over toward his full lips, tracing them, then pressing a path gently downward toward his neck, making a trail toward his chest. He was so handsome, so dear. All at once, a large hand caught hers, and when she gazed upward, she witnessed his smile.

He brought her fingers to his lips, where he pressed a wet kiss against them. And, at this exact moment, she thought she had never been happier. Without speaking a word of this to him, she made a pledge to herself at this moment, to love him, yes, but to protect him from the ravages and the stinging tongues of other men and women. Always, she determined, right or wrong, she would take his side.

Sensuously, she returned his smile.

With a hushed, husky voice, he murmured, "We have slept many hours, for already it is early morning."

"Is it? I didn't know."

"*Hau, hau*, it is so. Look upward, where the cracks in our shelter allow you to see the night sky."

"Shelter?" She gazed upward. How could she have missed that this man had built a small covering over them some time during the night? Yet she had.

"Look there, through this opening." He pointed. "Do you see that the sky has cleared and that the Seven Brothers' two stars are pointing downward and to the east, and that the remaining stars point toward the earth?"

"The Seven Brothers?"

"Constellation is the word in your language," he answered. "Your people call this grouping the Big Dipper. When those stars are pointing downward as they are, and at this time of year, it is early morning."

"Oh," she said, "I had no idea one could tell time by the movement of stars." She felt him shrug, but when he said nothing, she continued, "If it's early in the morning, then I guess I should return to the tent that I share with Jane, for I am certain my sister will be worried about me."

"Do not concern yourself with that. She is well. Iron Wolf is with her."

"What? Iron Wolf is there with her? Why?"

"Although I was not certain as to how the evening might end for us, I had hoped we might make love. Thus, I asked Iron Wolf to watch over your sister in case we were occupied elsewhere." He grinned at her.

But she didn't return his smile. Instead, she asked, "Is he merely watching her or is he sleeping with her?"

Wind Eagle laughed. "I do not believe that he is sleeping with her, because his honor will not allow him to betray my request of his aid. What I am trying to tell you is that he is standing guard over where she sleeps so that no harm comes to her. Being here with me, you are not there to protect her. He would stand his watch outside, I believe, not inside her lodge."

"Oh. I guess that's all right, then." She let out a breath. "But I didn't know that she was close enough to your friend that he would willingly provide this service for her."

"Have you never seen them together?"

"Yes, of course I have, but I didn't grasp that they might be romantically inclined." But was that true? Hadn't Jane only tonight admitted that she found Iron Wolf attractive?

"I do not state that they are in love," continued Wind Eagle. "I say only that when a man with eyes to see will witness them together, he will know that they each one admire the other."

"Does Mr. Iron Wolf know that she is with child?"

"He does. It would be hard for a man not to take note of this. I think he means to wait to see if the father remains distant from her."

"He will, I can assure you."

"You are certain of this?"

"I am."

"Then, if this is so," Wind Eagle replied, "and if the father does not make himself known soon, Iron Wolf might offer marriage to your sister so that her child is not fatherless upon its birth."

"Truly? Has your friend spoken to you of this?"

"*Hiyá,* he has not. But this is what I think."

"Has he told any of this to my sister?"

Wind Eagle shrugged once more. "I do not know. We will have to wait and see. Come, there is a creek nearby where we can wash our bodies and our clothing, for, if you look closely at your dress, you might find that it is soiled."

Luci felt blood rush to her neck and face, and she flushed.

"It is good," he spoke soothingly. "You now belong to me. But you might wish to remove the evidence of our romance from your clothing. If you do not feel you need do this, I have no worry about it."

She inhaled deeply. "I believe I do care. Let us hurry, and let us hope that there is no quicksand on its shores or within its depths."

His answer was simple: he merely smiled at her. "I do not think that there is quicksand there, for I have studied that ground well. Come," he began, "our little hut requires that you crawl out of it. On hands and knees now, do as I do and follow me." Crawling forward, he took her by the arm to guide her out of the temporary refuge, and both of them emerged into a balmy, summer night.

It must have been very early in the morning, for no birds sang, and even the sound of the crickets was sporadic in these woods. The sighing of the wind through the trees, soft and gentle, however, created the impression of camaraderie, not only with her husband, but with the environment around them. The ground beneath her feet felt soft and moist, and overhead, the sky had cleared and the carpet of millions, perhaps billions of stars twinkled and glistened in an otherwise black sky.

Looking upward, the spaciousness of the nature all around her affected her in a profound way, and she felt as though a part of her expanded outward, as though spiritually, she had become enriched because of this man. Indeed, she felt as if she had grown up.

Silently, he squeezed her hand before leading her in a southerly direction, and it wasn't until they had trod on that path for several minutes that she began to pick out the sound of the rushing, gurgling stream that must lie close at hand. After that, it wasn't long before they had both made footprints in the wet sand that led toward a gradual slope in the land, inclining downward to a creek that looked to her to be so shallow that it might be only three to four feet deep.

He bent down toward her and murmured quietly, "Do you like to swim naked?"

She gasped, and stuttered, "I...I..."

He laughed. "Please tell me that you do, for I intend to remove every bit of your clothing. Here we are, married for many hours now, and I have yet to see you standing before me, naked."

"But it's too cold to go swimming naked."

"Do not fear," he winked at her. "I intend to create much warmth within you very soon."

Gazing up at him, she shook her head at him and giggled.

He grinned. "I do not tease you when I say to you, that, when we are alone and together, I intend to keep you naked as often as you will allow me that pleasure."

"If that is true, then I fear we may have many children."

"*Hau, hau,* a man can hope. But come, you are still dressed in many clothes."

She sighed. "I fear that in my society, getting dressed and undressed is rather a trial. ut, if you are intent upon this thing, then we should begin at once."

"Let me tell this to you so that you have no doubt, that this is, indeed, my intention."

She chuckled. "Then, come, and help me, for the dress, the corset and even my chemise are tight and not easily removed by me, alone. Here, the dress is really a bodice and a skirt, and they are removed here," she pointed. "But as you see, beneath this is my corset, which will require you to untie and loosen it."

"My pleasure," he responded, as he began the rather lengthy process of undressing a fashionable, young lady...

CHAPTER NINETEEN

"*Why* do the white women wear so many clothes?"

"To improve our figure, I suppose."

He shook his head from side to side, perplexed. He said, "A woman needs no clothing to 'improve her figure.' She is perfect as she is, without the trappings of clothing."

"I would dare to disagree with you about that. Clothing, a little rouge, a little lipstick, usually makes a girl look so much better. Clothing can also hide flaws."

He grinned down at her. "Does a woman not know that these little flaws, as you say, are beautiful? hey should not be hidden."

"But then," she argued, "what would men do if women paraded naked in front of them at all times of the day? I do believe that no work would get done, whatsoever."

He laughed outright. "You make a good point. But, this man would very much like to see his wife standing before him without any clothing. I fear, I have dreamed of this moment with you."

"You have?"

"Ever since the quicksand fight, I have envisioned this."

"Well, you certainly hid your inclination from me. If I recall that time correctly, I believe that you saw me then without clothing."

"*Hau, hau*, this is true. But you were lying down, not standing, and I was not at that time, wishing to know you intimately, so I did not look at you then as I would like to see you now. Come, I believe we still have several layers more of clothing to remove from your body."

Amused, he laughed when he reached around behind her to untie her bustle. "So this is how the female of your race manages to obtain a rear that sticks out so far. And, here I thought that the white woman simply had a large backside."

She snickered. "Oh, please, don't tell me this is the first time you have undressed a woman in this, the American, culture. I even caught you with a young woman once."

"True, but did you not notice that she was still fully dressed?"

"No, I did not."

As he detached her bustle and petticoat, he turned her around to face him. "Come, let us not speak of other women or other men in this place. There are only you and I here, and whatever I did in the past, must now remain there. I did not tell you an untruth when I said to you that you are the only woman in my life now and the only woman I wish to have in my life in the future. I am in love with you, and I wish to see you, my wife, without the trappings of these clothes."

As he loosened her chemise and removed both it and her drawers, he heaved a deep sigh. He declared, "And now I can hold you next to me, with you as bare as you were the day you were born." He picked her up in his arms, and trod down the slight slope of the ground to the water's edge. "You are the most beautiful woman I have ever known, and now it is my pleasure to help you wash."

She shrieked. "Oh, my, it's going to be cold."

"But for a moment only, plus, I will not let you go, and my body will warm yours."

"And who will warm your body?"

"I need no such thing. Every day of my life, I have swum and bathed in water like this. I welcome the cold."

"Every day? Even in the winter?"

"*Hau, hau*, it is so."

"Then you are a brave man."

"I pray that it is so."

Quickly, he realized that she had spoken true. Although the water temperature did not even cause him to flinch, she, on the other hand, shivered in his arms. As the water splashed around his waist, playfully, he spun her 'round and 'round, holding her in his arms. Still, the cold water had her shaking physically. "Do you wish to engage in a game of water tag?"

"In the dark?"

"*Hau, hau,* it is the best time to play the game. It will heighten your perceptions."

"But I thought you were going to hold me closely to you so I don't freeze from the cold."

"And so I shall, if you desire it, but I think that if you take action, you will warm up more quickly."

He hadn't expected her to touch his shoulder, twist from him to swim quickly away, and call out, "You're it."

His laugh came from deep within him, and he easily reached out to tag her. But instead of moving away from her, he brought her in closely to him, saying, "I was wrong. I do not wish you to be even a small distance from me. Already, I miss you in my arms."

"I feel this way, also," she agreed. But then she added, "However, you must realize that soon we will have to part."

He brought her in close, and held her against him, as he murmured, "Say more clearly what you mean."

"What? Well, it's evident, isn't it?"

"What is evident?"

"That we will have to part—at least at night. We'll still be able to be with each other when we practice, and perhaps we can slip away from time to time, but—"

"I have not agreed to this. We are married now. You will stay with me in my lodge, or, if you are fearful of your sister being alone, I will live in yours."

"What?"

"Married people live with one another. I do not wish to be apart from you even for one night."

He heard and felt her sigh, and it wasn't long before she commented, "No, this cannot be. You do realize I must continue my disguise, don't you? That we are married changes nothing."

He paused. Had he heard her correctly? Had she really declared that their marriage brought no alteration to their lives?

He murmured, repeating, "Changes nothing?"

She nodded. "Indeed, all must continue as it is now."

How could those few mere words create the feeling within him that she had kicked him in the gut? Yet, he felt a pain shoot through him, and, for a moment, he thought he might retaliate with ugly words. But he didn't, and he carefully chose what he would next say. Softly, slowly, he argued, "I disagree. It has changed a great many things in our lives."

"I...I'm sorry. Don't you understand that what you are suggesting will bring great danger to me and to my sister?"

"I know only that you and I are now married, that you are mine, and that I will protect you from whatever danger you face. Do you think that I am so weak that I cannot do this?"

"Of course I don't have that opinion about you."

"*Wašté,* good. Then there is no other way for us but to tell the Showman the truth and to proclaim to all who would know, that we are married."

She sighed, and, putting her arms around his neck, she brought her body in even more closely toward his. "But what about my sister? Her baby? Can you protect them every moment of every day?"

"I would try."

"Yes, I know that you would. But you, like I, must practice and perform. Neither one of us could be there with her every moment of every day. No, there is no other way for my sister and me, but to hide who we are. Please try to understand: my sister's life, her honor, and her baby's life, as well as mine, might be in danger, and if I were to announce to the world at large who I really am, and very importantly, where I am. I don't know what might happen."

He stood very still as he cautioned himself to contain the anger still rising within him and the confusion that threatened to overwhelm him. Was it her intention to humiliate him? To marry him and then refuse his counsel, his protection? Was she already on that dangerous path to hurt him, as had two other beloved women in his life?

No. Despite his feelings that this was somehow so, he knew deep within him that she spoke true. She was afraid for the sister she loved; perhaps she was even fearful for herself. Still, even knowing this, mortification filled his being, and he felt urged to speak out in frustration.

Again, he cautioned himself. As the elders of his tribe had often advised, a man must guard his tongue, and a man must think his thoughts through before saying them aloud. For, as the wise ones also counseled, "Once words of fury are spoken, they cannot easily be taken back."

So it was at length that he began to voice his thoughts, and he said, "Although I did not wish to have this conversation with you this soon, I now believe that it is time for us to bare our hearts to one another, for it is true that we have secrets from one another. Come, I brought a few of the white man's towels and a buckskin blanket here, and they are on the shore. Let us go there and place both the robe and the towels around us to warm us as we tell each other the deep intimacies that we dare not say to another living soul. I would know why you feel there is danger in revealing who you really are."

He held her so closely in his arms that he felt when she swallowed, hard. She didn't respond in words; instead, she nodded.

He sighed. He had, of course, envisioned their morning spent in another, more pleasant way, but this conversation was, perhaps, more important. Indeed, already he could feel a barrier deepening between them. For his part, he wondered how could she marry him, say she loved him, and, in the same breath, imply that he was not man enough to protect her.

He didn't know, but he did realize that the only means to tear down the wall arising so quickly between them was to talk. It wasn't that he wanted to speak about these matters, it was more to the point to say that he must.

***

It was possible that in the past, being seated naked beside Wind Eagle might have caused her to feel vulnerable. However, because he held her so closely in his arms, she sensed that his purpose was not to exploit her, but rather to comfort her. Still, she felt reluctant to share the fear that still lingered within her heart, for, if she and Jane were to be discovered by the wrong people, a fate of imprisonment or worse might be visited upon them.

Thusly, she started her confession by asking a question. "Do you promise me that you will not tell another person what I am about to say to you?"

"I will not, unless there is a danger to you or your sister that might require my asking for another's aid, if a need arose to combat this enemy that haunts you. But even in this, I would seek to have you release me from my vow before I might take any action."

She nodded. "All right, then," she agreed, but still, she hesitated to bare her worries to him. When she revealed it all, might Wind Eagle scold her for deliberating shooting Hall in the thigh, so close to his private parts? Would her new husband wish he hadn't married a woman who could, and who would, maim a man in such a way? Or would Wind Eagle understand that she'd had ample reason to do so?

Still hesitant, she explained, "I fear that you might think better of having married me if I tell you what has happened to my sister and to me, for, in the past, many men have proven to me that they fear that I might turn my skills upon them."

"Never would I do that," he assured her. "I am already aware of your talent with a gun, and I do not fear it. *Hau, hau,* I admire it. Let me venture to ask about this act that you feel you must keep sheltered within your heart. Did you kill a man?"

"No," she assured him. "But I did shoot a man in a carefully protected spot." She placed her fingers on Wind Eagle's thigh in an approximate location to where she had landed that shot. "Here."

"Ouch!" was his instant reaction, as he jerked away from her touch.

She drew back her hand at once as she continued speaking, justifying, "I had good reason for what I did."

He hesitated, yet his voice was soft, and he murmured, "I know that you did, for I know your heart. Tell me now. Tell me what happened to you and your sister to drive you to run away from your home and to take part in this pretense."

She paused. "It is complex," she said at last, "but firstly, you should know that not only have I and do I 'take part in this pretense,' as you say, but it was also my idea that Jane and I do this, for I saw no way out of our dilemma."

"I understand, and I am on your side. Please tell me now."

She breathed in deeply. "It happened several months ago," she began, "when I found my young and underage sister pregnant by a man named Captain Timothy Hall. He is a man who is married to another woman. I discovered that he had convinced my sister that he and his wife were parted, and so, when he proposed marriage to my sister in order to seduce her, she said 'yes.' He lied to her."

Wind Eagle jerked his head quickly to his left, and he tightened his arms about her. But he remained silent.

"When Jane confronted Captain Hall with the reality of her pregnancy, he laughed about it, seemingly proud of his deception. It was only then that he confessed that he was still married and that he had no intention of divorcing his wife."

"You are right," Wind Eagle spoke up. "You had good reason for what you did to him. Know that in my tribe, if a man should rape a young girl in this manner, and lie about it, he is banned from the tribe forever. He must then go out and live alone. Often this causes his death. But come, there is more. I will remain silent and will listen to all you say."

Scooting in toward him as intimately as she could, she swallowed, took a deep breath, and continued, "When I first found out about my sister, I realized that something had to be done to defend our family's honor." A tear had pooled in her eye, and her lips shook as she spoke, yet she continued, saying, "We have no brothers in our family, and our father was, and still is, out of the country. So I did the right and proper thing: I challenged Captain Hall to a duel. Do you know what a duel is?"

He shook his head in the negative.

"It is a very old way of settling a dispute between two men by engaging in combat. This kind of fight has deep roots in our culture and has a long history, and so there are many exacting rules. For instance, both participants in the duel pick another man as a second combatant, in case he is needed. A time and a place are chosen for the duel, and upon even more particular rules, these two men shoot at one another. It is thought that the winner of the match is the one who is in the right. This may or may not be true, but this is the manner and the belief of the duel.

"I did everything right, according to the rules. I challenged Captain Hall in a public place; I chose a second, who would see to the matter, arrange the time and place and ensure that all the requirements for a duel were followed. My sister and I even furnished coffee and refreshments for us and for our enemy, as the laws governing the combat require.

"Upon command of my second, both Captain Hall and I fired our pistols; his shot missed me, but mine caught him in the shoulder, where I had intended it to land. According to the strict regulations of dueling, when first blood is drawn, the match is finished. Sergeant Smyth, the man I had placed in charge, declared the entire affair over, and I had turned away to lay my weapon aside, only to hear the report of Captain Hall's gun once, and then another blast. The second discharge caught me in the arm. Seeing that I was under fire and injured, I spun back around, aimed a good shot and hit Hall exactly where I had intended—close to the groin. I could have chosen a spot elsewhere on his body, and maimed him for life, but I chose not to do that."

Wind Eagle's arm, which rested on her shoulders, pulled her in closer to him. With his other arm, he reached out to her, and took her hand in his own. He squeezed that hand, but he didn't speak.

For a moment, her voice caught, and she couldn't easily continue the story. She felt like crying; she, the tough sister, the sister always in control, could barely keep her voice even. But, swallowing hard, she took courage and continued, "I grabbed Janie and placed her behind me, and, with gun drawn and aimed, we slowly backed away from the dueling field, for my coach was waiting for us on the street.

"Janie and I went at once to the nearest telegraph office and sent a wire to our father. Sergeant Smyth wrote a full report to him, but meanwhile, Sergeant Smyth also discovered that the newspaper had run a bad article on the duel, accusing me of treachery and cheating. You see, Captain Hall comes from a rich and powerful newspaper family, and, after what had happened, they printed a special edition of their paper that ran a story about me. In that story, they accused me of cheating, of shooting at Timothy Hall before the match between us had even begun. The article even said that I had injured him so that he could not defend himself. It was nothing but lies, of course, but because it was written up in a newspaper, many men believed it."

Again, Wind Eagle jerked his head to the left, and frowned. But he did not speak.

She continued, "Of course this had an effect, and it caused those men to take up the fight in Hall's defense. Plus, there were agents hired by the Hall family to encourage the crowd to do worse, to storm our residence that very night. Jane and I fled. But, we came to the understanding that the Hall family had hired detectives, also, and that they were actively searching for us. It was therefore needed that we disguise ourselves, and I'm afraid it was my idea that we become brother and sister. In this manner, we were able to trick those looking for us. We caught the first train that was leaving the city, then, without incident."

"Our first stop was here in New York, but our next train wasn't scheduled to leave for two or three days. We had no money, which meant we had no means by which to obtain food or lodging for the required few days wait. Nor could we easily leave the underground terminal, because all entrances were watched closely by the Halls' agents. It was then, as I stood upon the station's platform that I saw a poster advertising Buffalo Bill's show. It gave me an idea, and I thought that perhaps I could apply for employment with Buffalo Bill. And here my story ends, because I fear that you know the rest of my tale. Within a few hours of that decision, I met you through Buffalo Bill."

Wind Eagle didn't speak up at once. However, when she hesitated, and didn't say more, he asked, "Have you said all you wished to say?"

"Yes, for now."

"*Hau, hau.* And now I have a question for you: Do you know why this family has taken such great measures to try to capture you?"

"I'm not certain. Perhaps they fear my father's wrath? Both my father and Captain Timothy Hall are military men, and my father's position in the army far outranks Captain Hall's. It is to be assumed that my father, once he learns the particulars of this incident, will return home, will call for Captain Hall's arrest, and will convene a military tribunal that could imprison Hall for many years."

"Ah, yes, the white man's cages."

"They are not cages."

He didn't answer right away. However, at some length, he commented, "It is to be hoped that your father can set this matter right. But I am left wondering if Captain Hall's wife is also from a family who has great power."

"Perhaps. She is the daughter of a wealthy banker."

"I do not know what is a 'wealthy banker.'"

"Oh, sorry. You are so well acquainted with our culture that sometimes I forget that you have not been raised in it. A banker is a man or many men who keep other people's money as a service for them."

"Money? Gold or silver as Buffalo Bill pays us?"

"Yes."

He nodded his head several times. "I have heard of this kind of a man from several of the white people who have come onto our reservation. Are they not mentioned in your Good Book?"

"I'm not sure. Maybe they are."

"Is the family of this man's wife so powerful, that this snake, whom you call Captain Hall, might be worried that his wife would leave him? Is that why he and his family are continuing to pursue you and your sister?"

"I...I really don't know. Maybe, although I thought that the reason could be that Captain Hall's pride might be at stake, and that is what has caused him to lie about us and to harass us."

"Perhaps," said Wind Eagle, "but you and your sister are still fearful that he will discover where you are, and that he might still try to harm you. If it were simply his pride, he should have given up his pursuit of you by now, for you did not inflict a permanent injury upon him."

"In truth, he might not be trying to find us. I don't know. Maybe my fears are for nothing. Still, until Jane's baby is born, I must do all that is within my power to protect her and her child. And so we must remain as we are."

He paused for several moments. "You say that your father is out of the country?"

"Yes, he is. He is in charge of troops that are fighting in the Hawaiian Rebellion. I don't know when he'll be returning to the states. We did wire him, so I can only assume that when he is able, he will return and set this matter right. However, until that time, Jane and I must avoid capture by the powerful Hall family, because, truly, I don't know what to expect."

Again, Wind Eagle was silent. At length, he jerked his head to the left, and paused, before he inquired, "What is the name of this village where this happened?"

"Washington DC. My sister and I are from our nation's capital, and this took place there, mostly, although the duel occurred outside the city, in a state called Maryland."

"Washington DC?" He frowned. "You do realize that Buffalo Bill's Wild West is scheduled to bring this show to Washington DC on this tour?"

"Ah...no, I wasn't aware of that. I fear I have been so caught up in learning the new tricks for our performances that I have failed to pay attention to the schedule. Besides, within me is the hope that our father will return to this country and that he will find us and set this matter right, allowing both me and Jane to return to our old life."

Wind Eagle's arms tightened around her. "That old life, as you say it, must give way to the new, for your path and mine are now one."

206

"Yes," she agreed. "Yes, we are now of one path. Still, we have not reckoned with the wrath of my father. To be sure, it will be bent upon Captain Hall, but I fear that you may also feel his rage."

"Do you fear that I will cower like a woman before him?"

She couldn't help the short laugh that escaped her lips, for the idea was ludicrous. She said, "Absolutely not. Please understand that my reaction just now was not aimed at you; it was because the mere thought that you suggest is so outrageous, I can't even picture it."

"*Hau, hau.*" He pressed a kiss to the top of her head. "I am glad to hear that. Yes, your father and I will have much to speak of between us, but I welcome that time. I do not fear it."

"I believe you." She paused. "And now," she murmured, "it is your turn. You mentioned a little while ago, that you, too, have secrets from me. I have told you my own story, and I would now like to hear yours."

"And so you shall," he replied. "But first, we must talk about your deception, its needfulness, or not, and what our own actions must be until you can, at last, reveal who you really are. For I tell you true, that I will not long suffer us being apart."

Luci bit down hard on her lip and hoped desperately that he would not demand more of her than she could willingly give. She had determined, and she was still of that mind, that until their father arrived back in the states, neither she nor Jane could afford to make their whereabouts public. On that she would stand firm.

"Of course, your deception must remain as it is now until we are certain whether you and your sister are in danger or not."

As relief swept over her, she breathed out slowly.

"But," he continued, "it does not follow that we will not spend each night together, as any married couple should do." He grinned. "Never fear that I can fade into the shadows of the environment, be it day or night. I will teach you to do the same."

"Then you understand — really understand — why I must do this?"

"Of course. Did you think that I would not? The question is how you can continue with this deception, and yet be with me as the woman that you are, every moment of every day? But come, this is no great problem. Let us make our plans."

Luci couldn't help herself. She grinned.

CHAPTER TWENTY

*S*ome movement or sound caused her to awaken. Sleepily, Jane Glenforest pulled the coverlet up to her chin and glanced skyward at the canvas covering of the large tent, which was her own and her sister's quarters. It could be Luci, coming home at last. However, Jane didn't really expect Luci to return here tonight; indeed, it was her hope that her sister and Wind Eagle would settle their differences in an amicable and romantic way.

After all the time and attention she and Luci had dedicated to Luci's transformation from the image of a teenage boy to that of a seductress, it would be a fitting end to the evening. Hopefully, Mr. Eagle was appreciating their efforts.

Luci and Wind Eagle… The Wild West Show had certainly changed both her and her sister. Whereas before, Jane had believed her father's depiction of the degraded character of the Indian as true, she now wavered; there was another viewpoint of the wars with the Indians, mostly untold. Indeed, if she were truthful, she would admit to hoping for a permanent coupling between her sister and Wind Eagle.

After all, they were perfect for each other. Not only was Wind Eagle not intimidated by Luci's shooting skill, he also gazed upon Luci as though she were more precious than his own life. Did he realize that his affinity for Luci showed each time he reached out to touch her? That his insistence on her safety over his own was a telltale sign of his love for her? She supposed Wind Eagle thought it harmless to openly admire Luci during their practices. But Jane had seen those looks, those special gazes. She had even wondered what it might be like to be admired so greatly.

She sighed. So far, in her short life, her romantic episodes had turned as sour as fermented milk.

From out the corner of her eye, she was startled to catch an image, a shadow of a man; a man who was standing at the corner of her tent. She gasped, then held her hand over her mouth. Of course, it wasn't such an odd sight to witness a few men alert and stirring about at this hour of the night. There were several cowboys in the show who were known to be awake at all hours of the evening and early morning.

All she had to do, she told herself silently, was to wait for the man to go away; they always did. She waited. And she waited. This one, however, did not depart.

Still, thinking it unwise to be rash, she let several more minutes go by, and, when the man remained next to her tent, she knew there would be little chance that she would go back to sleep. Why did this have to occur tonight of all nights, when Luci wasn't here?

What should she do? Pretend he wasn't there? No, that wasn't possible. She was already aware of the man's shadow.

Should she hide? Perhaps. But where? These tight quarters didn't allow one to find cover.

Should she try to slip away? To crawl out under the canvas between the stakes at the back of her quarters? No, that wasn't possible. Her pregnancy was already pronounced, and her ability to squeeze under the canvas flaps without injury to the babe seemed impossible.

What to do, then? Did this man intend to harm her? It didn't seem likely, since, whoever he was, he wasn't attempting to enter her quarters. In fact, as she watched, she saw him bend down into a squat and pull a bag up from behind him, bringing it up and over his head. He reached inside that bag and brought out...what? Was that a pipe? An Indian pipe?

Or was it a knife?

No, not a knife. She could clearly see that there was a small bowl shape at the end of the object, and she watched as the man placed some sort of something...tobacco, maybe, within that bowl.

Who was this man? Was he an Indian? She had been here long enough now to have met several of the American Indians who worked with the show. Did she know this one?

Realizing that it was foolish to be caught without a weapon in this type of situation, Jane scooted toward the edge of the cot where Luci kept a small pistol. As silently as possible, she opened the case that housed it, and drew out the gun. Was it loaded?

Jane didn't possess Luci's skill with a weapon, but she did know a few life-saving facts about this particular gun, and she checked it now for its ammunition. Of course it wasn't possible to hide the sound of the clicks the gun made, and Jane was disconcerted to see that the man had arisen to his feet. He even turned his face toward the tent.

And then came the soft, low tones of a voice she recognized, as the man said, "Do not fear, Miss Jane. It is I, Iron Wolf, who stands guard over your sleeping quarters."

"Iron Wolf?"

"*Hau, hau*, it is I."

"What are you doing here?"

"My *kóla* has asked me to stand watch here tonight, to ensure your safety. It has not been my intent to frighten you, but when I came here, I became aware that you were asleep, and I did not wish to disturb you to tell you why I am here."

Jane was so relieved, she could barely understand all that he said, but she did grasp the first fact he'd mentioned, and she asked, "Your what? Who asked you to stand watch over me?"

"My *kóla*, my friend, Wind Eagle, asked me to do this favor for him."

"But why?" Jane frowned, but even as she asked the question, she knew the answer. "Oh, I think I might understand," she voiced. "He is with Luci, is he not? Then you understand about Luci?"

"*Hau, hau*, I have known about who she really is for some time. It is true that he might be with her."

"Then she will probably not be coming back here tonight?" Although Jane had said these words as a question, it was really more of a statement.

"I think that might be his hope. Meanwhile, he has asked me to ensure your safety this night. Do not fear. I will not harm you. You may go back to sleep, secure, knowing that I am here to protect you."

For the first time this evening, Jane became terribly aware that she had not lain down with heavy clothing covering her, for it was a warm night. Indeed, she was dressed in little more than her light blue chemise, and matching bloomers. Still, she was fully covered, and she decided she was dressed well enough.

Uncocking the pistol, she replaced it back into its case and closed the lid. Then she arose, tiptoeing toward the canvas "door," which was really no more than a slit that allowed for an opening in the tent. She pulled back a part of it, and stepped out into the night.

She was glad to see that the clouds had given way to a star-filled sky, and Jane inhaled deeply, appreciating the balmy feel of the air. Fearing to awaken others, she whispered, "Excuse my appearance, for I had been asleep."

"No need to be concerned, for you are beautiful as you are."

"But you haven't even looked at me," Jane observed.

He spared her a quick glance, then said, "As I expected, you are most beautiful, as you would be if you were to wear the ugliest of rags. But a man at this time of night, should not look at a woman too long. After all, her reputation is at stake, and it is not my wish to damage yours."

She sighed, then murmured, "How kind you are to flatter me, but I fear my reputation may already be tainted, for I am obviously pregnant. Still, I thank you for your compliment, especially since my appearance is not the sort of figure that is considered pretty."

"And you would be in error if you were to think this, for your beauty outshines all others."

She grinned at him, but he didn't see it, for he was looking in the opposite direction from where she stood. She asked, "May I sit with you? There are two chairs in my tent that we could bring out here. In that way, we might linger here together, and speak with one another."

"It would be my honor. I will need your permission to enter your quarters and gather these chairs, however."

"And you have it, Mr. Iron Wolf."

He jerked his head up and down in a brief nod, and disappeared inside the tent. When he reappeared, he held two chairs within his arms, which he quickly set up, placing them side by side.

Cautiously, slowly, she sat down in the chair closest to the entrance. She was now eight months pregnant, and she felt as though she were as big as this shelter that she shared with Luci. He, however, didn't seat himself in the extra chair. Instead, he took a cross-legged position on the ground beside her.

Gazing down at him, she sighed. Such a handsome fellow, he was. Although the night was black, for there was no moon in the sky at present, the millions of stars shed their light upon him, and caught at the strands of his dark hair, glittering there as though the top of his head were sprinkled with stardust. Suddenly the baby within her stomach moved, and she gasped.

At once his attention turned to her. There was a question within his eyes that she understood, although he didn't utter a word.

"It is the baby. He or she suddenly changed position. Here, give me your hand, for the babe is still moving."

He complied at once.

It was the second time she had ever touched him, and, as her hand lingered over his, she felt again that tingling sensation in her fingers; indeed, a sentimental type of warmth spread from her hand to the rest of her body. Its affect had a calming influence on her. She brought his hand to her stomach, where she spread his fingers over her stomach. The baby, it would appear, was trying to find a comfortable position and he or she jerked about. Her hand held his in place, as she asked, "Do you feel it? Do you feel it moving?"

He looked up at her and smiled. "I do. You honor me."

"Of course I honor you, because you are kind to me, and because I like you very much," she answered, still holding his hand against her stomach. "We are friends, are we not?"

He nodded. "*Hau, hau*," he murmured. "We are friends." He paused, and then quietly, he looked up at her and asked, "Where is your husband?"

The Eagle and the Flame

His question took her by surprise, for, although she was obviously with child, no one in the Wild West Show had ventured to ask her about her babe's parentage. She wasn't certain at first how she should respond. At length, however, gazing away from him, she answered, "I am not married." She couldn't look at him, so embarrassed was she. What must he think of her?

His hand on her stomach turned over to encompass and take possession of hers, and he came up onto his knees beside her. Gently, he put a finger beneath her chin, and brought her face toward his. He asked, murmuring quietly, "And the father? You are a beautiful woman, a woman any man would proudly call his own. Why did this man do this thing to you and then not claim you and his child, as he should?"

Jane bit her lip and looked down, away from him. Tears filled her vision, and she was aware that she could barely speak. She and Luci didn't talk about Timothy Hall, or what had happened between herself and that man. Jane was aware that the subject was not one that Luci would approach, perhaps fearing that she might cause Jane more pain.

Still, it was comforting to have someone show interest enough in her to ask her about what had happened. For a moment, she didn't know where to start, except to say, "I…I…" she hiccupped, and her voice shook with an unwanted, grief-inspired sentiment that seemed to start somewhere around her stomach, and cascade like a flood upward, toward her heart.

His hand tightened over hers. "I will do no more than listen, and what you tell me will not be said to another, unless you wish it. Do I need to tell you that I care about you, so that you might feel at ease with me? I promise you that I will not condemn you."

She cried. She couldn't help herself. This man's kindness, coupled with his soothing touch, seemed to trigger the latent emotion that had been building up inside her for all these months. The escape from Washington, DC had been so traumatic, that her ideas and thoughts on the matter hadn't yet caught up with her.

Timothy's rejection of her, as well as the realization that he had utterly betrayed her and used her, had served to break her spirit. And, it had all happened at a time when her emotions were anyone's guess, and when she'd needed that man the most. Worse, he had tried to injure or perhaps to even kill Luci.

The entire affair had left her stunned. To this day, she wavered between two conflicting emotions: the first was her fear that Timothy Hall might find her and bring about either her or her child's injury. Counter to this was the knowledge that her baby's fatherless birth would haunt her child throughout his or her life.

To this day, she sometimes wondered if it would have been better if she had thrown herself at the mercy of the Hall family. But no. The Hall newspaper chain had printed terrible articles about herself and about Luci; lies, lies and more lies.

How could she have ever thought herself to be in love with Timothy Hall? Worse, how could she have been so fooled by him?

Compared to the man sitting beside her, Timothy came up horribly lacking. The fact that Iron Wolf was an Indian warrior, who was, by all accounts, alien to her, made little difference to her. Indeed, their early morning talks throughout this past month had brought about a feeling within her, that, instead of being worlds apart, she shared many common ideas with him. For instance, they agreed that marriage should last a lifetime, that the raising of children was a man's and a woman's greatest calling, and that his concept of God, whom he called the Creator, was similar to her own. There were many other shared views, and it seemed to her that their ideas were harmonious, not discordant. Indeed, she liked him, and, if she were to be truthful with herself, she would have to admit that she was more than a little attracted to him.

As though to encourage her, he added, "I promise that what is said between us will remain between us, no one else."

"Yes," she said. "I know that, it's just — " She bit her lip, then sighed. "The father of this child told me he loved me, he even proposed marriage to me, and I truly thought we would marry. I knew he'd had a wife before, but he told me they were living apart, and so when he asked me to be his life's partner, I didn't hesitate. I believed him. Needless to say, he lied to me. He and his wife were not separated; they were living together, and I came forcefully to understand that I had been little more than a conquest for him." A sob interrupted her words, and worse, her nose began to run. "Excuse me," she interjected as she tried to arise, "I need to fetch my handkerchief."

"Here," he proffered, producing a piece of soft buckskin from his bag. "Use mine."

"I couldn't," she admitted. "I would soil it, and I do not wish to do that."

"It means nothing to me if it is dirtied, for I will simply wash it. But if you truly object, tell me where your handkerchief is and I will get it for you."

"It is on the table next to the cot inside my quarters."

Quickly he rose to his feet, and he was gone but a moment. Upon his return, he pressed the handkerchief into her hand. He sat down once again at her feet, only this time he took a position that was kneeling in front of her. Quietly, he murmured, "This man is a fool, but worse. It is an evil act he has committed against you."

By now the tears were streaming down her face, and she was beyond controlling them. Indeed, she couldn't speak. But she didn't need to.

He reached up to take her hand within his own, and he said, "This is a bad man and a foolish man. Tell me his name that I may know who he is."

"Timothy Hall."

He nodded, then repeated, "Timothy Hall. I will remember this name. But come, your baby needs a father."

"I know, it's only that I—"

"I will be that man, if you will let me. It is good for a child to have a father when he or she is born. It is important that the baby not be born without a man."

Jane stopped crying. Glancing down at this very handsome fellow—a man who apparently could have his pick of women—she doubted if she had heard him correctly, so she queried, "Excuse me, what was that you said?"

"Your child needs a father, a name that he or she can call his own."

"Yes, yes, but…"

"I would be that man. I will be father to this child of yours, if you agree. I am asking you to marry me. Will you?"

"Marry you?"

"Yes. Will you?"

Jane gulped, and after a brief pause, she answered, "I will if you truly mean it. Do you?"

"I do." He stood to his feet and stepped to her side. "Come, we must work quickly, for this show will be on the move in the morning, and my help will be required elsewhere. There is a man of your religion who travels with our show. He might marry us. Let us seek out this man and ask for his assistance, that your fear of birthing this child without a father will be at an end."

"You would honestly do this for me?" Her voice trembled, but she couldn't help its quivering.

"As you said, we are friends. What sort of man would I be if I left you hurting, when I could set your mind at ease?"

"But we're talking about marriage. People get married because they are in love with each other, and they usually stay married. Please, Iron Wolf, I like you so much that I couldn't bear to think that I might ruin your life. What if you were to meet someone else later in life who you love dearly?"

"You speak of a thing that is not and may never be, and you talk of love being needed between a man and a woman in marriage. I ask you, did I tell you that I was not in love with you?"

"Well, no, you didn't, but you also didn't say those simple, few words of love, either."

"Perhaps then now would be the time when I should tell you that I love you."

"I…I thank you for saying that, but I realize I am practically forcing you to say it."

He frowned. "Do you think I am lying?"

"It's not exactly lying, it's more like a little fib for my benefit, isn't it?"

"I do not know what this 'fib' is, but I tell you true that I love you. I have for some time now. Our talks each morning, while you await your sister, and I await my brothers, have caused me to greatly admire you. I have always respected your beauty, but your quiet demeanor and your kindness, despite your condition, showed me your courage. You made it easy for me to love you. I am sorry that I have not shown you my love and that I did not engage in what your people call romance. But, I did not know your story, and I thought that you were married, but that the father was caught up, elsewhere. It is unbelievable. What man, who is fully conscious, could be so foolish as to let you go?"

Jane barely heard what he'd said beyond his declaration of love, and she inquired, her voice still shaking, "You love me?"

"I do. Do not fear that you might not return my affection, for love will often grow, even though it is not present at the start."

"Oh, my." She cried.

"I am trying to help you, but know that you do not have to marry me."

"You don't understand, Iron Wolf. Why do you think I began to accompany my sister to her practices these last few months? It was not because of my sister, I promise you. My sister can take care of herself. It was because I wished to come to know you. I wanted to talk to you. I wanted to be with you."

He nodded, but upon his countenance was a look of disbelief.

"I still don't think you understand," she continued. "I love you, too, and have done so for quite some time now."

She hadn't even uttered the last word before he reached out to take her in his arms in what had to be the fiercest hug she could ever remember. Carefully he set her on her feet, then picked her up in his arms like a child. All at once he spun her around and around, and he laughed and he laughed. Jane couldn't help it. She laughed, too.

At last he stopped and had no more than set her onto her feet again, when he kissed her. Although it wasn't a passionate caress, Jane could tell he meant it. Jane felt her head spin, and a warmth of admiration for this man filled her, body, mind and soul.

How had something so good happen to her? She had been feeling so downtrodden, so sad, awaiting the birth of her child. And now happiness was practically exploding within her.

"We must find that man of the church now, for I am aware that in your world, a man must marry a woman in a way that your God allows, otherwise others do not recognize it. Come, let us hurry."

"Yes, yes, but I must change my clothing."

He looked her up and down, then sent a puzzled gaze into her eyes, which she understood without him having to voice his consideration.

"I am in my underwear," she explained. "Please give me a moment to dress, and then, yes, let us find that church and that preacher."

He brought her into his arms, where he hugged her closely to him. "Hurry," he urged. "I don't want another moment to go by without having you in my life."

She raised her head upwards toward his, silently asking for his kiss, which he complied with at once. "I will hurry," she agreed.

"*Hau, hau.*"

And Jane, placing another sweet peck upon his cheek, fled inside her quarters and dressed so hurriedly that she forgot to leave a note for her sister. But no worry, she would explain it all to Luci the minute she saw her.

CHAPTER TWENTY-ONE

*L*uci, still dressed as her feminine self, stepped out of the tent that she and Jane shared, and held the corners of the entrance flap together as though she expected it might open wide and reveal the shelter's inner sanctum. She could feel the blood rush to her cheeks as she gazed up at Wind Eagle.

Wind Eagle raised an eyebrow as though he were asking a question, but he said nothing.

Luci swallowed hard. "How has this happened? I thought you said that he wouldn't bed my sister?"

It was early in the day, around seven o'clock, and it was a busy morning. People were bustling about, speaking loudly, hurriedly taking down their tents or gathering up their possessions. However, no one, cowboy or cowgirl, showed even a passing interest in Wind Eagle and Luci. But why should they? The show was moving its headquarters today from New York to Philadelphia. There was too much to do to pay close attention to two people who looked as though they belonged together.

"Of what do you accuse me?"

"I'm not accusing you, I'm..." She blew out a breath in frustration. "What I am trying to tell you," she paused as she lowered her voice to a whisper, "is that your friend and my sister are together...in bed!"

When Wind Eagle didn't look in the least surprised, Luci raised her voice, but only a little. "You don't even look as though you didn't expect it. And yet, you said that he respected you too much to attempt to —"

"Luci! Please don't do this." Jane's voice came from behind her, and, when Luci turned around, she was met by the image of Jane, disheveled, scantily dressed and holding a robe together with one hand, while Iron Wolf stood at her side, his hand placed possessively on her shoulder.

Then, without skipping a beat, Jane uttered, "Iron Wolf and I have done nothing wrong. We are married. Though I admit that the minister didn't like having to perform the marriage ceremony between us, it is, nevertheless, done."

Luci couldn't remember a time in her life when she could think of no words to express herself, and it was up to Wind Eagle to say, "*Wašté,* good. May your days together be long and good. We are happy for you both." Then, turning to Luci, he changed the subject, and urged, "You must change your clothes, for, as you know, the show moves to a new location today, and you will be missed if you are not doing your part to help. All must be broken down and made ready to transport, and I will require your help with the ponies."

"Yes." Luci mumbled, nodding, and, finding her voice at last, she spoke out clearly, "I…I admit I am shocked, but I am also happy for you, Jane. Truly I am. It has been a worry of mine that your babe might be born out of wedlock, and I admit that I have not given the matter as much consideration as I should have. I thank you, Mr. Iron Wolf, and…" giving him a tentative smile, she murmured, "Welcome to the family."

Iron Wolf nodded in response. He did not, however, smile.

"But, Mr. Iron Wolf," continued Luci, "if you please, I have come here to change my clothing, and I cannot do it while you are present. Would you be so kind as to step outside the tent? I will be but a moment."

Iron Wolf nodded, and, applying a slight pressure on Jane's shoulder, he leaned down and said, "What my *kóla* says is true. We are moving camp today, and I am required to go and help the others, but I will make time to return here to your tent and do what I can to help you. However, since news of this sort seems to find a voice on the wind, it may be that our marriage could even now be known by the women of my tribe, and if so, they may extend a helping hand to you. Prepare yourself, because now that we are wedded, you might find yourself the center of attention from our women."

Jane smiled. "That would be most welcome."

With a hug, he whispered quietly in her ear, "While I am gone, do not forget that I love you."

"Never," Jane murmured back.

He smiled, stepped away from the tent and took his place beside Wind Eagle, where the two of them turned to leave.

"I will wait for you at the corral," Wind Eagle uttered to Luci, as he fell in step beside Iron Wolf.

"Yes," agreed Luci. "At the corral."

***

"My dear, dear Jane," Luci murmured to her sister as soon as the two men were out of hearing range. "What happened last night? When I left you, you were a single gal...and now — "

"Iron Wolf was watching over me last night," Jane replied, interrupting her sister. "And, when I became aware of his being here, I went to talk to him."

As Jane paused, Luci gently took her sister by the arm, and, turning her around, they both stepped inside their quarters, where, for a moment, Luci thought they might speak without fear of being overheard.

"I'm sorry, Jane," Luci said, once they had settled down and had each taken a seat. "I really didn't know about your feelings for Iron Wolf. It's true that I've seen the two of you together at practice, but I hadn't really *noticed* what was occurring between the two of you. But, marriage? What happened?"

Jane hesitated for a moment, her lips shaking. However, at length, she said, "We talked for a while, and when he asked me where my baby's father was, I'm afraid I told him the truth. It was then that he asked me to marry him. At first I thought he simply pitied me, and when I told him that he needn't feel sorry for me, he declared that he was in love with me and that he had been of that frame of mind for quite some time. But, he hadn't felt it his place to act upon his feelings toward me because he thought my husband was simply caught up somewhere else. He didn't expect me to be in love with him, also. But, Luci, I am. I have loved him for weeks and weeks now. He is kind, he is gentle, yet he is also a warrior worthy of praise. We are so happy, Luci."

As her sister spoke, Luci noted that Jane could barely keep back her tears. "I haven't wanted to tell you, Luci, but I have been so afraid of giving birth to my baby out of marriage. Since your duel, everything has happened fast, and I've felt so bad that my baby would be born without a father. And now, I am happy for the first time in many months, and I feel as if I might burst."

Luci scooted her chair up to Jane's, and, reaching out, she took Jane's hand in her own. "I really didn't know, Jane. I have been so caught up in my own problems that I fear I haven't been here for you."

"I knew you might feel this way. Please, don't feel bad. I could have said something to you, but I chose not to. But now… Oh, Luci, I love him so."

Luci nodded. "I can see that. I am very happy for you…for the both of you. I am beginning to fear, however, what Father may do when he discovers that both of his daughters have married into a group of people whom he is certain is an enemy."

"Both of us?"

"Yes, my darling sister. Last night Wind Eagle and I said our marriage vows in his tribe's honored way, with only God as our witness." She paused. "Is that how you and Iron Wolf married, or did I hear you say that a minister had performed the marriage ceremony?"

"It's the latter, Luci. We found and woke up the chaplain who attends to the Sunday services here with the show. He was not happy about our insistence on getting married, but he performed the ceremony anyway. It was Iron Wolf who insisted we marry in this way, for he felt only then would the baby be born within the sanction of marriage. He was afraid if we did it any other way, that the white people would not honor it."

"I am glad about that," Luci commented. "He is a smart man. It will also be harder for Father to come between the two of you, since you have the approval of the Church."

"And you, Luci, will you want a church wedding?"

"I don't think so. Do you forget that I must remain in disguise? Maybe some time in the future, but then again, perhaps not. I am of the opinion that God was there with us when we said our vows. I need no approval from anyone else."

"But don't you fear what Father might do?"

"I don't, Janie. After all, I have reached the age of majority, and, so doing, I should not have to seek my father's opinion, although I admit that I would like his good graces."

As they paused, there came a scratch at the tent's canvas opening, and, looking up, Luci saw that there were several Lakota women smiling and chattering at each other, and they were waiting outside. One of them spoke up, saying in English, "We have come to help our Assiniboine brother's bride. May we come in?"

Luci smiled. Iron Wolf had certainly predicted this occurrence with great insight. It was she who said, "Please do come in, but give us a moment."

"*Haŋ*," the Lakota woman said, and all of the women settled down it seemed, though they were still chattering at one another in a dialect that neither Luci nor Jane understood.

"I will gather up 'Louie's' clothing and change somewhere deep in the woods. I do believe, little sister, that you have many hands here, waiting to help you."

"Yes. And, Luci, I am so very happy."

Luci smiled, kissed her sister on the cheek, and, taking up her boy's pants, shirt, boots and hat, she opened the tent's flap, bid her sister a hurried, "good-bye," and sped in the direction of the wooded glen.

***

"We will stay with the ponies during the journey the Iron Horse makes to the village of Philadelphia," Wind Eagle explained to Luci after they had spent the day settling each horse into its stall onto the many and varied stock cars. "It is never easy transporting the wildlife. They don't understand what is happening, and often, when we move camp, their needs are ignored. We have lost horses and buffalo on these kinds of journeys. So you and I will care for some of the Indian ponies. Others will watch over the other animals and see to their comfort while we are on the move."

Luci nodded. "Will we look after the needs of the Indian ponies in one of the cars, or will there be two or three? There are so many horses in the show."

"We are assigned to only one "house" that the Iron Horse pulls, and, as you have seen, the other "houses" for all of our animals are at the front of the train."

"Yes, I did observe this. Is there a reason for it?

"*Hau, hau.* Riding close to the biggest, blackest and the main Iron Horse provides the smoothest ride, and, because the animals are all anxious, it makes their journey a little easier. Buffalo Bill's show is often moving camp, and he has learned that each one of the animals require care and attention on these journeys. Without it, we have lost some of our most prized friends."

"I'm glad that Buffalo Bill has seen to the needs of his animals. Do you know how long it will take us to get to Philadelphia?"

"I believe the Showman announced that the trip there should take two days because the train must move slowly, due to the animals needs. We will be traveling both day and night, although there will be many stops to ensure the animals are well. All this I say to you to show that we will be tasked with many chores, since all of our ponies will require plenty of food and water, as well as attention. They will need care and love from people who are familiar to them. We will be all that to our ponies."

Luci nodded. It couldn't be easy moving hundreds of performers, as well as the buffalo, the elk, the bears and horses. The guest seating and the hundreds of tents, alone, took up two open train cars, and, because the entire cast of the show was going to be on the move for the next few days, several dining cars had joined the procession. A good many sleeping cars took up the rear of the train, and this was where the majority of the cast and their families would travel.

But, despite the grandness and the impossibility of moving so many people, animals and possessions, within a relatively short time, the entire project was loaded onto the long column of the train. At last the show was ready to begin the journey.

Luci had been forced to leave Jane in the care of Iron Wolf for the entirety of the trip, but, since he was needed watching other animals, Luci had been pleasantly surprised when a group of five Indian women had attached themselves to Jane; they were intent on helping the new bride to move. Not only had they dismantled Luci and Jane's tent, they had done it so quickly, that Luci was certain that even her father, with all his military style and exactness, would have been impressed.

"Wait here while I check on Stormy Boy," Wind Eagle ordered Luci, as he vaulted up into the car where the ponies were installed. He had been gone no longer than a few minutes when it happened. Luci had been bent over, checking the ground for any possible gear that might have been dropped or overlooked. She had seen a leather strap and had squatted down to pick it up, when, from out the corner of her eye, she had caught sight of a man dressed in a black frock coat. Odd, she thought. It was a warm day.

It was when he'd opened a newspaper and brought it up to hide his face that she noted in particular that he wore a bowler-style hat, which was pulled down low over his forehead. Was he a Hall agent? Was he looking for her and Jane? Stealing another glance in his direction, she noticed that he wore the typical short, sideburn moustache that seemed to be a feature of the Hall family detectives.

Her stomach dropped, prompting her to feel a little dizzy. And, as she stood up with the leather strap in her grip, she noticed that her hands shook.

So, here was the truth at last. The great Hall family was still looking for herself and Jane.

Realizing she needed to seek the shelter of the stock car without appearing suspicious, she forced herself to take the long, slow strides of a boy to bring her level with the stock car. Soon, she was able to pull herself up into the car, and, as she tried to disappear behind the many horses, she hoped that she had not drawn attention onto herself. Once inside the car, however, she made a straight path to Wind Eagle, and, without explaining too many details, she said simply, "They are here. They are looking for us."

At first Wind Eagle appeared confused by her words, but then, a look of understanding appeared upon his countenance, and he commanded, "Show me where they are."

"I only saw one, and I can't point him out to you because that might draw attention to me. But he's outside, moving from car to car. He's wearing a dark suit, black coat and a bowler hat. He has a moustache that curls up at its ends."

"*Wašté.* Do not fear. I will ensure he does not see me, but I wish to have a look at him. For you, turn your back and begin brushing one of the ponies farthest from the door. Do not turn around, do you understand? Do not turn around."

She nodded, and, while she stepped to the back of the car and opened a stall, she prayed that she hadn't given herself away. But what of Jane? Luci had ensured that Jane was wearing her dark-haired wig, but was that enough? No. However, she was now surrounded by several of the Indian women, and she might be mistaken for being Indian.

Wind Eagle returned to her within minutes. "I have seen him," he stated matter-of-factly. "I must leave you for a moment so that I might warn Iron Wolf of the danger."

Luci nodded.

"The Iron Horse should be starting out soon, so I must work quickly. Do not leave this 'house,' or as you call it, the car, and do not turn around or speak to anybody. Pretend you do not hear well, if needed."

Again, Luci nodded.

Wind Eagle had been gone for no more than several minutes, when the train began to slowly move, swaying back and forth. Of course the animals reacted with a cacophony of neighing; worse, there were a few of the ponies who attempted to tear down their stalls. What should she do?

Certainly, she needed to calm the animals, but Wind Eagle had been exact when he'd told her not to move around the car. Although she did not like the idea of following his order, for good or for bad, she stayed put.

Luckily, Wind Eagle returned quickly, and he began the process of visiting each animal separately, speaking to every one of the ponies in a voice that Luci recognized as one that would give them comfort and courage.

Only moments later, one of the attendants rattled the train's car door shut. Good, Luci thought, and she breathed out in relief. Soon, Wind Eagle approached her.

"We are safe for the moment," he said, stepping up next to her. "But we will need to be wary. My friends tell me that the man you saw has already approached the Showman, and asked him many questions about two sisters who were on the run from justice. But Buffalo Bill was too distracted, and paid the man little attention."

"Good."

"However, that bad man will try again as soon as we reach our destination in Philadelphia. My friends and I will do all we can to block this man so that Buffalo Bill will not give him audience. We must acknowledge, however, that he will keep trying, and there may be more like him. Your sister can hide herself amongst my people; she can wear her dark-haired disguise, and dress like us so that she looks Indian. But you..." His gaze scanned her features critically. "You must perform, and we must practice. Perhaps if you keep your head down, and wear your hat with the stampede string drawn tightly under your chin, you will go unremarked. Maybe you should also wear your hair like I do, braided, pulled back, and clipped away from the face, so that if your hat were to blow away, you would still have the appearance of a boy."

"It could work."

"*Hau, hau,* it might. But we must be careful. You are never to leave my side; this will not be too difficult, since we are together for practices, as well as performances. Do you know that if something happens, if someone grabs you, you are to scream?"

"Scream? Me? I think not; I can defend myself. I am no sissy, and I don't need to shout out for someone else to come to my rescue when I can take care of myself."

"And there you are wrong, my wife. I do not question your ability to defend yourself, but consider that there may be more of them, and, after all, a man is usually many times stronger than a woman. Also, if there are a few of them, you could be overwhelmed. You are to scream so that I and everyone else around us are alerted to the danger."

Luci nodded. "All right, I will scream."

He grinned at her. "You promise?"

She sighed. "Yes, husband mine. I promise."

"*Wašté*," he muttered, then he winked at her. "You will not leave this 'house' on our journey. I will bring you nourishment from the dining car, and you will have your meals here. Here, also, you will sleep..." he smiled, "...with me."

"Where? Is there a stall here for human beings?"

He laughed. "At the front of this 'house,' we will make our bed." Again, he winked at her. "It should be a pleasurable journey."

When she shook her head at him, he chuckled, before turning away from her to approach and to soothe yet another pony. Luci, watching him, followed his example and entered the stall of a different pony, applying a similar kind of care. After all, there were sixteen horses that were traveling in this car, and it was her duty and Wind Eagle's to watch over and to ensure that, at the end of their trip, every animal was happy and healthy...including their two friends, Sure Foot and Stormy Boy.

***

"Little Red Riding 'Horse' said to the big, bad wolf, 'What big eyes you have...'" Luci inserted the word horse, for hood, believing the ponies might like to hear the story of a horse in the role of the heroine. "And so," she continued, "the big, bad wolf ran out of Grandma's house, never to be seen again. And they all lived happily ever after."

Luci gazed around the train car. At last, the ponies were quiet. Most were asleep. In addition to the story told to one and all of them, each horse had been rubbed down, fed, watered, and told in no uncertain terms that the journey was temporary and that soon they would arrive in the new town, where they would be placed again into the more familiar corral. It was a point of pride that, even though the show travelled to many different cities, the animal's enclosure, much like the performers' quarters, would be set up the same as before. The familiarity made for a calmer, happier environment.

"Good-night, my darling Sure Foot," murmured Luci, as she put down the soft brush, and, taking the horse's head in her hands, she kissed his nose gently. "Fear not, for during this entire trip, I will be here in this same car with you." Luci turned, blew out the lantern and opened the gate to the stall, but her gaze was backward, and when she rammed into Wind Eagle, and when his arms came around her, she was pleasantly surprised.

He brought her in so closely to him that she could feel the imprint of his hard, masculine body upon her, and when he whispered, "There is another animal you must calm tonight."

"Oh? Is there? And where is this beast?"

"Right here in your arms," he uttered. "Come, I have made our bed and I am thinking that it might be a while yet before we sleep."

She *tsked, tsked*. "What are you suggesting?"

"I will show you," he uttered as he turned her toward him, and, pulling up her shirt, he did not hesitate to adore her. Soon the shirt, each button undone, came off and was thrown aside. Next, the material that she used to wrap around her breasts unraveled and fell to the floor, and, with this gone, her chest became fully exposed to her husband's wandering touch. "Let me remember to thank the men of your society, who do not feel it necessary to wear so many clothes."

"Yes," she uttered, but the sound of her voice was more of a sigh than the spoken word. Indeed, she felt as if her bones were melting. When the suspenders that held up her britches fell from her shoulders, those pants, which had been supported by the fastenings, fell to the floor, leaving her standing before him in nothing but the boots upon her feet; boots which he removed easily.

At once, his hands seemed to touch her everywhere and when his fingers found her womanhood, she swooned in toward him. Soon, he whispered, "Your body is ready for me; are you?"

"Oh, yes."

He picked her up and rested her backside against one of the many posts of Sure Foot's stall. Pushing his breechcloth aside, he brought her up over him, wrapping her legs around him

"Ah, for more light so that I might see you better, my wife," he uttered.

"We have all of our lives before us, my love. If you desire, you may keep me naked when we are alone." She giggled slightly.

"*Hau, hau*, but I wish to watch you now as you experience our love."

"There are many lanterns in this car, my husband, and I believe we are allowed to place them where we like."

He laughed softly, and, as he became a part of her, she wondered at the happiness that filled her heart. Would they love each other with this same, intense passion even in old age? Somehow, she thought it might be so.

Her breasts were on a level with his lips, and he did not hesitate to honor them, as well. Holding her up by her legs and buttocks, he danced with her as he strained against her, giving her all of him. They kissed, they touched, they loved, and soon, Luci felt her body pushing toward that ultimate joy. Would this be the time when they would conceive another life? The thought was immeasurably pleasant. Oh, to have a child by this man.

She whispered, as she bore against him, "I love you so much, my darling. Never, ever doubt it. For all my life, you are my love."

It was at that moment that he spilled his seed within her, and, as they fell together off that high precipice of lovemaking, she heard him utter, "I, too. I, too."

Happily, she smiled.

But Wind Eagle didn't miss a beat. Without setting her onto her feet, he lifted her up farther and carried her to the forward section of the car.

The Eagle and the Flame

This part of the stock car was already partitioned off from the rest, so that those persons who were watching over the livestock might obtain some sleep, as well as enjoy a little privacy. The little room smelled heavily of straw and hay, as well as the general scent of a barn. In one corner of the area was a water basin, a water pitcher and towels. In another part were table and two chairs. Several trade blankets, as well as a buffalo-hide robe that possessed the scent of leather, were laid out over a bed of straw that dominated the center of the little space. By the side of those several blankets and buffalo hide were four lanterns that could be lit.

Wind Eagle placed her squarely on top of the spacious buffalo robe, which she discovered was curiously soft, then he set to work lighting the lanterns. Soon, a soft glow filled the little room.

"Ah," he stretched out the word, then he winked at her, "the better to see you with, my dear."

Luci grinned. "Now, who's been listening to my fairytales? I am not Little Red Riding Horse, and you are certainly no wolf."

"Are you certain of that, my wife? After all, your hair is red, your Indian name is Oi'le Kitaŋla, Little Flame, and I feel as hungry for you as my kóla's namesake."

She giggled. "Come here, my husband. The evening is still young and we have so recently been married...."

And, as might have been predicted, Wind Eagle complied. But before he lay down, he knelt at her side and said, "Did I mention that Sure Foot is now your pony?"

"My pony?"

"A wedding present. But also, it is easy to see that Sure Foot would miss the many fairy stories that you tell him each night if he were to remain mine, and, since I do not know all of these tales, I must give him to you." He smiled.

"Oh, my. My own pony... Thank you. I will love him, I promise, almost as much as I love you, and that is a great deal, my husband. But, why do you say that you don't know the fairytales? I have heard that your people have many legends."

"Ah, that they do, but I do not have your beautiful voice, which is needed to calm the pony."

She shook her head. "You flatter me."

"No, truth. Now, you say you love me a great deal. Are you ready to show me that love? Now?"

"Of course, my darling, of course."

He grinned at her, and, as the evening turned to the black of night, she kept good her promise.

CHAPTER TWENTY-TWO

This evening's performance in Philadelphia was to be the first
exhibition of the speeded mounted shooting since Stormy Boy's accident.
After a week of steady practice, both Wind Eagle and Luci had agreed
that he was ready. Wind Eagle had put the little Cayuse through his
paces, leading the pony first through all the motions slowly. Only a few
days ago, Stormy Boy had shown an enthusiasm for the same movements,
but at a fast clip, which signaled that he was ready to learn more.

It had taken several more days to accustom Stormy Boy to doing the
learned steps amidst the noise of the gun blasts. At first both Luci and
Wind Eagle had practiced the event using no ammunition, simply clicking
their guns at the right moment. And, when the pony had become skilled
at that, Luci and Wind Eagle had begun using the black powder blanks.
Lately, at Wind Eagle's insistence, a new item had entered into Stormy
Boy's performance — ear plugs. So pleasant was the change in the pony's
behavior, Luci had made similar ear plugs for Sure Foot.

The performance tonight was only minutes away, but before leading
Sure Foot into the arena, Luci checked briefly to ensure that her hair,
which was braided and pinned up high, was still safely hidden
underneath her cowboy hat; she had even secured the cowboy hat to her
hair with hairpins and had pulled the stampede strings in tightly toward
her chin.

As Wind Eagle had insisted, she was to keep her head down and her
hat pulled low over her forehead. That way it would be harder to tell who
she was. Not that there was much evidence that there was danger; she
hadn't seen that agent for the Hall family again. Indeed, he seemed to
have disappeared. Even upon reaching Philadelphia, the man hadn't

materialized, and, according to their Indian sources, he hadn't attempted to contact Buffalo Bill. Most likely he had moved on.

Still, there was no need to flirt with trouble.

"Do not fear that the same might happen tonight as it did in the New York Harbor," cautioned Wind Eagle, who, she noted, looked the part of a plains warrior. He didn't always paint his face for their exhibitions, but he had done so tonight, and red paint covered his cheeks and forehead, while a streak of red paint covered his chin, and was tabbed down his nose. He had even painted Stormy Boy's head, with a streak of red paint going from his eyes to his nose. Also, he had attached feathers to Stormy Boy's lead rope and reins. "Our ponies are more learned now than they were then, and this is our last act for today," continued Wind Eagle. "I think we were wise to leave the mounted shooting until the end of our performance instead of the beginning. It is fast, dangerous and exciting, and it is a good ending to our routine." He grinned at her sensuously, his tone teasing, for all his fierce looks. "Also," he went on to say, "once it is done and our ponies are brushed down and settled, we will have much time to ourselves." His smile broadened. "It is good that you can no longer share your sister's quarters. Now you will have to spend your nights with me, as a good wife should."

Luci rolled her eyes and glanced heavenward. Nevertheless, it was true. Jane and Iron Wolf had moved into the tent that had once been the two sister's quarters. This had left it up to Luci to find her own housing, but Wind Eagle had quickly taken charge of that problem, and had settled her into his own lodge. It couldn't have worked out better if Wind Eagle had planned it to be this way all along.

Luci decided theirs was a perfect sort of "honeymoon," if one could call it that. Although the show had only been settled in for a few weeks, already she and Wind Eagle rarely left one another's side. They worked and practiced together, they shared their meals, they played together, they traded good-hearted banter, and late at night, when no one else was around, they made love, renewing their vows within the privacy of Wind Eagle's lodge.

Luci couldn't remember a time when she had been happier. Even Jane bubbled over with bright and cheery emotion of late. Interestingly, no one appeared to pay much attention to the unusual marriage between Iron Wolf and Jane. There had been rounds of congratulations, of course, but mostly, after the crew had passed on their good wishes, they had left the two newlyweds alone.

Luci supposed that it was to be expected. There were simply too many men in the show who were married to Indian women. It must be that the sight of a mixed marriage went unremarked, because here, it was commonplace.

She smiled and sent Wind Eagle an impassioned look, as she purred, "I so look forward to our evenings...after the show."

He laughed. "Are you nervous?"

"I am," she confessed, "but not because of the event. I still worry about the Hall family's agents."

"I do, too," he agreed. "But come. We will let the speed of this last shooting match release our worry. Not that we will ever let down our guard."

Luci checked the holsters that she kept in position directly in front of her. She glanced toward Wind Eagle and smiled. "Let's make this event exciting, and show Buffalo Bill what we can do."

For answer, Wind Eagle winked at her. "*Hau, hau,* let us do that, but do not think for a moment that our act will be as sensational as what I have planned for us after the show — and all within our own private tepee."

And, to Luci's laughter, Buffalo Bill rode out into the middle of the arena, yanked his hat off his head, and announced their act.

"Here we go."

Together, as one, they waved to the audience. The familiar screams from the many young females, who were seated up front, had ceased to be annoying to Luci. Instead, she had trained Sure Foot to use the noise as a cue to break into a run. Stormy Boy did the same, and to a dizzying speed, she and Wind Eagle weaved in and around each other, firing shot after shot at the balloons.

It was rare that they missed their mark, and tonight was no exception. As they paused while the attendants set up another group of balloons, Luci smiled at Wind Eagle, then said, "Shall we bet? Whoever gets through the maze first on this second round gets a back rub from the other. Deal?"

"Deal."

Within a matter of minutes, the balloons were set up again, and neither Luci nor Wind Eagle hesitated to urge their ponies into a run. This pace was faster than the first run-through, and Luci felt exhilarated at its end, especially since she was aware that Wind Eagle had deliberately let her win.

"What fun!"

"It will be almost as pleasurable as what we will be doing later tonight after that backrub."

She giggled. "On this third and final run-through, let's say that the last one through the maze has to rub down the other's pony. Agree?"

"Of course."

And they were off. With their horses running at top speed, darting in and around each other, the further difficulty of shooting at targets over and over and in three different sets, added that dangerous element to their act that they knew Buffalo Bill would appreciate. Still, although this part of the act was dangerous enough to gain attention, it was also exhilarating.

He won, being the first one through the maze, but Luci didn't care; win one, lose one. Besides, she loved each moment spent with Sure Foot and Stormy Boy.

All too soon, the exhibition was done, and it had been accomplished accident-free. Luci let out her breath, unaware until then that she had been holding it. The crowd seemed exhilarated by what they had seen, and several people stood to their feet, clapping in appreciation. As both she and Wind Eagle said their goodbyes to the audience in the usual fashion—by waving—the young girls in the front row seats screamed their excitement.

At last they exited the arena. They had both dismounted when Buffalo Bill caught up to them.

"Spectacular! Just spectacular! Never seen anything like it. I'm going to increase your pay — both of you."

Luci might have responded, but from some distance away came the urgent summons of one of the managers. Buffalo Bill sighed deeply in apparent exasperation, then said, "Yes, yes, Nate, I'll be there in a minute." He clamped Wind Eagle on the shoulder. "Always some emergency once the show is on, don't you know. Gonna increase your pay is what I'm gonna do. Keep it up, you two. Knew it would be a good show if I could get the two of you together. Yes, yes, I'm coming." And, without awaiting a reply, he turned and was gone.

Wind Eagle glanced at Luci, and together, they grinned.

***

"And when the prince kissed the princess, she awakened, and, seeing the prince standing before her, so dear and so handsome, she fell instantly in love with him," Luci's voice was soft as a summer wind as she finished her tale to Sure Foot and Stormy Boy. "They married, and from that moment on, they lived happily ever after. The end."

Darkness had fallen upon the land at last. The show was over for the day, and most of the public had already departed. However, a few of the guests had remained in their seats because they had been invited to the opening night party, which was due to begin momentarily. Most of the performers had completed their work, but Wind Eagle and Luci lingered over their chores, brushing and pampering both Sure Foot and Stormy Boy.

"I thought I was to see to Stormy Boy's grooming this evening. You did, after all, win that bet."

"*Hau, hau,* it is true, but I have better plans for the evening than to linger here and watch you brush down Stormy Boy. But, if you prefer, I will let you finish his care. Ah, but then you might never know what sort of loving I have on my mind."

She looked up at him and grinned. "You flirt."

Wind Eagle simply smiled. "With you, always."

Luci laughed, while that now familiar and delicious, happy feeling swept through her. Glancing up briefly, she was pleased to witness a beautiful, clear night. There was only a half moon tonight, and she believed that it was slowly waxing. Millions, maybe billions of twinkling pins of light in the sky contributed to the silvery illumination that shone down on the land. Having grown up in the city where stars were not well seen, Luci was often struck by the beauty of the night sky in rural America, where the stars littered the blackness of the night as though they attempted to compete with the sun.

She inhaled the fragrance of the grassy and oxygen-filled air with pleasure. The dance must have begun at last, for the sound of the trumpets, trombones, woodwinds and percussion filtered through the warm, night air. Still, the music was loud enough, even at this distance, that Luci found herself bopping up and down to the beat of a jig.

"Do you want to go to the party when we finish here?" asked Wind Eagle.

"No, not particularly. Do you?"

He grinned. "I think not. As I have said many times tonight, I have a much more pleasant idea of how I would like to spend the evening with my wife."

Luci giggled. "Then I guess we had better finish our work as quickly as possible. I am almost done here. What do you think, Mister Sure Foot?"

Sure Foot snorted and switched his tail.

"Yes, yes, I know. I have yet to ensure you have plenty of water and hay, just in case there is too little grass in this pasture. I have not forgotten."

Sure Foot neighed in answer.

"You finish up while I pick up the hay and fill the water trough," Wind Eagle volunteered as he petted Stormy Boy on the nose, then he bent to breathe into the pony's nostrils.

"I have seen you and Iron Wolf do this before. Why do you sometimes breathe right into the pony's nose?"

"It calms the horse," he answered, "and lets him know that he is loved. If you ever watch wild ponies who have not yet known man, you will see them do this to each other. It strengthens the bond between each of the horses, and it does so between the human and horse, also."

"I didn't know that."

He winked at her. "Now you do. I will bring the hay and water."

***

"*A pá itó!*"

Wind Eagle suddenly grabbed hold of Luci and pulled her through an opening in the canvas tent that covered the tiered bleaching boards. It was a dark corner between the back of the customer seating and the canvas, and it smelled heavily of spit, stale food and dirt. However, he didn't stop there; he guided her farther into the maze, toward the seating boards lowest to the ground.

"What?"

He placed a finger over her lips, shaking his head back and forth in the negative. Bringing her finger to his lips, he said, without uttering a sound, "Stay here." And he was gone, leaving Luci alone and bewildered.

Luci crossed her arms over her chest and shivered. What was wrong? She and Wind Eagle had finished their chores at the corral, and had been walking "home," which was, at present, his tepee. He had been teasing her, and she had been laughing and giggling as though she were a much younger girl, when he had uttered an exclamation and had pulled her into the cover of the tiered customer seating.

She wasn't left long wondering why there was the sudden change of their plans, for Wind Eagle returned within a few moments. He drew her in close to him and whispered in her ear, "There is danger. I do not know what kind of threat this is or its source. I know only what I have perceived. You are in some sort of peril."

"You mean the Hall family agent? But I've seen nothing of that man for weeks now."

"I know. I, too, have not had a glimpse of this person, nor have any of my friends. Still, I think I should take you to your sister, who is being looked after by our women. Perhaps you can lose yourself with them, as has your sister. That will permit me to discover the danger without worrying about you."

"But, you forget," she argued, "that if there is danger, I would rather be with you."

"Do not do this," he whispered. "Not now. I can discover more easily what the problem is if I know you are safe. If you are with me, my attention will be spread between defending you and discovering what menace is afoot. I might make a mistake."

She sighed. "Oh, all right. But I don't understand. You know that I don't need you to defend me. I am no tenderfoot, and I can take care of myself."

"*Hau, hau,* it is not in my mind to disparage your ability to aim and shoot. But keep in mind what I have said before; several men could overwhelm you, take your weapon and use it against you." He reached up toward her, placing a finger beneath her chin, forcing her face up to his. "I love you. Please do as I ask." His lips were only a fraction of an inch from hers, and, like the lover he was, he did take advantage of the position, kissing her gently. "Do as I say."

All at once, the canvas tent opened with violence, thrust back by what appeared to be strong arms, while several lanterns swept in from the darkness outside. Luci pressed her body up close to Wind Eagle's and snuggled her face against his chest.

"They were at the corral only minutes ago. They have no choice but to come this way in order to get to his tepee. You," the man with the loud voice pointed a finger, "go to his lodge and wait for them. You, Miller, come with me. We're going to search underneath these bleaching boards. They might have received word of our being here and... Wait!"

The light of a lantern fell fully on Luci and Wind Eagle. "There they are. I've found 'em, sir! I've found 'em!"

Wind Eagle whispered, "You are to bend down and hide beneath the lowest of these boards. Now."

"What goes on there?" the low, harsh voice barked. There was no mistaking the authority in it.

Several more lanterns fell upon Luci and Wind Eagle, the light bright in contrast to the blackness surrounding this place, and, like a spotlight on a prison wall, that beam illuminated them. Quickly, Wind Eagle placed Luci behind his back, keeping one arm around her in a protective gesture. Then, he turned and faced the enemy. He drew his revolver. Luci did the same.

He whispered urgently, "You are to obey me now. Bend down and scoot into a place to hide."

"I heard that. It's too late for that, young fellow," bellowed that same severe voice.

"Father?" Luci ventured. Had her father returned from Hawaii? It could be. It sounded like him. "Father, is that you?"

"Of course it is. What is the meaning of this, Lucinda? Come out from behind this young fella. And where is your sister?"

"Stay where you are," ordered Wind Eagle.

"Young man!"

"It's my father," uttered Luci. "It going to be all right. It's my father."

"And so we meet," murmured Wind Eagle beneath his breath. But Luci did hear it, and more, when he said, "The trouble begins."

She supposed Wind Eagle was right. From this point onward, there could be turmoil for them. But she wouldn't think of that now; possibly Wind Eagle might win over her father's support. Although unlikely, it was still worth a try; if she could but forestall the clash of wills between her father and Wind Eagle, her father might be able to bring Captain Timothy Hall to justice.

"By the way, Lucinda," commented her father, "that was some shooting you did tonight. You, too, young fellow. Maybe no one else would have noticed, but I recognized your style, my girl. And you were riding. Where did you learn to control a horse like that?"

"Daddy!" Lucinda didn't answer his question. There wasn't time. She stepped out from behind Wind Eagle, and ran to her father, straight into his arms. "Oh, Daddy, I've missed you. But you're here now. At last, you're here. But come, before you say another word, I've something very important to tell you."

"Yes, yes, all in good time. I've found you, but where is Jane?"

"I'll tell you about that momentarily, but Daddy, listen, and don't yell at me until you hear me out. Daddy, there's no other way to state this, except to say, I'm married."

"You're what? Married?"

"Yes, I'm married. Wind Eagle," she gestured from the younger man to the elder, "this is my father. And, Daddy, this is my husband, Wind Eagle."

CHAPTER TWENTY-THREE

*W*ind Eagle glanced quickly from one of the white man's fittings to another as he sat in a chair within the most luxurious train car he had ever seen. Quickly, he memorized each desk, chair and gun case, on the chance that he might need the information later or that he and his wife were to be attacked now. On the alert, he saw that the red curtains were pulled over each window in the car; he took notice of the heavy, wooden desk with a single pistol laid upon it. He observed with some distraction that it was loaded, and that Luci's father stroked it as though it were a favorite pet.

The air inside the car held the heavy scent of a cigar, which sat poised on a dish at the side of the desk. A single trail of smoke trickled upward from the cigar, and ashes had accumulated at its end. It did not escape Wind Eagle's regard that he had not been invited to smoke, and he silently protested the rudeness of the white man's councils.

How different were Indian councils, where even an enemy was not only invited to smoke, but was expected to. Would words of truth be spoken here tonight? Who would know? Without the peace pipe and each man's vow to the Creator to keep his tongue straight, there was no guarantee that what would follow would be words from an honest heart. There was only the cigar, which held no meaning whatsoever...except, perhaps, to insult him.

Three men stood next to Little Flame's father, the man to whom others referred to simply, as General. The general was seated, but the other men were standing stiffly by him, as well as at every entryway into this car. And oddly, although Wind Eagle had been disarmed upon entry to this car, he was the only one so disadvantaged. All the soldiers within this room stood prepared with not one, but several pistols and a sword.

Each was also uniformed in blue. Wind Eagle realized with mounting distress that these men were representatives of the dreaded Long Knives, or Blue Coats, the same sort of enemy who had killed his mother.

He set his lips together and concentrated on other aspects of this special "house." It was as opulent as the kind of setting he had been treated to when he had been introduced to the Queen of England. Indeed, this one looked to be as grand as that one.

The car was paneled utilizing an unusual wood; there were pictures on each wall and on the partition directly in back of the general's desk were two swords, crossed. The main color of the room was red, and the atmosphere reeked of adversity. It was a war room—a grand one—but a war room, nonetheless.

Who was the general at war with? Wind Eagle suspected it was he, and that he sat within the enemy's lair.

He attempted to swallow his prejudice toward the general and these Blue Coats, but it was difficult. He knew that he must, however, endeavor to put the bad emotions aside, for he was well aware that this man was Little Flame's father, and no good would come from holding the general to account for the actions of others against his own people.

One of the general's men had pulled up two chairs in front of the general's expansive desk, and Wind Eagle currently sat in one of those chairs, while Little Flame had taken her seat in the other. Wind Eagle brought his attention back to the conversation between the general and his daughter. So far, Wind Eagle had been excluded from their talk, as though he were too unintelligent to be consulted.

"Married, are you?" The general repeated the question he had asked of his daughter several times. Even a casual glance could not miss the obvious, thought Wind Eagle; that the general bore a strong resemblance to his daughter; his hair was red, as was his beard, and it was scattered with white. His eyes were gray, the same color as his daughter's; his lips were full and his oval facial shape was similar to his daughter's. No one, seeing the two of them together, could dispute the familial resemblance.

He wore a blue coat like the soldiers who served him, but the general's jacket bore many golden buttons sewn on in twin rows, up and down his coat. There was a patch of gold embroidery at the shoulder of his uniform, which seemed to distinguish it from the other soldiers' outfits.

Little Flame hadn't answered her father's question at first, but now, after the two of them had shared some courteous words, it appeared that this main topic of concern would be asked over and over until the general had garnered a response from Luci. And so, at some length, she said, "Yes, Father, I am married."

"What church?"

"A wooded, country church, Father, with the only witness to our vows being God, our Creator."

"Then you're not really married, is that what you're telling me?"

The comment was meant to intimidate, and Wind Eagle quickly decided it was time to ignore the general's discourtesy toward him, which included speaking to a woman instead of to him, as one man to another. Forget the fact that Luci was his daughter, it simply wasn't done when in council.

And, so it was Wind Eagle who answered that question, and he did so with as little harshness as possible, saying, "We are married, General. We are married according to the custom of my tribe, the Assiniboine. The Creator was our witness. He is the only one needed to make our marriage real and acceptable, since it is He who sanctions our vows."

"Nonsense," the general responded. "All *civilized* people know that a marriage can only be considered done properly, and both people married, in a church of God."

"And so it was, sir," responded Wind Eagle as respectfully as he was able spit out the words. "It was a church which was put there by the Creator, himself, and He heard our words of love and our pledges that we said to one another. We meant every word we uttered. She is my wife. I am her husband."

The general frowned at him; he paused, clicking the fingernails of his right hand on the desk. After a moment, he asked, "Lucinda, how could you do this to me? You know I wanted you to marry a military man."

Wind Eagle didn't allow Little Flame a chance to answer that question, and he spoke up at once, saying, "She has, sir. It is only that it is *our* Assiniboine military, not *yours*."

"Enough!" The word was bellowed with enough force to have blown down a house of straw, thought Wind Eagle. "Young fella," continued the general, "do you think I don't know what you're doing? Trying to keep me from talking directly to my own daughter?"

"As is my right, sir. I am the man of the family, and you are speaking of our marriage. Would you have me hide behind my wife's skirts?"

The general's face reddened in the wake of that particular statement, and he looked as though he might have blown down a house of sticks, as well, so angry was he. "I see how it's going to be. Yes, I understand now that we need to settle this matter tonight. Well, good, we'll speak man to man, but I will not permit Lucinda to be present during our discussion. After all, it is the man of the family who decides its fate—" After a slight pause, he smiled menacingly at Wind Eagle. "Isn't that right, boy?"

"Daddy, no!"

The general looked directly at Luci. "Lucinda, it was in my mind tonight to rescue you and Jane and to take you both home. I wished a happy reunion between us. But this…this has taken me by surprise. And it is not a good surprise. Frankly, I am shocked. You must know that I would never approve of this man."

"I know, Father, and I'm sorry it has come as a blow to you."

"But an Indian, Lucinda. How could you marry an Indian?"

"Father! Wind Eagle is sitting here before you. Please do not speak of him in a derogatory manner; not in front of me, and especially not in front of him."

The general didn't utter a word for several moments, and, in truth, he looked as though he might explode and blow down that house of bricks, as well. However, when he spoke, his voice was even, and he articulated his words meaningfully, saying, "Very well. Your point is taken. But, Lucinda, your *husband* and I must speak man to man. We have matters to discuss that are only for our ears. You must admit that there are some familial affairs that concern only the men, and must be discussed without the interference of the feminine gender." The general shot him a sharpened glance. "You understand that, don't you young fella?"

"*Hau, hau,*" was Wind Eagle's only response.

"I'm afraid that reunion I had envisioned will have to wait, Lucinda. Where is your sister? Can you go to her while this *boy* and I talk?"

"Her sister is with my people." Wind Eagle answered the question.

"Why?"

"They are protecting her."

"Against?..."

"Evil men."

The general narrowed his eyes, then without releasing his stare at Wind Eagle in any way, the general ordered, "Smyth, take Lucinda to the Indian camp, where she is to join her sister and await my next orders. Meanwhile, this young man and I will '*pow-wow*' here in my office."

"Father, this is all so unnecessary," Luci protested. "This is my marriage, too, and my future you will be discussing. I should be here to listen to what the two of you have to say to one another."

"No, Lucinda." The general folded his hands in front of him in such a way as to make the shape of a tent. "As hard as it might be to understand, this *youngster* and I need to speak to each other, alone. When we are done, you will be called here."

Luci didn't speak. Instead, she looked sideways at Wind Eagle, her countenance pleading with him to allow her to stay.

Sympathy for her played war with what he knew had to be. There would be no peace here until he and the general spoke to one another privately, for there was presently a great deal at stake, including a need for a plan to alleviate the danger to his daughters. And, so he said, "Your father is correct. We must be allowed to discuss…matters of general concern to the family. I will come to you when we have finished. The night is long, and I think we still may have much of the evening before us." He winked at her and grinned, hoping that his usual teasing would allay her fears.

Lucinda turned away, her countenance sad, as she accused, "And you, Anthony Smyth, I thought you were *my* friend, not my father's."

"I am friend to you both, and you know it." Sergeant Smyth spoke to her as if he were her brother and she were his to discipline. "You are a general's daughter and I am also a soldier, under orders."

"Judas," she muttered under her breath. But she nonetheless arose from her chair, ignoring Smyth's proffered arm. "I will be in the Indian section of this camp, awaiting you both."

"Yes, yes," was the general's only response.

Wind Eagle nodded, bestowing upon her his best attempt at a good-hearted wink.

***

"I'm going to come right to the point with you, young man, and be blunt," the general blurted out, as soon as Lucinda and Sergeant Smyth had stepped through the exit.

Wind Eagle didn't answer.

"Are you a pervert? Did you believe when you married my daughter that she was a he?"

"*Hiyá.* I do not know what this word, pervert, means, but I can tell you true that I have known from the first moment I met your daughter that she was female, and a female old enough to bear children."

"So you say, but I don't believe you."

Wind Eagle cautioned himself against the annoyance rising up within him, and he tried to give the general quarter. After all, it was to be expected that his new father-in-law would be upset. He had lost a daughter to a man whose people he had fought and killed. No mistake; their relationship might always be stormy, but this style of "talk" was clearly a form disrespect, and, it was also an interrogation, a mild form of torture to the Indian mind. Indeed, Wind Eagle was almost to the point of speaking as brusquely as the general.

Still, it was not his duty to cause their future relationship to become worse by giving back to his father-in-law in kind. So, he chose his words with care, and he said, "Father-in-law, you must know that there are easily distinguished differences between men and women."

"Obviously."

"Besides the usual. But on the chance that you do not recognize the other telltale signs, let me relate to you a few of the obvious ones that can be seen by anyone if he will but look. Your daughter's pointing finger and her ring finger announced loudly to me that 'he' was a 'she.' Her forehead, which, like a child's, is straight up and down, told the truth of her sex. A man's forehead, unlike a woman's, is usually slanted back. The smallest part of her waistline is too high above her navel to be confused with that of a man's. But the most distinct difference that showed me at once that 'he' was a 'she' was her scent."

"What? Her scent?"

"*Hau, hau.* A woman's natural body odor is different from a man's, and an Indian who is trained to notice these tiny differences, cannot be fooled by a boy's clothing and general manners."

"Now see here, are you trying to tell me that you thought from the beginning that my daughter smelled bad?"

Again, Wind Eagle cautioned himself against demonstrating the mounting anger within him, and he uttered as calmly as possible, "*Hiyá,* I did not say she smelled bad. All men and women have a scent that is almost impossible to detect, but if a man is trained to distinguish the subtle differences, he can tell the disparity between a man's fragrance and a woman's. I was never fooled by her disguise."

"I see," said the general, looking down at a paper on his desk, and, opening a drawer, he drew out several gold coins. "So you say. Now, what is it that you want from me? I'm assuming you married her for some reason. What is it you require? Perhaps money to send home to your family?" He patted the gold as if it were a treasure. "If money is what you require, that can be arranged. Do you have another wife at home who needs the cash? Children?"

Wind Eagle frowned. "I have no other wife and certainly no children...yet."

"Ah, yes, that leaves money as the object of your affection, doesn't it? I thought as much. Again, I will be blunt. How much do you require from me so that you may walk away from this 'marriage'?"

"Money? Walk away? Why would I?..." Enough was enough. Wind Eagle rose to his feet, and, pacing forward, he placed his hands on the general's desk. "It is to be understood that you are shocked at learning that your daughter is married to a man you do not approve of, but do not think that you may insult me as though I were a young boy who is unaware of the evil of your accusations. Yet, despite your words, you are my father-in-law, and there are matters we must discuss, one of them important and urgent, and it is yet unknown to you."

"How fitting a tirade!" The general shot up to his feet. "You don't need to pretend with me, *boy*. I know your people for what they are: parasites, unable to live without the handouts from the white man. I think you protest too much. I would say that you are pretending outrage so that you may hold out for more money from me. Know this, young man. I don't intend to give you more than what you deserve, if that."

Wind Eagle straightened up to his full height and placed his arms over his chest. Chin raised, he countered, "Your talk to me is bad. Your talk about your daughter is bad. You should be more careful with your tongue, Father-in-law, for some remarks, once said, can never be taken back. Is it truly your intention to imply that your daughter is not winsome? That I have any other reason than love to have married her? Know this: I don't want your money. I don't want your advice, and our meeting is at an end. If you will call off your dogs who guard every entrance and exit of this car, I will take my leave from you."

Wind Eagle swung around and stepped toward one of those exits, but the soldier who guarded it barred his way by shoving a rifle in Wind Eagle's face. Wind Eagle glanced askance at his father-in-law. "Do you have other bad words to say to me? If not, permit me to leave."

The general placed his fists on his desk and leaned forward from the hip, and, although his face was a deep color of red, his voice was calm, as he stated, "It seems to me, young man, that you are off the reservation. You are, aren't you? You know that's a crime, don't you? Why, if it were up to me and I were in your place, I'd take the money and run. Now. For, if you remain here and insist that your marriage to my daughter is real, I intend to round you and your friends up and send you all back to your reservations...or worse. We have jails for your kind of people."

Wind Eagle narrowed his eyes. "If you do this, you may very well lose that girl you seek to control, for she will follow me."

"Not if she is unable to."

Wind Eagle executed a hundred and eighty degree turn so that he faced his father-in-law. He took a step forward. "Speak so that I and others may understand what you are truly saying. What are you threatening toward her?"

Suddenly a commotion arose in the entryway, where there appeared to be a fight in progress. Several soldiers fell to the ground, a few more followed, and to the flurry of thrown punches, an Indian man — a little beat up, yet still wrestling — stepped into the room, and, seeing Wind Eagle, he uttered, "*Iyá nitáya nitáwicu taŋka!* "

Blue Thunder! Blue Thunder was here and was distressed? What had he said? Due to the blue coats shouting and the general chaos, all Wind Eagle had heard was the last word; something about "the sister." Little Flame's sister? Jane?

Yes. Had he said that Jane had been taken? There was no time to determine what had or had not occurred, however, so Wind Eagle took Blue Thunder by the arm and stepped away from the entry. Not wishing his father-in-law or any of the soldiers to hear or have knowledge of the subject of their talk, Wind Eagle switched to "speaking" in the quick, abbreviated language of sign. He asked by holding his right hand parallel to his shoulders and turning the hand right and left, "Question: Jane was taken?"

With his right hand, index finger pointing up, Blue Thunder moved that finger down and to the left, the sign for, "Yes."

"Who took her?"

Blue Thunder pointed to a white flag in the room, and signed, "A white man and two Mexicans."

Wind Eagle signed, "Question: Was the man in the long coat and round hat also there?"

252

"No one saw him."

"Question: Does our friend, my sister-in-law's husband, know?"

"Yes," he nodded, then signed. "He is already trailing them."

"It is good. And my wife?" He spoke her name, "Oí'le Kitaŋla," then he switched back to sign and asked, "Question: Is she with our women?"

"I did not see her there."

Wind Eagle frowned, thinking fast. He gestured in sign, "She was taken there by a Blue Coat. Question: Did you see her with the soldier?"

"I did not."

"What's going on here?" The general had come forward to stand shoulder to shoulder with Wind Eagle.

"This is my kóla," explained Wind Eagle. "He tells me that your daughter, Jane, has tonight been taken away by an enemy."

"Rubbish!"

"Your other daughter, my wife, may also be missing," continued Wind Eagle as though the general hadn't spoken. "My friend and I will go at once to find both trails left by your daughters and see if they merge. It matters not if their trails are two or combine into one, for we will follow the trail or trails and hopefully will find your daughter or daughters unharmed. You may come or not, I do not care."

"You lie."

Wind Eagle didn't miss a beat, and he said, "Father-in-law, this is what I've been trying to tell you in our council here tonight. Your daughters are in danger."

And, with nothing more to be said or argued, both Wind Eagle and Blue Thunder bullied their way through the blockage of soldiers, and exited. No one stopped them.

CHAPTER TWENTY-FOUR

*A*ll human beings bear a scent that can be distinguished by other life forms. Yet, there was not a second to spare to allow for a sweat bath, which was usually required to wash away that human fragrance, especially important if the enemy had brought dogs with him. Soon, however, Wind Eagle and Blue Thunder discovered that it didn't matter. By the tracks left upon the earth here, it was clear that the captors had no canines.

It was typical, also, that a scout took a few moments to camouflage himself. But there wasn't an instant to spare for that ritual, either. Besides, it wasn't necessary here at the start of their tracking.

Wind Eagle picked up the trail made by Little Flame and the soldier named Smyth, and ran quickly along it, with Blue Thunder following alongside him. It was easy to see that the soldier and Luci had stepped near the bleaching boards, and it was there that the prints showed that a struggle had taken place. Two of the kidnappers had attacked Little Flame, and the soldier called Smyth had been struck from behind. It was all there in the prints left over the earth. Further, Smyth had been dragged beneath the boards, and, following that trail, they saw that Smyth had been dumped deep underneath the lowest of the seating boards. He was on the ground, lying still, but he was still alive when they found him, and Blue Thunder and Wind Eagle administered care for him with what they had at hand. Then, with quick consultation, both men decided it would be best that one of them escort the soldier back to the general's quarters. Blue Thunder volunteered.

It was so agreed, and, while Blue Thunder left to attend to Sergeant Smyth, Wind Eagle quickly found the point where three men in total, plus

Jane and Little Flame, had all come together. One trail to follow; it was good.

From what was to be read here in their tracks, Wind Eagle could see that two of the three men were heavy, but even considering this, the evidence left over the earth showed that Little Flame had put up a struggle.

He smiled, as admiration for his wife's determination and courage overflowed within him. However, as Wind Eagle had often cautioned, these men were bigger and stronger than she, and he saw where she had been grabbed from behind, brought under control, disarmed and hauled along with the others.

The evidence over the earth was unmistakable: they had mishandled his wife. Wind Eagle's anger flared at the obvious fact, and he felt as hot and as vengeful as his warrior ancestors. Yet, he also knew that his good sense as a scout held no use for bad emotion, for it was well-known that to let hatred overcome one's mind was a path to defeat. Exercising the finest self-control he could muster, he deliberately put those ugly emotions from him.

After all, it was clear by their tracks that the two girls, although kidnapped, were still alive. Also, he remembered that Iron Wolf was following their trail, although his kóla had erased his own impressions from the earth.

It was then that Wind Eagle let his awareness become a part of the "spirit-that-moves-through-all-things," and, as he had been taught by the elders of his clan, he could perceive the recent past impressions that had been left here over the earth. From these invisible impacts, it was possible for Wind Eagle to utilize that form of communication known to the ancient scouts, and passed along to the upcoming generations, and in doing so, he knew that Iron Wolf was trailing these thieves, yes, but also he realized that Iron Wolf expected his friends to follow as reinforcements.

Then, with an expansion of attention, he became aware of Iron Wolf's thoughts, even at this distance, and he received Iron Wolf's silent, wordless communication. Iron Wolf would await his two kólas before he would act. Indeed, he would only take action if there were a threat to the girls.

It was good, and, with that thought, the silent communication ceased. Running along the trail left here, Wind Eagle didn't bother to hide his own prints, since Blue Thunder would follow. He did see that the kidnappers' tracks led to a known path through the woods, and Wind Eagle was well into the thickets when Blue Thunder caught up to him.

When on the scouting trail, communication was done by the language of sign, alone, and Blue Thunder gestured, "The soldier wished to come with me, but his head injury needed healing, and the white man put him in the white man's medicine lodge."

"And my father-in-law?"

"He is mustering a few of his Blue Coats in preparation to finding the girls."

Wind Eagle smiled. "I wish him well," he signed. "Come, do you see these tracks? The kidnappers are doubling back, while over there—" He pointed, "they try to erase their real trail. But they are not true scouts. They do not do this well, and I can see that they are not far ahead of us. They are hampered by the women and their many horses. Iron Wolf awaits us; I believe he has them in his sights."

Blue Thunder nodded, and he signed, "We must not become complacent and think that because they are hindered by the women and too many horses, that they are not dangerous, or that they might not elude us. We should expect the worst."

Wind Eagle nodded. "You speak well. Come, let us find a stream and paint our bodies with charcoal and mud, so that we might fade into the woods without detection. Then, we will quickly follow this trail and meet up with Iron Wolf."

"Good," Blue Thunder gestured.

***

Neither he nor Blue Thunder slept this night; they used the hours of darkness to trail the enemy. After all, the captors were traveling by horseback, and it was only during the blackness of the evening that Wind

Eagle and Blue Thunder could make up time, as well as move undetected through the forest.

It was now early morning, and the sky in the eastern part of the heavens was awash in the gray mist of dawn. Although Wind Eagle followed the trail over the land, his senses were stretched outward to the world around him, in case anyone else were in this forest.

That was when he felt the thunder of hooves in the distance. Taking a moment away from the scant tracks that he followed, he stood up straight and trod to the edge of a cliff, facing east, which overlooked a wide valley. A moment later, Blue Thunder joined him.

Off in the distance could be seen a troop of perhaps five or six blue-coated soldiers, led by what looked to be Little Flame's father. Wind Eagle might have found humor over their attempt at scouting, were the circumstances of the moment less dangerous. For he was well aware that any man, even one badly trained, would see what these men did not; they could not hide their presence or the direction of their current course. Even a white man would have been able to escape from that troop.

Wind Eagle could only wonder about that small assembly of Blue Coats. They must have left in such a hurry that they hadn't been able to hire an Indian scout, and, without that scout, they were accomplishing little more than going about in wide circles.

"My father-in-law," he signed, shaking his head. "He acts as though he expects the enemy to find him, instead of elude him."

"They are lost," gestured Blue Thunder. "Should we join them and bind our skills to theirs?"

"No," he signed. "I do not wish to be distracted, for I would be reunited with my wife as soon as possible. And, let us not forget that her sister is carrying a babe. We must get to them as soon as we can. For the moment, my father-in-law can remain lost. Come, our enemy had to stop for the night, and we did not. These tracks show that they are not far ahead of us."

"Wait," signed Blue Thunder. "Look there! The general waves a white flag. It looks to me as though he knows he is lost and he asks for our help, for he knows we are trailing the kidnappers. Shall we give him our aid?"

Wind Eagle sighed. It was true that Wind Eagle held little affinity for this man who was his father-in-law, and he didn't wish that man to join him. The general wasn't needed, and he certainly wasn't wanted.

Yet, what choice did he have? He *was* her father.

Wind Eagle gestured in sign to Blue Thunder, "Yes, we have no choice now. Let us wash the dirt and mud from our bodies and go down there. A word of caution before we allow ourselves a council with them: None of the Blue Coats may join us. If the general wishes to accompany us, he may do so, but it will be on our terms, not his."

Blue Thunder nodded, signing, "So be it."

***

Luci was frustrated. Not only was she disarmed, she was distraught, knowing that her strength would never overcome that of those two huge bullies. Worse, the handsome, young cowboy who had once courted Jane, Will Granger, seemed to be the "brains" behind the kidnapping. Only now did Luci recall that Jane had once mentioned Granger's friends, and that they had made her feel ill at ease.

Luci hadn't given that remark its due at the time; she had discounted the knowledge. Now, she wished she'd looked further into it.

Why Granger? What connection did he have with the powerful Hall family? Was Granger simply being paid, or were there deeper roots between the cowboy and the Hall family? Or perhaps worse, did this kidnapping have nothing to do with the Hall family?

The other two men in the abduction party were huge, at least in weight, and they looked to be Mexican, not Indian. Both seemed to be of medium height, but it was hard to tell their real stature, because the cap of their sombreros reached high toward the sky. They were each one of them clothed in smelly, dirty-brown breeches, a loose shirt, and each of those men wore a blanket and a belt of ammunition over that shirt. She heard one of the men being called Pedro; he was easy to distinguish because he wore a red hat. The other was Ramiro, and his sombrero was brown.

All three of these men, including Granger, had strapped a gun belt to his leg, and each of those belts held two holsters and two guns. Singularly, the men possessed his own rifle, which each man had placed either beside him or over his legs, for they were all sitting upon the ground, boots toward the fire.

It was early morning and the mist of a sunless dawn hung over the grasses where she and Jane reposed. They were both of them wet from the dew, and tired, for neither of them had been able to sleep through the night.

Luci didn't care about her own comfort, but Jane? Jane was eight months pregnant, and the lack of sleep might tax her spirit and her body. To try to lessen the effect of the cold, Luci sat next to her sister and took her into her arms. Not only did she hope to impart her body heat, but perhaps comfort, as well.

Luci saw that the kidnappers had camped in a small meadow, overshadowed and almost hidden by trees of oak, maple, ash and many other plants and shrubs that Luci didn't recognize. Some of these trees however, were huge, and their shade caused the meadow to be cool, dark and worst of all, wet.

The horses were tethered nearby and Luci could hear them munching on the grass, but she also knew that any attempt to run to those ponies in an effort to escape was wasted, especially for Jane. But what other option did they have?

Should she try to disarm the men? Did she dare to leave Jane even for a moment in an attempt to do so?

While she was trying to envision other means of escape, the Mexican in the brown hat had leaned forward, over the fire, with a pan in hand. It appeared that this man, Ramiro, had it in mind to cook breakfast. The smell of his efforts, however, was not pleasant, for the odor of the food was foul and offensive.

She noticed the red-capped man had placed his rifle to the side, instead of holding it in his lap. Could Luci grab that rifle and get off three shots before one of them could shoot at her? Or worse, shoot Jane?

Maybe. But what if they killed her? What then would happen to Jane?

Luci squirmed as she sat arm in arm with her sister. Luckily, they had positioned themselves as far away from the kidnappers as possible and had been allowed to do so.

Embarrassingly, Ramiro had insisted on accompanying them this morning, as both she and Jane had needed to attend to bodily matters. The scent of that man, which had smelled of dried body excrement, including sweat, had made Luci feel as though she might vomit. But she didn't. Instead, she stepped as far away from him as he would allow.

It was Ramiro now who was walking toward them, and, coming within reach, he squatted down in front of her and Jane, offering them some of the food. And, even though it might have felt demeaning, both girls accepted that food. It was either that or go hungry.

Luci had been silent toward her captors during their long trek here, but she decided it was time to speak up at last. It might help. And, so she asked Will Granger, "Where are you taking us?"

"To the train station," he answered. "Don't worry. I wouldn't harm a hair on your sister's pretty head. We are simply escorting you both to the train, which is awaiting you."

"Train? The same one that Buffalo Bill uses?"

"I don't think I can answer that."

"I wonder why," Luci mumbled under her breath. "Can you tell me where that train—the one that you're taking us to—might be heading?"

"I don't think so. Now, I apologize for the manner in which you both had to be taken. But it's all for your own good. No one means to harm you. You'll see."

Amazingly, Granger's smile looked to be young and innocent, and Luci wondered if his naiveté were real, or if this were an act meant to put both her and Jane off their guard.

Jane had been so quiet since their kidnapping that it was surprising when she spoke up, saying, "I cannot travel so far today. I am with child, and it is due soon."

"Yes, yes, I know. We all know," replied Granger. "How could we not? But what we do must be done. All I can promise you is that you both will be treated like royalty once we get to the train."

"Will you swear to that?" asked Luci, for she doubted Granger was the brains behind this kidnapping, and if, indeed, he weren't, it would follow that he would have no knowledge of what was intended. She asked, "Will you be accompanying us?"

Will Granger looked contrite and momentarily angry before he visibly reined in his emotions, setting his lips together in such a babyish pout, Luci wondered at his age.

"I cannot go far," Jane protested. "Already the baby has dropped into a birthing position, and I can barely walk, let alone ride a horse. I cannot go." This last was accompanied by a scream so loud that even the men looked taken aback. Jane grabbed hold of her protruding stomach.

"Jane," asked Luci, "is the baby coming?"

"I don't know. This is my first child. But that pain was real and was terrible."

Luci stood up. "You!" She pointed to red-hatted Pedro. "Go gather me some water, and you—" She directed her index finger at Ramiro. "Build a fire—a big one, and boil that water that's going to be brought to you. And you, Will Granger, you are to run back to Buffalo Bill's show and get the physician...now!"

"I will not," stated Granger. "I cannot."

Luci glanced from one to another of the men. Not one of these three had moved. Indeed, they looked a little inane, and seemed to be smoking some sort of weed in a pipe that they passed back and forth. What was it? Certainly not tobacco. And, this activity between them seemed to cause all three to suddenly find humor in their situation, for they were giggling with each other as though they were children.

What was that weed? Was it some sort of drug?

Dear Lord, it might be. And, if it were a drug, she reasoned that it was useless to ask any of them for help, for they would be incapable of giving aid, even if she could convince them to do so.

What was she to do? She bit her lip, thinking hard.

It appeared that she was stuck here with not only the dirtiest and vilest of men, but perhaps the stupidest, also. What were they doing smoking some kind of weed after engaging in a kidnapping? Did they think no one would try to follow?

Are any of you going to do it?" She addressed the men. "Are you going to help me?" Not one of those men responded.

In the end, it was Luci who stood up and stepped forward to take up a nearby bucket that would hold the water she needed. She said, "If none of you are going to come to our aid, I'm afraid you will have to let me have my way, for my sister is having her baby. Now. Do you understand?"

Her only answer from the three of them was more snickers, although after a fit of ridiculous laughter, Will Granger said, "We will watch."

"How *good* of you." Although her intention was sarcastic, the emotion was lost on these men. "I'm fetching the water now."

With a hand gesture, Granger urged her on, and Luci, disgusted with them all, turned away.

"Jane, I must be the one to get some water to boil, as you can see. Do not worry that it is I who must attend to you. When we were still in Washington, I had taken the time to study the technique of birthing. All will be well. I'm sure of it. Now, I must go to the stream to get some water, and then I'll stoke the fire so that it is a bigger blaze."

"Yes," said Jane. "I understand."

Luci nodded, then turned away to trod in the direction of the stream. Luckily it wasn't far away. Stepping through the grasses, rocks and the late flowers of season, she gained the tiny shoreline of the creek and bent to urge some of the water into the bucket. It was then that something brushed against her arm. She pushed it away, but when the touch returned, she looked down and almost screamed in surprise. But she didn't yell out, and she was glad that she hadn't, for it was Iron Wolf who had come to squat beside her. However, she couldn't help the gasp that escaped her lips.

Iron Wolf held up his finger for silence, and, taking the bucket from her, he gave her a leather pouch full of water. Then he "spoke" to her, but the language was in gestures, and she didn't understand. Still, he persisted, and at last she was made to understand that he meant to bring her the water she needed. He would leave that pail along the path to the stream.

Bringing her fingers toward his lips he said, without sound, "Your husband comes. Do not fear."

At once, she felt herself calming, and she nodded at Iron Wolf; her way of showing him she understood. Arising, she stepped back toward Jane. But before she took the leather pouch to the fire, she whispered quietly to Jane, "Iron Wolf is here. He means to help us."

"Good," replied Jane with a sigh. "I knew he would follow. And now, I need worry no more, for, between the two of you, I know I am in good hands."

Luci smiled, and she squeezed Jane's hand. "Yes, all will be well now."

But was it true? Luci realized that she might have read papers and books on the subject of delivering babies, but she had never done it. Would her aid be good or bad? She could only hope that it would be good and that there would be no complications.

Unbidden, she recalled that their own mother had been lost to them in the act of giving birth. She bit her lip and said a silent prayer, begging the Lord for a steady hand and a good usage of her knowledge.

"And please, dear Lord," she whispered, "keep Jane safe in your hands and alive."

CHAPTER TWENTY-FIVE

"We move along the trails invisible to all but the most aware scout," Wind Eagle said to the general as they stood next to a stream that ran through the woods. "You must look as though you are part of the environment." He stripped off the clanking metal buttons that the general wore on his uniform and threw them away, aware that he was enjoying this perhaps more than he ought. He almost smiled, and he had to remind himself that he was not at war with the general…at least not yet.

"Indians!"

"Son-in-law," reminded Wind Eagle.

"Son-in-law or not, I want it known that I didn't agree to have my uniform and my medals, my buttons, my sword, my belt and even my spurs thrown away."

Wind Eagle winked at the general. "Nothing, not one thing on your person must make noise, or do you wish to announce yourself to the enemy?"

The general didn't answer.

"Now, Father-in-law," Wind Eagle continued, and there was a smile in his voice, "if you do as we say, after we rescue the girls, I will lead you back here to find these things for you."

"You expect me to believe a promise from an Indian?"

"An Indian who is your son-in-law," said Wind Eagle. He shrugged. "Time will tell if I will do this or not, but you must act as we tell you to, or none of that will come to pass." Again, he winked.

"Stop that, young man. Do you think I am a commoner that you can make laughing faces at me?"

Wind Eagle laughed outright. But he quickly brought himself under control, presenting a serious demeanor to the general, at least for the moment. "Of course not," he answered, then he couldn't help himself, and he grinned. "Come, your camouflage is next. It is very important."

"Camouflage? What do you have in mind now?"

By way of answer, Wind Eagle picked up some mud from the nearby stream, and slapped it onto the general's uniform. That wasn't all. He repeated the process, then, gathering some clay, he worked several handfuls of the orange-colored muck up and down the general's now mud-splattered uniform. By way of decoration, he showered some grass and twigs over the mud and clay, trying to curtail himself from enjoying this too greatly. Blue Thunder followed up the procedure by streaking charcoal over the mud, clay and twigs, even over the general's hands. Wind Eagle finished the camouflage by streaking charcoal down the general's nose.

"Now, this I know I did not agree to. You are not only staining my uniform, you seem to be delighting in doing so."

"And so I am, General. So I am," answered Wind Eagle honestly. "But let me remind you that you did agree to this. Under the white flag you said that whatever our terms were, whatever you had to do, you would do, so long as we led you to your daughters. These are our terms. You must look so much like the environment that a man, looking straight at you, would look through you. Come, we are finished. Let us move out into the environment. Are you ready?"

"Of course I'm ready."

"Good."

Quickly Wind Eagle and Blue Thunder camouflaged themselves in much the same manner, but it was done within minutes. And, as the small party began to move along the path, Wind Eagle instructed the general, "You are to walk this way with first the toe upon mother earth, followed by the rest of the foot. You are to bend at the waist as you stalk the path. Do not stand up straight, for you make yourself a target. Do you have any questions?"

"None."

"*Hau, hau*. Each one of us will carry the rifles that we took from your men, two each. Are you ready to go?"

"Didn't I just say that I was?"

For answer, Wind Eagle merely grinned.

***

As Luci stepped back into the clearing, she knew at once that there was trouble. Not only were the Mexicans and Granger laughing uncontrollably, but in Ramiro's demeanor was a chilling look that Luci recognized, and it was not good. What did that man have in mind? Did Ramiro think that she and Jane were defenseless? It might appear as though they were, but if he tried anything, Luci would die before she would let him harm Jane or her baby.

Luckily, she knew that Iron Wolf was here to help them; that he held the entire camp within his sights, although he lingered unseen in the shadows. She also knew that he, too, would die before he would let anyone harm his wife.

Luci took up her pouch, brought it to the fire and set it aside. Several logs were stacked by the fire, and she picked up one of those to spread over the fire. That was when it happened.

Ramiro slowly came up to his feet. He swayed a bit, but he stepped forward, toward Jane.

Luci looked at the others, spotting exactly where their weapons were. Next to Will Granger was a rifle. If need be, she could get to it quickly, turn and fire off a shot. She froze in preparation, keeping Ramiro within her line of vision.

Ramiro was laughing. "What kind of baby will you have, pretty girl?" he asked and then he snorted. "Will it be a fine Mexican baby? Or is your husband a white man like my *amigo*, Granger? Ah-h-h...," he seemed to answer his own question. "I think it is a white baby. I don't like white babies." He drew his gun, and Luci made a lunge to the side to get at Granger's rifle. She had it in her hands, she pointed it with her finger on the trigger, and she fired, but the shot went wild because Granger suddenly jerked the weapon out of her grip. Worse, he grabbed hold of her, and, although she bit and clawed and tried to slip out of his hold, he

266

held her fast. She reached over to grab his gun; he laughed and threw her away.

Ramiro continued, "I think I will kill that baby and implant my own seed within you," continued Ramiro. "So much better are Mexican babies." He pointed his gun, and Jane, sobbing and crying, placed her hands over her stomach.

Luci, free now, shot forward, toward Jane and the baby, placing herself directly in front of them, and, closing her eyes, she waited for the worst....

***

Wind Eagle heard that shot, and premonition caused his stomach to plummet, his senses screaming. Luci was in trouble. She was in the line of fire. He knew it.

Forget the carefulness of the trail; forget his father-in-law. Like his namesake, Wind Eagle burst forward in the direction of the sound of that rifle. Blue Thunder didn't miss a pace; he was sprinting beside Wind Eagle, and silently, they each one knew that together, they would thwart this enemy. In both men's hands were two rifles.

Within seconds they came to a path that led toward the sound of that gunshot, and from far away, Wind Eagle saw his wife, his love, shoot forward across the camp, and put herself between the gun of a Mexican and Jane. Wind Eagle's heart fell; he was still too far away to shoot accurately. He sped forward.

Suddenly, he beheld Iron Wolf, who plunged forward from out of the tree line, and, with the speed of his forward motion, he used his body as though it were a weapon. With a quick foot, Iron Wolf kicked the gun out of Ramiro's hand, and, with that same forward momentum, he threw Ramiro to the ground.

Wind Eagle had no more than come within shooting range when he saw Will Granger pick up a rifle and point it toward Iron Wolf. But before Granger could pull that trigger, Wind Eagle blasted the weapon out of his hands, knocking Granger's rifle to the ground, and, at the same time, injuring Granger's hand.

The Eagle and the Flame

Wind Eagle threw down the expended rifle and moved away fast, in case there was a rain of fire volleyed in his direction. Blue Thunder threw another rifle at Wind Eagle, which he caught, as they both sprinted to a different position. He paused for a moment and looked out upon the camp, seeing that another Mexican, the one in the red hat, had drawn his gun and was looking wild-eyed toward the forest at Wind Eagle's former position. The kidnapper pointed his gun in that direction, and Wind Eagle didn't hesitate to shoot the weapon right out of the red-hatted criminal's hand.

That same Mexican drew his other gun and aimed it toward the forest again, but Wind Eagle and Blue Thunder had both anticipated this, and they each one fell to the ground to sprawl forward, at a fast, crawling motion, until they reached a position on the far side of the clearing.

This time, his second revolver drawn and aimed toward the spot where Wind Eagle had just fired from, the abductor shot wildly into the trees and bushes. But it was all for naught.

Shifting his attention briefly to Granger, he saw that the man was injured, but there was a light of insanity that radiated from his eyes that Wind Eagle recognized as dangerous. Granger was standing, holding a deadly revolver in his hand and he looked ready to use it on anything that moved. Seeing this, Wind Eagle didn't hesitate a second to unload a line of fire at that firearm. Granger's revolver fell to the ground on the first round, and Granger, even more wild-eyed with stunned disbelief, retreated fast, turning around and running away, leaving the scene of the battle so hurriedly that his clothes caught and tore over thorny branches of the shrubbery. But not even a briar patch would deter him, for he was speeding away as though the devil himself were after him.

Wind Eagle nodded to Blue Thunder, who returned a gesture that showed he had duplicated Wind Eagle's intention, even though not a word had been spoken between them. Placing a hand on Wind Eagle's shoulder, Blue Thunder squeezed briefly, then turned to track Granger through the woods.

Meanwhile, Iron Wolf and Ramiro were engaged in a deadly struggle over the ground, both reaching hard and fast to obtain a knife that had been left beside the fire. Wind Eagle was on the point of blasting that knife to pieces, when he beheld that Luci had become aware of the same problem and had run toward that knife to kick it away.

But her actions had drawn attention from the Mexican in the red sombrero. Wind Eagle watched as that man aimed his pistol at Luci, and, as rage filled Wind Eagle, he quickly aimed at that man and sent off a shot that catapulted the pistol from the man's hand, while again injuring the enemy's hand in the process. Good. He had intended that.

Immediately, the red-hatted foreigner held up his hands in a gesture of surrender, and, when the enemy in the brown sombrero realized he was losing the wrestling match with Iron Wolf, he quit the fight and turned to flee from the camp. At once, the red-hatted criminal joined his compatriot in the escape. Wind Eagle couldn't help smiling at the picture the two of them made as they fled uphill and over a ridge, scaling it as though they were half mountain goat.

Wašté. The bad men were gone. No one had been killed, but the thugs had certainly beheld better days. They were whipped. Wind Eagle breathed in a sigh of relief, and turned around to watch as his father-in-law stepped out of the woods, making his path toward Wind Eagle.

"That was fast thinking and good shooting, young man," the general complimented, though it seemed grudgingly given. "I saw what you did. You saved my daughter's life."

Wind Eagle nodded briefly once, then added, "And my world."

"Don't think I've seen shooting that good in a while."

"It is what I do. But if you look closely, those two kidnappers are making a trail, and it might lead us to their master. If you were to follow them on one of those horses on the other side of the clearing, perhaps you might outrun them and capture them. In that way, it is possible that we could discover who is responsible for this terrible wrongdoing."

The general nodded. "Is that an order you're giving me, young man?"

"A suggestion."

"Sounded like an order to me. Can't say as I like it, but it's a reasonable request, *boy.* If you'll excuse me, I'll go secure one of those horses." He turned then to rush toward the horses, and, saddling one, he rode out of the camp at once, his mission clear; he would trail those two fleeing men.

Wind Eagle inhaled deeply as he watched his father-in-law leave. Was the trouble between them over, he wondered, or was it only beginning?

As Wind Eagle stepped farther into the camp, he pulled his thoughts up short. So filled was he with the energy needed for fast action, it wasn't until the present moment that he realized he had almost his love. Almost, she might have gone the same way as his mother and sister.

Indeed, if he had been a few seconds late, she might now be gone. As his eyes met hers across the camp, a jolt of reality hit him: the worst had not happened. She had not gone the way of his relatives, and, so great was his relief at this recognition, he felt close to tears.

She was still on the ground, having rolled away, out of the line of fire, and as he stepped toward Luci, he wondered if he were going to cry like a young child. He certainly felt like it.

When he reached her, he fell to his knees beside her, and, taking her in his arms, he was aware that the tears he had hoped to restrain, were streaming down his cheek.

"I could have lost you," he murmured. "Like my mother and like my sister before you, I could have lost you. But here you are, you are still alive." He gathered her in his arms, and, hugging her, he repeated, "You are still alive."

"Yes," she answered, "thanks to you and your uncanny ability to always make your shot. Still, had you been a little late…"

"But I was not. You are here with me; you are in my arms, in my life, and, what's more, we are committed to each other. Our paths are one. I love you, my wife. I will always love you."

Her arms were around his neck and she was hugging him so tightly, he thought she might never let go. And, then she said, "I, too, my darling. I, too."

He smiled. Together they cried.

***

"Luci! Iron Wolf!"

Jane's screams had Luci jumping up and running toward her sister. She had almost forgotten her plight because of the urgency in battling the criminals.

Jane yelled, "Luci, I think the baby is coming, and I'm scared. Is Iron Wolf here?"

"I am," returned Iron Wolf, kneeling on one knee beside her. Luci watched as he took hold of Jane's hand and moved closer to her. Looking up at Luci, he said, "I helped a woman from our tribe deliver my sister's baby. This happened because times were bad for my tribe, and we had no one else to help. I remember the words of the old woman well, and she told my sister to squat in order to deliver the baby. It is a natural position, and she said that it made for an easier birth for both baby and mother."

Luci nodded. "I believe you may be right. Let us do that. The baby has to move down the birthing canal, and so it only makes sense to aid its passage by using gravity. Iron Wolf, please help Jane to get up and into a squatting position. Wind Eagle, please boil as much water as you are able to carry, and then boil some more."

Wind Eagle jumped up, and, taking hold of the leather pouch, which was still beside the fire, he placed it close enough to the fire for the water to boil. Then, having done so, he hurried out of the camp in the direction of the stream.

"Jane, I will need you to push the baby out when I tell you to. But first, let me examine the birth canal to ensure that your passage is open enough to allow the baby out. Iron Wolf, while I do this, go help Wind Eagle."

Iron Wolf complied at once and hastily left camp. Jane nodded at Luci, who quickly examined her, and said, "The birth canal is wide and open. The baby is ready to be born. Are you ready to begin the birthing process?"

"Yes. But only if Iron Wolf is here. Where is he?"

"I am here," assured Iron Wolf who rushed forward, and, stepping up close to Jane, he helped her rise up into a squatting position.

It seemed to Luci as if the next several hours dragged by, but soon, it happened. As Jane strained with one last push, the baby arrived, headfirst. A new life had come into the world, and, as its cry announced its coming onto this earth, Luci couldn't help but observe that what had started off as a horrible and terrible crime, had transformed into the most beautiful miracle of life.

And, Luci couldn't help it, she cried.

***

The dim light of evening had fallen upon the land when General Glenforest rode into the encampment. Luckily, he owned more than one uniform, and he was happy that he was able to come back to his daughters' encampment and present himself in the more favorable light of the general he was.

He had been successful in his quest to apprehend the Mexicans, and, after capturing them, he had turned them over to his own military for questioning. He didn't linger there, however, to field questions as to why he looked like a walking bush. With mud, clay, twigs, leaves and branches sticking out all over him, he had looked more like a tree than a man.

He didn't explain; instead, he had returned to his quarters where he had bathed and dressed in another uniform. Happily, he had emerged from his quarters, sporting a dress uniform of blue, complete with embroidery on his shoulder and two rows of gold buttons falling down his coat. The hat he had placed on his head was wide brimmed, and a belt of gold braid held his sword, which fell down to rest alongside his left thigh. He wore blue trousers with a gold stripe lining the outward side of his pants, and on his feet were shiny leather boots that extended up and over his knees.

He had enlisted his own surgeon to accompany him, and, as they rode into camp, they both looked exactly like what they were: military. Quickly, both men dismounted. With his surgeon two steps behind him, the general approached his daughter, Jane, who was smiling happily up at that Indian, a man who, even now, was returning her grin, and speaking softly to the baby, which he held in his arms.

"Jane," began the general, "I have brought my surgeon, Doctor Tenner, to attend to you. Doctor, this is my daughter, Jane." He ignored the Indian. "Although you girls might like to go back to your home tonight, I believe that it is best that we spend the night here, in this clearing, and travel to Buffalo Bill's camp in the morning."

"Thank you, Father," murmured Jane. "I believe that will work well."

"Thatta girl," acknowledged General Glenforest as he gave these temporary quarters a quick glance, deciding at once that both his daughters and their Indian *husbands* looked much too content. Indeed, in his absence, the clearing had been made to look as though it were as cozy as a home.

According to his own Intelligence people, that Indian, Iron Wolf, was supposedly Jane's *husband*, and he was holding the new baby boy, who was wrapped in a soft piece of buckskin. By his side lay Jane, the new mother, and, although she was on the ground, she appeared to be well taken care of and happy. She was stretched out fully atop a warm, cushy buffalo robe that appeared to be as soft as a mattress. Toy Indian trinkets lay all about the camp, from a tiny bow and arrow to a buffalo-hide rattle, which was neatly beaded in a typical Indian pattern of blues and oranges. Even a cradle board, again adorned with beadwork, lay next to Jane.

It was obvious to the general that either Wind Eagle or that other Indian fellow had ridden back to Buffalo Bill's camp. There, they had gathered a supply of blankets, trinkets, and warm robes for the night ahead. The scene that was spread out before him was one of peace and harmony.

The general scowled. He didn't like it. Not one bit.

This was not the life he had envisioned for his daughters. In his own mind, he had envisioned them both marrying well and marrying military men…the United States Military. Indeed, he felt urged to scream out his frustration and disapproval. But, he also knew that the time to act was not now. Let everyone present believe that all was well. And, it would be well—at least it would be from his own perspective…if not theirs.

Lucinda was nineteen and on her own. So be it. The fact that Mr. Eagle had saved her life tonight might earn him the privilege of not being under the general's scrutiny. Their marriage he would leave be for now.

But Jane... Jane was another story. She was underage. She was still under his, her father's, protection.

How could a girl so young know her own heart? Within his own mind, the general was certain that the Indian lad who had married her had also misled her. What was it he wanted? Money? An easy life? He must have other intentions, since the general could think of no other reason why a man who had the eye of many young females, would tie himself to a pregnant woman—made pregnant by another man.

And, so it was his responsibility as her father—indeed, it was his duty- to ensure that both she and the baby were well taken care of, and that their lives in the future would be filled with happiness within the boundaries of the world that he knew and loved. So, yes, he had made his plans, and they were good ones. In truth, what he was going to do he felt certain was for the best. He was sure of it.

***

Luci watched her father with some misgiving. She knew her father well enough to realize that his frown signified that he was not happy, and, despite his attempt at pretending to be pleased, she was certain it was a lie, a mere mockery.

Still, he could wait, for she had another concern more urgent. And so, as General Glenforest came down upon his knees to sit next to Jane, Luci reached toward Wind Eagle, and whispered, "I must speak to you."

He nodded.

"Not here. I fear what I need to say is between only the two of us. Perhaps over there," she pointed, "on the opposite side of the camp, we might find more privacy, for it leads into the woods."

"*Wašte.* Wait here while I ensure that the place is safe. If it is, I will give you a signal like this..." He flicked his hand. "Do you understand?"

"I do."

"*Wašte',*" was all he said, and he was gone.

It took longer than she would have expected, but at last, he motioned to her that it was safe. Rising up to her feet, she stepped across the camp and disappeared into the woods, whereupon Wind Eagle immediately took her into his arms.

He hugged her tightly to him, and she relaxed against him, at least a little. He whispered in her ear, "You did well, my wife. No one would ever know that you have never before delivered a baby."

"Thank you. That is kind of you to say. I must admit, however, that I am glad it is over and that both the baby and Jane seem to be doing well. But, my darling, there is another matter that is on my mind, and it is about something that you said. Earlier you mentioned that your mother and your sister had perished long ago, and that this somehow reminded you of me? Is it right that you were afraid that what had befallen them might have been my fate here today?"

"*Hau, hau*, it is true."

"Is this the secret you have been holding back from me?"

"Ah, you have caught me, my flamed-haired wife. Perhaps I should have told you this when we first married, but the time to do so never appeared to me. It is a long story and a sad one, and I think that when I tell it to you, you might understand, at last, my reluctance to fall in love with you, a girl who dresses herself in the clothes of a boy. But come, there is no reason for us to remain here in the cold of the woods. Let us go back to camp and warm ourselves around the fire, and when we are comfortable, I will tell you about my mother and my sister. But do not think that I am weak if you see a tear in my eye. Sometimes, even we boys cry."

"Yes, my dear husband," she answered, and she allowed Wind Eagle to lead her back into the clearing, where they stoked up the fire until it was a warm blaze. And, after they had made themselves as comfortable as possible, Wind Eagle began his story. But first, he reached for her hand, that action telling Luci more than any other that what had happened to him had scarred this man deeply. And, so it was that Wind Eagle told her of his secret fear, admitting that the death of these two women who had been close to him, had hardened his heart, not only against the Blue Coats, but also against any woman who would ever use the pretense of being a boy to bring about a means to an end.

When his confession was over, Luci hugged him and held him closely, not speaking for a long time. At length, however, she murmured, "No wonder you cautioned yourself against me. Indeed, it is to be wondered that you fell in love with me at all, for there were so many reasons that you should not."

"Ah, but there were more causes — and many of them quite pleasurable — why I should be in love with you, for you are a woman with a big heart, my wife, and I am a lucky man to have you."

"Oh, my darling, Wind Eagle, I love you so. I will always love you, even if times become tough for us, and they may. Even then, my darling. Even then."

***

The women were asleep and Wind Eagle was standing guard over the camp when Blue Thunder returned, slipping silently into a seat next to Wind Eagle. A moment later, Iron Wolf joined them. Using the language of sign, Wind Eagle asked, "What did you learn, my friend?"

Blue Thunder answered in the same manner, signing, "I followed the bronco cowboy several miles both east and south. His path led to the tracks of the Iron Horse, where there were two 'houses' being pulled, one of them filled with blue coat soldiers. The bronco cowboy met with several of these soldiers and I have their descriptions if you require them. Within a short while, two of those Blue Coats took the bronco cowboy away from the train and into the woods. There, they killed him and dumped his body into a creek. When the two soldiers came back to the train, they were greeted by others with handshakes, and I heard one man say all is well. There were only two train cars and one engine, no more. The Iron Horse pulled away, going south. I did not follow it, but came back here to report what I saw and what I heard."

"Here, now," came the voice of the general as he paced across the encampment toward them. "What are you three fellows doing over there so close to the woods? Is there something secret going on between you?"

It was Wind Eagle who answered the general, and, in a low tone of voice, he said, "Have a seat, General. Blue Thunder has returned with news about the bronco cowboy whom he followed. Perhaps you might be interested to hear what he has to tell us."

"Indeed, I would. What did you discover, Mr. Blue Thunder?"

Wind Eagle remained silent as Blue Thunder verbally repeated the same details to the general, and, when Blue Thunder had finished, the general asked, "Were all the men on both trains soldiers?"

"*Hiyá*, no," Blue Thunder murmured.

"So only one of the two cars was peopled by soldiers. Who was in the other car?"

"They were all men in that car. No soldiers. No women. There were both young men and old. That is all."

Wind Eagle observed the general discreetly, seeing his father-in-law's frown. What was the general thinking that caused him to freeze and catch his breath? At length, the general spoke up, but his voice was hushed as he uttered, "This is a turn of events I never expected. It looks as if there is more foul play afoot here than I would have considered. For soldiers to be involved with a man who had recently kidnapped my daughters, and then to kill that man, speaks of conspiracy to commit murder, perhaps something even more criminal and sinister than that, if there be such a crime. But I will need more evidence and more information if I am to determine why this has happened, and, if there is more here to uncover than a desire to get even with my daughters." He drew in a deep breath. "Now, boys, what are your plans? Have you any?"

It was Wind Eagle who answered, saying, "Tomorrow, we will all return to the Show, including the new mother and the baby. We will ask questions of other cast members. Who are those two Mexicans? General, what did you discover about them, if anything?"

"Nothing that would help us to understand what has caused this. I caught both of them and turned them over to my troops to question. But even under a heavy volley of questions, my people came away with no answers. Whoever is behind this did not tell those two men why they were kidnapping the women."

"It makes no sense," said Iron Wolf. "If there were no reason for taking them, why did they do it?"

The general paused, and Wind Eagle became alert to the distasteful look his father-in-law cast at Iron Wolf. However, after that short break in the conversation, the general answered, saying, "My men did obtain other information. It would appear, boys, that they were offered an unending supply of drugs and five hundred dollars each in American money. This we did learn. But why, you ask? We still don't know."

Iron Wolf nodded, saying nothing verbally. However, his gaze at his father-in-law was guarded.

"*Hau, hau,*" Wind Eagle said into the tense atmosphere of their council. "We know about the loco weed. We believe that this is why those men threatened the women. They were crazy in their minds."

"Makes no difference why they did it," replied the general. "A crime is a crime, and both those men are being deported back to the Mexican government, where they will await punishment by their government."

"Are they still here that we may speak with them?" It was Wind Eagle speaking.

"No. We sent them back at once. Now, boys, tomorrow, I intend to take Cody into my confidence and ask for his help in protecting my daughters. I will leave a guard here to watch over them, but it is temporary. Mr. Eagle, I think it best that I confess to Cody the truth about Lucinda and who she really is, but I will ask him to help us continue her disguise. As her husband, you will need to approve my plan to keep her looking like a boy for a little longer."

Wind Eagle paused, for he had intended to seek out Cody, also, but for the opposite reason. He said, "I, too, had decided to seek out the Showman, but my thoughts on the matter are different from yours. I had hoped that Little Flame might throw off her disguise. Why do you believe she should continue the pretense? When she was taken by the kidnappers, she was dressed as a boy, so the disguise did not protect her."

"I don't know that as a fact, young fellow. Besides, there is another reason for her to continue her masquerade. This show is traveling to

Baltimore soon and then to Washington, DC, Lucinda's hometown, and she is well-known there. This pretense, as you put it, will protect her."

Wind Eagle nodded.

"As I have already said, I do not understand what this trouble is about," continued the general, "but I intend to discover the scheme in its entirety. A word of caution: I suspect that lies will be told about me, about Lucinda and Jane, and also about you men. I believe, also, that there are those who will deceive me, and perhaps you, as well, for it appears that Captain Hall has friends among many soldiers, as well as with men placed in high positions in the government."

Wind Eagle nodded, as did Iron Wolf and Blue Thunder.

"It is my hope, Mr. Iron Wolf," said the general, his stare at Iron Wolf cold and austere, "that you will permit me to offer my own temporary quarters to Jane and the baby, so that they might be taken care of by my surgeon. Since you claim to be her husband, I would ask…" The general's lips tightened, "I would ask that you will allow this." It was no question. "You may of course visit when your duties are not calling you elsewhere."

Wind Eagle noted that Iron Wolf paused for a time longer than was common in a council. Also, within his gaze was caution. "It is well what you say, and I will see her and my baby often."

The general didn't provide an answering response to Iron Wolf's acknowledgment. Instead, he cleared his throat, and uttered, "Until tomorrow, then, gentlemen."

"*Hau, hau*," answered both Wind Eagle and Blue Thunder. Iron Wolf, however, remained silent.

CHAPTER TWENTY-SIX

"General Glenforest, welcome to my humble abode. To what do I owe this privilege?" Bill Cody stood up to greet the general and offered his hand.

"Sit down, Cody, sit down," ordered General Benjamin Glenforest, shaking that proffered hand, and he looked at the handsome celebrity with an air of censure, for, in his own view, this was a man out of uniform. Be that as it may, this was not the reason why he was here, and, as soon as Cody sat down, the general did the same. Taking a moment to settle himself into the chair, he paused, then uttered, "I assume by now that you are aware that I am the father of Jane Glenforest and her brother?"

"Yes, sir, I am. I hear that Jane had her baby?"

"She has."

"Ah, I must remember to send her and her husband my hearty congratulations."

The general narrowed his eyes. There it was again, that Indian being addressed as his daughter's husband. To Cody, however, he answered, "Yes, you do that. May I come directly to the point of my visit?"

"By all means."

"I will be leaving tonight by way of my own train, for I brought my regiment here with me. I intend my daughter, Jane, and her baby, to accompany me."

"And her husband, Michael Iron Wolf?"

"He will remain here where he is needed as part of the show."

"I see," said Cody guardedly. "Is he aware of your plans?"

"He is not, and I don't intend him to know of them." Here the general looked long and hard at Cody. "Do I make myself clear?"

"Yes, you do, General. You are aware, are you not, that they were married within the church?"

"Yes, I am aware of that. But I am not letting that stand in my way. Not where the welfare of my daughter is concerned. She and the babe will go with me. My surgeon will see to her and the baby's health and needs, and she will be under my care until she comes of age. Do you understand?"

"Yes, sir."

"Good. Now that we have that taken care of, there is the matter concerning my other daughter that I must speak to you about."

"Other daughter?"

"Yes. The sharpshooting boy whom you know as Louie, is my elder daughter, Lucinda."

"What?"

"Yes, indeed. Don't mean to brag, but I'm the one who taught that gal to shoot."

"A gal? Are you telling me that Louie is a girl?"

"Yes."

Cody paused. "I promise you I didn't know."

"I realize that you didn't, and, by hiring Lucinda, you did her, her sister and me a favor that I will not forget. However, I am in need to ask another favor of you."

Cody inhaled deeply, narrowed his eyes, but said, "By all means, General."

"It is this: Both of my daughters are in trouble because of a misunderstanding that happened while I was out of the country. I don't know yet why there is so much trouble about it and why there are men who have been hired to find them. Did you know that the girls were kidnapped yesterday?"

Cody looked to be honestly shocked. He shook his head. "I did not."

"Well, they were, and I don't know why. Now, while I am determined to take Jane and her baby with me, Lucinda will stay here with her husband—"

"Husband?"

"Yes, husband." The general coughed, then continued, saying, "To make a long matter short, Charles Wind Eagle knew all along that 'he' was a 'she.' The two of them fell in love and married. Meanwhile, Mr. Eagle and Mr. Iron Wolf, as well, found out about the men hired to find Lucinda and her sister. Because they are both close to my daughters, they have both been attempting to protect the girls. Something sinister is going on, Cody, and I don't intend to stay in the dark about it for long. One man, Will Granger, is already dead."

"What? Granger is dead?" Cody pounded his fists on his desk, and his face took on an ashen color. "Why, he's the best bronco I've ever had with the show. Where am I going to get another one like— This is terrible news, General."

"And yet, as you are in charge here, it is my duty to inform you of this. Yes, I'm sorry to be the bearer of bad news, but Granger was, indeed, one of the kidnappers, and now he is dead, not by my hand or by my men, but by soldiers who are unidentified as yet. Soldiers… Who gave them their orders? And what orders were they? Why was he killed? And, why were my daughters kidnapped? So many questions, and I have no answers, for, as I have already said, I have been out of the country.

"Now, Mr. Cody," continued General Benjamin Glenforest, "I am asking that you, in my absence, watch over Lucinda. You should know that I told her husband that she must continue her disguise as a boy. This is for her protection, since this show will be traveling to Washington DC, a place where she is well known. Her husband, one of the best shots I've ever seen, will, no doubt, protect her. But I will leave a guard here, nevertheless. That guard is to be short-lived. When you leave to go back to Nebraska for the winter, the guard will be discharged of the duty here. Will you honor me with this service I ask of you, and watch over Lucinda for me?"

Cody stood up and offered the general his hand. "Of course I will."

The general followed Cody up and took that proffered hand. "Neither Charles Wind Eagle nor Lucinda know about the guard that I am leaving here, and Lucinda does not know that I have talked to you about her true identity. Let's keep it that way, shall we?"

Cody smiled. "Yes, General, sir. You have my word of honor on that."

And, having obtained Buffalo Bill Cody's word, the General took his leave.

***

As Wind Eagle awaited an audience with his father-in-law, he tried to concentrate on what he hoped might ensue between himself and his wife's father, rather than what he feared could happen. He had washed his face and body clean of any remaining camouflage and war paint, understanding that the general did not grasp why an Indian warrior painted his body. The man was unaware that the colors and symbols helped to give a warrior confidence and strength; that it announced a fighter's daring deeds and that it provided the needed camouflage in an otherwise hostile environment. Indeed, this lack of understanding between them also caused a spiritual separation, as well; one that Wind Eagle recognized well. It was because of this last that Wind Eagle had decided to erase the symbols of war from his countenance. After all, he did not wish war upon his father-in-law now or in the future. Rather, it was his desire to ease the tension between them, allowing his father-in-law's antagonism to gradually fade.

Wind Eagle had donned his best clothing, wishing to appear rich enough to afford his wife and any family yet to come. This was the white man's world, a foreign domain to him, yet he understood it well enough to know that a father, regardless of culture, needed to be reassured that his daughter's husband was able to take care of her and their future children.

Besides, pride and the American Indian's tradition of honoring the bride's father, would not allow him to escape his duty to provide gifts. Thus, Wind Eagle stood under a noon-day sun, dressed in his best garb of traditional white buckskin.

His white leggings fell down to his moccasins, which were also sun-bleached white and beaded with blue and red beads. His white doeskin shirt reached below his knees, covering his breechcloth that was worn beneath. Over his shoulders was thrown a white buckskin cape, and, in his left hand he held a lance, which was also made into a bow; it was an object of great honor. He had placed his war shield over his left shoulder, and, although there were two beads at each side of his face, holding his bangs in place, he wore no feathers in his hair. In his right hand, he held a peace pipe, recently made. He looked exactly what he was: a proud, Assiniboine Warrior.

Iron Wolf stood beside him, also dressed in his best apparel. Although his regalia was of a tan color, it was beautifully decorated with white, orange and green porcupine quills. His doeskin shirt hung down below his knees, and was fringed, while his leggings reached past his footwear to the ground. Tan moccasins bore the same beaded design as his shirt. Thrown over one shoulder, he wore a buffalo robe, and, in one of his hands he carried a long rifle, while in his other, he held a quiver full of arrows.

Both men had left the majority of their hair loose and long, like a lion's mane, to match this solemn occasion. The ever-present bangs were left long in the center of their foreheads and beaded at the side.

After they had been left waiting for what must have been an hour or more, a blue-coated soldier approached them, waved them on, and it wasn't long before they stepped into the general's headquarters, which was, at present, the same train car which Wind Eagle remembered from a few days past.

"Good day, *boys*," said the general, who stood to his feet. "To what do I owe this meeting?"

"We come," replied Wind Eagle, "to bear you gifts, for we wish to live, each one of us and separately, with your daughters."

With this said, Iron Wolf stepped forward and presented General Glenforest with a quiver, beautifully beaded with orange, white and green beads. Next he removed his buffalo robe from around his shoulders and presented it, as well. And, lastly, he held out his rifle, along with ammunition, laying it on the general's desk. With a simple nod, he stepped back, having spoken not one word.

Wind Eagle took a pace forward, and said, "We present these gifts to you in honor of your daughters. We would live with your daughters in peace and in harmony for all our lives. This lance I give you," he continued, "is a token of my respect. Only an esteemed warrior is allowed its use. This white robe I wear…" he took it off his shoulders and placed it on the general's desk, "…is for you. And, this pipe of peace is recently made by my own hand. It was created for you. Lastly, these…" Producing a pouch, he took out several buttons, trinkets, a belt and metals that the general had lately lost, and placed them before him. From under his clothing, he brought out the general's sword that had been lost at the same time, and placed it, too, on the desk. "…I return to you, as promised."

This said, he stepped back, coming to stand again beside Iron Wolf.

General Glenforest gazed first at one of them, then at the other, his look hard, direct. "Well, well, *lads*, it seems you have surprised me. But come now, all these presents are not necessary."

Wind Eagle spoke up at once, saying, "It is our custom and our duty to present gifts to the father of our brides. We have each one of us spent what idle hours we have fashioning these gifts, for it is well known that the father of the bride will miss his children. It is our way to try to ease that pain."

"How…kind," said the general, but the look in his eyes, and the harshness of his voice betrayed his true reaction, and that response and its severity was not missed by Wind Eagle.

"Now, Mr. Iron Wolf, I assume you have also come here to see my daughter, Jane, and her baby?"

"*Hau, hau*," stated Iron Wolf.

"Then step this way, *boy*, step this way. Oh, and Mr. Eagle," the general looked over his shoulder. "I thank you. You may go."

Wind Eagle acknowledged his father-in-law with a nod, but he was troubled. It seemed simple…too simple, and he was not in a good mind about that.

It was easy to see that the general was not pleased with either one of them. Something was wrong. But what?

Because he didn't know, Wind Eagle chose to ignore his father-in-law's order, and, instead of leaving, he pulled up a chair and sat down, prepared to wait.

***

"Young man," said the general as he came back into his personal quarters, the one which was clearly a war room. "I see that you are still here and have chosen to disregard my order to leave."

Wind Eagle nodded, his gaze downcast, as was proper Assiniboine etiquette. He remained seated.

"I am unused to my men disrespecting my orders."

Again, Wind Eagle nodded, although he reminded the general of his own status, stating, "I am not one of your Bluecoats. My loyalty lies elsewhere, as you know."

"Yes, so it might appear, yet your people are conquered, and, if you know what's good for you, you will give your oath of loyalty to your victor."

"Never."

The general frowned, seated himself behind his desk, and, opening a cigar box that lay upon the desktop, he slowly picked out a cigar and lit it. He did not offer a smoke to Wind Eagle, and Wind Eagle was reminded again of the intended insult. Wind Eagle, however, spoke not a word.

At length, the general asked, "Do you wish to pow-wow with me?"

"I do." Wind Eagle said no more; he waited instead for his father-in-law to speak.

"Very well, then. What's on your mind, *boy*?"

"The bronco cowboy…" Wind Eagle paused.

"Yes? What about him?"

"Why was he killed, and by your own Bluecoats? Since there is no war in this part of the country, why were those Bluecoats here, so close to the Showman's arena?"

"I don't know the answer to your question, but I intend to find out all that and more — and soon — and, know this: they were not *my* soldiers. They were under no orders from me."

Wind Eagle gave a brief incline of his head as acknowledgement. Then, he asked, "Why did the bronco cowboy steal away your daughters? Where was he taking them? To whom? What were they to him?"

"I might ask that question of you, young fella."

"And I would have to answer in a similar manner as you, and say that I do not know, but I intend to discover the reason. You realize that until this is solved, your daughters are not safe?"

"Of course, and I don't need you to remind me of that."

"If you discover a fact of importance, I would ask that you inform me of it. You know where I am, and the white man has many ways of quick communication."

The general hesitated for a long moment. At last, he uttered, "I am under no obligation to tell you anything, *boy.*"

"Are you not? And yet, you expect me and my *kola,* Iron Wolf, to protect your daughters without insight into the reasons for the danger to them?"

Again, his father-in-law hesitated. Many moments passed, and still neither man spoke. At length, Wind Eagle offered another thought, and he said, "As my elders have cautioned, 'In matters of safety, it is an unwise man who does not share what knowledge he might have with his friends.'"

"I am no friend of yours."

"Are you certain that is true? In this single instance, we share one desire: the safety of your daughters. On that score, we are of one path, and to that end, we are friends, as unlikely as that might be. I do not like it, either. But, for your daughters' sake, you must think on this, and so must I."

"On the day when I am in need of suggestions and orders from a young man many years my junior, is the day when I will cease to be an army man." The general rose to his feet. "Our meeting is at an end. I have nothing more to say, and I request now that you leave me."

Wind Eagle didn't respond to these curt words, except to come up to his feet. He raised his right hand in the universal sign of a truce, then said, "Before I go, I must repeat that you and I must think well on the idea of becoming allies in this matter. Since two or more are better than one against an unseen enemy, we should not discount the other."

"That will be enough, *boy*. I have not asked for your advice, and I do not wish it. Go now."

Wind Eagle said not another word, but turning, he silently strode from the general's quarters. As he stepped outside, however, his thoughts turned inward. So, he and his two *kola's* were still working on their own. Somewhere out there the real deceiver lurked in the shadows, perhaps even now plotting against the Assiniboine people.

But how were he and his *kola's* to find this person? He didn't know, but he did wonder about one aspect of their problem: why did he feel as if his wife's trauma mirrored the plight of his own people? Was the enemy which threatened her life the same evil force that would cause his people's destruction?

Perhaps. However, on one point he was certain: only by following that path to the end would he be able to answer that question. He rolled the thought again through his mind. Could it be true? Did his own people and his wife and her sister face the same or a similar enemy?

Indeed, in his heart, he believed it might be so....

CHAPTER TWENTY-SEVEN

It happened during the opening ceremony. One moment, Iron Wolf had been performing his feats of trick riding, the next, Iron Wolf had guided his pony next to Wind Eagle's, had laid his hand upon his friend's shoulder, and had said, "I must go."

Wind Eagle understood. All was not right, and he knew, without it being said, that the problem was Jane's father.

He nodded at Iron Wolf, and uttered, "I understand. We will do your stunts for you as best we can. Perhaps it is not as bad as we fear. Go!"

In response, Iron Wolf nodded briefly once, then galloped from the arena with all due speed.

***

Luci was certain that tonight's mounted shooting exhibition was their best performance yet, and she felt the exhilaration of danger, combined with the skill and speed that came from accomplishing this part of their program. Wind Eagle must be experiencing much the same, she thought, for he was laughing.

The audience was honoring them with a standing ovation, and, in response to their enthusiasm, both she and Wind Eagle waved furiously back to them. After a moment Wind Eagle observed, "It is well that our performance is good. Soon, after we are finished with our performances here and in your village of Washington DC, I will seek a conference with the Showman and confess all, including our marriage and the danger to you and your sister. Although I believe your father spoke of some of these things to the Showman, it might go better for you and for us together, if we speak directly to him. But through it all, we must ensure that you continue in your disguise, for while you wear your boy's clothing, it is believed that you are safer."

"Yes, my husband. As you say, my husband."

Wind Eagle grinned, and, within his eye was a wicked light as he added, "Did I tell you what I have planned for us after the show tonight?"

Luci giggled. "Yes, you have, my dear husband. Come, let us hurry and settle these ponies in for the night, for I must admit that I am anxious to be in your arms. I am hoping your plans for the evening go well."

Wind Eagle smiled at her and gave her that irresistible wink, and, as the band played out the popular tune, "I Dream of Jeannie," he took up the melody and promised in song, "I dream of Luci with the flame-colored hair. Indeed, I dream of Luci. Tonight," he grinned, then added, "…let me show you how I intend to fulfill my dreams."

Together, they laughed, and, as they led their ponies toward the corral, they joked and teased each other, promising many pleasant deeds to be done this night and many more to come. And so it came to be….

THE END

Karen Kay

A Note on
Mounted Shooting or Western Mounted Shooting

Research has shown that the competitive sport of Western Mounted Shooting is most likely a recent invention of the rodeo. However, there is evidence that mounted shooting had become a part of the Wild West shows in order to show real life historical events. The present day event of Mounted Shooting is done singly, not as a race between two people. Here's what Wikipedia has to say about it:

"**Cowboy mounted shooting** (also called **western mounted shooting** and **mounted shooting**) is a competitive equestrian sport involving the riding of a horse to negotiate a shooting pattern. Depending on sponsoring organizations, it can be based on the historical reenactment of historic shooting events held at Wild West shows in the late 19th century. Modern events use blank ammunition instead of live rounds, certified to break a target balloon within twenty feet."

Author's Notes on Language

The Assiniboine are originally a northern branch of the Sioux or Dakota American Indian tribe, although they long ago quarreled with their fellow tribesmen, and then went their own way. But their language didn't change because of their split from the tribe. Now, because I could not find many of the words that I sought in the Assiniboine Language, I have used the following as a guide for this book.

     1)   When I could find the Assiniboine word for a thing or an action or a name, I used it. These words were obtained from several different sources: *The Assiniboine* by Edwin Thompson Denig; and *Assiniboine Words*, an online source.

     2)   When I could not find the Assiniboine word or words, I used the Lakota Dictionaries, which are: *Lakota-English Dictionary* by Rev. Eugene Buechel, S. J. and edited by Rev. Paul Manhart, S. J.; and *Everyday Lakota*, An English-Sioux Dictionary for Beginners by Joseph S. Karol; Red Horse Owner's Winter Count.

As a further note, the book, *The Assiniboine*, is written by Edwin Thompson Denig as a report to Henry Rowe Schoolcraft, which dates to around 1854. He writes that, to his knowledge, the Assiniboine separated from the Lakota/Dakota sometime around 1760, and not later than 1777. As Mr. Denig comments, and this is quoting from this book: "…their language with but little variation is the same (as the Lakota/Dakota tribes)…"

So it is because of this historical notation, that I have taken the liberty to use Lakota words when I could not find the appropriate Assiniboine word. It is my hope that this adds a depth of authenticity to the story.

A Further Observation
Regarding Language and
Regional English

Perhaps you might have noticed the different usage of the words, "supper" and "dinner" in my story. The differences, I believe, are historical and today are regional.

In the story, "supper," is used as being the evening meal, and "dinner" is used as being the noon-day meal. Interestingly, at this time in history, the use of those two words is correct.

When I was growing up in the southern section of the Midwest, these words were used as I have done so in this book. Believe it or not, there are distinct and different definitions for the word, "dinner" today, depending on the part of these United States one might come from.

When I moved away from the Midwest, I was at first confused by the difference in definitions of the very same word, and it took me a while to sort it out.

So, because this book takes place in the latter part of the nineteenth century, I am using these words as they were employed during this time period, and also as I came to know them when I was growing up. Here is how those meals were known, and used in this story:

Breakfast — Dinner — Supper

In other parts of the country, I came to know these meals described as:

Breakfast — Lunch — Dinner

When first referenced in this story, I define this word, "dinner," as it was known at this time and place — as the mid-day meal — but I thought I might give more definition of these words at the end of the book, to help with any confusion, if there were any. Believe me, when I first moved away from the Midwest, the difference in definition confused me.

Eventually, I worked it out, of course, but I figure there's no reason to put you through that confusion, also. And, so I am hoping that this note at the end of the story will be an aid to understanding the use of these words.

Karen Kay

2019

Below is an image of an Assiniboine Warrior painted by Karl Bodmer sometime around 1833 or 1834. Bodmer later wrote, "Over there I had friends." Notice, if you would please, the "bangs."

About the Author

Multi-published author, Karen Kay, has been praised by reviewers and fans alike for bringing the Wild West alive for her readers.

Karen Kay, whose great grandmother was a Choctaw Indian, is honored to be able to write about a way of life so dear to her heart, the American Indian culture.

"With the power of romance, I hope to bring about an awareness of the American Indian's concept of honor, and what it meant to live as free men and free women. There are some things that should never be forgotten."

Stay in touch with Karen Kay by signing up for her newsletter;

https://signup.ymlp.com/xgbqjbebgmgj

Find Karen Kay online at www.novels-by-karenkay.com

Enjoy an excerpt from IRON WOLF'S BRIDE, a novel coming soon

IRON WOLF'S BRIDE

An Excerpt

By

Karen Kay

CHAPTER ONE

Buffalo Bill's Wild West Show

Late Summer 1888

Philadelphia, PA

That man had stolen his bride and his new born son.

Slipping down from his Cayuse pony, Iron Wolf squatted over the ground to examine the place where his father-in-law's Iron Horse had recently been located. Was it only yesterday that he had visited his bride, Jane, and his new-born son here? But, the entire train, or Iron Horse, which consisted of only five cars, was gone. How long ago had it left?

He could see no trace of it in the distance.

Had Jane wished to go?

Never. He knew her heart.

Admittedly, his father-in-law had shown in words and in actions that he disapproved of his youngest daughter's marriage to an Assiniboine Indian. But to take her away like a dog in the night…

Was this action supposed to teach him that Jane didn't wish to remain married to him? To throw him away?

It did the opposite. He knew his wife loved him, and, that were she able, she would never allow this. But she had only recently given birth and was now bedridden. She had obviously been unable to stop her own father.

Further, did his father-in-law wish to paint him, Iron Wolf, in a bad light? As though to say to Jane that her new partner could not protect her and take care of her? And, experienced though he was in the ancient practice of scouting, if he couldn't catch up to that Iron Horse and steal her back, would Jane's military father tell even more lies to her? Might he say to her that her newly wedded partner didn't care? Or worse, that he was too stupid to find them?

Of course these ideas and incidents were intended. But he, Iron Wolf, would trail them; he would find them. And, even though he felt despair in his heart, he would do it.

To another it might appear an easy task…at least at first. But Iron Wolf knew that intertwining tracks from other trains might cause him unusual delays. Thus, he decided that he had better quicken his pace and begin his work at once.

With the ease of one who is familiar with the skill of scouting, tracking and riding, Iron Wolf jumped up, landing on his pony's back, and, directing his faithful animal to follow the tracks, he set out to overtake the train before it intersected with tracks from other trains.

***

"My darling, Jane," murmured Jane's father, General Glenforest. "Forgive me if I am staring at you as though seeing you for the first time. You look so much like your beautiful mother, who has been gone from us all these years. Sometimes when I look at you, I see her, for she was a beautiful woman, with blond hair the same color as your own."

"Thank you, Daddy," whispered Jane, placing her hand within her father's. As she lay in bed, she turned her head to smile at her newborn son, who was in her arms. "I am indebted to you for allowing me the use of your sleeping car. I am awaiting Iron Wolf to finish his performance with the show and to come here tonight. Have you seen him?"

"I have not."

"Well, no matter. I know that as soon as he is finished, he will come to me." She placed her finger against the baby's hand, and his tiny fingers closed around it. She smiled. "He is perfect, is he not? We have yet to name him. But we have time. Did you know that it is not always a custom within Iron Wolf's culture to select a name for the baby at birth? But our baby will have a name soon. Are you sure you haven't seen my husband yet?"

"I have not. Now, Janie, I know of no other way to tell you this except to come out with it bluntly. I do not mean for your marriage to Iron Wolf to last."

"I know that," she said, and, turning slightly, she smiled up at her father. "Yet, it will. Wait and see."

"Janie, I don't think you understand me. I am saying that the marriage won't last because I am taking you and the baby away from that man."

"Oh, Daddy, please." Jane frowned up at her father and pouted.

"Don't look at me like that," he said. "There is trouble here at Bill Cody's show, and you and your sister barely escaped with your lives only a few days ago. No, until I discover the source of the danger, you are coming with me."

"There is no need for that, Father. Iron Wolf will protect me and our baby."

"I disagree with you. But, regardless, you are still my daughter, and, because you are not yet of age to marry without your family's permission, I intend to take you away from here, out of the line of fire."

"Father! Don't say that. Besides, what you say isn't true. Luci approved of my marriage, and, since she is my sister, I did have permission. After all, you weren't here."

"I am the head of our family, Jane, and I am here now. It doesn't matter to me if she gave her blessing to your marriage or not."

Jane glared up at her father.

"I don't think you yet understand, so let me be clear," said General Glenforest. "I am taking you far away from here. We will be leaving the

States. As you know, I have a younger sister in England, and I am certain that she will be able to take you and the babe into her care until this danger passes."

Perhaps it was due to so recently giving birth, but Jane was having a difficult time understanding her father's logic, and so she asked, "And Iron Wolf? He is coming, too, isn't he? He is my legal husband."

"That he may be, but he is not coming. I will say this only once, so please listen. Iron Wolf is not this child's biological father. He is Indian, and, because he is Indian, he does not deserve to be married to you."

"That's not true, Father. Do you not know that without Iron Wolf, my babe would have been born outside of marriage? But, even aside from that, without Iron Wolf, I would now be dead, for he defended me against that kidnapper who was aiming a gun at me and my baby."

General Glenforest grunted before stating, "That may be. But Mr. Iron Wolf is still not coming with us."

Jane bit her lip, trying to recall the exact phrases she had so often uttered in the past to cause father to capitulate to her wishes. Yet, she couldn't remember even one of those expressions, and so she reverted to defiance. She said, "If Iron Wolf doesn't come with us, then I will not go with you, either. He is my husband. I love him, and I will stay here. I refuse to leave."

"You already have."

"What?"

"Do you think that the sway of the train is due to the wind? It is not. We are already well on our way."

"What?" Jane looked quickly toward the window, but the curtain was closed. "Where are you taking me?"

"To New York, where we will set sail to England."

"Well, I guess you'll be going alone, because *I won't go*. Somehow, in some way, I will find a way to leave and return to my husband."

"You have no choice, Jane. I am your father and you are underage. Besides, I promise that if you don't go with me, I will ensure that your 'husband' is arrested by the police. It is a crime for him to be off the reservation."

"He has a letter from Buffalo Bill."

"Yes, he may have that, but my authority extends far beyond Bill Cody's interests, and I can assure you that if I wish to do it, your Mr. Wolf can and will be arrested and will be sent back to the reservation."

"No!" How could this be happening to her so soon after giving birth? She loved Iron Wolf with all her heart; she also loved her father. Suddenly the elation she'd felt since giving birth dimmed.

Tears were already blurring her vision, yet, with a force of will, she determined that she would not let her father see her cry. So it was that in a shaky voice, she muttered, "Father, how can you do this to me? You may think you are hurting Iron Wolf, alone, but you forget that I love him dearly. Please, Daddy, don't do this."

To his credit, her father hesitated, but then said, "How can you know that you love him? You are only fifteen, which is much too young to know your heart."

"I am sixteen."

"Are you now? That's right, I missed your birthday while I was gone. But, Jane, sixteen is still very young. I am certain that given time, you will forget him, and that you will come to think of this as a bad time in your life."

"No, Father, you are wrong. It is not a bad time in my life and I won't forget him; I will remember always that when I was destitute, Iron Wolf rescued me, and, when I had no one who seemed to care about me, he came to me."

"Any young man worth his weight would have done that."

"That's not true. There were…are many young men with the show, but none of them gave me so much as a second glance. No one. Don't do this, Father, for Iron Wolf is an honorable man."

Her father rubbed her hand. "You are young, Jane. Too young to know your own mind. here will be others you will love. You'll see. Know this, you will come with me. This is an order, for I must ensure your safety and that of your baby. And, you will adhere to my wishes."

Jane withdrew her hand from her father's and looked away from him as she requested, "If that is so, then at least bring me pen and paper, so that I might leave a note for Iron Wolf, and please, before you go, help me to sit up that I might write it."

Her father nodded and assisted her into a seating position.

Once properly situated, Jane demanded, "You will ensure that this note is delivered to Iron Wolf." It was not question. "You must promise this to me, for I no longer trust you, Father."

Her father paused momentarily, then held up his hands in surrender. But before he stood to his feet, he said, "I do what I do for the best. I think, once you are away from here, you will understand that."

Tears were pooling in Jane's eyes, but she refused to shed them in her father's presence. "I will never understand it, Father. Now, please bring me pen and paper."

He nodded and bent to kiss her forehead, but Jane scooted out of his reach, turning her face away from him. She did, however, watch him leave the "room," listening to the loud clang of the train's heavy door banging shut.

She stared at the closed door long after her father had left. From deep inside, she found a thread of courage and she determined that she would not cry until she had written that note. Later, out of her father's presence, she would give in to her grief. But not now.

Whispering to herself, for she wished no one else to hear, she murmured, "I will return to you, Iron Wolf, my love. I did not use you as you may come to think that I did. Truly, I love you, and I promise you this, I will return."

***

Iron Wolf at last admitted that he had failed. There were so many train tracks intersecting each other. For two days he had followed several different tracks, only to realize that none of them was the one that the general had used.

It had been a long time coming, but at last he admitted that what he was doing wasn't producing anything except frustration. But what could he do?

Asking that question caused him to look inward, giving him a possible answer: he had been so focused on his lack of experience with the white man's iron horse, their tracks and the busy vibrations of cities, that he had forgotten that a scout has many avenues of communication, and that speaking was only one of those. Taking the buckskin reins of his pony in hand, he led it to a patch of ground where lush grasses grew, and, letting the animal feast upon the treat, Iron Wolf sat down, cross-legged.

Closing his eyes, he let his focus expand outward in the way of the ancient scouts. He searched for her, silently seeking for her in the spiritual realm.

"Is that you, Iron Wolf?" she asked in a form of communication without words.

"It is I. I look for you. Where are you?"

"New York Harbor. My father is taking me and our son to England."

"Where is this harbor?"

He saw a picture of the place in her mind's "eye." He knew this harbor, for he had sailed into it only months ago, he being part of Buffalo Bill's Wild West Show. But where was it from here?

She continued, using only thought, "It is on the Hudson River, where it empties into New York Bay. We leave in the morning."

"I will come to you. Look for me. Keep me in your thoughts so I might more easily find you."

"I will."

That ended their unspoken communication. He would go there at once.

***

People rushed by him without looking at him, and the noise on the street confused him. Above him were wires crisscrossing the street, and, on the street where he trod, vendors sold their wares, their barking voices drowning out any other sound. Those merchant wagons were everywhere, littering the street and causing jams, as a multitude of humanity rushed furiously around the obstacles. The speed in this town was dizzying to Iron Wolf, but each lackluster face he saw was even more troubling. These people noticed nothing, not even the wealth of the kinship of other living beings around them. Each person he looked at appeared to be enchanted, as though held by some evil force.

Buildings rose up on each side of the street, towering over him, and, with the structures reaching toward the sky, Iron Wolf felt closed-in. Everywhere, and on every street corner, resided children of various ages; they were hungry, they looked tired and they acted as though they had no one in the world who loved them or who cared for them.

He had seen similar faces like these on the streets in England, where children shivered in the cold and starved because of lack of food and the means to procure it. Unfortunately, the plight of these youngsters before him now looked all too similar to those in England. What was wrong with the white man's cities that it pushed its youth out onto the streets to fight with each other over crumbs of bread?

And, while these infants were clearly weak from the abuse of hunger, there were numerous men and women who passed by this young humanity as though these juvenile, dirty faces didn't exist. Worse, Iron Wolf had already seen these wealthy men and women parading their well-fed dogs and other pets through the streets of this city.

These men, he thought, might be rich in material goods, but they were vacant in compassion. Such cruelty to the young was unknown to Iron Wolf and his people. In an Assiniboine village, children were treated as though each child were the kin of all the people.

Looking at these youngsters in this city of New York, he lost his heart to them. But, though he wished to, he dared not stop to give them aid; not this morning. His mission was to rescue his bride and bring her home...to his lodge within the Wild West Show.

He glanced around. Where was New York Harbor from here? The noise and confusion was so great that he could not determine which way would lead him to the harbor and to *her* ship. She had said that they were to set sail this morning. Was he too late?

He attempted to ask one man for help, but that man rushed on by without speaking. Iron Wolf tried again. Surely someone would help point him in the right direction. But, it was not to be.

At last, he saw a boy who was perhaps seven years old; he was sitting alone upon a street corner. He didn't appear to be in the good graces of the other boys who were either fighting amongst themselves or were shouting out words like…, "Extra. Extra. Read all about it. Get your paper here."

Leading his pony by his buckskin reins and ignoring the other boys, Iron Wolf approached the small lad, and, squatting down beside the child, asked, "Can you tell me how I might find New York Harbor?"

The young boy looked up; his eyes widened, as though in fear. Iron Wolf understood, for he was dressed in his Indian garb, complete with quiver, bow and arrows.

Iron Wolf said, "I mean you no harm. I am trying to find New York Harbor."

"Gee, mister, are you a real Indian?"

"I am. Will you help me? Do you know the way to New York Harbor?"

"Sure, mister. Can you read street signs?"

"No."

"Okay. Go up that way…," he pointed, "…about two blocks. Golly, do you know what a block is?"

"I do."

"Good. Turn left and go straight about 10 or more blocks. Once you get to the water, turn right. You'll see it then. Lots of ships there."

"I thank you." Reaching up behind him, Iron Wolf removed one of the eagle feathers that he wore in his hair. He handed it to the youngster, saying, "This is the feather of an eagle. The eagle is sacred to my people, the Assiniboine, for it is told to us that the eagle saved our world long ago. This feather…it is now yours."

The boy stretched out a hand to accept the gift. He smiled. "Thank you, mister. What tribe did you say you were from?"

"The Assiniboine."

"Gee, I wonder if anyone will believe that I talked to a real Indian?"

Iron Wolf grinned back at the boy, then said, "The eagle feather might cause others to think you speak the truth. May the Creator watch over you and help you."

Rising up to his full stature, Iron Wolf took his leave and trod in the direction the boy had pointed out. It was good, because, following those simple directions, it wasn't long before he spotted the ships. Still leading his pony, he broke into a trod, expanding his awareness outwardly to find her. Which ship was hers?

"Where are you?" he asked without words.

"I am here, in the harbor."

He saw in his mind's eye her location.

"But hurry, Iron Wolf," she entreated. "Our ship is starting to pull out of port."

Running forward, his progress was hampered by the longshoremen who worked at the port. Wood, boards, machines stood in his way, causing him to side step them, his pony following his lead.

Iron Wolf beheld the one ship that was only now starting to pull away from its dock. He quickened his pace, racing forward. Could he jump the short distance to the vessel and pull himself up to its desks? Yes, he could and he would.

Looking outward, he saw that many boards were piled up next to the ship's dock and that they formed a slight rise. Enough to give him speed and leverage. ron Wolf raced toward that place, pausing only to ask one of those strange and burly longshoremen to hold his pony.

"Iron Wolf!" He heard Jane's shouted words over the noise around him. "Hurry, Iron Wolf! Please! We are leaving!"

He looked up and beheld his bride with their baby in her arms. He saw her give their son to her father to hold, for the general was standing at her side. She leaned over the railing and shouted, "Hurry!"

That was all the incentive he needed to spur him on, and, speeding toward that tall pile of boards, Iron Wolf ran up it and took a flying leap toward the ship, his arms stretched outward, his legs moving as though they would help him to fly. For a moment, he felt as though he were a bird.

He was going to make it!

He reached out toward the ship's railing. He was there. His fingers touched the railing's wooden frame. His fingernails scratched it.

But there was little to no grip for him to hold onto. With arms and feet outstretched and shuffling about to give him momentum, he bent forward, seeking a place to latch hold of.

But it was not to be. The ship moved away slightly, and, as it did so, Iron Wolf slipped down, the railing now out of his grasp.

He fell down with a loud splash into the water, and, within only a few minutes, a small boat approached him, several men there reaching out to pull him up into the boat. A blanket was produced by one of those men, who set it around Iron Wolf's shoulders.

"That was quite a leap, young man," observed an older gentleman, one of the longshoremen. "Never seen anything like it. Wish you had made it."

Tears stung Iron Wolf's eyes. He had been so close to rescuing her. And now she was gone. He couldn't even see her anymore, although he did believe that he heard her wails over the sound of the waves.

As he watched the ship gradually fade into the distance, his voice was shaky as he answered the older man, saying, "I wish, also, that I had 'made it.'"

The man patted him on the shoulder. "She'll never forget 'ya. Your attempt today will remain within her heart forever. Now, come on, young fella, let's get to shore, and, if'n you'll let me, I'll buy 'ya a cup of coffee."

Iron Wolf nodded. It was all he could do, for words failed him.

She was gone.

ISBN 979-8-63686-333-5

Made in the USA
Middletown, DE
03 January 2021